The Complete Classical Wisdom Collection (Vol. 5)

*On the Nature of Things, Fear and Trembling &
The Genealogy of Morals — Exploring Existence
from Epicurean to Existential*

A Modern Translation

Adapted for the Contemporary Reader

Lucretius | Søren Kierkegaard | Friedrich Nietzsche

Translated by Tim Zengerink

Table of Contents

Preface - Message to the Reader

What If You Could Help Rebuild the Greatest Library in Human History?

Thousands of years ago, the Library of Alexandria stood as the crown jewel of human achievement — a sanctuary where the collected wisdom of every known civilization was gathered, preserved, and shared freely.

And then, it was lost.

Through fire, conquest, and the slow erosion of time, humanity lost not just books — but ideas, dreams, discoveries, and stories that could have changed the world forever.

Today, the Library of Alexandria lives again — and you are invited to be a part of its restoration.

Our mission is simple yet profound:

To rebuild the greatest library the world has ever known, and to translate all timeless works into every language and dialect, so that no seeker of knowledge is ever left behind again.

By joining our movement to rebuild the modern Library of Alexandria, you become part of an unprecedented mission:

- **Unlimited Access to the Greatest Audiobooks & eBooks Ever Written:**

   Instantly explore thousands of legendary works—Plato, Shakespeare, Jane Austen, Leo Tolstoy, and countless more. All instantly available to read or listen, placing a complete literary universe at your fingertips.

- **Beautiful Paperback & Deluxe Editions at Printing Cost**

  Own any title as an elegant paperback, deluxe hardcover, or stunning collectible boxset—offered to you at true printing cost, delivered straight to your door. Build your personal Library of Alexandria, crafted for beauty, built for durability, and worthy of proud display.

- **Fresh Translations for Modern Readers—in Every Language & Dialect**

  Enjoy timeless masterpieces reimagined in clear, contemporary language—no more outdated phrases or obscure references. Alongside the original versions, we're tirelessly translating these classics into every language and dialect imaginable, ensuring accessibility and understanding across cultures and generations.

- **Join a Global Renaissance of Literature & Knowledge**

  You directly support expanding our library, publishing deluxe editions at true cost, translating works into all global languages, and bringing humanity's greatest stories to people everywhere. By joining today, you're not just preserving a legacy of masterpieces; you set in motion a powerful wave of literary accessibility.

Become a Torchbearer of Knowledge.

Join us for free now at **LibraryofAlexandria.com**

Together, we will ensure that the light of human wisdom never fades again.

With gratitude and a shared love of knowledge,
The Modern Library of Alexandria Team

Visit:

www.libraryofalexandria.com

Or scan the code below:

Introduction

From Atoms to Anxiety:
Ancient and Modern Reflections on Human Meaning

The search for meaning is the central pursuit of philosophy. Across centuries and civilizations, thinkers have wrestled with the fundamental questions of existence: What is the nature of reality? What is the purpose of life? What role do fear, faith, and morality play in the human condition? In The Complete Classical Wisdom Collection (Vol. 5), we bring together three radically different, yet deeply interconnected, meditations on these themes: Lucretius' On the Nature of Things, Søren Kierkegaard's Fear and Trembling, and Friedrich Nietzsche's The Genealogy of Morals.

These works span over two thousand years of philosophical inquiry—from the Epicurean physics of the Roman world to the existential anxieties of 19th-century Denmark and the radical critique of morality in Nietzsche's late modern Germany. Each author, in his own way, challenges conventional beliefs and opens new paths for thinking about reality, morality, and the self. This volume is not unified by a single doctrine, but by a shared commitment to asking the most important questions, and to following those questions wherever they lead—even into discomfort, paradox, and darkness.

This introduction will guide readers through each text, situating it in its historical context, unpacking its central arguments, and highlighting how the three authors speak to one another across time. Though their conclusions often diverge, their works converge in calling us to live more consciously, more honestly, and more courageously.

Lucretius and the Liberation of the Mind

Titus Lucretius Carus, a Roman poet-philosopher writing in the 1st century BCE, authored De Rerum Natura (On the Nature of Things) as both a scientific treatise and a spiritual manifesto. Drawing on the teachings of the Greek philosopher Epicurus, Lucretius sought to free humanity from the fear of gods, fate, and death by explaining the world through natural causes.

For Lucretius, everything that exists is composed of atoms—indivisible, eternal particles moving through the void. This materialist vision rejects supernatural explanations, affirming that all phenomena, including the soul and consciousness, arise from the interaction of atoms. Death, therefore, is the dissolution of those atoms—it is not something to be feared, for it is simply the end of sensation.

The poem is both beautiful and austere. Lucretius combines poetic language with precise philosophical argumentation. He describes the birth of the cosmos, the origins of life, the mechanics of perception, and the illusions of religion. He aims not only to inform but to console. By understanding nature, we can overcome irrational fears and live lives of tranquility (ataraxia).

Lucretius' work stands as a bold affirmation of human reason against superstition. His Epicureanism emphasizes the pursuit of modest pleasures, the cultivation of friendship, and the acceptance of natural limits. He insists that the path to happiness lies not in riches or divine favor, but in understanding the true nature of things.

In an age of religious dogma and existential uncertainty, On the Nature of Things remains a powerful reminder of the liberating power of knowledge. It invites us to see the universe not as a stage for divine punishment, but as a vast, lawful, and ultimately impersonal field of matter in motion—beautiful in its indifference and empowering in its clarity.

Kierkegaard and the Leap of Faith

In stark contrast to Lucretius, Søren Kierkegaard (1813–1855) confronts the terror and mystery of existence through the lens of faith. Often considered the father of existentialism, Kierkegaard wrote Fear and Trembling under the pseudonym Johannes de Silentio in 1843 as a meditation on the biblical story of Abraham and Isaac. The work explores the paradox of faith: how can one believe in the absurd? How can one act against all ethical norms out of obedience to the divine?

Kierkegaard distinguishes between two kinds of life: the ethical life, governed by universal moral rules, and the religious life, which transcends the ethical through a personal relationship with the absolute (i.e., God). Abraham's willingness to sacrifice his son is not ethically defensible—it is, Kierkegaard argues, a "teleological suspension of the ethical." Abraham acts not from reason or moral principle, but from absolute faith in the divine command.

This "leap of faith" is not irrational—it is supra-rational. It requires the individual to embrace inward passion, paradox, and risk. The knight of faith walks alone, misunderstood by others, and must find peace not in justification, but in radical trust.

Fear and Trembling is both poetic and philosophical. Kierkegaard does not provide systematic arguments but unfolds a series of reflections, paradoxes, and imaginary variations on the Abraham story. His aim is not to explain faith, but to make us feel its dread and awe. He challenges modernity's easy assumptions about religion, ethics, and individuality.

While Lucretius seeks certainty through science, Kierkegaard embraces the uncertainty of existence. He sees anxiety not as a problem to be solved, but as the gateway to spiritual growth. Faith, for him, is not comfort—it is the highest form of courage.

Kierkegaard's existential vision continues to influence theology, psychology, and literature. His exploration of inwardness, choice, and meaning speaks to all who wrestle with the tension between reason and belief, freedom and commitment, despair and hope.

Nietzsche and the Birth of Moral Psychology

Friedrich Nietzsche (1844–1900) is perhaps the most provocative thinker in this volume. In The Genealogy of Morals (1887), he sets out to uncover the hidden origins and psychological underpinnings of Western morality. His goal is not to defend any moral system, but to expose how our values have been shaped by history, resentment, and power.

Nietzsche identifies two primary moral systems: "master morality" and "slave morality." Master morality, rooted in strength and nobility, defines "good" as what affirms life, power, and excellence. Slave morality, born of weakness and resentment, defines "good" as what is humble, meek, and equalizing. Nietzsche argues that Judeo-Christian morality, especially in its emphasis on guilt and sacrifice, is a form of slave morality—a reactive response to power rather than a creative force.

In his genealogical method, Nietzsche traces how moral concepts like guilt, conscience, and punishment emerged not from reason, but from social and psychological processes—particularly the internalization of aggression. He introduces the idea of "the ascetic ideal," whereby suffering is given meaning as a sign of virtue. This, he argues, has stunted human vitality and distorted the will to power.

Nietzsche does not offer a new morality. Rather, he calls for a "revaluation of all values." He seeks a future beyond good and evil, where individuals create their own values through strength, creativity, and honesty. His writing is aphoristic, poetic, polemical, and intentionally unsettling. He aims to provoke, to awaken, to shake the foundations of inherited belief.

The Genealogy of Morals is both a work of critique and a vision of renewal. Nietzsche's diagnosis of guilt, resentment, and herd conformity remains profoundly relevant. He warns against the hidden coercions of morality and calls us to reclaim our instincts, affirm life, and become who we are.

For Nietzsche, philosophy is not an academic exercise—it is a spiritual warfare. It is the courage to look into the abyss and laugh. It is the will to say yes to life in all its pain and grandeur.

Contrasts and Convergences: A Philosophical Triad

Lucretius, Kierkegaard, and Nietzsche do not agree. Their metaphysical assumptions, their styles of argument, and their visions of the good life differ dramatically. Yet they each offer powerful tools for self-understanding and cultural critique.

- Lucretius teaches us to dispel fear through knowledge, to embrace the finite, and to live in harmony with nature.
- Kierkegaard teaches us to face uncertainty with inward passion, to recognize the sacred in the absurd, and to risk everything for love of the absolute.
- Nietzsche teaches us to question the origins of our beliefs, to resist herd morality, and to affirm our will to power as a creative force.

These are not philosophies of comfort. They are philosophies of awakening. Each demands that we examine our assumptions, confront our fears, and choose how to live. Each challenges us to grow—to move beyond inherited dogma and toward personal authenticity.

In reading these texts together, we engage in a dialogue across the ages—a dialogue about existence, responsibility, meaning, and transcendence. They invite us not to follow a single path, but to reflect, wrestle, and decide for ourselves.

Welcome to The Complete Classical Wisdom Collection (Vol. 5). May these works disturb your complacency, deepen your inquiry, and strengthen your resolve to live not by habit or fear, but by thought, courage, and wonder.

Of The Nature of Things

Titus Lucretius Carus

Book I

Proem

Mother of Rome, delight of gods and men,
Dear Venus, who beneath the stars that glide
Fills the vast oceans and fertile lands with life.
Through you alone, all living things are conceived,
Through you they rise and see the great sun above.
Before you, Goddess, as you draw near,
Stormy winds retreat, and heavy clouds disperse.
For you, the Earth blooms with fragrant flowers,
For you, the calm waters of the seas smile,
And the serene sky glows with soft light for you.
When springtime dawns and gentle west winds blow,
The birds of the air, moved by your power,
Announce your coming, O divine one,
And wild herds leap joyfully through the fields,
Or swim freely in rushing streams.
Every creature feels your spell,
Following wherever you choose to lead them.
Through seas, mountains, rivers, and green forests,
You inspire love in every heart.
Through your power, life is born again,
Each kind producing its own.
And since you alone guide the universe,
And without you, nothing reaches the light of day,
Nothing beautiful or joyful can exist,
I ask you to share in this work I now write.
It is for Memmius, whom you have graced
With every virtue and charm.
Grant my words an immortal beauty,
And bring peace to the lands and seas.
You alone can calm the rage of war
And bring harmony to humanity.

Even mighty Mars, the god of war,
Cannot resist your eternal power.
Often, he throws himself into your arms,
Overcome by love's unending pull.
There, gazing at you with longing,
His strength and ferocity fade.
With your words and embrace,
You can soothe his fiery heart,
And guide him toward peace.
O glorious Goddess, grant peace to the Romans,
A peace that this troubled time so desperately needs.
For without peace, I cannot focus on this work,
Nor can the noble Memmius attend to the needs of the state.
While humankind lay crushed across the lands,
Burdened beneath Religion's heavy hand,
She loomed above, her terrifying face
Glowering down from the boundless skies.
But it was a Greek who dared to stand,
Who first raised mortal eyes against her power.
Neither the fame of gods nor lightning's flash,
Nor the thunder's roar from ominous skies,
Could shake his will. Instead, these spurred him on,
Filling his fearless heart with fiery resolve
To tear apart the barriers of Nature's gates.
Through his courage and wisdom, he prevailed.
He journeyed far beyond the flaming walls
That marked the boundaries of our known world,
Exploring the vast, unmeasured universe.
From there, he returned as a conqueror,
Revealing truths of what can come to be,
What cannot, and by what unchanging laws
Each thing is bound, held firm through endless time.
And thus, Religion now lies trampled down,
And his triumph lifts us toward the heavens.
I know how hard it is to shape in Latin verse

The profound discoveries of the Greeks,
Especially since our language lacks the words
For concepts so strange and new.
Yet your worth, and the joy I expect from your friendship,
Urge me onward, despite the toil it brings.
Through sleepless nights, I search for fitting words
And verses to reveal, in shining clarity,
The hidden truths that lie at Nature's core.
So I ask you to come with an open mind,
Free from distractions, focused, and untroubled,
Lest you dismiss my offering too soon,
Before understanding its meaning and worth.
For this is for you: the ultimate law of gods and skies,
The origin of all things, the seeds of creation.
From these, Nature brings forth all that exists,
Nurtures it, multiplies it, and finally,
Returns each thing to its primal state when it ends.
These fundamental elements we call
The atoms of creation, seeds of matter,
Or primal bodies—the building blocks of the world.
I fear you may think we walk an impious path,
Wandering into thoughts that defy the sacred.
But often, it is religion itself
That leads to the foulest acts of humankind.
Recall the tale of Aulis, where the greatest chiefs,
The leaders of the Danaans,
Defiled the altar of the virgin goddess Diana.
They stained it with the blood of Agamemnon's daughter,
Slain in cruelty.
She felt the garland upon her maiden hair,
The ribbons falling gently to her cheeks,
And saw her grieving father by the altar.
The priests, hiding the knife, stood by in silence,
While the crowd wept at the sight of her.
Terror-stricken, her legs gave way,

And she fell to the ground. Even her role
As the first to call him "father" could not save her.
They lifted her trembling body
And carried her to the altar—not with hymns
Or joyful songs for a wedding day,
But as an innocent girl, condemned by sin.
On that day, her father struck her down,
Turning his daughter into a sacrificial offering,
All to gain favorable winds for the fleet to Troy.
Such are the horrors that blind faith can bring.
And there may come a time when you, too,
Driven by the fear of omens and prophecies,
Will seek to break away from us.
Even now, these seers weave false dreams,
Threatening your plans and filling your life with fear.
They wield such power because men do not know
That all suffering could have an end.
If they did, they would find strength,
A way to stand firm against such terrors.
But as it is, no tools, no knowledge exist,
Because people fear eternal torment after death.
They do not understand what the soul truly is—
Whether it is born with the body,
Or comes into us at birth,
And whether it dies with us,
Or journeys to shadowy caves in the underworld.
Perhaps, as some say, it passes into animals,
A belief even our great poet Ennius held,
Who first brought the laurel crown of Helicon
To the Italian people, earning eternal renown.
Yet even Ennius, in his immortal verse,
Speaks of the dark halls of Acheron,
Claiming no souls or bodies return from there,
Only pale, ghostly figures.
He tells how Homer's spirit rose to him,

Weeping bitterly,
And revealed the secrets of Nature's origin.
Let us, then, with steady minds,
Seek to grasp the truth of the skies above—
The laws that guide the sun and moon.
Let us study the forces that drive life below.
But most of all, let us strive to understand
What the mind and soul are made of,
And what it is that terrifies us so deeply,
Whether in the grip of sleep or illness,
That we see and hear, as if close by,
The long-dead, whose bones rest beneath the earth.

Substance is Eternal

This fear, this darkness in the human mind,
Cannot be dispelled by the rising sun,
Or the bright rays of morning's light,
But only by understanding Nature and her laws.
And Nature begins with this truth:
Nothing is ever created from nothing.
People fear the unknown because they look at the sky and earth,
Unable to explain their workings,
And believe divine powers must be at play.
But once we understand that nothing comes from nothing,
We can begin to see the truth of how all things arise—
Not through the tools of gods, but through natural laws.
Imagine if anything could come from anything:
Fish might spring from the land,
Humans might rise from the sea,
Birds might burst fully formed from the air,
And wild creatures might roam,
Producing offspring of entirely different kinds.
Fruits would grow on random trees,
And life would exist without order or reason.

But this does not happen,
Because all things are born from fixed seeds,
Each following its own nature and origin.
Why else would roses bloom only in spring,
Grain ripen in summer,
And grapes mature in autumn?
It is because the seeds of life combine at the right times,
And the earth, ready and fertile,
Brings forth her creations when conditions are just.
If things came from nothing,
They could appear at random,
Without cause or season,
And grow without nourishment or time.
Imagine if life sprang up without any process:
A baby could immediately grow into an adult,
Or a tree could suddenly emerge from the ground,
Fully grown.
But Nature does not work this way.
Everything grows gradually,
Preserving its kind through steady development,
Feeding and flourishing only from its own matter.
This shows us that nothing can grow without a source,
Just as crops need rain to thrive,
And living things need food to survive.
Without these, life would cease to sustain itself.
Thus, it is more reasonable to believe
That all things share fundamental elements—
Like the letters that form many words—
Than to think anything can exist without origins.
Why doesn't Nature create humans tall enough
To walk across the seas,
Or strong enough to tear down mountains,
Or capable of living forever?
Because all things are made from fixed, unchanging matter,
Bound by the rules of their creation.

The fields we till yield more crops than those left untouched,
Not because of miracles,
But because our labor awakens the seeds within the earth.
If nothing required seeds or care,
The earth would spontaneously produce
More beautiful and abundant forms on its own.
So, admit this truth: nothing comes from nothing.
All things have their origins,
And all return to their basic forms when they end.
Nothing truly perishes into nothingness.
If something were completely mortal,
It could vanish instantly without force.
But we see that everything endures
Until an external force breaks it apart
Or internal decay dissolves it.
If time could destroy all matter completely,
Life would never return.
The earth could not sustain us with food,
Nor could rivers and oceans remain full,
And the stars would lack fuel to shine.
But because matter is eternal,
The world continues to renew itself.
Even rain, which seems to vanish,
Returns as crops, trees, and fruit,
Feeding animals and humans alike.
Cities thrive, children grow,
Forests echo with birdsong,
And cattle rest content in the fields.
From these cycles of life,
Nature creates one thing from another,
Never allowing anything to exist
Without the death of something else.
And now, since I have taught that things cannot
Be born from nothing, nor, once born,
Return to nothing, doubt not my words,

Though your eyes cannot see the smallest seeds of matter.
Consider instead those forces we know exist,
Yet remain invisible to sight.
The winds, unseen, lash against our faces,
Driving great ships to ruin and tearing the clouds apart.
They whirl wildly across the land, scattering trees,
Or roaring through the mountains with deafening blasts.
Their howls shriek ominously as they wreak destruction,
Though we cannot see them, their power is clear.
Like rivers swollen by heavy rains,
The winds sweep all before them.
The torrents rush down from the hills,
Carrying fragments of trees and rocks,
Crashing against piers and bridges with unrelenting force,
Until even the strongest structures give way.
The waters surge, hurling debris far and wide,
Destroying all that stands in their path.
Just so, the winds scatter and break,
Driving everything before them,
Or spiraling into whirlwinds,
Lifting all they catch in their twisting grasp.
The winds are unseen, but they are no less real,
Their works and ways as mighty as the rivers.
We know, too, the scents of things that reach our noses,
Yet never see their particles come.
We feel the warmth of fire, the chill of frost,
And hear the voices of men,
Though their forms are not visible to our eyes.
These, too, must be made of matter,
For only physical things can touch the senses.
Consider how clothing hung by the shore grows damp,
The moisture seeping in unseen.
And when laid out beneath the sun,
The fabric dries, yet we see not the water depart.
It scatters into particles too small for sight.

Or take the ring worn on the finger,
Thinning slowly beneath with passing years.
Drops falling from a roof wear grooves into stone,
And the iron plowshare, dragged through fields,
Wastes away little by little, unseen.
Even the stone-paved roads grow smooth
From the countless steps of passing feet.
Bronze statues at the city gates
Have hands worn thin by the touch of many travelers.
We see the marks of time upon these things,
But we cannot see the tiny bits that break away.
In the same way, Nature builds all things,
Adding little by little, unseen by any gaze.
No eye can trace the growth of trees,
Or the steady maturing of life,
Nor can we see the gradual decay
As time and age wear all things down.
Salt waves gnaw at towering cliffs,
But the smallest changes escape our sight.
Thus, Nature works through forces unseen,
Her processes hidden, yet ever present.

The Void

But know this: creation is not crammed or blocked,
For in all things, there exists a void—
An empty space, intangible and unseen.
This truth, once known, will guide you often,
Saving you from endless doubt and wandering,
And from losing faith in what I have explained.
If there were no void, nothing could move,
For matter's nature is to block and halt.
Without an open space to flow into,
No thing could shift or find a starting place.
But look at the world—the oceans, the land,

The vast expanse of the heavens above—
So much moves in so many ways before our eyes,
And if there were no void, all would be still,
Matter trapped, compressed, unable to stir.
Even the most solid things are not without void.
In rocks and caves, water trickles through,
And beads of moisture collect like tears.
Trees grow, bearing fruit in their season,
As nutrients pass upward from the roots
Through trunks and branches to nourish every part.
Voices penetrate walls, reaching our ears,
Frost seeps into our very bones.
Such things are only possible because of void—
For bodies must have space to pass through.
Why else do some objects weigh more than others,
Though their sizes appear the same?
If a ball of wool and a lump of lead
Contained the same amount of matter,
They would weigh the same. But they do not.
Lead is heavier because it holds less void,
While the wool, full of emptiness, weighs less.
The difference in weight reveals the truth:
Matter and void are always intermingled.
Some argue that water gives way before fish,
Allowing them to swim by creating space.
They claim the water rushes back to fill the gap,
And so, they say, motion is possible
Even if everything is completely full.
But this belief is false.
Where could the fish move if no space existed?
And how could water shift aside
If the fish had nowhere to go?
Without void, nothing could begin to move at all.
When two solid bodies strike and separate,
A gap forms between them, filled by air.

But even air, rushing in with gusty speed,
Cannot fill the gap instantly.
It moves to one place first, then spreads to the rest.
Some might say this happens because air condenses,
But they are mistaken. If air were compressed,
It would create voids elsewhere as it shrank,
And no true filling would occur.
Without void, air could not collapse on itself,
For matter cannot contract infinitely.
Thus, despite objections, the truth stands firm:
There is a void in all things.
I could present many arguments to prove this,
But these few examples should suffice.
They are the footprints that will guide you,
Like a hound tracking a hidden trail.
Once you sense the path, you can follow it,
Thought by thought, uncovering hidden truths.
But if you stray or hesitate,
Even by a little, I warn you, Memmius,
You may find yourself lost.
Still, fear not: I will pour forth proofs in abundance,
Drawing from the wellspring of my mind.
Yet time moves swiftly, and I worry
That life itself may leave us
Before I can reveal to you
Every answer your questions deserve.

Nothing Exists Per Se Except Atoms and The Void

But now, to continue weaving the tale begun,
All of nature, self-sustained, consists
Of two main things: of bodies and the void
In which they rest and move about.
For common sense among all humankind
Declares that body must exist.

If this deep-rooted belief should fail,
We'd have no foundation to prove anything else,
No place to begin our reasoning.
And without the void—empty space,
Where bodies move and find their place—
Nothing could exist or change position.
As I have shown, without such space,
Motion would be impossible.
Beyond these two—bodies and void—
Nothing exists that is separate from both.
There is no third kind of thing in nature.
Anything that exists must be something—
If it can be touched, no matter how slight,
It adds to the sum of bodies, large or small.
If it cannot be touched and allows all things
To pass through it unhindered,
Then it must be what we call the void.
Moreover, whatever exists must either act,
Be acted upon, or provide the space
In which things move and exist.
Bodies act and are acted upon;
Void provides the space to move.
Thus, there is no third nature, no other kind,
Besides bodies and void,
That can be sensed or understood
By the reasoning of the mind.
Name whatever you like throughout creation;
You will find it is either a property of these two,
Or an accident caused by them.
A property is something inseparable from a thing,
Without which it cannot exist:
Weight belongs to rocks, heat to fire,
Flowing to water, tangibility to bodies,
And intangibility to the void.
But poverty, wealth, slavery, freedom,

War, peace, and other such conditions,
Which come and go while the nature of things remains,
These we rightly call accidents.
Even time does not exist by itself;
We perceive its passage through changes in things:
What has happened, what is happening now,
And what will come next.
No one feels time apart from motion
Or the stillness of objects.
When we speak of Helen's abduction,
The siege and fall of Troy,
We do not claim these acts exist by themselves,
But rather as events tied to people and places.
Those who lived them have long since passed,
Carried away by the relentless flow of time.
Thus, all past actions are accidents—
Some of humankind, others of the world.
Without matter and the space of the void,
Even the fire of love that burned
In the heart of Alexander of Troy,
Ignited by Helen's beauty,
Could not have sparked that great conflict.
The wooden horse would never have been built,
And the fires that consumed Troy
Would never have risen from its ruins.
From this, you see that every act and event
Does not exist on its own.
It is neither a body nor the void,
But an accident of both—
Dependent on the matter and space
Where all things happen and exist.

Character of The Atoms

Bodies, once more,

Are of two kinds: some are primal seeds,
The indivisible germs of all creation,
And others are unions formed by these primal seeds.
Those primal seeds, the first building blocks,
Cannot be destroyed; they endure by their own solidity.
It may seem strange to think that anything
Could possess a truly solid frame,
When lightnings pierce through walls of houses,
Voices and shouts travel through barriers,
Iron glows white-hot in fire,
And even rocks burn and shatter under fierce heat.
Rigid gold softens and melts in the flames,
Bronze yields and flows under intense heat,
And warmth or cold seeps through silver cups.
Hold such a cup in your hand, and you'll feel
The warmth or chill of the water within,
Passing through the metal's shining surface.
So it seems nothing is truly solid.
Yet reason and the nature of things compel us
To see that there must exist
Bodies of solid, everlasting structure—
The seeds of things, the primal particles
From which the entire universe is built.
First, we know there are two kinds of things:
Bodies, and the space where bodies exist.
Each is distinct and cannot mix with the other.
Where there is empty space, no body can be,
And where a body resides, there is no void.
Thus, the primal particles must be solid,
Free of any void within.
But since void exists in all created things,
Those things made of solid matter
Must have spaces between their parts.
No matter can contain void within itself
Unless it is formed of tightly bound particles.

Only matter with a solid structure
Can hold and shape the void.
Therefore, matter, with its enduring solidity,
Must be eternal, even if all else—
Every creation in the universe—dissolves away.
If there were no void at all,
The world would be a single, solid mass.
Without matter to fill empty spaces,
The world would be nothing but a void.
Thus, nature is a balance of body and void,
With neither being entirely full nor empty.
There must be particles capable of alternating
Between the empty and the full.
These particles cannot be broken from the outside
By blows or cuts, nor torn apart from within.
They cannot be destroyed by fire, cold, or dampness—
The forces that erode weaker things—
For without void, nothing can be crushed,
Split apart, or broken down.
The more void within a thing,
The more vulnerable it becomes to destruction.
But the primal particles, being entirely solid,
Stand unshaken.
If matter had not been eternal,
Long ago, all things would have perished,
Returning to nothingness.
And from nothing, nothing could ever be created.
But since I have shown that nothing comes from nothing,
And nothing returns to nothing,
The primal seeds must possess an immortal frame.
When anything meets its end,
It is dissolved back into these seeds,
Which remain, ready to build anew,
Supplying the universe with the materials
For endless creation.

Bodies, once more,
Are of two kinds: some are primal seeds,
The indivisible germs of all creation,
And others are unions formed by these primal seeds.
Those primal seeds, the first building blocks,
Cannot be destroyed; they endure by their own solidity.
It may seem strange to think that anything
Could possess a truly solid frame,
When lightnings pierce through walls of houses,
Voices and shouts travel through barriers,
Iron glows white-hot in fire,
And even rocks burn and shatter under fierce heat.
Rigid gold softens and melts in the flames,
Bronze yields and flows under intense heat,
And warmth or cold seeps through silver cups.
Hold such a cup in your hand, and you'll feel
The warmth or chill of the water within,
Passing through the metal's shining surface.
So it seems nothing is truly solid.
Yet reason and the nature of things compel us
To see that there must exist
Bodies of solid, everlasting structure—
The seeds of things, the primal particles
From which the entire universe is built.
First, we know there are two kinds of things:
Bodies, and the space where bodies exist.
Each is distinct and cannot mix with the other.
Where there is empty space, no body can be,
And where a body resides, there is no void.
Thus, the primal particles must be solid,
Free of any void within.
But since void exists in all created things,
Those things made of solid matter
Must have spaces between their parts.
No matter can contain void within itself

Unless it is formed of tightly bound particles.
Only matter with a solid structure
Can hold and shape the void.
Therefore, matter, with its enduring solidity,
Must be eternal, even if all else—
Every creation in the universe—dissolves away.
If there were no void at all,
The world would be a single, solid mass.
Without matter to fill empty spaces,
The world would be nothing but a void.
Thus, nature is a balance of body and void,
With neither being entirely full nor empty.
There must be particles capable of alternating
Between the empty and the full.
These particles cannot be broken from the outside
By blows or cuts, nor torn apart from within.
They cannot be destroyed by fire, cold, or dampness—
The forces that erode weaker things—
For without void, nothing can be crushed,
Split apart, or broken down.
The more void within a thing,
The more vulnerable it becomes to destruction.
But the primal particles, being entirely solid,
Stand unshaken.
If matter had not been eternal,
Long ago, all things would have perished,
Returning to nothingness.
And from nothing, nothing could ever be created.
But since I have shown that nothing comes from nothing,
And nothing returns to nothing,
The primal seeds must possess an immortal frame.
When anything meets its end,
It is dissolved back into these seeds,
Which remain, ready to build anew,
Supplying the universe with the materials

For endless creation.
So primal seeds possess a solid unity,
Without which they could not endure
Through endless ages and infinity of time,
Ensuring the replenishment of worn-out worlds.
If nature allowed things to break apart forever,
The bodies of matter would by now
Have been reduced so completely by ancient decay
That nothing new could ever be formed,
No living thing could grow, or reach its prime.
For everything is destroyed more quickly than it is made,
And so, if infinite time has passed already,
It would have shattered and dissolved all things long ago.
There would be nothing left to rebuild or renew
The world we see around us today.
But notice this: a fixed limit must exist
To prevent the breaking down of matter.
We see it in the way everything is continually renewed,
Each in its season, each reaching its peak,
Its flower of life, before it fades.
Again, if there were no boundary
To the decay of the material world,
Then all bodies, of every kind,
Would have endured from the beginning of time
Until now, untouched by destruction.
But if, as you believe, they are fragile by nature,
It makes no sense that they could have lasted so long,
Enduring through endless ages,
Subject to the countless blows of chance and change.
So, observe in this account of creation
How, even though the particles of all matter
Are solid and unbreakable,
They combine to form things that are soft:
Air, water, earth, and fiery vapors.
This is made possible by the void within things,

Which allows them to flow and function.
If, however, the primal seeds themselves were soft,
It would be impossible to explain
How such solid things as basalt and iron
Could ever be formed.
Without a firm foundation of solidity,
They would lack the strength to exist at all.
The primal seeds, powerful in their simplicity,
Remain solid and unyielding.
When tightly bound together,
They create objects of unbreakable strength,
Able to endure against all forces.
Moreover, every kind of thing in nature
Has fixed limits for its growth and lifespan.
Nature has decreed what each can do,
What each can never do.
No fundamental change occurs; everything abides
Within its limits, passing on its traits,
Spring after spring. The birds reveal their stripes,
Their spots, their forms, unchanging in their kind.
This proves that all things must be made
Of matter that cannot be altered or destroyed.
If the primal seeds could be conquered or changed,
Then nothing would be certain—
No living thing could be reliably born,
Nor would there be laws to govern
What each thing can and cannot do,
What boundaries they cannot cross.
The generations, kind after kind,
Could not so faithfully reproduce
The habits, motions, and ways of life
Of their ancestors.
Thus, primal seeds remain unchanging,
Bound by eternal laws,
Ensuring that all things retain their nature,

And life continues without disruption.
Of that first matter, which our senses cannot see,
There exists a smallest point, a limit beyond division.
This indivisible minimum of nature is not
A thing apart, standing on its own,
Nor can it ever be so, for it is always part of another—
A first and single element, from which others align,
Joined in close-packed order, forming
The essence of all matter.
These smallest particles are not separate,
But tightly bound to one another,
Unable to break away from the whole.
Thus, the primal seeds possess a solid unity,
Their indivisible parts tightly joined,
Not by mere combination, but by their eternal singleness.
Nature preserves these seeds as the foundation of all things,
Allowing no rupture, no decrease, no decay.
Moreover, if there were no minimum size,
Even the smallest bodies would be infinite,
For a half of a half could still be halved endlessly.
What, then, would be the difference
Between the whole and the smallest part?
None—for both would consist of infinite pieces.
Reason denies this, for the mind cannot grasp
A boundless division without end.
Thus, we must accept that there are smallest, indivisible units,
The minimums of nature.
And if these exist, we must also accept
That primal particles are solid and eternal.
For if Nature, the creator of all things,
Broke everything into parts so small
That they lacked any structure or substance,
She could not build anything anew.
What lacks parts cannot form connections,
Cannot possess the weight, motion, or collisions

Necessary to create and sustain the world.
Thus, these indivisible seeds—solid, eternal,
And irreducible—serve as the building blocks
Of all creation, enabling things to exist
And continue through infinite time.

Confutation of Other Philosophers

Those who claim that fire alone is the substance of all things,
That the entire universe arises only from fire,
Have strayed far from the truth of reason.
Foremost among them is Heraclitus,
Famed for his cryptic words that dazzle the foolish,
Though serious seekers of truth find little wisdom there.
For the ignorant are often drawn to that which is obscured,
Marveling at distorted language,
Believing as truth whatever flatters their ears
Or comes wrapped in fine and polished phrases.
But how, I ask, can the infinite variety of things exist
If all comes from fire, simple and pure?
It matters not if fire is condensed or rarefied;
Its nature would still remain the same—
Burning heat in every form.
When compressed, the fire might burn hotter;
When dispersed, it might burn more gently.
But beyond such changes, nothing else could arise.
Certainly not the vast variety of earth's forms
Or the diversity of all we see.
If they admit a void exists,
Fire could indeed be condensed or rarefied.
But fearing the contradictions this would create,
They reject the idea of void,
Straying far from the path of truth.
Yet if void were entirely absent,
All matter would be compact and immobile,

A solid mass without motion or change.
Fire could not cast its light or heat outward,
Proving that its particles are not tightly packed.
And if they claim fire transforms into other things
Through some combination or alteration,
Then fire itself would cease to exist,
And with it, all heat would perish.
From nothing, the world could not arise again,
For if anything changes beyond its bounds,
It dies to what it was before.
Thus, something must remain unchanged,
A foundation enduring beneath the world's transformations,
Ensuring all things do not collapse into nothingness.
Primal particles exist, eternal and unchanging,
Which rearrange themselves to create new forms.
Through their motion, order, and connection,
Matter transforms, taking on new natures.
But these seeds themselves are not fire,
For if they were, no transformation could occur.
Even if particles shifted, left, or joined anew,
If they all retained fire's nature,
Only fire would ever be created.
Instead, primal bodies collide and combine,
Their motions and arrangements giving rise
To fire, or to other forms entirely,
Changing what they produce without themselves
Becoming like the things they create.
To say that all is fire, and nothing else exists,
Is a thought bordering on madness.
For the senses, which perceive fire,
Also perceive all other things just as clearly.
If fire alone is real, the senses would be deceived,
Yet it is through the senses that we know fire itself.
How then can we trust fire while rejecting all else?
This reasoning is flawed and self-contradictory.

Why dismiss everything else but allow fire?
Or, equally absurd, deny fire and accept all else?
Both paths are equally misguided.
Those who claim the universe is made of fire,
Or air, or water, or earth alone,
Have wandered far from the truth.
Even those who mix air with fire, or water with earth,
Or claim all four elements combine to create all things,
Miss the mark.
Empedocles of Acragas first introduced this idea,
A thinker from the three-cornered isle of Sicily,
Surrounded by the mighty Ionic seas,
Where the waves crash against the rugged coasts,
And swift ocean currents divide the land from Italy.
Here, Charybdis swirls in its deadly grasp,
And Aetna rumbles with fiery wrath,
Threatening to spew its flames anew,
Hurling lightnings skyward in a fiery storm.
Though Sicily is rich and bountiful,
Renowned for its strength and heroes,
It has produced nothing more revered or divine
Than this one man.
His lofty voice, inspired and pure,
Sings of truths so great and profound,
That he seems more god than man.
Yet he, and those others mentioned before,
Though lesser in insight, skill, and wisdom than he,
Even as they unveiled much noble truth,
And spoke from the heart's shrine,
Pronouncing holier and sounder responses
Than ever issued from the Delphic oracle,
Still stumbled over the question of first elements,
And great was their fall—great minds brought low.
First, they denied the existence of void,
Yet still allowed for motion in things,

And admitted the existence of soft, fluid forms—
Air, dew, fire, earth, animals, and grains—
All composed without the presence of void.
Next, they claimed no end exists to the division of bodies,
No boundary to the cutting down of matter.
They refused to see that all things must have limits,
Even the smallest particles invisible to sight.
If the boundaries of the unseen are real,
Then surely there must be minimums,
Beyond which division cannot go.
Moreover, they held that the primal germs were soft,
Subject to birth and decay, mortal in their being.
If that were true, then all things
Would eventually dissolve into nothingness,
And from nothingness arise again,
A cycle contrary to reason and truth.
Their doctrines, thus, stand far from reality.
Further, the primal bodies they propose
Are hostile to one another,
As poisons mixed and opposing forces clash—
Rains, winds, and lightning scatter in storms,
Driving each other apart in chaos.
If all things are made of four elements,
And dissolve back into the same four,
How can these elements be called primal?
By the same reasoning, all things themselves
Could be considered the seeds of the four.
For fire, earth, air, and water
Constantly transform into one another,
Interchanging their forms and natures
Throughout eternity.
Yet, if fire, earth, air, and water meet
Without losing their distinct natures,
They cannot form the world we see:
No breath, no trees, no living things.

Instead, this wild heap of elements
Would display their separate forms—
Air visibly mixed with earth,
Unquenched heat clashing with water.
To create the world, the primal germs
Must have hidden, unseen qualities,
Free from alien elements that might distort
Or weaken the new forms they create.
But these thinkers start from the heavens.
They claim fire becomes the winds of air,
Air gives birth to rain,
Rain forms the earth,
And the earth returns, reversing the process:
Moisture becomes air, air becomes heat,
And the cycle continues endlessly,
From the heavens to earth and back again.
Yet the primal germs cannot act in this way.
There must be something immutable,
Unchanging, to prevent the world
From dissolving into nothing.
For any change beyond natural bounds
Brings instant death to the thing that was.
Thus, the things they describe—
Fire, air, water, and earth—
Must themselves derive from other,
Unchanging and indestructible elements,
To avoid the collapse of all things into naught.
Why not, then, suppose that there are bodies
With a nature so fixed and enduring
That they can create fire,
And with a slight change in arrangement,
By adding or removing a few,
Or altering their motion and order,
They can give rise to air, water, earth, and all,
Interchanging forms forever?

"But look," you say, "the facts are clear to see—
All things grow into the winds of air,
And everything is nourished by the earth.
Unless the seasons bring their timely rains,
Filling the soil beneath dark thunderclouds,
And unless the sun provides its warmth and light,
No grains, no trees, no breathing creatures grow."
True—and unless man takes in food and drink,
His body would waste, his strength would fail,
And life would dissolve from bones and flesh alike.
It is beyond doubt that we are nourished
By certain things, just as other things are fed
By sources unique to their own natures.
This happens because the many primal seeds,
Shared among countless things, are mixed in different ways.
It's no surprise, then, that diverse things
Are sustained by diverse sources.
Moreover, it matters greatly how the primal seeds
Are combined with one another—what positions they take,
What motions they give and receive among themselves.
These same seeds form the sky, the sea, the land,
Rivers, the sun, trees, and living beings,
But their combinations and movements differ,
Producing endless variety in what is made.
Consider even these verses here,
Made from letters common to many words.
Yet each verse and word differs in meaning and sound,
Simply because of the order in which the letters are arranged.
If such variety can arise from mere letters,
How much more can the primal seeds of matter achieve
Through their infinite combinations?
Now let us examine the "homeomeria"
Of Anaxagoras, a concept with no name
In our Italian tongue, though the idea itself
Is not difficult to explain.

Anaxagoras claims that all things are formed
From minute versions of themselves:
Bones are made of tiny bones, flesh from tiny bits of flesh,
Blood from drops of blood, and gold from grains of gold.
He imagines earth as bits of earth,
Fire as tiny fires, water as tiny waters,
And so on with all substances.
Yet he denies the existence of void in things,
And allows no limit to the division of matter.
On these points, he seems no less mistaken
Than those we discussed before.
Moreover, the particles he describes are too fragile—
If these primordial particles are the same in nature
As the things they form,
And if they are subject to the same decay,
What could prevent their annihilation?
What would endure against the grip of death?
The fire? The water? The air?
The blood, the bones? None of these,
For all would share the mortality
Of the objects we see perish before our eyes.
Yet the proofs above already show
That nothing can return to nothing,
And nothing can arise from nothing.
Since food nourishes and builds the body,
You must understand that our veins, blood, and bones
Are formed from particles unlike themselves.
If someone claims that food contains tiny particles
Of veins, bones, and flesh,
Then all food—solid or liquid—must itself
Be made of these same varied substances.
Thus, bread or water would need to contain
Small bits of bone, flesh, and blood.
If everything that grows from the earth
Were already contained within it,

The earth itself must be composed
Of all these different materials,
Holding within it the diversity of life it sustains.
Apply the same reasoning to other things:
If flame, smoke, and ash lie hidden in wood,
Then wood, too, must be a compound
Of many alien substances,
Containing these forms unseen.
Here lies a subtle way to evade the truth,
One that Anaxagoras claims for himself.
He argues that all things are mixed within all,
And only that which dominates in number
Or lies nearest to hand comes into view.
But this idea is far removed from reason.
If it were true, then grains, crushed by millstones,
Should sometimes yield a trace of blood,
Or fragments of other substances that nourish our bodies.
Rocks grinding against each other
Should ooze with gore. Similarly, herbs
Ought to drip with sweet milk,
Flavored like that from a ewe's udder.
Breaking clods of earth would reveal
Scattered bits of grains, leaves, and roots.
Splitting logs of wood should uncover
Ash, smoke, and hidden fire.
But since experience shows none of this occurs,
It proves that things are not mixed with things in this way.
Rather, seeds, shared by many things,
Are combined in countless ways within all matter.
"But," you say, "on windy hills,
The treetops sometimes rub together,
Driven by fierce southern gales,
Until they blaze with bursts of flame."
True indeed—but fire is not stored inside the wood.
Instead, the seeds of heat lie dormant,

And when friction draws them out and unites them,
The fire is kindled, igniting the forests.
If fire were already formed and hidden within the trees,
The flames could never remain concealed.
They would constantly burn the woods,
Reducing all the forest to ash.
This shows, as I explained earlier,
How much depends on the arrangement of seeds—
How they are combined with others,
What positions they hold,
And what motions they give and receive.
For these same seeds, rearranged,
Can create both fiery and wooden things,
Just as a small shift in the letters of a word
Produces entirely different meanings.
Consider again: if everything you see
Could only exist by containing particles
With exactly the same properties as the whole,
Then your argument destroys the very seeds of things.
You would have to claim that the primal germs themselves
Could laugh, shed tears, or express emotions,
Like living beings breaking into fits of laughter,
Or weeping with salty tears down their cheeks.

THE INFINITY OF THE UNIVERSE

Now listen further! Attend with sharper mind!
I know how dark the path may seem,
But the hope of praise has struck my heart,
Piercing like a thyrsus deep into my soul.
At that moment, sweet love for the Muses stirred,
And now, inspired, I wander boldly,
Exploring paths untrodden by others,
Discovering pure, untouched fountains of thought.
I drink deeply, I pluck fresh flowers,
And weave for my brow a crown of truth,
Taken from lands the Muses have never adorned.

First, I teach of great and mighty things,
Stripping away the strangling coils of fear,
Freeing the mind from dread religion's grasp.
Next, I sing of the darkest themes in words
Made clear, imbued with the charm of the Muses,
For good reason:
As doctors, when treating children with bitter wormwood,
Coat the rim of the cup with sweet honey,
So the unthinking child may drink,
Unaware of the bitterness within,
Yet emerge strengthened and healed,
So too have I, knowing these truths may seem harsh,
Dressed them in sweet verse, the honey of the Muse,
Hoping to hold your mind long enough
To guide it toward understanding
The nature and order of all things.
Now that I have explained how solid matter,
Eternal and unyielding, flies forever
Through infinite time,
Let us examine whether these seeds,
And the space they inhabit,
Are finite or infinite in nature.
We must explore the vast expanse of void,
The boundless abyss where all things occur.
The sum of all existence has no limits,
For if it did, it would need a "beyond."
And a "beyond" cannot exist without something
To border and contain it.
If there were a boundary, we must ask:
What lies beyond it?
If you say "nothing," then the boundary itself is void,
And void is infinite.
Imagine you stand at the edge of this supposed limit,
And hurl a spear beyond.
Does it fly onward, piercing the beyond,

Or is it stopped by some unseen wall?
Either answer proves there is no boundary,
For if the spear flies, space continues;
If it stops, something beyond resists it.
Thus, the universe stretches endlessly,
Without an edge or limit to contain it.
If space were finite,
The infinite weight of matter
Would collapse into a single point,
And the universe, unable to spread,
Would not exist. There would be no sky,
No sun, no earth, no seas.
Instead, matter is in constant motion,
Flowing from all directions, endlessly supplied.
Even the mighty thunderbolts
Cannot traverse this infinite void
Nor find an end to their course.
Things bound things, but nothing bounds the All.
Air surrounds mountains, sea ends at land,
Land meets the sea again—but the totality
Has no outer limit.
The nature of all existence is infinite,
Balanced by body and void.
If it were otherwise,
The universe would collapse,
Matter scattered without union,
Unable to form the world we see.
Primal particles, eternal and in motion,
Have tried every possible arrangement
Since time immemorial,
And through their collisions and unions,
The world as we know it emerged,
Sustained by the ceaseless supply of seeds.
The rivers replenish the seas,
The sun warms the earth to bring forth life,

And breathing creatures grow and thrive.
But these cycles depend on infinite space
And an endless reserve of matter.
If the supply were finite,
All things would dissolve,
As creatures die without food.
The blows that unite the universe,
Though·constant, cannot preserve it all;
Some particles escape,
And new ones must take their place.
Thus, an infinite supply of matter,
Moving through infinite void,
Is the only way the universe persists,
Boundless, eternal, and ever in motion.
In these matters, my dear Memmius,
Do not yield to the common and mistaken claims:
That all things press inward to a single center,
And thus the nature of the world stands firm,
Unshaken by any outward blows,
Incapable of being divided or dispersed.
They argue that all heights and depths
Constantly press toward this central point—
As if anything could rest upon itself,
Or support itself in this way.
They also contend that the heavy bodies
Beneath the earth are somehow pressed upward,
Resting upside down upon the underside of the earth,
Much like the reflections we see in water.
They claim that living creatures beneath us
Walk head downward, yet do not fall
Into the sky below, just as we do not
Spontaneously fly upward into the heavens.
According to them, when those creatures
Look toward their sun, we see our stars of night.
And they believe their seasons of the sky

Mirror our own, with days and nights divided equally.
But these are vain dreams, embraced by fools,
Born of perverse reasoning and false beliefs.
For in a boundless world,
There can be no fixed center.
Even if such a center existed,
Nothing could settle there permanently,
For no force would hold it in place
More than any other could dislodge it.
The void itself, infinite and yielding,
Allows no fixed position, no resting point.
It must give way equally to weights,
Wherever their motions lead.
In the void, bodies cannot remain still,
Deprived as they are of any force to anchor them.
Nor can void offer support,
For its nature is to yield and give way.
Thus, no craving for a center
Could bind things together in such a manner.
Moreover, those who claim that not all bodies
Press toward the center,
But only earth and water—
The seas, rivers, and all things
Encased in earthly form—
Contradict themselves.
They argue that thin air and hot fire
Are driven outward from the center,
And that this outward motion feeds the ether,
Filling it with bright stars
And fueling the sun's flame in the sky.
They suggest that heat, fleeing from the center,
Gathers above and creates these celestial fires.
Yet this same logic would demand
That tree branches could not sprout leaves,
Unless their nourishment rose slowly upward

From the earth below.
These claims, built on faulty reasoning,
Crack under scrutiny,
For the world, boundless and infinite,
Knows no center, no fixed order of weight or motion,
And no single point to which all things gravitate.
Lest, like the winged flames of fire,
The walls of the world dissolve and flee,
Scattered into the boundless void,
And all that exists should follow after—
Lest the heavens, with their thundering vaults,
Burst apart and splinter skyward,
And the earth, slipping from beneath our feet,
Collapse into ruin. Its solid mass,
Torn apart along with heaven's wreckage,
Would scatter its primal seeds,
Drifting forever through the immeasurable void,
Leaving behind no trace, no remnants—
Only desolate space and invisible atoms.
For wherever you imagine the primal seeds lacking,
That very place becomes the doorway of death,
Through which all matter will rush and scatter
Outward, into nothingness.
If you reflect on these truths,
Guided by reason with but little effort,
One thing after another will reveal itself,
And the path will grow clear before your gaze.
No blind night will obscure your understanding,
Nor hinder your vision of nature's farthest reaches.
Thus, one truth will light another,
And knowledge will kindle torches of its own.

Book II

Proem

It is sweet, when on the vast and stormy sea
The winds churn up the waves, to watch from land
Another's struggle, distant from your own,
Not because we take delight in others' pain,
But for the joy of seeing troubles spared from us.
It is sweet, too, to witness mighty armies
Clashing in battle across the open plains,
While we ourselves are safe from risk and harm.
Yet nothing is more sweet, more goodly,
Than to stand on the high, serene plateaus,
Fortified by wisdom's walls, and look below
At other men, wandering far and wide,
Searching in vain for life's elusive path.
Some strive for genius, others chase after rank,
Laboring through days and nights in endless toil,
Seeking power, mastery over the world.
O wretched minds of men! O blinded hearts!
In what great dangers, in what shadows of life,
Do you waste your fleeting years!
How can you not see that Nature seeks for nothing
Except to keep pain from the body
And fill the mind with peace, free from fear and care?
We see, then, that the body needs but little:
Only enough to drive away pain
And provide a modest share of simple joys.
For Nature craves no lavish luxury.
It is no less sweet, if golden statues
Do not line the halls, holding lamps aloft,
If the house glitters not with gold and silver,
And no gilded ceilings resound to the lyre.
It is enough to recline with friends on soft grass,

By a flowing stream, beneath the shade of a great tree,
Refreshing our bodies with simple pleasures—
Most sweet of all when springtime graces the earth,
Sprinkling flowers across the green.
Nor will a fever leave your body sooner
If you toss upon a couch of purple silk
Than if you lie on a poor man's humble bed.
Since treasures, rank, and glory bring no ease
To the body's sufferings,
They bring no more comfort to the mind.
Unless, perhaps, you find joy in the sight
Of your legions gathering on the Field of Mars,
Or your fleets deploying across the seas,
The spectacle momentarily silencing
The fears of death and dispelling dread.
But if we reflect, we see this pomp is hollow—
A mockery, a fleeting show.
The dread of death does not fear swords or armies,
Nor does it shrink from golden thrones or purple robes.
Even amidst kings and rulers of the world,
Dread walks undaunted, mingling among them.
Can there be any doubt that such fears arise
Not from wealth or power, but from the mind itself?
For all of life labors in the dark.
Just as children tremble in the shadows of night,
Fearing what they cannot see,
So do we, in the full light of day,
Dread things no more real or terrible
Than the phantoms children invent in the dark.
This terror, this darkness in the mind,
Cannot be dispelled by the rising sun,
Nor by the bright arrows of morning light.
Only nature's laws, understood,
Can bring such fears to an end.

Atomic Motions

Now come, and let me guide your steps
To untangle how the primal seeds
Give birth to all the varied world,
And how, when formed, it dissolves again—
What force compels these acts, and what speed
Drives the seeds through the vast, infinite void.
Attend closely and yield to my words.
For matter does not cling together tightly,
Nor is it packed so dense as to remain unchanged.
We see how everything ages and decays,
How time erodes all things,
How objects wither and pass from sight.
Yet the total sum of matter endures,
Unharmed, because the seeds departing from one
Diminish it, while joining another,
Replenishing what they reach.
This endless exchange ensures the world's renewal:
What dies in one place gives life to another.
Thus, nations rise and fall, generations pass,
Each one like a runner handing on
The torch of life to the next.
But if you believe the primal seeds can stop
And, from rest, give birth to motion anew,
You stray far from truth's path.
For all seeds move through the infinite void,
Driven by their own weight or struck by others.
When these seeds meet and clash,
They often rebound, leaping apart,
Solid and unyielding in their nature,
Nothing behind them halting their motion.
Consider further: nowhere in the vastness
Of all existence is there a bottom,
No final resting place for primal seeds.

The infinite void extends without measure,
Boundless in all directions.
Thus, primal seeds can never find rest;
They are forever driven by ceaseless motion.
Some collide and rebound, leaving gaps;
Others cluster more tightly,
Their shapes interlocking in firm bonds.
Those bound closely form the roots of rocks,
The brute strength of iron, and other dense matter.
The seeds that leap far apart, leaving large gaps,
Create thin air and the radiant light of the sun.
And many others, cast off from unions,
Wander the void, unlinked and unaccepted,
Without a place in the structure of things.
This ceaseless dance of seeds mirrors
What we see with our own eyes:
When sunlight streams into a darkened room,
Tiny motes are revealed, tumbling in the light,
Battling, colliding, parting,
Chased up and down in endless motion.
From this, imagine the ceaseless tossing
Of primal seeds in the mightier void—
A small reflection of their vast, unseen dance.
These tumbling motes in sunlight
Hint at the hidden movements of primal matter.
For even in the smallest specks,
You can see how unseen blows
Drive them to change course,
To rebound, to scatter in all directions.
This restless motion begins with the primal seeds,
Moving of their own accord.
From their blows, they stir the smallest unions,
Closest in size to themselves,
And these in turn move the next larger bodies,
Until motion climbs stage by stage

To reach the objects visible to us.
Thus, from the unseen atoms,
Motion spreads outward, step by step,
Until it reaches the world we observe,
Though the original forces driving it
Remain hidden from view.
Do not wonder, Memmius,
Why, while the seeds of things are in constant motion,
The world as a whole seems to stand still,
Except when its entire frame visibly moves.
The nature of these primal atoms lies
Far beyond the reach of human senses;
Since we cannot see them,
Their movements remain hidden from our eyes.
Consider even the things we can observe—
How often their motions are concealed by distance.
On a far hillside, flocks of sheep may graze,
Wandering as the dew-drenched grass calls to them,
While lambs, full-bellied, frolic and lock horns in play.
Yet from afar, all appears as a still white blur,
A motionless gleam against the green hill.
Or imagine mighty legions spread across the plains,
Engaged in mock warfare, their polished brass
Gleaming in the sun, the ground trembling
Under their rhythmic march. Their shouts echo
From mountain walls to the stars above,
While cavalry charges send tremors through the earth.
But from some high vantage point,
The great army appears at rest,
A shining stillness upon the fields below.
Now consider the speed of matter's atoms,
And from this example, learn how swift they move:
When dawn first sprinkles light across the land,
And birds flit through the forest,
Filling the air with their liquid notes,

The sun rises, and suddenly its light
Spreads to clothe the world in radiance.
Yet, the sun's light and warmth do not travel
Through a void; they push through the dense air,
Slowed as they cleave the waves of atmosphere.
These rays move as a mass, tangled together,
Each particle restraining the others,
Checked by resistance as they advance.
But the primal atoms, solid and indivisible,
Travel through the void unhindered.
Unbound by external forces,
They race straight toward their goal,
Swift and unimpeded.
Their simple, compact nature allows them
To move far faster than the sun's light,
Covering vast expanses of space
In the time it takes sunlight
To fill the sky with its glow.
There is no need to trace each atom's path
To understand the laws of their motion.
Yet some, ignorant of matter's workings,
Claim that the seasons and the fruits of the earth
Exist only by divine will,
That gods adjust the world's workings to suit mankind,
Providing grains, life's pleasures, and the allure of love
To ensure the propagation of the human race.
They argue that the gods created all things for man,
But in doing so, they stray far from reason.
Even without knowledge of primal seeds,
I dare assert—by observing the heavens,
And by countless other proofs—
That the world was not crafted by divine hands
For humanity's sake.
For great are the flaws with which the world is burdened.
These faults, Memmius, I will later explain in detail.

For now, let us continue unraveling
The nature of motion and the truths it reveals.
Now, let me show you this truth, Memmius:
Nothing corporeal can rise upward by its own force
Or move against gravity's pull.
Let not the upward leap of flames deceive you,
For they ascend not by their own will,
But are driven by external forces.
Flames grow upward as they consume fuel,
Just as trees and plants reach skyward,
Though their weight always presses downward.
When fire climbs through a house,
Leaping from beams and timbers,
It is not moving freely—
It is pushed upward by the heat beneath.
Have you not seen how blood spurts upward
From a wound in the body,
Or how water hurls back timber and beams,
No matter how forcefully they are pushed beneath its surface?
The deeper they are submerged,
The more violently they rebound,
Emerging far above the surface,
Yet their weight always pulls them downward.
So too with flames:
Though they seem to rise,
Their motion results from external forces,
Not from an intrinsic upward pull.
Look to the meteors sweeping the skies,
Trailing long lines of fire.
Do not their flames follow paths provided by nature?
Do not stars fall toward the earth,
And does not the sun,
Though high in heaven,
Send its heat downward to warm the ground?
Lightning, too, cuts through the rain,

Zigzagging from cloud to earth,
Its fiery energy descending.
In all this, we must also grasp this truth:
As the atoms fall through the infinite void,
They do not always follow perfect straight lines.
At indeterminate times and places,
They swerve ever so slightly from their paths.
Without this subtle deviation,
All atoms would fall endlessly downward,
Parallel like raindrops in a bottomless void,
Never colliding, never creating anything.
Some argue that heavier atoms fall faster,
Striking lighter ones to create the collisions
That bring the world into being.
But this view falters,
For in the void, where no resistance exists,
All atoms, regardless of weight,
Fall at the same speed.
In water or air, heavier objects fall faster
Because the medium resists lighter bodies less.
But in the void, where nothing resists,
All move equally, without obstruction.
Thus, no collisions can occur simply from weight,
And without collisions, nature could create nothing.
Therefore, atoms must swerve slightly—
A minute deviation, almost imperceptible.
This swerve, slight as it is,
Allows them to meet, collide, and create motion.
Without this swerve,
All movement would be predetermined,
Each motion linked to another in an unbroken chain,
And free will would not exist.
But we see it does.
When we move as we desire,
It is not because of external force

Or predetermined cause.
Consider the horses at the starting gate:
They rear with eagerness to race,
But their bodies do not leap forward at once.
Their matter must first be roused,
From the mind's command to the limbs,
Until their motion matches their will.
Contrast this with motion forced upon us,
When external blows drive us against our will.
In such cases, our inner force resists,
Pulling back on the reins,
Redirecting the body's course
To align with our desires.
This power to resist,
To act freely despite external forces,
Must originate in the atoms themselves.
If the primal seeds lacked this capacity,
All motion would be fixed,
A mere consequence of weight and impact.
Thus, we see that freedom—
The ability to act without compulsion—
Is born of the atoms' subtle swerve.
In no fixed place or time,
This slight deviation breaks the chain of necessity,
Allowing for choice, will, and the creation of all things.
The stock of matter has never been more tightly packed,
Nor has it ever been divided by wider gaps.
For nothing can be added to it, and nothing can be taken away.
Thus, as the elemental particles move today,
So they moved in ages past,
And so they shall move forevermore.
What was born long ago shall be born again,
Under the same conditions and laws,
To grow and flourish according to Nature's
Unchanging and eternal decrees.

The sum of all things cannot be altered,
For nothing exists outside the universe—
No place for matter to escape,
No external source to supply fresh atoms,
To intrude upon the established order,
Change the essence of things,
Or reverse their motions.

Atomic Forms and Their Combinations

Now come, and grasp what follows:
Understand the countless forms and shapes
Of the ancient seeds of the universe.
They differ vastly, not just in a few cases,
But in endless variety.
These primal particles do not share
A single uniform appearance.
It is no wonder, since their number is infinite,
As I have shown—without limit or sum.
It must follow that they cannot all
Be marked by the same outline or shape.
Consider humanity, the flocks of fish
Swimming silently in streams,
The joyful herds grazing the fields,
The wild beasts, and the myriad birds—
Some flitting through water-bound haunts
By rivers, springs, and pools,
Others darting from tree to tree
In untamed forests.
Take any creature you choose,
From any kind or group,
And you will see each one differs in form,
Distinct from all others of its kind.
Without this diversity,
Mothers could not recognize their young,

Nor offspring their mothers—
Yet we see this happen every day,
As clearly among animals as among humans.
Behold, at the altars of the gods,
Where incense burns,
A yearling calf falls to the ground,
Its breast streaming warm blood.
Meanwhile, the orphaned mother roams
The green woodlands,
Searching the earth for her lost young.
She tracks its cloven hoofprints,
Scanning every place for signs,
Until, finding none, she halts.
Filling the leafy paths with her cries,
She returns to the stall,
Driven by relentless longing.
Not the tender willows,
Nor the fresh, dew-kissed grass,
Nor the gentle streams
Gliding along the banks
Can soothe her or ease her pain.
No other calves grazing nearby
Can distract her heart—
Her mind clings fiercely
To what is known and hers alone.
So too, the young of goats,
With their bleating throats,
Seek out their horned dams,
And the lambs their ewes.
Unfailingly, each finds its place,
Pressing to its proper teat,
As nature wills.
Even among grains of wheat,
No single kernel is identical to another—
Some subtle difference

Marks each one apart.
Likewise, on the seashores,
Where soft waves kiss the thirsty sands,
You will find no shell or conch
Perfectly alike in shape.
Thus, the seeds of all things,
Born of nature, not crafted by hand,
Do not conform to a single pattern.
They drift, diverse in form,
Each shaped uniquely,
Without a fixed mold or design.
It is easy to understand, dear Memmius,
Why the fires of lightning penetrate more deeply
Than the flames we kindle from earthly pine.
The celestial fire is composed of finer particles,
More subtle and delicate,
Allowing it to pass through spaces
That our denser fire cannot breach.
Consider how light passes through the horn
Of a lantern, while rain is kept at bay.
This is because the particles of light
Are finer than those of water.
Observe also how wine flows swiftly
Through the holes of a colander,
While olive oil moves sluggishly.
This happens because the oil's particles
Are larger or more entangled,
Slowing their separation and movement.
The same principle applies to all matter—
Finer particles move freely,
While larger, hooked elements are slower to pass.
Notice how honey or milk pleases the tongue
With its smooth and rounded nature,
While wormwood or centaury repels with bitterness.
The agreeable substances are formed of smooth atoms,

While the harsh and sharp are made of jagged shapes,
Tearing at the senses as they enter the body.
All sensations arise from these differences:
Smooth forms bring pleasure,
While rough forms cause irritation and pain.
Consider the difference between the sound
Of a sweet melody played on strings
And the harsh screech of a saw—
Surely, their atoms differ in shape and structure.
Likewise, the odors that pierce the nostrils
From burning flesh are not the same
As the fragrant scent of saffron or incense.
The pleasant and the foul, the beautiful and the vile,
Are all made of different forms,
With smoothness producing charm,
And roughness creating distress.
Some sensations lie between these extremes—
Such as the tartness of wine or the bitterness of herbs.
These arise from elements that are neither entirely smooth
Nor fully hooked, but slightly angled,
Tickling the senses without tearing them.
Fire and ice also differ in the shapes of their atoms,
As their effects on the body clearly show.
For touch, above all, is the ultimate sense—
Whether pain or pleasure arises
From something external or internal,
From collisions of atoms or their orderly flow.
Touch alone reveals the true nature of matter,
Showing how diverse forms cause diverse sensations.
The hardest substances—diamond, flint, iron—
Are built from hooked atoms,
Interlocked like branches,
Resisting blows and force.
Meanwhile, liquids, with their smooth and rounded atoms,
Flow freely, their particles unable to cohere.

Popcorn kernels in the hand flow like water,
Their roundness enabling easy movement.
Yet even in fluids like ocean brine,
Rough particles are mixed with smooth ones,
Giving the bitter taste.
The rough particles do not cling together,
But their globular nature allows them to roll
And still rasp the senses.
Proof of this mixture lies in the separation
Of sweet water from salt.
As water filters through the earth,
The rough, briny particles cling to the soil,
While the smooth, sweet ones flow freely,
Emerging as fresh springs.
Smoke, clouds, and flames also disperse easily,
Made of atoms that are not tightly linked.
Their pointed forms pierce through air,
Stone, and body alike,
Yet remain unbound to one another.
Having explained these truths,
Let us turn to another:
Though atoms vary in shape,
Their variations are finite.
If their forms were infinite,
Some seeds would grow infinitely large,
For endless variation would require endless parts.
Imagine atoms composed of three parts—
Rearranging their top, bottom, left, and right
Will yield only a finite number of shapes.
To create new forms, additional parts would be needed,
And with each new form, more additions required.
This would lead to infinite size,
Which we know cannot exist.
Thus, atoms are finite in form,
Bound by nature's laws,

And their differences, though vast,
Do not extend to infinity.
Now consider this, Memmius:
The dazzling robes of barbaric lands,
Their hues steeped in the Meliboean purple,
Dyed with the shellfish of Thessaly,
Would pale beside brighter, newer colours,
If such could be conceived.
The radiant feathers of peacocks,
Their golden generations streaked with brilliance,
Would be overshadowed by a fresher splendor.
The scents of myrrh, the sweetness of honey,
Would lose their allure.
Even the swan's song,
Or Apollo's hymns upon the lyre's strings,
Would be silenced by a sound more divine.
If ever something finer than the finest,
Or loathlier than the worst,
Could emerge to the senses,
The balance of things would be undone.
But such is not the case.
All things are bounded, limited—
Their forms, colours, scents, and sounds
Confined by nature's eternal laws.
The extremes of heat and cold
Stand fixed upon the path of seasons,
And between them lie every shade,
Every degree of warmth and chill.
Creation itself is governed by this law,
Differing only by finite changes,
Bound always by the limits of frost and flame.
From this truth, let us draw another:
The primal seeds of things,
Though varied in shape and form,
Are infinite in number.

Since their shapes are finite in kind,
Those sharing the same form must be infinite,
Else the supply of matter would fail.
From everlasting to today,
These eternal atoms endure,
Unbroken by time's ceaseless blows,
Sustaining the world without end.
Though some creatures are rare,
Like the elephants of India,
Whose ivory walls shield the land within,
They thrive elsewhere in abundance,
Balancing the scales of life.
Even if we imagined a being unique,
One of its kind across all lands,
Its existence would still require
An infinite reserve of matter
To form, to grow, and to sustain itself.
Without infinite seeds of its kind,
How could it survive in the vast chaos of the void,
Amidst the countless tides of matter?
Just as after a mighty shipwreck,
The ocean scatters beams, oars, and splinters of wood
Across distant shores,
So too would finite seeds,
Flung through endless ages,
Fail to unite or persist.
Yet we see things born,
We see them grow and thrive.
This proves the infinite nature
Of the primal seeds in every kind,
Providing the matter for all existence.
Neither creation's forces
Nor destruction's power reigns eternal.
Birth and death wage an unending war,
A balance of forces in ceaseless struggle.

Sometimes life's vitality prevails;
Sometimes it is overcome.
At the edge of life's beginning,
The cries of infants pierce the dawn,
While the laments of death
Echo in the shadows of every night.
Day and night, birth and death,
Have ever been entwined.
Hold this truth firmly in mind:
Nothing visible or known to us
Is made of a single kind of seed.
Everything is composed of mixed elements,
And those with more powers and properties
Contain the greatest diversity of seeds.
The earth, above all,
Holds within her the seeds
Of water, fire, and life itself.
From her springs the cool rivers,
The blazing fires of Aetna,
The grains and trees that nourish mankind,
And the grasses and pastures
That sustain the beasts of the wild.
For this, she is called
The great mother of gods,
The parent of beasts and men.
The ancient poets sang her praises,
Hailing her as the source of all creation.
Seated in her chariot above the airy realms,
She drives her team of lions, teaching all
That the vast earth hangs poised in empty space,
Needing no other earth to hold its weight.
To her chariot are yoked the wild beasts,
Symbolizing that even the most savage offspring
Must be tamed and guided by a parent's care.
A turret-crown encircles her head,

Signifying her fortressed cities,
For she sustains their strength and safety.
And today, adorned with the same emblem,
Her sacred image is borne solemnly
Through many lands, worshipped as divine.
Nations far and wide revere her as
The Idaean Mother, following the ancient rites.
They escort her with Phrygian bands,
Honoring the legend that grain first spread
From those regions to the world.
To her they dedicate the Galli,
The emasculate priests, to show
That men ungrateful to their mothers,
Or violators of her sacred majesty,
Are unfit to bring life into the world.
The Galli come, with wild frenzy,
Beating hollow cymbals and tambourines.
The blaring horns cry out with raucous bray,
And the pipes stir their minds to madness
With piercing Phrygian melodies.
They bear sharp knives, wild symbols of their zeal,
Meant to terrify the impious
With the fearsome power of the goddess.
When the Mother is carried through the cities,
She blesses all with silent grace.
People line the streets, scattering coins of brass and silver,
Showering her and her attendants
With a snowfall of roses.
Armed troops accompany her,
Known to the Greeks as the Phrygian Curetes.
Dancing with bloody mirth,
They clash brass on brass,
Their crested helmets nodding fiercely.
This armed procession recalls the story of Crete,
Where, as the tale goes, the Curetes drowned

The infant cries of Zeus with their rhythmic dance,
Beating their weapons to shield the child
From Saturn's devouring jaws.
Others say the armed retinue honors
The Mother's lesson: that men must defend
Their homelands with valor,
Guarding their parents with courage and pride.
Yet such tales, however beautifully told,
Stray far from reason.
The gods must dwell in eternal peace,
Untouched by mortal woes,
Needing neither our gifts nor our service.
The earth, insensate and eternal,
Is no goddess, but rather the source
Of life's materials. She holds within her
The seeds of countless forms,
Birthing all that lives and grows.
Those who name the ocean Neptune,
Or call the grain-crops Ceres,
May speak in metaphor,
So long as they keep their souls
Free from the stains of blind religion.
Look to the flocks, the herds, and the horses,
Grazing together on a single plain,
Beneath one sky, drinking from one stream.
Each lives in its own form and nature,
Faithfully repeating the traits of its kind,
Generation after generation.
In every plant and every river,
In all creatures great and small,
Diverse materials and seeds reside,
Shaped uniquely to form their distinct natures.
Every living being, without exception,
Is composed of bones, blood, veins,
Moisture, flesh, and muscle—

All built from elements
Diverse in shape and form.
Even fire, when it blazes,
Reveals its secret power:
Atoms within its frame
Release heat and light,
Scattering sparks and embers wide.
If you examine the world with reason,
You will see how everything hides within itself
The seeds of many forms,
Diverse and interwoven.
Observe how certain things are given
Colour, flavour, and scent combined—
Chiefly in burnt offerings,
Where fire reveals the hidden essence
Of their nature.
Thus, all things must be composed of diverse shapes.
The smell of scorching enters our senses,
While the bright color from dye remains apart;
And flavor, distinct from both,
Affects us differently still.
From this, it is clear that color, flavor, and scent
Are made of differing elemental shapes.
These varied forms combine into one,
And things exist through the mingling of seeds.
Yet not all things can combine in every way,
For if they could, monstrous forms would arise—
Half-human creatures with beastly parts,
Or trees growing from the bodies of men,
Sea creatures fused with land animals,
And the earth giving birth to Chimeras,
Breathing fire from hideous jaws.
But such beings are never born,
Because all things come from fixed seeds
And follow a fixed ancestry.

Nature ensures that each creature,
From the food it consumes,
Absorbs only the atoms suited to its kind.
These atoms, once within,
Join and produce the proper motions
That sustain the creature's life.
Meanwhile, nature expels foreign particles,
Those unsuitable for the body,
Which cannot integrate or support its functions.
Invisible bodies are cast out,
Impulsed by the force of blows,
Unfit to bond or sustain vital motion.
These laws do not bind living forms alone;
They govern all things, everywhere,
Distinguishing and defining the world.
Just as all things in creation are,
In their very nature, each unlike the other,
So too must their atoms differ in shape.
Not because only a few share the same form,
But because, as a general rule,
No one thing is exactly like all others.
In these verses, you see many elements
Common to many words—letters repeated,
Yet the words and lines remain distinct,
Built from different combinations.
Not every word is made of identical elements,
But rather, each has its unique pattern.
So it is with all things in nature:
While many seeds are shared across forms,
Their specific combinations
Create entirely different wholes.
Thus, humankind, grains, and joyful trees
Are each composed of distinct atoms.
Moreover, since the seeds differ,
So too must their intervening spaces,

The pathways they form, their connections,
Weights, impacts, collisions, and motions.
These distinctions do not merely define
The living forms of the world;
They also separate the ocean from the land,
Hold the heavens apart from the earth,
And maintain the harmony of all things.

Absence of Secondary Qualities

Thus must you understand that primal seeds,
The basic forms of things, lack hue and dye.
Do not suppose that white things shine because
Their atoms too are white, nor black things dark
Because their seeds are black. This thought is false.
For matter holds no colour of its own—
Neither like the objects formed nor unlike.
And should you think that mind or sense imparts
A hue to these first bodies, you are lost,
Far from the truth. For even those born blind,
Who've never seen the sun or light of day,
Can feel and recognize through touch alone
The forms of things, though colours mean no more.
What we perceive in dark is yet untinged;
No colour comes to us when light is gone.
If every colour shifts and changes shape,
And nothing keeps its hue unaltered still,
Then primal seeds cannot be stained with hues,
For they must hold their form eternally,
Or all would crumble back to nothingness.
A change in essence spells the end of things.
Thus, seeds must be devoid of tint or shade,
Or all we see would vanish into void.
Yet though they lack all hue, these primal forms,
By their arrangements, make all colours bloom.

A blackened thing may turn to gleaming white
As atoms shift, combine, and rearrange—
Much like the ocean changes, dark to light,
When winds upheave and churn its tranquil waves.
But if the sea were made of only blue,
No storm or motion could transform its hue.
If primal seeds could bear the stain of red,
Or green, or white, or blue, then just as shapes
Of cubes retain diversity within,
Each ocean wave would show a patchwork hue,
A thousand shades at odds with one another.
But objects we behold are pure in tone—
No patchwork waters shimmer in the sea.
Furthermore, colours do not birth themselves.
White does not come from white, nor black from black,
But rather, all derive from varied seeds,
Combined and altered in their size and shape.
And since no colour lives without the light,
These primal seeds, which dwell in shadowed void,
Must ever lack the vivid glow of hues.
See how the hues of doves and peacock tails
Shift subtly with the angle of the sun.
The green of emerald mingles with the red,
The golden bronze gives way to glowing white,
Depending on the play of beams and rays.
So colours are but fleeting forms of light,
A product of the sun's swift-moving touch.
Moreover, objects worn and torn to bits
Lose colour as they crumble into dust.
A linen cloth, unraveled thread by thread,
Reveals how dyes dissolve and fade away
Long before matter falls to primal seeds.
Thus, colours vanish as their forms degrade,
Proving they do not dwell within the core.
As not all things emit a sound or scent,

Nor all can touch or taste, so not all bear
The property of colour. Mind alone
Can sense and know these things without such traits.
And primal seeds, the building blocks of all,
Must lack both sound and scent, both warmth and cold,
For they emit no essence from themselves.
Just as a fragrant balm must first be mixed
With oil devoid of scent, lest it corrupt
The pure and subtle perfume it should hold,
So too must primal seeds be free of hues,
And scents, and flavours, lest they alter forms.
The seeds are bare, their power unadorned,
Yet from them rise all things in varied hue.
The rest; and yet, since all these things are mortal—
The pliant, being soft of body and yielding;
The brittle, with frames that crumble into dust;
The hollow, full of pores and easily broken—
They must be separate from primal elements,
If we are to establish an immortal foundation
Beneath the world, where the sum of all safety
And stability may rest, lest all things
Return to nothingness and perish utterly.
Now also, whatever we observe possessing sense
Must undeniably be formed of elements
Devoid of sense themselves. And the evidence,
So clear and immediate to all who see,
Does not refute this notion nor oppose it;
Rather, it leads us to this truth by hand,
Compelling belief that all living beings
Are born from lifeless elements, as I assert.
Indeed, we see live worms arise from foul dung
When the soaked earth rots after heavy rains;
And everything changes form in the same way.
Behold: rivers and grass, and lush pastures,
Are transformed into cattle; the cattle, in turn,

Into our own bodies; and from our bodies,
Wild beasts and winged birds grow mighty.
Thus nature converts all food into living forms,
Creating senses in these frames,
Just as she transforms dry logs into flame.
Do you not see, therefore, how greatly it matters
In what order the primal seeds are arranged,
With what other seeds they mix and combine,
And what motions they give and receive?
But now, what doubt strikes your sceptical mind,
Forcing you to argue against belief
That sense can arise from senseless atoms?
Surely, it is this: you see liquids, earth, and wood,
Even when combined, fail to create feeling life.
Thus, it will be helpful to remind yourself:
I never claimed that sense is born
Under all conditions or from every substance
That composes things capable of feeling.
What matters here is first the size of the seeds
That make up the thing endowed with sense;
Then, the shapes they carry; and finally,
Their positions, motions, and arrangements.
In wood and clods, these conditions are absent.
Yet even these, when softened by the rain,
Can give rise to writhing grubs, because the atoms
Within them, disarranged by the new factor,
Recombine in such a way as to create life.
Next, those who claim that sensing beings can
Only be formed from other beings that feel,
When soft they fashion them, for all sensation
Is linked with flesh, with sinews, and with veins—
And these, as we observe, are formed soft,
Endowed with frames destined to perish.
Yet even if they could endure forever,
Their sense would still be partial, tied to parts,

Or they'd be judged to share a sense akin
To that which animates the living whole.
But parts alone cannot themselves perceive,
For every sense within each member points
Back to the unity of something greater.
A severed hand, or any limb removed,
Cannot sustain sensation of its own.
Thus, these parts must resemble living beings
To hold the power of sense within themselves,
Each part in harmony with vital feeling,
Sensing all things precisely as we do.
If so, how could they serve as primal seeds,
The indestructible roots of all creation?
For living beings are subject to decay,
And mortal things cannot eternal be.
And even were they, by their unions all,
They'd yield but swarms of living things alone—
A chaos thronged with men, beasts, herds, and flocks.
For simply by conglomeration none
Can birth a thing new-made and separate.
And if, within a living frame, they lose
Their own sensation, taking on another,
Why grant them such a quality at all,
Only to strip it from them afterward?
Recall the proof: we see that fowls' eggs change,
Becoming chicks; and teeming worms arise
When sodden earth is drenched with soaking rain.
It's plain that sense can spring from insensate things.
And if some argue sense can thus emerge
By change, or through a certain kind of birth,
Know first: no birth occurs unless there comes
A union of the elements before,
No change unless they intertwine and meet.
For sense cannot inhabit any frame
Before its living nature is composed—

Since all its matter, scattered and dispersed
In rivers, air, and earth, cannot unite
To form the vital motions needed to
Ignite the spark of sensing life within.
And further, if some violent external blow
Strikes hard enough, it shatters every frame,
Confounding mind and body, as the seeds
Are loosened from their order and their motion halts.
Until these structures shake and scatter wide,
Undoing the vital threads of life itself,
The soul is driven out through every pore.
What else, when struck, could matter possibly do
But break apart, loosening from itself?
And yet, when gentler blows disturb the frame,
The vital motions often can prevail—
Restoring order, calming chaos, calling
Each part back to its proper place again,
Quelling the near dominion of death's sway,
And kindling once more sensations almost lost.
Else how could life reclaim its footing near
The very brink of death, turning away
From that abyss, rather than fully passing?
Furthermore, pain arises when matter,
Jostled within the body's joints and vitals,
Quivers and shakes against its natural state.
Delight, by contrast, blooms when all returns
To proper place, and smoothness soothes the form.
Thus primal seeds can feel neither pain nor joy,
For they lack the composition required
To suffer or to savor sweet delight.
If sense were necessary in all things
That lend sensation to the living whole,
What then of those fixed elements from which
Humanity is formed? Shall we believe
They laugh aloud, or weep, or question what

They themselves are made of? By such logic,
Each primal germ would need to come from others,
Endlessly regressing into nonsense.
Follow this reasoning: if a laughing man
Need not arise from laughing elements,
Nor thinking minds from sapient seeds, why, then,
Cannot sensation spring from senseless things,
Joined and arranged in proper form and motion?

Infinite Worlds

Once more, we all are born from seeds of heaven,
That same great Father, who bestows on earth,
Our nurturing mother, drops of liquid life,
Impregnating her womb to bear her broods—
The golden grains, the joyous shrubs and trees,
The human race, and all the wild beasts' kin.
She yields the food that feeds all living frames,
Sustains their lives, and helps them propagate;
Thus earning well the name of mother true.
What springs from earth sinks back to earth again;
What's sent from ether, homeward speeds once more
To heaven's embrace. Yet death annihilates
Nothing entirely: bodies never perish.
She only breaks their bonds, and then re-forms
The primal seeds in fresh configurations.
Thus, forms and colours shift, sensations come
And go, and life itself takes fleeting shape.
So thou may'st learn how much it matters, friend,
With what companions, in what structure held,
The primal seeds unite, and how they move.
For nothing that we see adrift today,
Born or destroyed, remains in its essence
Fixed within the eternal atoms' core.
Why, even in these verses that I craft,

The meaning rests on where and how I place
Each letter: sky and sea, the lands and streams,
The sun, the grains, the trees, and living forms—
All take their being from these same base shapes.
And what distinctions simple order makes!
So too in nature: change the intervals,
The ways of motion, paths, and weights, or bonds
Between the seeds, and all must change in turn—
The things themselves must differ utterly.
Now to sound reason turn thy open mind.
Strange truths demand a readiness to hear,
For they present the world in novel guise.
Yet nothing is so simple, at the start,
That it seems easy; nor so great, at first,
That it astounds forever. Mortal men
Soon grow accustomed, little by little,
To marvels vast and wondrous as they are.
Consider how the heavens stretch above,
The bright, clear skies, the constellations' dance,
The moon's soft glow, the blazing sun's fierce light:
Were these revealed to mortals suddenly,
If unforeseen, what wonder would there be!
What awe-struck whispers would the nations share!
Yet now, though grand, they scarcely draw our gaze.
So, cast not reason from thy mind in scorn,
Nor spurn this truth because it seems so new.
Instead, with sharpened judgment weigh its worth.
If it prove true, then yield thy heart to it;
If false, prepare thy arguments with care.
For now my human mind seeks far beyond,
To fathom the vast reaches lying past
The ramparts of this world, the boundless void,
Where thought itself leaps forward, swift, unbound.
First, understand that the universe has no bounds—
No end above, below, nor to the sides,

As reason shows and Nature's truths proclaim.
The infinite abyss of space extends,
And countless seeds, unnumbered, ceaselessly
In endless motion drift throughout the void.
It's folly, then, to think this earth and sky,
This single world of ours, were formed alone,
While all those seeds beyond remain inert,
Their power unused, their purpose left undone.
For just as seeds collided here by chance,
Combining randomly, without design,
To form this world, so countless other worlds
Must rise in other realms of boundless space.
For matter flows abundant, free, and vast,
And space lies open, offering no restraint.
Thus, many earths, suns, skies, and seas exist,
And races born of myriad kinds abound,
Scattered across the cosmos, endlessly.
No single kind of thing exists alone,
For all are members of a greater race—
Beasts roaming mountains, men upon the plains,
The fish in streams, the birds that skim the air—
Each springs from countless like itself. And so,
The earth and stars, the sun and moon, are joined
By countless others of their kind, unseen,
Scattered in regions vast beyond our ken.
Perceiving this, thou'lt see that Nature moves
Free from the tyranny of haughty gods.
No hand divine directs her course, nor voice
Commands the sum of her immeasurable frame.
For who could guide such boundless realms, or wield
The reins of endless matter, sky, and fire?
Who could at once light myriad suns, or shake
The heavens with thunder, while still tending all?
Indeed, how often has the lightning struck
The temples of the gods, or storms laid low

Their shrines, while blameless mortals bore the blows
Of such chaotic, aimless acts of force?
These sights, more reasoned than all fabled tales,
Reveal the truth: Nature herself, unbound,
Creates and ends, assembles and dissolves,
Without divine direction or decree.
From time's first dawn, new matter has flowed in,
To build the earth, expand the heavens' vault,
And fill the sea. Each element combines,
Joining its kind—earth thickening with earth,
Moisture merging with moisture, fire with fire.
This ceaseless process, guided by no will,
Extends the universe and shapes its bounds.
Yet limits hold: each thing can grow no more
When Nature reaches her appointed end.
For when the inward flow of nourishment
Equals the outward loss of vital seeds,
The body halts its climb, and life begins
Its slow descent toward decay and death.
As growth recedes, the tides of age prevail,
And what expands with ease now wastes away,
Unable to sustain its former strength.
So all things perish: either worn by time,
Eroded by external blows, or drained
By dwindling stores of life. Their fleeting forms
Are carried off by Nature's endless flow,
While she, unbroken, works to forge anew.
Thus, too, the mighty walls of this vast world
Shall crumble down, their ramparts stormed and breached,
Their fragments scattered through the boundless void.
For food sustains all things, renewing life;
Yet now no food suffices to uphold,
No veins contain the measure that is needed,
No Nature yields as much as time demands.
Even now, the earth—so weary, worn with age,

That once bore forth all life in teeming floods—
Now scarcely brings to birth her smallest forms.
She who of old gave life to mighty beasts,
And nourished every race upon her plains,
Now falters in her power to renew.
For never from the heavens' vaulted heights
Did golden chains let mortal beings down,
Nor did the sea, nor rocks lashed by the waves,
Bring forth these lives; the earth, the mother, bore them—
She still sustains, as once she gave them birth.
It was her hand that first bestowed the grain,
The joyful vineyards, and the pastures green,
Which now, though aided by our tireless toil,
Reluctant grow, their bounty slow and scant.
We yoke the oxen, wear our bodies down,
And spend the strength of sturdy farmer's hands;
The iron tools grow dull, and yet the soil
Grants little yield, begrudging every ear.
The aged ploughman shakes his head in grief,
And sighs to see his labours yield no gain.
He dreams of days long past, when life was full,
When less was asked, and yet the earth gave more.
He praises now the fortunes of his sires,
And, prattling on, recalls how simpler men
Once lived in plenty on their smaller fields.
The vine-planter, too, with weary heart, laments,
And rails against the seasons and the skies,
Not seeing that all things, by slow degrees,
Are fading, wasting, slipping to their end.
For all that's born must journey to the tomb,
Each worn and spent by time's unyielding march.

Book III

Proem

O thou who first did lift so bright a torch,
Illuminating dark paths of human thought,
Thy wisdom shines a beacon, guiding men
To seek the true and shun the shades of fear.
I follow thee, great glory of the Greeks,
Not as a rival, but a devotee,
Eager to tread the noble paths thou laid,
As one who loves the master's work would do.
For how can sparrows vie with mighty swans,
Or lambs unsteady match the coursing steed?
Thou art the father, fountain of our truths,
Bestowing precepts from thy treasured scrolls.
As bees do sip the blossoms of the fields,
We drink thy golden wisdom, ever fresh,
A feast for thought, eternal in its worth.
When thy profound, godlike reason first unveiled
The workings of the universe entire,
The terrors of the mind were swept away;
The walls of this vast world fell open wide,
Revealing all the wonders of the void.
The gods emerged in their celestial calm,
Free from our woes, their peace untouched by strife,
Dwelling in realms beyond the winds and storms,
Where neither frost nor tempest breaks their rest.
No longer does my gaze behold the shades
Of Acheron, nor does the earth's expanse
Obstruct my view of all that lies below.
Through thee, I find a new and holy awe,
A trembling joy at nature's perfect law,
So plainly laid before the eyes of men.
And now, my verse must turn to delve the soul,

To teach the nature of the mind and life,
And banish fear of Acheron's dark gates,
Which clouds with dread the brightness of our days,
And poisons life's delights with shadowed grief.
For though some claim they dread not death itself,
Declaring shame and poverty their fears,
Their actions and their prayers betray the lie.
Exiles, fugitives, and outcasts alike,
Despised and stained with every wretchedness,
Still seek the gods with sacrifices grim,
Offering prayers and rites in bitter straits.
Their words, their masks, fall shattered in despair,
Revealing minds enslaved to fear of death.
The lust for wealth, the hunger after power,
The endless toil that leads to fleeting gain,
These too are rooted in the dread of death.
Men, fleeing want and disgrace, heap corpse on corpse,
Amassing riches at the cost of kin,
Hardened by fear to acts of cruel despair.
From envy, hatred grows; from greed, deceit;
From dread of death, the bonds of trust are torn,
And every virtue trampled underfoot.
For children fear the shadows in the dark,
And grown men tremble at the light of truth.
This terror of the mind, this ancient night,
No dawn can chase away, no gleam of gold,
But only wisdom, grasped through nature's laws.

Nature And Composition of The Mind

First, let us probe this question: the mind,
That intellect which governs human life,
Is part of man, no less than eyes or hands,
No less than feet or any vital limb.
But some declare its seat is nowhere fixed,

And name it "harmony"—a state derived,
Not of a part, but from the whole entire.
Thus do they claim that health within the flesh,
Although no single part can claim its seat,
Is yet the body's state. So mind, they say,
Resides as harmony, diffused throughout.
Yet, mightily, I hold their error plain.
For oft the body, seen and palpable,
Is sick, yet in the mind a joy remains;
Or else the mind in sorrow lies entrapped,
While limbs and frame enjoy a sweet repose.
Just as the foot may throb while head is whole,
So too the mind or body feels alone.
And when in slumber deep, the weary limbs
Lie lax and void of sense, the mind within
Still stirs itself, in dreams it wanders far,
Embraces phantoms, joys, and suffers cares.
Consider this: when body is undone,
With flesh consumed, the limbs still sometimes hold
A semblance of their life; yet, when a breath
Or heat's small remnants from the frame are gone,
All life departs, the structure falls to dust.
Thus life depends not on all parts alike,
But on those seeds of warmth and vital wind,
Which, fleeing, leave the body dead and cold.
So too the soul, a corporeal thing, must be,
A part within the body, not mere "harmony."
And now, since nature of the mind and soul
Dwells in the body as a vital part,
We must dismiss this notion borrowed hence
From Heliconian minstrels—let it serve
For music's art, not for the seat of life.
Mind and the soul, though joined as one, yet show
A double nature: one the sovereign power,
Which we call "mind," residing in the breast,

Where joy and terror spring and reason rules;
While through the limbs the soul obeys the mind,
A scattered presence moved by its command.
The mind alone perceives, and when it stirs,
It stirs itself, and neither body nor soul
Necessitates its mirth or pain; and yet,
When struck by fiercer shocks, the whole must feel:
A trembling spreads, the pallor pales the skin,
The voice is lost, the tongue falls silent, ears
Ring loudly, darkness veils the failing eyes,
And limbs collapse, as terror wracks the frame.
At times, such fear may even bring to death.
Thus, clear it is: the soul, conjoined with mind,
Forthwith transmits the mind's disturbance through
The limbs and body, proving them entwined.
From this, too, follows that the soul and mind
Are of a corporeal substance, since they move
And move the body, which no act can touch
Except by physical force. The spear that strikes
Our frame may miss the life itself, yet still
May stagger thought and set the mind adrift,
Till strength returns. Such anguish of the mind
Proclaims its nature too must be corporeal.
Thus have I shown the mind and soul, as parts
Of man corporeal, hold sway within,
And not as fleeting "harmony" dissolved
When man himself dissolves into the void.
The nature of the mind and soul, I tell,
Is wrought of finest particles, so small
And light, their motion outruns all we see.
For nothing moves as swiftly as the mind:
What it proposes, it begins at once,
Far faster than what hands or eyes can do.
Thus, such agility must spring from seeds
Exceedingly fine, smooth, and round, to move

At even the slightest touch or impulse weak.
Observe the flowing water: with a breath,
Its waves respond, for all its stock consists
Of rolling, rounded forms. Yet honey moves
Much slower; its structure, rougher, clings together,
Its atoms larger, rougher than the stream.
The lightest breeze will scatter poppy seeds,
Yet cannot shift the weight of stones or grain.
So by this rule, the smoother and more fine
The body's seeds, the swifter its response;
The rougher and more heavy, the more still.
Since mind is swift beyond all else we know,
Its seeds must be the smallest, roundest kind.
This truth, once grasped, illuminates the rest.
When life departs, when mind and soul withdraw,
The body's shape and weight remain unchanged.
All goes with death but sense and vital heat.
Thus, the soul's form must be compact and fine,
Its atoms woven subtly through the veins,
The nerves, the very marrow of the limbs.
For just as fragrance fades without a trace,
Or savour leaves the food yet alters not
Its weight or form, so soul, composed of seeds
So delicate, departs unseen, unfelt,
Leaving the body's outward semblance whole.
Yet soul and mind are not one simple form.
An aura subtle mingles there with heat,
And heat with air—a triple nature bound.
Heat, being rare, permits the airy seeds
To intermingle, forming one fine weave.
But these alone could never yield the sense,
The thought, the consciousness that life requires.
To this must join a fourth, unnamed, unknown,
More mobile, smooth, and subtle still than all.
This fourth conveys the motions that awake

Sensation; it is stirred the first, and then
Transfers its impulse to the heat and air,
Which rouse the blood and nerves, and finally
Reach to the marrow, spreading joy or pain.
Thus, sensation courses through the flesh,
Yet rarely penetrates beyond the skin;
For when it does, the soul, perturbed too much,
Begins to scatter through the body's pores.
So fragile is the balance that sustains
Our life, and yet, by nature's wise design,
Most shocks are stopped before the vital core,
Preserving life and granting us repose.
The soul and body, intertwined as one,
Hold shared dominion till their joint life's done.
Their union, like the fragrance in the myrrh,
Cannot be parted lest the whole deter.
From birth, the seeds of life are closely bound,
With mutual motions all their sense is found.
The soul, though fine and made of smallest parts,
Instructs the body, guides its vital arts.
Through every vein and nerve, it weaves its thread,
And, with the body, learns the path it's led.
For when the mind is struck by joy or pain,
The body echoes, stirred in every vein.
No single part can sense apart sustain,
Nor can the soul alone perception gain.
Each motion, thought, and sense is mutual born,
Each to the other bound till death is sworn.
To rend the soul away would break the frame,
And leave the body ruined, robbed of flame.
Like fragrant frankincense destroyed by force,
The sundered life cannot retain its course.
If any claim the body feels no pain,
And sense is soul's domain alone to reign,
They clash with fact: for eyes perceive the light,

And bodies flinch at wounds or burning blight.
Should soul alone be keeper of the sense,
The body's part would claim no consequence.
Yet, when the soul departs, the frame decays,
For it no longer serves the vital ways.
To say the soul peers outward, through the eyes
As through mere doors, with truth cannot align;
For when the light's too bright, we squint and fail,
And doors, unhampered, would not thus prevail.
If eyes were only portals to the mind,
Then with them closed, we'd clearer vision find.
From birth, the soul and body learn to share
Their powers, as each depends upon the pair.
No sense arises from a single source,
But through their blending comes the vital force.
Thus, see the truth: their lives are intertwined,
And neither lives without the other's kind.
The soul and mind, as partners deeply twined,
Compose the essence of our mortal kind.
Though mind stands sovereign, holding life's command,
The soul, its ward, obeys its guiding hand.
Without the mind, the soul cannot remain;
Together they depart, as life does wane.
Democritus, though wise, yet missed the trace,
Proposing soul and body's shared embrace.
For soul, more subtle, scattered, light, and few,
Cannot by bulk the body's form imbue.
Its primal seeds, dispersed with gaps between,
Are finer still than dust, or gossamer seen.
Thus, sensations come with measures vast,
For countless atoms must their signals cast
To stir the soul and make its presence felt,
By pounding motions where their clashes melt.
The body's coarser elements require
More frequent hits to kindle soul's desire.

The mind, however, reigns above the soul,
Its intellect retains the body's whole.
If mind remains, though limbs are torn apart,
Life lingers still, sustaining vital heart.
Yet when the mind is lost, the soul takes flight,
Abandoning the frame to death's cold night.
As vision rests upon the eye's clear core,
Its pupil bright, though injured parts implore,
So too the soul and mind in union dwell,
Each vital to the other, bound as well.
Destroy the mind, the soul will cease its claim,
And life's bright flame will vanish all the same.
This sacred bond, this deep entwined duet,
Sustains the frame, where life and soul are met.

The Soul is Mortal

The soul and mind, united, frail, and bound,
Are mortal both, as proofs in nature found.
Now hear, as sweet toil yields these truths to thee,
How they arise, dissolve, and cease to be.
The soul, composed of atoms small and fleet,
Exceeds in fineness smoke or vapor's sheet.
Like incense curling high from altars' glow,
Its substance, subtle, swiftly tends to go.
When vessels break, their liquids spill or seep;
When fog disperses, winds their fragments keep.
So too the soul, if loosed from mortal clay,
Fades quicker still and scatters far away.
The body forms the soul's supporting vase;
When shattered, both dissolve to void and space.
If blood's escape leaves veins and flesh undone,
How shall mere air, more tenuous, hold as one
The fragile soul? It parts as body fades,
Like mist dissolved by morning's warming rays.

Observe, as age unfolds, the mind and frame
Together grow, and together bear the same
Inevitable decay. In tender youth,
The mind is weak; in age, it seeks no truth.
When limbs grow frail, and strength begins to wane,
The mind too falters, tethered to the strain.
Disease, which plagues the flesh, afflicts the mind;
Their fates are linked, as nature's laws designed.
Grief, fear, and madness seize the mind with might,
And such afflictions end in death's dark night.
For as the body's pangs the soul confound,
So mortal pains the fleeting mind unbound.
See how the fiery wine within can weave
Its chaos through the veins, make strength deceive:
Limbs stumble, tongues stammer, eyes grow dim,
And thoughts are drowned as senses fade and swim.
If such a transient cause the mind can shake,
A greater blow its fragile bonds would break.
Witness the man who, seized by sudden throes,
Writhes, sputters, foams, and in convulsion goes.
The soul, disturbed by body's dire distress,
Reveals its nature: mortal, powerless.
Thus mind and soul, as body, find their end,
To winds dispersed, where primal atoms blend.
The soul, when ravaged, foams as if to spew
Its essence forth, like waves in tempest's brew
Where winds compel the seas to rage and toss.
It groans, torn by the poison's cruel cross,
Which drives the seeds of voice in hurried flight
Through well-worn paths, escaping to the light.
Reason falters; mind and soul are rent,
Their harmony undone, their strength near spent.
Yet when disease retreats, its venom fades,
The man, though reeling, slowly sense regains.
Thus, mind and soul, when trapped in fleshly frame,

84

Are fragile, wracked by sickness and by shame.
How then could these, exposed to open air,
Immortal battle with the winds out there?
The healing arts restore the mind's distress,
Confirming mortal roots in its recess.
For what can alter nature's primal plan
Save rearrangement of its form and span?
Yet what is deathless cannot lose or gain;
Its essence fixed, unchanging will remain.
But mind, when changed by sickness or by cure,
Shows mortal bounds no shift can long endure.
Mind and body, bound in common fate,
Are vessels joined, their essence integrate.
As severed limb or eye cannot persist
Detached from life, they rot and cease to exist.
So, too, the soul apart can never be,
For bound it is in body's frailty.
The union prospers both in life's design;
No sense endures if one must disentwine.
As eyes removed no longer see the day,
So soul and mind, alone, would lose their sway.
For deep within the body they're confined,
Their motion trapped in flesh, their fate entwined.
Once freed, the soul dissolves to mist or air,
Unable life's sensations to repair.
The frame disbands, its essence seeps away,
And mind and soul to scattered winds decay.
Thus death, the sunderer of life's tight bond,
Dissolves the soul to fragments far beyond.
When life departs, the body's ruin tells
How mind and soul had intertwined so well.
No single moment marks their swift retreat;
They fail in parts, their dissolution discrete.
Were they immortal, they'd not shrink nor flee,
But shed the frame, intact, like snakes shed skin to free.

Yet even in life, the soul can seem to fade,
A shadow tottering in the frame decayed.
When faintness grips, the body bends and falls,
The mind withdraws, and silence fills the halls.
How then, when loosed from fleshly bounds, can soul
Retain its essence, stripped of life's control?
Such truths unravel error's feeble guise:
The mortal soul cannot immortal rise.
Its fragments lost, its tethered power dissolved,
Its fleeting life, in body's ruin, resolved.
If soul immortal entered with the birth,
Why hold we not the memories of earth
Before we lived this life? Why no recall
Of deeds once done, if soul retains it all?
Should mind so alter, every trace effaced,
Is this not death by other name replaced?
Thus, what was once, hath perished, gone to naught,
And what now lives, by nature's hand is wrought.
Why, too, does soul, if death it cannot know,
Shrink not entire, as body comes to woe?
When limbs grow cold and sense retreats from skin,
Why gathers it not close, held safe within?
Yet no such seat of concentrated soul
Appears to rally when the dying toll
Creeps slow through flesh; instead, as parts decay,
The soul, like breath, dissolves and drifts away.
Observe the field where soldiers clash in fight,
And chariot scythes bring ruin in their might:
A severed arm still twitches on the ground,
A foot, cut free, its curling toes astound.
The head, once hewn, maintains its gaze, until
The final spark departs and all is still.
Shall we then claim each fragment keeps its soul?
Would many souls inhabit but one whole?
Absurd! The soul, as body, splits and dies,

Its mortal nature shown before our eyes.
And mark the serpent, sliced in writhing parts,
Its severed lengths still animated, starts
Each toward the other, jaws in futile quest
To join again and soothe the wound's unrest.
Are these now hosts of souls in pieces spread?
Or was the single soul, like body, shed?
What of the man who fades as death encroaches,
Each limb in turn the chill of death approaches?
The nails turn blue, the feet lose sense and life,
The creeping cold ascends in gradual strife.
The soul does not withdraw to one last place;
It fragments, like the body, and efface
Itself entirely as breath slips to the winds—
No trace remaining where its presence thins.
And if, as some may falsely hold, the soul
Gathers its essence inward, makes it whole,
Then should the seat of such collected power
Burn bright with life, a final blazing hour.
But no such spark, no focus of the mind,
Emerges; only dissolution blind.
Thus mortal must the soul be, since it dies
In step with flesh, its parting seen through eyes.
Lastly, if immortal were the soul,
And births it entered whole, its sacred role,
Why not retain some trace of lives before,
Some memory of what came ere this shore?
Yet blank our minds, and naught remains to show
The footprints of the paths we used to know.
If memory's power has wholly changed or failed,
What is that but death by other veil?
Thus must we see, from reason's steadfast guide,
The soul that was is gone; what lives, new-tied.
Moreover, if the soul should enter frame
Just at the moment body springs to life,

Why does it grow as if by nature's aim,
Entwined with flesh, with blood, with nerves so rife?
If it were foreign, placed as in a cave,
And not a partner fused with living form,
How could it share the pain the body gave—
The aching tooth, the ice-cold water's harm?
The body's flesh, its bones, its very teeth
Share with the soul the joys and pangs of sense.
From this, 'tis clear, they're twined, not placed beneath—
Not transient, but born of joint essence.
And when the soul departs, dissolving ties,
It cannot leave the body whole, unscathed.
The weaving threads of life it thereby flies,
And with the severance, both are unmade.
If soul, as some might fancy, trickles in,
Seeping through pores, absorbed through all the frame,
Then it, like water mingling, must begin
To scatter, perish—merge and lose its claim.
For what dissolves within another's form
Cannot survive, nor hold its own estate.
Thus, too, the soul, from dissolution born,
Finds in the body's death its destined fate.
And what of life within the corpse's clay?
Does soul remain, or leave its seeds behind?
If fragments linger when the soul's away,
Then soul is mortal, as its parts unwind.
But if it flees intact, with none to stay,
Whence crawl the worms, the teeming forms of life?
Does soul from outward bring these beasts to clay,
Or bubble they from death's dissolving strife?
Should souls descend to animate decay,
How could one soul give rise to such a host?
Are treaties made in realms where spirits play,
Where first to come claims entry, others lost?
Or must they toil to forge new forms from seeds,

Dismissing peace to war for mortal needs?
The fox's cunning, lion's raging heart,
The deer's innate and ancestral fleeing—
Each shows the mind with body grows, takes part,
In traits inborn, not later entering being.
Were souls immortal, swapping forms at will,
The hawk might quake before the gentle dove,
The stag might hunt the hound through forest still,
And men might shun their hate, and beasts learn love.
If souls retain their wisdom, why do men
Not bear the knowledge of their prior state?
The child begins as blank, and only then
Through growth and frame learns reason, small or great.
Were soul unchanged, a steed's newborn would know
The mastery of gallops through the plain.
But minds are shaped by bodies, as they grow,
And when they falter, minds too feel the strain.
And if the soul with body wax and wane,
Must they not share a common mortal thread?
For what immortal would such growth sustain,
Or flee from age, as though by frailty led?
And why should countless souls await in strife
To fill the forms of creatures yet unborn,
Contending madly for a fleeting life,
While others linger in immortal scorn?
No treaties bind the souls in such a race;
No orderly descent could guide their ways.
Instead, as body wanes, so wanes its grace;
And soul, entwined with flesh, fades with its days.
For bound together, born as one, they die,
The mortal shell and mind, beneath the sky.
Again, a tree can't flourish in the air,
Nor clouds reside beneath the ocean's swell,
Nor fish take root upon the fields of earth,
Nor blood course through the rigid veins of stone,

Nor sap in boulders thrive: all things are fixed,
Bound to their proper natures and their place.
So too the mind cannot exist alone,
Apart from body, nor sustain itself
Without the thews and pulsing streams of life.
Were it conceivable to stand apart,
It might as well take root within the head,
The chest, the feet—no matter where it dwelled—
So long as it remained a part of man.
But even here, within this mortal frame,
The soul and mind are stationed and confined,
Each in its own domain, to grow and act.
How then imagine them to dwell apart,
Unbound by blood and body, yet endure?
To think the mortal bound to the divine,
Entwined, enduring both decay and time,
Is folly's height. What could be more opposed—
The fleeting joined with the eternal flame?
If soul were deathless, it would surely stand
Immune to blows, impervious to decay,
Its essence formed of indivisible parts,
Like primal seeds we've spoken of before.
Or else, like void, it might escape all harm,
Unyielding to the touch of any force.
Or, lastly, it would be eternal still,
For lack of space to scatter and dissolve—
As is the sum of all, boundless and whole.
But should one claim the soul eternal proves
Through some defense against dissolving blows—
That naught can harm its essence, or that harm
Is felt and then expelled before it breaks—
Such claims dissolve when viewed in mortal life.
For when the body sickens, so does soul;
And when the frame endures its biting pains,
The soul, in tandem, bears the torment too.

The past, as well, torments the soul with guilt;
Old crimes resurface, gnawing bitterly.
Add to these woes the frenzy of the mind,
Its sinking into torpor, or its loss
Of memories once cherished and retained.
Even sleep—a brief oblivion each night—
Suggests how soul can waver, fade, and sink.
What then of death, which ends all mortal ties?
How could the soul survive, when even here
It quakes beneath the weight of fear and pain?

Folly of The Fear of Death

Therefore, death to us is nothing, nor a thing to fear,
For the nature of the mind is mortal and no more.
Just as in the ages long before our birth,
When Carthage's hosts clashed in mighty war,
And the trembling world hung in uncertain fate,
We felt no pangs, nor knew the strife of nations.
So, when the union of body and soul dissolves,
And we are no more, nothing can harm or touch us,
Even if earth and sea should merge in chaos
And heaven tumble down upon the ruins.
For once dissolved, the senses cannot suffer,
Nor the self lament its own extinguished light.
If perchance one fears the soul may linger still,
Detached from body but imbued with feeling,
Let them reflect: it is only in this union,
This bond of soul and body, that life and pain exist.
When this bond breaks, the self is gone forever,
Its motions stilled, its thoughts dispersed to naught.
Even were time to gather our scattered atoms,
Rebuilding our frame and reigniting life,
That second self would not concern the first—
For the thread of memory, once severed, cannot join.

The selves we were in yesterdays long past
Are nothing to us now; we grieve them not.
Reflect on this: the atoms that form us now
Have wandered many times before, forming
Countless shapes and lives, only to dissolve again.
If we recall no pain from those lost selves,
Why should we dread the loss of this one now?
For only the living can feel harm or woe;
Death, which ends life, bars such feelings too.
He who grieves his future corpse is plagued by folly,
Imagining his self in lifeless flesh,
Picturing his body torn by beasts or fire.
Yet no one exists within the corpse to suffer;
No self remains to mourn its disarray.
The dead feel nothing. What harm is there, then,
To lie in flames, or earth, or brutes' wild jaws?
Why should the honeyed tomb, the icy slab,
Or crushing soil torment what cannot sense?
Consider this, then, to free the mind from grief:
"Thee now no more the warm embrace shall welcome,
Nor children's laughter fill thy heart with joy.
Thou shalt no longer strive nor hold dominion."
But add: "And thou no longer carest for these things."
For he who sees that death is endless sleep,
A rest eternal without pang or longing,
Will lay aside his fears of what may come,
Knowing the mind's release is but repose.
Death is sleep eternal, a scattering of self,
The atoms dispersed, their motions ceased forever.
And just as sleep demands no self or being,
So too does death demand even less—
For none awaken once life's icy pause has struck.
This too, men often say, reclining at their ease,
Amid the wine cups, garlanded with blooms awry:
"Brief is this joy we mortals glean; it flies

Too soon, and once it's gone, it comes no more."
As if, in death, the worst of all our ills
Were parched tongues thirsting, or some lack endured.
But if, perchance, great Nature raised her voice,
And thus reproached us with a stern rebuke:
"O mortal, what afflicts thee so that thou
Dost yield to plaints and tears in face of death?
If all the days behind thee brought delight,
And all thy life was not a wasteful flow,
Why not, content as one who leaves a feast,
Depart from life with calm, untroubled heart?
But if thy joys were squandered, unfulfilled,
And life offends thee, why prolong the chain,
Only to lose again what once seemed sweet?
Why not make end, and free thyself from toil?
For naught remains that I can give thee now,
No new delights, nor days unlike the past,
Though thou shouldst conquer all the bounds of time,
And endless years should stretch before thy feet."
What could we answer to this just appeal?
Would not her words stand firm, her counsel true?
Yet should some elder soul, grown ripe with years,
Lament his fate with louder cries than fit,
Would not her voice rise sharper still to chide:
"Cease your weeping, fool! Restrain your moans!
The sum of life's delights is now fulfilled;
Yet ever you disdain the goods at hand,
While craving more that cannot come to you.
Thus, life has slipped away, incomplete, in vain,
While death now waits beside you, close at hand.
Why linger here, unsated of the feast,
When time has come for you to make your way?
Yield with grace, and give your place to those
Who follow, as once others made room for you."
Justly, I think, would Nature reason thus,

And rightfully reproach; for ever new
Must rise from old, and one thing give to others
Room to grow and thrive. None are consigned
To black Tartarus—no endless void devours—
But substance ever serves the generations,
A ceaseless chain of life that rises, falls,
And rises yet again.
Look back: before our birth, the eternal past
Was nothing to us—silent, unperceived.
So, too, shall time to come, when we are gone,
Mirror that past, unbroken and serene.
What horror lies in that? What grief can stir
At such a fate? Is it not calmer far
Than any dreamless sleep, untroubled and secure?
And truly, those torments they tell of in Acheron,
The depths of the underworld, are here in life.
No Tantalus, struck by empty fear,
Cowers beneath a rock suspended in the air;
But rather, a baseless dread of the gods
Plagues humanity, and each fears the fall
Of misfortune that fate might send their way.
No vultures feed forever on Tityus,
Sprawled out in Acheron, nor can they find
Eternal banquet in his mighty breast.
Even if his limbs spanned the whole wide earth,
He could not endure perpetual pain,
Nor nourish such devourers endlessly.
Instead, our own Tityus is the lover
Torn by relentless anguish, gnawed within
By unfulfilled desires, his soul laid bare.
And we see Sisyphus, not in some distant hell,
But here among us—he who strives for power,
Who courts the people's favor, seeks the rods,
The axes of high office, only to fall,
Beaten, dejected, time and time again.

This is to push the stone with wearying toil
Up the steep hill, only for it to roll
Back down again into the plain below.
Likewise, to sate an ungrateful mind,
To fill it with pleasures yet find it never full—
As the seasons bring forth their varied fruits,
And still we hunger endlessly for more—
Is like the Danaids in their endless task,
Pouring water into a sieve that never fills.
Cerberus, the Furies, Tartarus' dark pit,
And its fiery waves—they exist not there,
Nor ever could. But here on earth we see
The fear of justice, the dread of retribution.
The dungeon, the scourge, the infamous leap
From the rock of shame, the rack, the flames, the lash—
All these are real, and yet, even in their absence,
A guilty conscience wields its own cruel whip,
Tormenting the mind with fear of what may come,
Of heavier punishments after death's veil falls.
Indeed, the fools' own lives are Acheron on earth.
Say to yourself at times: "Even good Ancus
Left the sunlight behind, though greater than I.
And kings, lords of vast dominions, have fallen,
Yielding their power to the grasp of death.
He, too, who bridged the sea with his armies,
Who marched his cavalry over the waves,
Mocking the roar of the ocean's tides,
Poured out his soul, no less than the lowliest slave.
Scipio's son, terror of Carthage, lies
In the dust, his bones mingling with the earth,
No different from the humblest in his house.
Add to this roll the discoverers of arts,
The companions of the Muses, such as Homer,
Who now sleeps, sceptered no longer, among the dead.
Democritus, seeing his mind grow dim with age,

Gave himself willingly to death. And even
Epicurus, who surpassed all men in wisdom,
Extinguished like a star beneath the sun's bright light.
Wilt thou, then, hesitate and shrink from death,
When life itself is but a living death for thee?
Thou who in slumber dost waste the greater part
Of thy brief years, and even awake dost dream,
Haunted by phantoms, burdened by empty fears,
Unknowing what ails thee as cares toss thee about,
Like a drunkard staggering, mind clouded, astray."
If men could feel, as deeply as they bear
The weight that presses heavy on their minds,
The causes of their anguish and their grief,
And why their hearts are burdened so with woe,
They would not live as now, so lost, so blind,
Uncertain what they seek, yet seeking still,
Endlessly shifting place, as though escape
Could lighten what they cannot leave behind.
The man who tires of home flees from his halls,
Only to find no solace far away;
He hastens back, his weary steps retraced,
And finds no joy at home. He speeds along,
Driving his chariot down to country fields,
As though to douse some blazing fire—and yet,
Upon arrival, yawns or falls asleep,
Seeking escape in dreams, or rushes back
To town again, in restless, aimless flight.
Thus every man flees from himself—his self
That none may flee, for it clings ever close,
Loved and loathed, and always misunderstood.
Sickened and weary, man knows not the cause;
But should he see it clearly, then, at last,
All else forgotten, he would seek to know
The nature of the world, for here the stakes
Are more than fleeting moments—they are all

Of time, eternity, and mortal fate,
What lies beyond the shadow cast by death.
And yet, when all is said, what madness drives
This fevered lust for life that grips us so,
Binding us fast in terrors and in toils?
Death is unyielding; none may turn its course;
Its hour is fixed, and we must face its gate.
Yet still we labor at the selfsame tasks,
Repeating, circling back, forever bound,
Finding no new delight to forge from life.
The things we long for, when they are denied,
Seem best of all; yet when at last they're ours,
Some other want consumes us, and we thirst
For yet another fleeting dream. We chase,
Unceasing, life's illusions, yet remain
Ever unsure what future days may bring,
What chance may hold, or what the end shall be.
Nor can we, by prolonging life, reduce
The span of death awaiting us; no hour
Can we subtract from what eternity
Has claimed, nor steal one moment from its grasp.
Thus, mortal man, live out thy numbered days,
As many as thy lot allows; yet still,
Eternal death awaits thee, just the same.
He who has died but yesterday shall lie
No shorter time in death's eternal shade
Than he who passed a thousand years before.

Book IV

Proem

I wander far afield, sustained by thought,
Through untrod paths of the Pierian Muse,
Where none before has ventured. Here I thrive,

Delighting in untainted springs, to drink
Their waters deep; I joy to pluck new blooms,
To weave a crown of fresh, ungarlanded flowers
For this my brow, from regions yet untouched
By hands of men or homage of the Muse.
First, for I speak of mighty themes, and strive
To free the mind from coils of dread belief
That fetters it with fear. Then, too, I frame
Clear song on darksome topics, touching all
With the Muse's charm—a purpose fair and true.
For just as healers, seeking to bestow
A bitter draught of wormwood on young boys,
First sweeten all the rim with honeyed gold,
That childish folly, coaxed by pleasant taste,
Might take the healing bitter to the heart,
And be restored to health through gentle guile:
So I, perceiving that my doctrine seems
To many harsh and heavy, filled with dread,
And seeing how the common throng recoils
In horror from it, have adorned my words
With melodies of Muse and honeyed song,
To charm and hold thy mind upon these truths,
Till thou hast learned the nature of all things
And understood their purpose and their worth.

Existence and Character of The Images

But since I've taught already of what kind
The seeds of things must be, and how distinct
In varied forms they flit, with motion stirred
Eternal, shaping all, and since I've shown
The nature of the mind, its bond with flesh,
Its growth, its life, its final dissolution,
I turn now to a theme of utmost weight:
That there exist those forms, those airy shapes,

The images of things—these subtle films
That skim the outer surface, scale-like, thin,
And through the air flit lightly, here and there,
To stir our minds, awake or lost in sleep.
These, when we dream, or in the shadows peer,
Take on strange shapes of wonder, forms of dread,
And move us deeply, making some believe
That souls escape from Acheron's dark bounds,
That shades walk forth among the living still,
And part of us persists beyond the grave.
But no—when mind and body are undone,
Their elements return to primal seeds,
And naught of us remains to roam or wail.
I say that from all things there stream abroad
Fine effigies, faint images, like skins,
Shed from their outermost. These waft and glide
Through space, unseen, until they strike our sense
And conjure shapes that stir our intellect.
This truth, though subtle, reason makes it plain.
Behold the visible: the smoky wreaths
That curl from burning logs, the heat that waves
Above a fire, the sheen a serpent sheds—
All these are proofs that surfaces give off
Thin layers, parts, or vestments of their form.
And finer still, these effigies may pass,
Unseen, unbroken, as a perfect whole,
Bearing the shape and semblance of their source.
Consider too the hues of stretched-out awnings,
Which, in the sunlight of a theatre,
Diffuse their colors on the crowd below.
These dyes, sent forth from surfaces, attest
That objects cast their essence out in streams,
And finer still than color's subtle glow
Are those thin shapes that form the mirrored world.
The images reflected in a glass,

In water, or a polished plate of bronze,
Prove that such forms exist. They come to us,
Invisible in single frame, but dense
When many flow in constant, quick succession,
To recreate the likeness of the source.
Thus, effigies of objects stream and move,
Too slight to see alone, yet strong enough
To fill the senses with their fleeting touch.
Consider now the size of smallest things:
Some creatures are so minute that even less
Than their third part evades the naked eye.
What then of organs nestled deep within?
How fine their fibers, smaller still the seeds
That form their essence, life, and thought itself!
And scents confirm this truth: a bitter herb,
The southernwood, or wormwood's pungent leaf,
Exhales its tang from surface to the air.
A touch, though faint, releases subtle streams,
Proclaiming that the smallest parts exist
And act upon us, though they stay unseen.
Then why not rather grasp that countless images
Flit everywhere, in endless modes, unseen,
Bodiless, through the vast expanse of air?
But lest thou think these images arise
From objects only, know that others form,
Self-born, within the airy skies of earth,
Shaped and reshaped in countless fleeting forms,
Shifting appearances at every turn.
Behold the clouds that gather thick on high,
Darkening the serene expanse of heaven.
We see their shapes—giants, beasts, or mountain peaks—
Rolling across the sun and trailing shade.
Such forms, though momentary, show how swift
And manifold are images that arise,
Flow forth, and vanish into nothingness.

Forever from all things an outer stream
Flows forth—thin films, textures of form and hue.
When these strike objects, as with polished glass,
They pass, unbroken, forming mirrored shapes.
But roughened surfaces, like wood or stone,
Rend these effigies and scatter them.
Yet when they meet smooth mirrors, nothing breaks;
Instead, they bounce back, reflecting forms.
So swiftly does this process play, that ere
Thy eye perceives, the mirrored shape appears,
Proof that such images from objects flow,
Fine, fleeting, and incessantly renewed.
Think, too, how light from sun to earth arrives
In but a moment, filling all the world.
So must the images of things be borne,
In manifold directions, swift and sure,
Answering each surface turned to meet their path.
For sudden storms obscure the tranquil sky,
And blackened clouds, as if from Acheron,
Surround the heavens in a murky night.
Such vast assemblies of forms and fleeting shades—
How small a part is any single image!
Now mark the swiftness of their flight through air.
Objects of lightest mass, of smallest form,
Move swiftest—like the beams of sun and heat.
These particles, propelled by endless blows,
Pass freely through the spaces of the air,
Pushed by the force of those that follow close.
Thus too must images in swiftness move,
Their rareness and their lightness bearing them
Through boundless space, with nothing to impede.
Consider this: if rays of sun can pass
From heavenly heights to earth in but an instant,
What of those images that merely skim
The surface, hurled away without delay?

How much more swiftly must they travel forth,
Unbarred by obstacles, propelled by force!
Thus do we see, as stars reflect in pools
Beneath the open sky, the images
Of heaven's constellations flash below.
So swift the journey of these phantom forms,
From ether's height to earth's awaiting gaze.

The Senses and Mental Pictures

Bodies send streams perpetually to sense—
Be it scent, heat, or spray from ocean waves
That gnaw at walls along the briny coast.
Voices, too, disperse their sound through air,
While taste's sharp tingle meets us by the sea
Or bitter wormwood stirs the tongue's recoil.
From all things, streams of nature radiate,
Each borne incessantly, filling space around.
So ceaselessly our senses are engaged,
Alert to see, to smell, to touch, to hear.
And since we grasp a square by touch in dark
As surely as in daylight's clearer view,
It follows both are caused by images,
By forms that strike the senses in their kind.
Thus sight and touch confirm: these outer films,
These tenuous effigies, must dart from things,
Fitting the shape of objects that they leave.
These images, invisible yet real,
Traverse the air in countless forms and hues,
Yet only through the eyes their truth is caught.
Wherever sight is turned, they strike the gaze,
Revealing form, position, and their range.
For when they speed, they displace the air between,
Driving it through the channels of the eye,
Until the force informs us: "This is near,"

Or: "This lies farther off," gauged by the length
Of air displaced before their brushing flight.
Marvel not that we see a single thing,
Though countless particles in streams converge;
For as the wind upon us strikes as one,
Though countless breaths compose its moving force,
Or as a rock touched shows its solid form,
Not hue or dust, so does the image tell
The unified impression of the whole.
And why, within a mirror, deep and clear,
The world reflects as though removed in space?
Understand the mechanism at play:
The image strikes the glass and, bouncing back,
Displaces air between our gaze and it.
This air conveys the vision, making seem
The shape we see recedes behind the plane.
Thus twofold airs—the nearer and the far—
Grant depth to vision in the glass's truth.
And when the right becomes the left in view,
The cause is simple: images rebound,
Reversed as masks when cast upon a frame,
Returning to present the opposite.
From glass to glass, reflections ripple on,
Till twisted angles multiply the forms
And further turn the left to right again.
Or curved mirrors keep the right aligned,
Bending the image back with faithful cast.
These images seem joined to us in step,
Walking our gait, mimicking our stance,
Because from regions whence we turn away
No more are they reflected back to sight.
Bright light repels the gaze; the sun confounds,
Its mighty beams descending swift through air,
Assaulting eyes and breaking their fine threads.
Seeds of fire within such piercing rays

Strike pain upon the sight, much as disease
Can taint the vision of the jaundiced eye,
Painting the world with hues of sickly yellow.
From shade, we glimpse the luminous beyond,
As light flows swiftly in to cleanse the dark,
Opening pathways for the images
That stream from objects in the sun's embrace.
But from the light, no gaze can pierce the dark,
For heavy shadows flood the eye instead,
Blocking the subtle channels vision needs,
Thus rendering the obscured world unseen.
When from afar we gaze upon the towers
Of cities squarely built, they seem as round.
This happens since the distant angles lose
Their sharp distinction, softened by the air
That blunts and scatters their advancing forms.
When edges fade, the stones appear as shaped
By some turner's wheel, though faintly so,
Not truly rounded, but with shadowy semblance.
Likewise, our shadow seems to follow us,
Matching our steps and mimicking our form,
Though it is naught but air deprived of light.
When we obstruct the sun's rays on the ground,
The earth, reft of illumination there,
Gains shadow while our movement clears a path
For sunlight to return. Thus shadows shift,
Illusions born of constant interplay
Between the light and our obstructing forms.
But senses do not err in such events.
Their task is only to perceive the place
Where light exists or shadows fall; they serve
Our reason, which must judge what truth lies there.
Blame not the eyes for faults of mind or thought,
Nor deem all senses prone to errancy.
A ship at anchor seems to move when we

In motion pass; the hills and fields appear
To flee astern as sails drive forward flight.
The stars seem fixed in heaven's arching dome,
Though ever in their paths they circle wide.
The sun and moon, steadfast to our view,
Yet sweep across the sky in ceaseless course.
Between two mountains' peaks, a gap reveals
A fleet's escape, though distance blurs their truth,
Making them seem a single island joined.
Children, dizzy from their games, perceive
The spinning world as whirling round their heads,
And roofs and walls as threatening to fall.
At dawn, the sun appears near mountain crests,
Its fiery orb tinging their rugged tips,
Yet oceans stretch vast leagues between the two,
And countless lands divide their seeming nearness.
A shallow pool, mere inches deep, reflects
The heavens' breadth, as if beneath the earth
A mirrored sky lies sunk in endless space.
In rivers swift, the standing horse appears
To drift upstream, its motion all reversed,
As if the flowing waters bore it back.
A portico, though level in its length,
Contracts into a cone when seen afar,
Its columns narrowing to a vanishing point.
The distant sun, rising or setting, seems
To leap from waves or plunge into their depths,
A trick of sight for those who lack the scope
To see the wider world of land and sea.
Ships anchored in the port seem strangely bent,
Their hulls submerged appearing curved or torn,
While masts above the waterline stand straight.
Winds shifting clouds at night give constellations
The false appearance of another course,
Though stars remain upon their fixed orbits.

With pressure underneath one single eye,
The world appears to double—twain the lamps,
Twain the forms of all about the room.
In sleep, we wander far in dreams, convinced
We wake and move, though still our bodies lie
Enclosed in night's unbroken, silent dark.
These errors spring from mind, not sense itself,
Which perceives what is but adds no falsehood.
The mind, by inference, confuses truth,
Conflating what it sees with what it thinks,
And thus belief, untethered, twists the facts.
Yet senses faithfully convey the world—
The rest is in our reasoning alone.
If one should claim that nothing can be known,
He cannot know if even this is true,
Since he admits to knowing naught at all.
With such a one, no dialogue remains;
He stands inverted, feet where head should be.
Yet grant he knows this single point—I'll ask:
From whence comes knowledge of the true and false?
What test has proven doubtful things distinct
From certain truths, if all the world he sees
Has shown no sign of what is truly real?
The senses first must form our grasp of truth,
For no criterion, higher, more secure,
Exists to judge the senses false or true.
What greater arbiter than these can stand?
Shall reason—born of senses, rooted there—
Contradict its own foundation, sense,
And prove itself as false as what it doubts?
Or shall the ears reproach the eyes, or touch
Deny the ear, or taste refute the skin,
Or scent dispute the tongue? Not so, indeed.
Each sense its sphere commands: the eye for sight,
The ear for sound, the tongue for taste, the touch

For warmth or cold, for soft or hard, and nose
For smells. Distinct their powers and tasks remain,
And none can convict another of deceit.
No sense can disprove itself, for trust
Is due to each in equal measure still.
What sense reports is true—its own domain
Is sovereign, judged by none but what it shows.
If reason falters, failing to explain
Why distant towers seem round though near they're square,
It harms us less to theorize amiss
Than to renounce the senses' primal faith.
For life itself would crumble, if we dared
Distrust what senses plainly show. Without
Their guidance, how would we avoid the brink
Of cliffs or other dangers? How discern
The safe from perilous paths?
As buildings fail,
If plumb-lines deviate or squares mislead,
So too must life collapse if senses err.
Reason, like bricks mislaid, would topple all,
And life, unmoored, would falter in the void.
Thus, those who war against the senses' truth
Are vain, their arguments as false as flawed.
Now let us show how senses recognize
Their objects, each perceiving its own realm.
A sound, a voice, is heard when, striking ears,
It moves the sense through matter of its own.
For sound, as much as voice, must have a form,
A body, since it strikes and scrapes the ear.
Who shouts or screams will feel their throat grow rough,
The windpipe rasped, the passage tightly strained
As thicker streams of sound push through their bounds.
This friction, proof of sound's corporeal force,
Shows sense and body joined, their union sure.
Thus, senses stand as sentinels of truth,

Their trust the bedrock of our lives and thought.
No greater judge than these can guide our way;
No stronger proof exists to light the path.
Voice and words, indeed, are made of matter,
For they can tire the body, cause its loss.
Prolonged discourse, from morning's early glow
To evening's shade, drains strength and wastes the frame,
Especially when loud with ringing shouts.
Thus voice must be corporeal, a force
Whose particles escape and wane with use.
The nature of a voice—its smooth or rough—
Depends upon the shapes of primal seeds.
A trumpet's hollow roar is rough and harsh,
While flutes of Berecynthian pipes emit
A buzzing boom, and swans' lament at dusk
Pours forth a liquid wail. From deep within,
We force these sounds; the mobile tongue crafts words,
And lips, through shaping motions, give them form.
So, when the voice has little space to cross,
It reaches ears distinct and clear, intact.
But over distance, air confounds its form,
And winds distort its flight, dissolving words—
A scattered sound is heard, but sense is lost.
One voice may rouse a multitude of ears,
Its single burst divided into parts,
With each fragment carrying the tone and form
To waiting listeners. What misses ears
Is lost to winds; what strikes on solid walls
Returns as echoes, mocking our own calls.
In lonely places, cliffs reflect our cries,
Returning words in mimicry, as though
Companions called from distant, unseen paths.
At times, the rocks repeat a single cry
Sixfold or more, their echoes bounding back,
Conjuring myths of fauns or woodland gods,

Their revels breaking silence with their song.
Thus, myths arise in lonely, shadowed woods,
Born of men's fears or need to fill the void.
Yet, no marvel lies in sound that passes
Through walls unseen, for voice can thread through gaps
And winding passages where sight may fail.
Doors closed may dull the words but let them through,
For voice, unlike an image, does not break
When turned aside; it travels, bending paths.
Its many parts divide and scatter wide,
Like sparks from fire bursting into flames,
Filling hidden spaces with their din.
But images, sent forth in straight lines,
Cannot pierce walls; hence why the eye sees naught
Though ears may catch the sound from beyond.
Now turn to taste and tongue, the seat of flavor.
When chewing food, we squeeze out subtle streams,
As one might press a sponge soaked full with water.
These streams disperse within the porous tongue,
Whose intricate paths discern the smooth or rough.
Smooth bodies please, caressing as they pass;
Rough ones sting and irritate the sense.
Yet flavor's pleasure halts at tongue and palate;
Once food descends the throat, the joy is gone,
Its role reduced to fueling flesh and frame.
What matters is digestion, nourishment—
Not how the taste was savored at the start.
Thus, voice and taste, though tied to body's bounds,
Reveal the nature of corporeal forms:
A union of material and the senses,
Where matter flows to touch, to speak, to feed.
Indeed, where one from overwhelming anger
Is struck by fever, or otherwise
Feels the intense force of some illness,
There, the whole body is thrown into disarray,

And the arrangement of its parts shifts—
So the things that once brought certain tastes
No longer do so, while others take their place,
More suited now to enter the pores
And create sourness. Both types, in truth,
Are found together in honey—
Something we've already proven before.
Now come, and I'll explain how smells
Reach and affect the nose.
First, it's important to know
That countless tiny particles
Stream from objects and spread freely,
Touching everything around them.
But each living thing is affected differently;
Some are drawn to one scent, others to another—
All because their senses are built differently.
Bees are led by the scent of honey;
Vultures by the smell of corpses.
Dogs follow scents to track wild animals,
While the white goose,
Which saved the Roman citadel,
Can smell the presence of humans from far away.
In this way, each creature is guided
By the smells suited to it—
To find food or avoid poison,
And thus continue to survive.
But this variety isn't limited to smell
Or even to taste. The way we see things
And the colors we perceive
Aren't the same for all creatures.
For example, lions—fierce as they are—
Can't bear to look at a rooster.
The rooster, with its flapping wings,
Chasing away the night,
And calling out to announce the morning,

Drives the lions to flee.
This is because the rooster's body contains particles
That, when they enter the lions' eyes,
Pierce them with unbearable pain.
Yet, these same particles don't harm human eyes,
Either because they don't penetrate
Or because they pass through so quickly
That they can't linger and cause damage.
To speak again of smells:
Some travel farther than others,
But none go as far as sound or voice—
Not to mention light, which travels faster still.
Smells move slowly,
And disappear as they mix into the winds.
First, because they are released with effort
From deep inside objects (we know this because
Grinding, breaking, or burning something
Releases stronger smells,
Showing that odors come from deep within).
Second, smell is made of larger particles than sound,
Since it cannot pass through stone walls,
While sound easily can.
This is why it's harder to locate the source of a smell—
It cools and scatters in the air,
So that by the time it reaches us,
It's weakened and harder to trace.
Even dogs, skilled at tracking scents,
Can sometimes lose their way.
Now, let me explain how images move the mind.
Countless thin images of objects
Float in every direction, so fine
That they merge in midair,
Like strands of spiderweb or thin sheets of gold.
These images are far thinner
Than those that strike the eyes,

For they pass through the body's pores
And directly affect the mind,
Triggering sensations.
This is why we see things like centaurs,
The monstrous Scylla, or Cerberus—
Or even the faces of people long dead.
These images form partly from the air,
Partly from objects around us,
And partly from combinations of shapes.
For example, no real centaur exists,
But when the image of a man and a horse
Come together, they combine to create one.
In the same way, other strange shapes are formed,
And when these light, subtle images strike the mind,
They stir it, creating vivid impressions.
This happens just as it does with sight:
As the eyes see objects through films,
So too does the mind perceive them
Through even finer, subtler films.
This explains why we can "see" things like lions
Not just with our eyes,
But also with our minds.
When we sleep, the body rests,
But the mind stays active,
Still affected by these films,
Which is why we dream of people or things,
Even of those who are no longer alive.
The senses, asleep, cannot tell truth from illusion,
And memory, also dormant,
Doesn't remind us that these visions aren't real.
So, we believe what we see in dreams.
And further, it's no surprise that images appear
To move their arms and other parts in rhythm.
Often in dreams, we see them doing this.
When one image disappears,

And another takes its place in a new pose,
It seems as if the first image changed its gestures.
This change must happen quickly—
So fast, and with so many images available,
That in the briefest moment the mind can perceive,
Countless pieces of images arrive to replace the old.
Sometimes, an entirely different image appears.
What seemed to be a woman might suddenly
Turn into a man.
A new face or even a different age may appear,
But sleep and forgetfulness
Make sure we don't question this strange shift.
There's much to explore and explain here,
If we truly want to understand.
First, why does the mind,
When it decides to think of something,
See that thing immediately?
Do the images wait for our command?
Does an image appear
Exactly when we wish it to—
Whether we think of the sea, the land, or the sky?
Do scenes of gatherings, parades, feasts, or battles
All form instantly at our word?—
Even when, at the same time and place,
Another mind might be thinking of something
Completely different?
And what of this:
When we dream of images moving,
Stepping forward in rhythm,
Swinging their arms with smooth, quick motions,
And turning their heads as they keep time—
Are these images truly skilled in art,
Wandering around with perfect training,
Just so they can perform for us at night?
Or is this the truth instead·

In even the smallest moment of time we can imagine—
The time it takes to say a single word—
There are many smaller moments hidden within,
Which reason can uncover.
So it is that in the briefest instant,
Countless images are nearby, ready to appear,
Each one in its own form.
When one image vanishes,
And another takes its place in a different pose,
It seems as though the first image changed its movements.
And because these images are so delicate,
The mind focuses only on the ones it chooses to see,
While the rest disappear entirely,
Except for the ones the mind prepares itself to notice.
The mind does prepare itself,
Hoping to see what comes next—
And that's why this happens.
Haven't you noticed how the eyes,
When trying to see something very small,
Will strain to focus,
Unable to see clearly otherwise?
Even with ordinary objects,
If you don't pay attention,
It's as if they are far away and out of reach.
So, it's no wonder that the mind ignores the rest,
Except for what it has chosen to focus on.
In this way, we draw big conclusions
From small details,
And often trap ourselves in our own misunderstandings.

Some Vital Functions

In these matters,
We ask you to avoid one great mistake:
Do not assume that the eyes were created

So we could see, or that thighs and knees,
Designed to bend and rest upon the feet,
Were made so we could walk smoothly ahead.
Do not think that forearms joined to upper arms,
Or the hands on either side,
Were given to us so we could handle tasks.
This way of thinking is backwards,
For nothing in the body is made for a purpose;
Rather, things are born, and their uses follow.
No one could see before eyes were created,
And no one could speak before the tongue existed.
The tongue came into being before speech,
And ears existed long before they heard sound.
All our body parts, it seems, were there
Before they were put to any use,
So they could not have been made for their uses.
Instead, fighting hand-to-hand,
Twisting and breaking joints,
And wounding limbs with blood and gore,
All existed long before
Shining spears were invented.
Nature taught humans to avoid injuries
Long before the left arm was trained
To lift a shield for protection.
And resting the tired body
Came far earlier than soft beds.
Quenching thirst existed long before cups.
The things made to help us live—
Like beds, shields, and cups—
Were created later, for their usefulness.
But senses and body parts were different.
They existed first and only later
Revealed their uses.
This is why it's impossible
To argue that our senses and limbs

Were created with specific purposes in mind.
Likewise, it's not surprising
That all living creatures seek food
As part of their nature.
I've already explained how tiny particles
Stream out constantly from objects,
In countless forms and patterns.
This is especially true for living beings,
Whose constant motion sends particles out—
Through breath when they pant,
And through sweat when they toil.
The body loses material this way,
Growing weaker, and pain follows.
So, food is consumed to restore the body,
To fill in the gaps in the joints,
And to renew its strength.
Food enters the body and satisfies
The open hunger running through limbs and veins.
At the same time, liquid spreads
To every part of the body that needs moisture.
It calms the burning heat inside,
Quenching the fire that scorches us.
This is how thirst is washed away
And hunger is eased.
Now, let me explain
How we can step forward when we wish,
How we move our limbs,
And how our bodies carry their weight.
Listen closely.
First, an image of walking
Appears in the mind, as I said before.
This image inspires the will to act,
Since no one acts without first imagining
What they want to do.
When the mind decides to walk,

It sends a signal to the soul,
Which is spread throughout the body.
This happens easily,
Because the soul is closely connected to the mind.
Next, the soul sends a signal to the body,
And step by step,
The whole body begins to move.
At the same time, the body adjusts,
Allowing air—so light and nimble—
To flow through open pores
And spread everywhere inside.
These two forces, working together,
Move the body forward, like a ship
Driven by both oars and the wind.
There's no mystery here.
Even the smallest, finest particles
Can move something as large as the human body.
The wind, though invisible and delicate,
Drives massive ships.
One hand can steer such a ship,
And a small rudder can turn it wherever you please.
Likewise, heavy loads, large and numerous,
Can be lifted and moved
By pulleys and wheels with minimal effort.
Now, how sleep spreads its calm
Through our limbs and gives the mind a break from its troubles,
I'll explain in verses sweeter than many others—
Like the soft song of a swan,
Much better than the loud clamor of cranes
Among the airy clouds of the south wind.
So, give me your sharp attention and an open mind,
So you won't deny the truth of what I say
Or turn away in disbelief,
Unable to grasp these spoken truths.
Sleep comes mainly when the energy of the soul

Has scattered throughout the body,
Some of it leaving outward,
And some retreating deep inside.
This makes our limbs loosen and droop.
There's no doubt that the soul gives us our senses,
And when sleep blocks those senses,
It's because the soul is disturbed and partly expelled.
But not entirely—
Otherwise, the body would collapse into
The cold stillness of death.
If no part of the soul were left within,
Even in hiding, like fire buried under ashes,
How could the senses reawaken?
Just as flames rise again from hidden embers,
So too does sense return when the soul stirs anew.
Now I'll explain how this strange state happens,
How the soul becomes confused
And the body grows weak.
Listen carefully so my words don't vanish into the wind.
First, the outer parts of the body,
Exposed to the touch of moving air,
Are constantly struck by tiny gusts.
For this reason, most creatures
Are protected by skin, shells, tough calluses, or bark.
But this same air also affects the inner parts
When creatures breathe in and out.
Thus, the body is buffeted both inside and out,
As the air's blows enter through tiny pores
And reach the body's core elements.
Over time, this leads to a kind of collapse.
The fundamental particles of body and soul
Are thrown into confusion.
When this happens, some of the soul is expelled,
Some retreats into hidden recesses,
And some scatters throughout the body,

Unable to unite or move together.
Nature blocks the pathways and connections,
And so the sense withdraws deep inside.
With nothing left to support it,
The body weakens, the limbs grow heavy,
The arms and eyelids droop,
And even as you lie in bed,
Your knees buckle and lose their strength.
Sleep often follows eating,
Because food has a similar effect to air,
Spreading through the veins as it's digested.
The deepest sleep comes when you're full or exhausted,
Because the body's particles are most disrupted then,
Bruised by the effort of work or digestion.
Thus, three things happen:
The soul sinks deeper,
It is partially expelled,
And its movements become scattered and divided.
Whatever tasks a person focuses on most during the day—
Whatever they've spent time on or strained their mind over—
Often appears in their dreams.
Lawyers dream of pleading cases and citing laws.
Commanders dream of battles and leading troops.
Sailors dream of struggling against the wind.
Even I dream of writing this book,
Studying the nature of the world
And recording what I discover here on these pages.
So every pursuit and art tends to appear in dreams,
Mocking and taking over the minds of men.
Even animals are affected.
Horses, though stretched out and asleep,
Will sweat and strain as if racing for a prize.
Hunting dogs, in their soft slumber,
Will suddenly move their legs, growl, bark,
And sniff the air as if catching the scent of prey.

Sometimes, even when awake,
They chase after imagined stags,
Believing they see them fleeing ahead,
Until the illusion fades and they come to their senses.
Young puppies, bred for the home,
Sometimes jerk awake,
As if startled by unfamiliar faces.
The fiercer the breed,
The more intense their dreams and actions in sleep.
Birds, too, will flee in the night,
Flapping their wings in fear,
Dreaming of hawks swooping down to attack.
Even humans,
Whose minds tackle great challenges,
Will continue their mighty tasks in sleep.
Kings dream of storming cities or falling into captivity,
Fighting on the battlefield,
Or crying out as if their throats were cut.
Some wrestle and groan,
Filling the air with wild cries,
As if attacked by lions or panthers.
Some speak aloud in their sleep,
Revealing their plans or even confessing their crimes.
Others dream of dying,
Or of falling headlong from a mountain,
And wake up frantic and confused,
Their minds still shaken from the dream.
A thirsty man might dream
Of sitting beside a spring or river,
Drinking deeply, trying to gulp the entire stream.
Children, overtaken by sleep,
Might dream they're lifting their clothes
Beside a chamber pot,
Only to wet the bed and soak
Their fine Babylonian sheets.

Young men, just entering adulthood,
With their bodies newly producing seed,
Are often visited in sleep
By images of beauty—
Visions of fair faces and radiant forms
That stir their bodies and release the seed,
Leaving stains behind as if the act itself
Had truly been carried out.
And as said before,
That seed is awakened in us when mature age
Has strengthened our bodies…
Just as different causes bring motion to different things,
So too does one force stir the human seed,
Driving it to flow out from the man.
As soon as it leaves its starting place,
It moves through the whole body, passing
Through the limbs and frame,
Gathering in specific parts of the muscles.
It energizes and excites the man's genitals.
The aroused regions swell with seed,
And with this comes the desire to release it
Toward the object of longing,
That which the body so eagerly seeks—
The object that love has made the mind obsessed with.
Almost every man is drawn toward his own wound,
And the blood flows toward the place from which
The blow of love was struck.
If the source of desire is near,
That fiery passion reaches directly for it.
In the same way, someone struck by Cupid's arrows—
Whether by a boy with soft, delicate limbs
Or by a woman radiating love
Through every part of her body—
Strives to reach the one who caused his longing.
He burns to unite with them,

To release into their body
The fluid that was stirred within his own.
For this silent craving promises a sense of joy.

The Passion of Love

This craving is what we call Venus in us.
From this arises all the charms of love.
From this, the first drop of joy seeps into human hearts—
A joy soon followed by cold, creeping worry.
Even if the one you love is far away,
Images of them linger near,
And their sweet name echoes in your ears.
But you must push these images away,
Chase off whatever feeds your love,
Turn your mind elsewhere,
And release the seed gathered within you into other bodies.
Do not cling to thoughts of a single love
Or hoard your desire for one pleasure—
This only brings pain and unavoidable sorrow.
For just as a wound, if nourished,
Grows deeper and harder to heal,
So too does love burn more fiercely each day.
The suffering worsens with time,
Unless you counter the wounds of love with new blows—
Soothing them while they are fresh
By pursuing other loves freely
Or redirecting your restless mind elsewhere.
The man who avoids love entirely
Still enjoys the gifts of Venus.
He takes the pleasures free of penalties.
Indeed, the joys of Venus are purer
For those with a calm, steady soul
Than for those sick with love's torment.
Even in the moment of passion,

Lovers are restless and uncertain.
They cannot decide where to first indulge their hands or eyes.
The parts they long for, they grip too tightly,
Harming the body they desire.
They press their teeth against her lips
And crush mouth into mouth with eager kisses.
This is because their pleasure is not pure—
It hides stings beneath it,
Urging them to hurt the very thing
That sparked their love-madness.
Yet Venus soothes the pain with tender caresses,
And the mix of affection tempers the fury of passion.
Lovers hope that the same body that kindled their fire
Can also extinguish it.
But nature insists otherwise.
For love is the one craving that grows fiercer
The more it is fed.
Food and drink enter the body
And can fill the parts that hunger for them,
Satisfying thirst and hunger with ease.
But beauty and charm send nothing real into the body—
Only fleeting images, empty and insubstantial,
A vain hope that often vanishes like smoke in the wind.
It is like a thirsty man dreaming of water:
He reaches for it, yet finds nothing to quench
The burning thirst in his body.
He chases illusions of liquid,
Straining in vain, thirsting even as he gulps down
The image of a stream.
In the same way, love deceives lovers
With empty images.
They cannot satisfy their lust
Just by gazing at the body they desire.
Nor can their hands, wandering across tender skin,
Draw out the pleasure they seek.

Even when they finally embrace,
Their bodies entwined,
Sharing the bloom of youth
And feeling the height of physical joy,
When Venus is about to sow her seed in the fields of woman,
They lock themselves tightly together,
Mixing saliva, breathing into each other,
Pressing teeth to lips.
Yet all this is in vain.
They cannot dissolve into each other's bodies,
Cannot fully merge or become one.
Often, they seem to struggle and strain for this,
Clinging desperately in Venus' grip,
Until their bodies seem to melt away,
Overcome by the force of their delight.
But when the lust stored in their muscles
Has been spent,
There comes a brief pause,
A momentary calm in the raging heat.
Yet soon the same madness returns.
The old craving burns anew,
Driving them to seek again what they cannot grasp—
An elusive remedy for their torment.
In this uncertain state, they waste away,
Wounded by a pain they cannot see.
To this, we must add
That they waste their strength and grow weak from the effort;
They spend their futile years
Living under someone else's control,
Neglecting their duties,
Letting their good reputation falter,
While their wealth is lost on luxurious things—
Babylonian tapestries,
Exquisite perfumes,
And dainty Sicyonian shoes

That adorn her feet.
Emeralds of green light are set in gold;
Rich purple dresses, worn often,
Grow shabby and soaked with Venus' sweat.
The hard-earned property of their ancestors
Is turned into headbands, fine headdresses,
And garments from Alidens or Cean isles.
Lavish banquets are laid out,
With rare cloth, fine food, games of chance,
Goblets, perfumes, crowns, and garlands.
All of this is in vain,
Because from the fountain of these pleasures
Always bubbles a drop of bitterness.
This bitterness torments them among their delights,
When their mind, stricken with remorse,
Gnaws at itself for wasted years and ruinous indulgence—
Or because she leaves them doubting her loyalty,
Dropping sly hints that burn like fire
And cling to their eager hearts.
Perhaps they think she looks at others too much,
Or notice a trace of a laugh on her face.
These troubles come even in successful love,
But in unrequited or failed love,
The miseries are too many to count.
This is why it's better to take precautions beforehand,
As I've already shown,
And guard against love's enticements.
It's easier to avoid falling into love's traps
Than to escape once entangled,
When you're caught in the strong nets of Aphrodite.
Even when you're caught with tangled feet,
You can still escape—
Unless you stand in your own way,
Ignoring the flaws of the one you adore.
People, blinded by passion,

Invent virtues that don't exist.
So, we see many crooked or unattractive people
Held in high regard by their infatuated lovers.
These lovers advise each other to honor Venus,
Thinking their friends are smitten with true beauty—
While blind to their own delusions.
A dark-skinned woman is called "golden like honey";
A dirty, smelly one is said to be "carelessly elegant."
The one with catlike eyes is "a little Pallas";
The skinny, wiry one is "a gazelle."
The short and pudgy woman is "charming, like one of the Graces";
The big, bulky one is "impressive, commanding admiration."
The stuttering one "has a sweet lisp";
The mute woman is "modest";
And the loud, sharp-tongued woman is "witty and spirited."
The scrawny, sickly one becomes "delicate";
The coughing, dying one is "fragile and refined."
A woman with a thick chest and heavy breasts is said to be "like
    Ceres nursing Bacchus."
The pug-nosed lady is "a feminine Silenus."
The one with swollen lips is praised as "a luscious kiss."
It would take forever to list all such delusions.
Even if her face is beautiful
And Venus' charm lights her whole body,
You must remember—there are others like her.
You lived without her before,
And she does nothing that others don't.
Even this woman, so praised,
Hides herself behind perfumes,
Which even her maids laugh at behind her back.
Yet the lover, shut out from her,
Lays flowers at her doorstep,
Anoints her doorposts with perfume,
And kisses the threshold in despair.
If at last he's admitted,

One whiff of her scent might drive him away,
Searching for excuses to leave.
His long-planned complaints dissolve,
And he curses himself
For ever believing she deserved so much devotion.
Women are aware of this,
Which is why they try harder to hide
Their less glamorous realities
From the men they wish to ensnare.
But no matter how they try,
You can uncover these truths with careful thought.
If she is kind and graceful,
Overlook her flaws in return—
This is only fair for mortal love.
Not every woman pretends to love.
Many genuinely desire shared pleasure,
Embracing their lovers with true passion
And urging them to enjoy love's race together.
Animals, too, feel this same instinct.
Cattle, birds, wild beasts,
Sheep, and mares all yield to males
Because their nature burns with desire.
They gladly accept the joy of Venus' embrace.
And don't you see how creatures,
Bound by mutual pleasure,
Struggle even against their bonds?
Dogs at crossroads, panting to separate,
Strain to pull apart
Even as Venus' chains hold them fast.
This wouldn't happen if not for the shared joy
That drags them back and holds them.
Thus, mutual pleasure ties them together
And binds them to one another.
When the male's seed mingles with the female's,
If the female seizes control,

The offspring resembles her more.
If the male's seed dominates,
The offspring resembles him.
Sometimes, the child is an equal blend,
Taking features from both parents.
This happens when the seeds mix harmoniously,
Aroused and driven by Venus' passion.
In some cases, offspring resemble grandparents,
Or even great-grandparents.
This happens because parents carry
Hidden traits passed down from their ancestors.
These hidden particles combine in different ways,
Producing features, voices, and hair
That reflect the family line.
A female child can come from a father's seed,
And a male from the mother's.
Gender, like faces and bodies,
Does not arise from a single source.
Each birth comes from two seeds,
And the child takes more from the parent
It resembles most—
Whether male or female.
Nor do the divine powers deny any man
The joy of fathering children,
So that he is never called "father"
By his sweet offspring,
Or spends his life in barren love forever.
This is what many believe,
And so they gloomily sprinkle altars with blood,
Making them fragrant with burnt offerings,
Praying that their wives may be made fertile
Through abundant seed—
But they trouble the gods and sacred rituals in vain.
For some men are sterile because their seed is too thick,
While others have seed that is too watery and thin.

The thin seed cannot cling to the right places;
Instead, it trickles away and is wasted.
Meanwhile, overly thick seed is unfit,
Either failing to shoot forth properly,
Not reaching the right place,
Or, even if it does, mixing weakly with the woman's seed.
The harmony of Venus' union matters greatly here.
Some men impregnate certain women more easily,
And some women conceive more readily with specific men.
Indeed, many women who were sterile
In previous marriages have later found mates
With whom they could bear children,
Blessing their homes with sweet offspring.
Likewise, husbands whose fertile wives
Could not bear them children
Have found other partners whose nature aligns with theirs,
Granting them sons to brighten their old age.
It is crucial that the seeds
Mingle harmoniously for procreation.
Thicker seeds must mix with thinner ones,
And thinner with thicker,
For successful conception.
Diet also plays an important role in this process.
Certain foods can thicken the seed within the body,
While others make it thinner and weaker.
Additionally, the way love is made
Matters greatly as well.
It is commonly thought that women
Conceive more easily in positions
Like those of four-legged animals,
With the breasts downward and the hips raised.
This posture helps the seed
Reach the proper places.
Women should avoid excessive motion or playfulness during
    intimacy,

As this can hinder conception.
If a woman moves too joyfully,
Arching her body and tossing herself wildly,
She disrupts the natural course of the seed,
Deflecting it from where it needs to go.
Courtesans often move this way intentionally,
Preventing pregnancy while increasing pleasure for their clients.
But such practices are unnecessary for wives,
Whose goal is often to conceive.
Sometimes, it happens—through no divine intervention
Or arrows of Venus—that a plain and unremarkable woman
Wins a man's love.
Her actions, accommodating nature,
And tidy habits can endear her to him,
Making her a companion for life.
Long familiarity can also foster love.
Even as a stone, struck repeatedly by gentle blows,
Eventually weakens and cracks,
So too does a heart yield to love
When exposed to kindness and habit over time.
Do you not see how drops of water,
Falling consistently on stones,
Eventually wear through them?

Book V

Proem

O who can craft with mighty heart a song
Worthy of the greatness of these discoveries?
Or who can find words strong enough
To give proper praise to the one
Who left us heirs to such vast treasures,
Discovered and revealed by his own effort?
Surely no mortal man could do this.

For if he must be named according to the majesty
Of these great findings, then he was a god—
Listen to me, illustrious Memmius—a god,
Who first discovered the way of life
Now called philosophy.
By his skill, he lifted life
Out of the wild waves of chaos and darkness
And anchored it in calm harbors,
In the light of reason and peace.
Compare this to the discoveries of others:
According to the tales,
Ceres gave us the gift of grain,
And Bacchus the juice of grapes for wine.
But even without these gifts, life could continue,
As some peoples live without them still.
But happiness and well-being were impossible
Without freeing the mind.
That is why this man rightly seems to us a god—
He who spread the sweet comforts of life
Across all lands, soothing the minds of men.
And if you think the labors of Hercules
Were greater than these,
Then you stray far from reason.
What harm could the mighty jaws
Of the Nemean Lion cause us now?
Or the Boar of Arcadia with its bristling hide?
Or the Cretan Bull, or the Hydra,
That venomous monster of Lerna,
Surrounded by its deadly snakes?
What threat could the three-bodied Geryon pose,
Or the Stymphalian birds of the marshes?
What danger is there from the fire-breathing steeds
Of Thracian Diomedes,
Roaming the lands of Bistonia and Ismara?
Even the great serpent,

Guarding the golden apples of the Hesperides,
Coiled around its tree with immense bulk—
What harm could it inflict on us now,
On the distant shores of the Atlantic?
None of these monsters,
Even if they lived and were undefeated,
Could bring us harm today.
For the earth still swarms with savage beasts,
And the forests and mountains
Are filled with dangers even now.
Yet we avoid those places with ease.
But if the mind is not freed,
What conflicts and fears rage within us!
How great the struggles and dangers of the soul!
The agonies of desire tear men apart.
How overwhelming the fears!
Pride, greed, and reckless indulgence
Bring endless slaughter in their wake,
Along with debauchery and laziness.
Therefore, the man who overcame these evils,
Who freed the mind with words alone—
Not with weapons—
Shouldn't he rightly be ranked among the gods?
All the more because he spoke
Of the immortal gods themselves
With divine wisdom,
Revealing the truths of the world
And explaining its nature.

Argument of The Book and New Proem Against A Teleological Concept

And now, following in his footsteps,
I continue his reasoning,
Explaining through my words the laws

That govern how all things are formed,
How they must follow those laws
And cannot escape the eternal decrees of time.
We've seen that among mortal things,
The mind is born from the body,
Fragile and unable to endure
Through the infinite ages.
We've also discussed how dreams bring images
That confuse the mind,
Making us think we see people
Who are no longer alive.
So far, we have come to this point:
The order of my plan now requires me
To explain how the universe itself
Is made of mortal matter, born in time,
And how its parts—earth, sky, oceans, stars,
Sun, and moon—came together.
I will also explain what living creatures
Sprang from the earth,
Which never came to life at all,
And how humans began to name things
And develop language to communicate.
I'll tell how the fear of gods arose in their hearts,
Leading to the creation of temples, altars,
Sacred groves, lakes, and idols of the gods.
I will also describe how nature guides
The courses of the sun and moon,
So that we don't mistakenly believe
That they move of their own free will,
Or that their paths are planned by gods
To sustain crops and life on earth.
Even those who know the gods live carefree lives
Sometimes wonder how things work,
Especially the movements of the heavens.
This doubt often drives them back to fear

And makes them believe again
In harsh, all-powerful gods.
Such men fail to understand
What can and cannot be,
And by what laws all things are bound,
Each with its proper limits set in time.
But now, lest I delay you with empty promises,
Look first at the sea, land, and sky:
O Memmius, see their threefold nature—
Three vast bodies, so different,
Yet all will one day be destroyed.
One single day will bring annihilation,
And the great structure of the world,
Which has endured for countless ages,
Will collapse.
I know this idea may seem strange and incredible,
That the sky and earth could someday end.
It is a difficult truth to explain,
As with any new idea,
One that cannot be seen or touched.
For the senses are the easiest way
To open belief in the human mind.
But still, I will speak.
Perhaps the fact itself will compel belief,
And you may soon witness a time
When the earth shakes with violent upheaval.
May nature, the great guide,
Keep these disasters far from us,
And may reason, not the events themselves,
Convince us that all things can be destroyed
And crash down in ruin.
Before I begin explaining this further,
I will share truths more solid and clear
Than anything the Oracle of Delphi ever proclaimed.
These truths will console you,

So you won't be trapped by religion,
Thinking that the earth, sun, sky, sea,
Stars, and moon must last forever,
Or that they are divine and eternal.
For some believe that those who explore
The truths of the universe
And challenge the heavens' walls,
Wishing to darken the brilliant sun,
Deserve punishment for their arrogance—
A belief as old as the myths of the Giants.
But this is far from true.
The sun, moon, and stars are not divine;
They are unworthy of being counted among the gods.
Instead, they serve as examples of things
That lack life, motion, and thought.
It is absurd to think
That judgment and reason could exist
In things like fire, water, or air—
Just as a tree cannot grow in the sky,
Clouds cannot form in the sea,
And fish cannot live on land.
Every part of the world has its place and purpose.
So too, the mind cannot exist alone,
Separated from the body.
If it could, why not imagine
A mind in the head, shoulders, or even the feet?
But since the soul and mind exist only in this body,
Arranged within its proper parts,
We must reject the idea
That they can survive outside the body.
They cannot dwell in rotting earth,
In the sun's fire,
In water,
Or in the distant reaches of the sky.
These elements have no divine sense,

For they cannot be quickened with life.
Likewise, you must never believe
That the sacred homes of the gods exist
Anywhere in this earthly world.
The nature of the gods is far too subtle,
Too removed from our senses,
And barely understood even by the mind.
Since they are beyond the touch of human hands,
They cannot grasp anything tangible to us.
For anything that cannot be touched itself
Can never touch something else.
This means their dwelling places
Must also be unlike ours—
Subtle and fitting for such a delicate essence.
I will prove this to you later in greater detail.
Further, to claim that the gods created
This magnificent world for the sake of humanity,
And that we should therefore praise their work,
Calling it worthy of admiration,
Or that it is sacrilege to question or overturn
What has been established by ancient divine will—
Such ideas, Memmius, are pure folly.
What gratitude could we offer
That would benefit the immortal, blessed gods,
Enough to make them act on our behalf?
Or what new reason, after so long a time,
Could persuade them—
Who have lived in eternal peace—
To alter their way of life?
It is those who are dissatisfied with the old
Who seek change,
But beings who have known only endless contentment—
What could spark in them a desire for something new?
And what harm would it have caused us
If we had never been born?

It's not as if we were trapped in misery,
Waiting in darkness for the dawn of creation!
Whoever has been born naturally wishes to live
As long as life is sweet,
But for those who never lived,
What difference does it make to them
That they were never born?
How could the gods have had a model
For creating the world in the first place?
How could they have conceived
What humans should be like,
Or imagined what they wanted to create?
How would they have known
The properties of the primal elements,
Or how those elements could combine
To form the world,
If nature herself had not first provided examples?
For countless ages,
The primordial particles of the universe
Have been in motion,
Colliding in every possible way.
By combining and separating,
They have continually tested
What could be created.
It is no surprise that they eventually settled
Into the arrangements we see today,
Sustaining the world through endless renewal.
Even if I did not know the nature
Of these primal particles,
I would still confidently assert—
Based on the patterns of the skies
And many other observations—
That the universe was not created
By any divine power.
The many flaws of nature make this clear.

First, consider all the regions under the vast sky.
Much of it is taken up by mountains,
Forests filled with wild beasts,
Cliffs, barren swamps, and oceans
That separate the lands with vast stretches of water.
Of the remaining space, nearly two-thirds
Are rendered uninhabitable
By unbearable heat or eternal frost.
Even the land left for farming
Would be overrun with brambles and weeds
If human effort did not resist it.
For survival, people have long toiled,
Sweating under the burden of their tools,
Splitting the soil with plows and mattocks,
Struggling to make the earth yield its bounty.
Unless we turn the fertile soil with the plough
And knead the earth, bringing it to life,
Crops would not grow on their own,
Rising into the free, bright air.
Even then, after our hardest labor
Has brought them to leaf and blossom,
The blazing sun may scorch them with deadly heat,
Or sudden rains, chilling frost,
Or violent winds may destroy and twist them.
Beyond this, why does nature foster
On both land and sea
The dreadful breeds of savage beasts,
Enemies of the human race?
Why do the seasons bring sickness and disease?
Why does untimely death strike so often?
Look at the newborn child:
Like a castaway washed ashore by raging waves,
He lies naked on the ground,
Speechless and in desperate need of help,
When nature first brings him

Into the light of day.
Torn from his mother's womb with birth-pangs,
He fills the air with plaintive cries—
A fitting beginning for one
Who must journey through so many hardships in life.
But all the flocks, herds, and wild beasts
Come into the world fully equipped.
They need no rattles,
No soothing words from a nurse's playful chatter.
They do not require different clothes
To adapt to changing weather.
They need no weapons or high walls
To protect what they have.
For the earth itself,
And nature, the creator of the world,
Provides abundantly for them all.

The World is Not Eternal

And first,
Since the bodies of earth, water, air,
And fiery exhalations (these four elements
That make up everything we see)
Are all born and have a perishable nature,
The entire world must also be understood
As perishable.
For truly, anything whose parts and pieces
Are born in time and have a limited lifespan
Must itself have been created in time
And must eventually perish.
So, when I see the largest parts of the world—
Its mightiest features—being consumed and renewed,
I know that the sky above
And the earth beneath had a beginning in time
And will, in time, come to an end.

And in case you think
I am making this claim lightly or to suit myself—
Because I argue that earth and fire are mortal,
That water and air also perish,
And that these are born again and grow anew—
Consider the evidence.
First, certain parts of the earth,
Parched by relentless sun
And trampled under countless feet,
Release clouds of fine dust,
Which the strong winds carry into the air.
Other parts of the soil are washed away
By heavy rains and swelling rivers
That erode their banks.
Moreover, whatever the earth gives
To nourish and grow life,
It takes back in return.
And since the earth, the mother of all,
Is also the common grave of all things,
You can see her resources diminish
Only to be replenished with new growth.
As for the sea, streams, and springs,
They overflow with fresh water
Again and again.
This endless renewal of water
Requires no explanation—
The constant movement of countless waters
Proves it clearly.
Whatever water rises up
Is immediately carried away,
So there is never an overflow.
This happens partly because
The strong winds and the sun's heat
Reduce the seas by evaporation,
And partly because water seeps underground

Through the earth.
Saltwater is filtered out,
And the fresh water gathers again
At the sources of rivers.
From there, it flows onward,
Pouring over the land through channels
Carved by ancient floods.
Now, about the air:
It constantly changes, hour by hour,
In countless ways.
Whatever rises as dust or vapor from things
Is carried into the vast ocean of the air.
If air did not, in turn, return to replenish things
By giving back matter as it absorbs it,
Everything by now would have dissolved
And turned entirely into air.
But the air is continuously created
From the things around us
And flows back into them,
Since all things are in a constant state of flux.
Likewise,
The endless source of liquid light,
The ethereal sun, floods the heavens
With a constant flow of new radiance,
Replacing the light as soon as it shines.
Whatever beams stream from the sun
Are lost the moment they fall elsewhere.
You can understand this from simple examples:
When clouds begin to pass beneath the sun
And seem to split its rays in two,
The lower beams disappear entirely,
Casting shadows wherever the clouds roll.
This shows that light constantly needs renewal,
With each beam perishing as soon as it flashes forth.
Without this replenishment,

Nothing could remain visible under the sun.
Even earthly sources of light, like lamps and torches,
Behave the same way. Their gleams dart forth,
Flickering alive with their flames,
While new light continually replaces the old.
The destruction of one flame
Is masked by the swift birth of another,
So the light never truly leaves the area it illuminates.
Thus, we must believe that the sun, moon, and stars
Emit their light from constantly renewing sources.
The flames that first rise always perish one by one,
Preventing us from imagining them as eternal.
Do you not see, as well,
How even stones are defeated by time?
How tall towers collapse into ruin,
And massive boulders crumble?
How the shrines of gods and their idols crack and decay?
Even divine power cannot hold back
The inevitable march of fate,
Nor can it defy the fixed decrees of nature.
Look at the monuments of heroes, now in ruins,
And hear them ask if you still doubt
That they too grow old.
See the shattered rocks falling
From high mountains,
Unable to withstand the forces of time.
If these had endured since eternity past,
Resisting every assault of the ages,
They would not suddenly collapse now.
Now, consider this whole world—
The vast structure surrounding the earth.
If it produces all things within itself,
As some claim, and reclaims them upon their destruction,
Then it must itself be born of mortal matter.
For whatever gives part of itself to sustain other things

Must eventually diminish and be replenished
When it takes things back.
Moreover, if the earth and sky had no beginning—
If they had always existed—
Why, before the Theban war or the fall of Troy,
Did no poets sing of other great events?
Why have so many heroic deeds been forgotten,
Lost to time, without eternal monuments to preserve them?
Surely, this is because the universe is new,
Having only recently begun.
Even now, some arts are still evolving.
New devices are continually being added to ships,
Musical instruments were only recently invented,
And the understanding of nature and the universe
Was discovered not long ago.
I, too, have only just begun
To express these truths in the Roman tongue,
Bringing this knowledge to my people.
But if you believe that all these things
Existed in the same way before,
Only to be destroyed by fiery eruptions,
Massive earthquakes, or floods
That overwhelmed the earth and its cities,
Then you must admit,
Defeated by the argument,
That the earth and sky will someday
Be destroyed as well.
For if such great catastrophes
Have afflicted the world before,
It stands to reason that some even greater disaster
Could cause its ultimate collapse.
This is no different from how we know
That humans are mortal—
Because we all suffer the same illnesses
That claimed the lives of those who came before us,

Removed from life by nature.
Whatever lasts forever must either
Resist all forces, being made of solid matter
That allows nothing to break it apart—
Like those seeds of matter
We've discussed before—
Or exist free from harm,
Like the void, which cannot be touched or struck.
The void endures because it cannot be broken,
And it provides no resistance to blows.
Alternatively, something could last forever
If there were no space around it
For its parts to break apart and scatter—
Like the universe as a whole,
Which has no external place
Where its pieces could flee or dissolve.
Nor are there bodies outside the universe
To strike it and destroy it.
But the world is not made of solid matter,
As it contains void mixed throughout.
Nor is it entirely void,
And there are still forces from the infinite beyond—
Mighty whirlwinds of matter
That could batter the world into ruin,
Or other catastrophic forces
That might shatter its walls.
There exists infinite space,
A vast and boundless abyss,
Into which the universe's foundations
Could be hurled and destroyed.
Some external force could still strike them
And bring everything to ruin.
Thus, the door to destruction is not closed
For the heavens, the sun, the earth,
And the deep seas.

It stands wide open,
Glaring at them with a monstrous grin.
This is why we must admit
That these things were born in time.
For objects made of mortal matter
Could not have survived
The countless assaults
Of infinite past ages without breaking apart.

Again, the four great elements of the world—
Earth, water, air, and fire—
Clash constantly in a fierce and endless war.
Don't you see that their struggle could one day end?
What if the sun and its heat
Finally gained control
And evaporated all the water?
They are constantly trying to do this,
Though they haven't succeeded yet.
The rivers, fed by endless seas,
Continue to replenish the water,
Threatening the world with floods
From the ocean's deep reservoirs.
But the winds and the sun's heat
Work to dry up the seas,
Hoping to stop the waters
Before they succeed in their goal.
This vast struggle continues,
Each force balancing the other,
Locked in battle over the fate of the world.
At times, fire has been victorious.
Once, as the tale goes,
Water ruled over the earth.
Fire triumphed in the story of Phaethon,
Who lost control of the sun's fiery chariot
And set the skies and lands ablaze.

Then Jupiter, in his wrath,
Struck Phaethon down with a thunderbolt,
And his father, the sun,
Seized the flaming reins,
Tamed the horses,
And restored order to the universe—
As the ancient poets of Greece tell us.
But this tale seems far from the truth.
Fire prevails only when
A greater number of fiery particles rise
From the infinite beyond.
At other times, fire is subdued,
Or it consumes the world
In burning heat.
Likewise, water has had its victories.
As the story goes,
Floods overwhelmed humanity,
Drowning men beneath their waves.
But when the force of water receded—
Its fury turned aside—
The rains stopped,
And rivers calmed their rage.

Formation of The World And Astronomical Questions

But now, I will explain how the gathering of first particles
Created the vast universe—
The earth, the sky, the endless seas,
The sun's path, and the moon's orbit.
It was not through some plan or deliberate thought
That these primal elements placed themselves
In their proper order.
Nor did they agree upon how they would move.
Instead, the particles of matter—

Countless and varied—
Have been moving and colliding
For infinite ages, driven by their own weight
And the constant blows they endured.
Through these endless movements and combinations,
The particles eventually formed unions and motions
That gave rise to the great structures of the world:
The earth, the sea, the sky,
And all living creatures.
In that ancient time,
The sun's blazing wheel had not yet risen
To light the heavens.
No constellations, no oceans,
No sky, no earth, no air,
And nothing that resembled the world we know.
There was only a chaotic mass—
A storm of disordered particles,
Colliding and conflicting with one another.
Their random motions and varied shapes
Prevented them from joining together
In stable and harmonious ways.
Over time, similar particles began to gather,
Separating into distinct groups
And forming the world's major elements.
The heavens lifted high above the land,
The sea spread out its waters,
And pure fires of the upper sky
Clustered together in their own realm.
First, the heaviest and most entangled particles—
The earthy ones—
Settled in the middle,
Forming the solid ground.
The more they interlocked,
The more they pushed out
The lighter particles,

Which became the sea, the stars, the sun,
The moon, and the boundaries of the world.
These lighter elements were made of smaller, smoother particles.
The fiery ether, escaping through countless pores in the earth,
Rose upward,
Carrying the stars with it.
This process is similar to how lakes and streams
Release mists into the air,
Or how the earth smokes
When the sun's golden rays at dawn
Begin to warm the dew-covered grass.
As these vapors gather overhead,
They form clouds,
Which weave a cover across the sky.
In the same way, the light, diffuse ether
Spread out on all sides,
Bending and curving into a dome
That encased everything below.
Next came the sun and moon,
Their globes suspended in the air,
Midway between the earth and the ether.
They were too heavy to remain aloft
In the highest ether,
But too light to sink to the ground.
Thus, they revolve in their paths,
Becoming part of the greater whole,
Like some parts of the human body move
While others remain still.
As these elements separated,
The earth collapsed inward,
Forming the vast basins
Where the oceans now stretch.
Day by day, the sun's rays and ether's tides
Pressed and shaped the earth,
Condensing it further toward its center.

This process squeezed out salty moisture,
Which flowed into the oceans,
And released particles of heat and air,
Which rose to form the bright, glowing heavens.
The plains sank lower,
While the mountains grew taller,
Their rocky foundations resisting the forces of compression.
Thus, the earth became stable,
Its heavy and coarse matter settling at the bottom,
Like dregs sinking in a liquid.
The oceans, air, and ether above
Were left pure and separate,
Each lighter than the one beneath it.
Ether, the lightest and most fluid of all,
Floats above the winds,
Unaffected by their chaos.
While the winds below clash and whirl,
The ether glides steadily,
Carrying its fires in a smooth and constant motion.
The steady flow of ether
Is like the Pontus sea,
Which moves with fixed tides,
Maintaining its endless rhythm as it glides forward.
And so,
For the earth to remain at rest
In the middle of the universe,
It must lose weight gradually and shrink,
Being connected from its very beginning
To another substance below it—
Bound tightly to the vast realms of air,
On which it depends and where it resides.
For this reason, the earth does not weigh down
On the air beneath it,
Just as a man's body does not feel
The weight of his own head pressing on his neck,

Or the body's full weight pulling on the feet,
We do not notice the earth pressing on the air.
Instead, we feel only external weights—
Those placed upon us—causing discomfort,
Even if they are lighter than our own body.
This shows that the inherent nature of a thing
Always determines its effect.
Thus, the earth is no foreign object
Dropped from another universe
Onto alien air.
It was formed alongside the air
As part of the world's creation,
Just as our limbs are part of our bodies.

***

Furthermore, when the earth is shaken violently
By a great thunder,
It also shakes everything above it.
This could not happen unless the earth
Was firmly connected
To the air and sky.
They are bound together with common roots,
United since their origin.
Don't you see how the subtle energy of the soul
Supports the heavy weight of the body?
It does this because it is joined to the body,
Bound to it as one.
In the same way,
What power could lift our body into a leap
Without the energy of the mind guiding the limbs?
So, you see how a subtle force,
When connected to something heavy,
Can be incredibly strong—
Just as the air is bound to the earth,
And the mind to the body.

***

Now let us consider what makes the stars move.
If the heavens spin as a massive sphere,
Then it must be that air presses on the poles—
Both above and below—
Holding and enclosing them in place.
Additionally, air might flow across the top of the sphere,
Pushing it in the same direction as the stars,
Or it might stream beneath it,
Turning the sphere upward,
Much like rivers turn waterwheels.
It's also possible that the heavens remain still
While the stars themselves move,
Perhaps driven by swift currents of ether
Encased within the sky.
These ether tides might flow
In search of escape,
Carrying the stars along their paths.
Or, it could be that an external stream of air
Flows from a distant source,
Driving the stars onward,
Or that the stars themselves
Move under their own power,
Traveling wherever their "fuel" invites them,
Sustaining their fiery bodies as they go.
It's hard to say with certainty
Which of these causes moves the stars in our world.
But I can show that in the universe at large,
Different worlds may follow different plans.
One of these causes must apply here,
Moving the constellations we see.
Yet to determine which one is true
Is not an easy task—
It requires careful, step-by-step reasoning.

***

The sun's disk is likely neither much larger
Nor its blaze much smaller than it appears.
From the distances at which light and heat reach us,
Neither the flame's size nor its brightness
Seems diminished.
Thus, the sun's heat and radiance
Touch our bodies just as they appear.
Its form and size, as seen from earth,
Are likely very close to their actual dimensions.
As for the moon,
Whether it shines by reflecting the sun's light
Or glows with its own radiance,
Its shape and size remain as they appear to us.
All distant objects seem blurred
When viewed through layers of air,
Yet the moon's bright and well-defined form
Indicates it is visible to us on earth
Exactly as it is.
Lastly,
The fires of ether—those stars we see from earth—
May be slightly larger or smaller than they seem,
But only by the tiniest margin.
Fires we see here on earth
Change size only slightly when viewed from afar,
So long as they remain bright and distinct.
Similarly, the stars above likely maintain
Almost exactly the size we perceive.
Nor should it surprise us
That the small sun can emit such vast light,
Flooding the oceans, lands, and sky,
Bathing the entire world in fiery warmth.
It's possible that the light comes from a vast wellspring,
A single source that spreads its radiance outward.

In this way, the fiery particles
From the entire world gather and flow together
To form a single, powerful stream of heat and light.
Do you not see how even a small spring of water
Can flood meadows and fields?
Similarly, the heat of the sun,
Though its fire may be small,
Can fill the air with fierce warmth,
Especially if the air is ready to be kindled—
Just as we see an entire field of grain
Or stubble catch fire from a single spark.
The sun, gleaming on high,
May also have an invisible fire surrounding it,
Unseen by the eye,
But adding greatly to the power of its rays.
There is no single, definite explanation
For how the sun moves from summer
To its winter position in Capricorn
And back again to Cancer at the solstice.
Nor do we fully know why the moon
Crosses the same distance each month
That the sun takes a year to traverse.
The most likely explanation comes
From the teachings of Democritus,
Who argued that objects closer to the earth
Move more slowly because
The rotational force of the sky weakens
As it nears the ground.
The sun, lying below the blazing stars,
Is left behind as the heavens whirl above it.
The moon, being closer to the earth than the sun,
Lags even farther behind.
The slower the motion of the heavens below,
The more the moon falls behind the stars.
This is why the moon seems to return

To the same position in the Zodiac
More quickly than the sun,
Since the stars overtake her more often.
It could also be that streams of air,
Blowing alternately at fixed times,
Push the sun from summer to winter
And back again.
One stream might drive the sun
Toward the cold of winter,
While another sends it back
To the heat of summer.
The same reasoning could explain the movement
Of the moon and stars,
Which may be carried along
By alternating air currents,
Much like clouds are blown
In different directions at different heights.
Why shouldn't the stars in the ether
Be moved by opposing streams of air,
Just as clouds are moved below?
Night envelops the world in darkness
When the sun, after its daily journey,
Reaches the farthest edges of the sky,
Its fires spent and weakened
By their long passage through the air.
Or it may be that the same force
That drives the sun above the earth
Then compels it to travel below.
Morning, at its appointed hour,
Spreads rosy light across the heavens,
Either because the sun, returning beneath the earth,
Prepares to rise and light the sky,
Or because fiery particles gather together,
Forming a new sun at the start of each day.
Some say the fires seen on mountaintops at dawn

Combine into a single orb,
Creating the sun anew each morning.
It's not surprising that fiery particles
Could stream together at a fixed time,
Reforming the sun's brilliance.
Many things happen at regular intervals:
Plants sprout and shed their flowers,
Children lose their baby teeth,
And young men grow soft beards at a certain age.
Even thunder, snow, rain, and winds
Follow fixed patterns,
Arriving in their seasons.
From the very beginning of the world,
These causes have operated in regular cycles.
And now, just as they did then,
These events continue to follow
Their fixed order and sequence.
Likewise,
Days may grow longer as nights grow shorter,
And nights may extend as daylight fades.
This might happen because the sun,
Traveling under the earth and across the sky,
Follows two arcs—one longer, one shorter—
Dividing the ether unequally.
As it moves, it adds light to one part of its path
While taking it away from another,
Until it reaches the point in the heavens
Where day and night become equal again.
When the sun is halfway between
The northern and southern winds,
The sky keeps its two goals balanced evenly,
Thanks to the steady position of the Zodiac,
Through which the sun travels in a year,
Illuminating the heavens and the earth
With its slanted rays.

This, at least, is what astronomers tell us,
Using their diagrams to chart the stars
And map the Zodiac's constellations.
Or perhaps the air beneath the earth
Is denser in some places,
Slowing the sun's fiery beams
So they cannot easily rise.
This would explain why winter nights linger so long
Before the many-rayed badge of the day appears.
It might also be that, as seasons change,
The fires that fuel the sun
Sometimes stream together more quickly,
Sometimes more slowly.
Thus, some claim that each day
A new sun is born at dawn.
The moon may shine because
It reflects the rays of the sun.
As it moves farther from the sun's position,
It reveals more of its light to us,
Until, opposite the sun across the sky,
It gleams fully.
When the moon rises,
It watches the sun set.
Then, as it moves closer to the sun again,
Its light fades gradually,
Its glowing face turning away from us.
This is how those who think the moon is a sphere,
Traveling between the sun and the earth,
Explain its phases.
Alternatively, the moon might have its own light,
Revealing its changing shapes
Through other mechanisms.
Perhaps another dark, invisible body
Travels with the moon,
Blocking its light in three different ways.

Or the moon could rotate on its own axis,
Half of it glowing with light,
While its spinning reveals and hides
Different parts of its surface over time.
This idea, supported by Babylonian astronomers,
Contradicts the theories of Greek astrologers.
Yet, both views could hold some truth,
And there's no clear reason to favor one
Over the other.
It's also possible that each day
A new moon is created and then destroyed,
Its shapes following a fixed sequence.
This would align with the regular cycles
We see in nature:
Springtime arrives with Venus,
And her winged companion leads the way.
Mother Flora follows,
Scattering colors and sweet fragrances.
Summer brings heat and the dry touch of Ceres,
Along with northern breezes.
Then comes autumn with Bacchus,
And finally winter,
Chilling the earth with its icy breath.
If so many things happen in fixed cycles,
It is not surprising that a moon
Could also be born and destroyed at regular intervals.
Similarly, the eclipses of the sun and moon
May have various causes.
Why should the moon be the only body
Capable of blocking the sun's light
By placing itself between the earth and the sun?
Couldn't another dark object,
Always invisible to us,
Be responsible for such phenomena?
And why couldn't the sun itself

Lose its fire temporarily
As it passes through regions
Hostile to its flames,
Only to regain its light afterward?
Likewise, when the earth casts its shadow,
Blocking the sun from the moon,
This might not be the only explanation for lunar eclipses.
Why couldn't another body
Pass below the moon
Or above the sun,
Interrupting their light?
Even if the moon glows with its own light,
Why couldn't it grow dim in certain parts of the sky,
Traveling through regions that weaken its radiance?

Origins of Vegetable and Animal Life

And now, to what remains!
Since I've explained how the motions of the sun and moon
Come about, and how they may falter,
Veiling the land in shadow
When they seem to blink,
Only to shine again with bright radiance,
I will return to the early days of the world.
I'll tell how the young earth, in her first moments,
Brought forth life, raising it to the light
And entrusting it to the winds.
At first, the earth gave rise to grass,
Covering the hills and plains
With green shoots.
The meadows sparkled with vibrant colors.
Then came the trees,
Spurred by a great impulse
To grow tall into the air.
Just as feathers, hair, and bristles

Are first to grow on animals,
So the earth first sprouted grasses and shrubs,
And later gave birth to countless living creatures
In countless forms.
These creatures could not have fallen from the sky,
Nor emerged from the salty pools of the sea.
Earth has rightly earned the name "Mother,"
Since all life comes from her.
Even now, life forms in the soil,
Shaped by rain and the heat of the sun.
It's no wonder that, in those early days,
More and larger creatures arose,
Born in the fresh, young years of earth and sky.
First came birds,
Hatching in springtime and leaving their eggs behind,
Just as crickets today shed their shells
And go on living.
Then the earth brought forth
Other living beings in abundance.
The land was rich with heat and moisture,
And in suitable places, womb-like cavities formed,
Attached to the earth by roots.
When the young creatures inside
Reached the age to seek the air,
They broke free, escaping the dampness of the ground.
At that time, the earth supplied them with food.
Like a mother's milk,
The earth's pores released nourishing juices,
Just as a woman's body produces milk
After childbirth.
These early creatures found warmth in the soil
And softness in the grass,
Without suffering from harsh cold,
Scorching heat, or violent winds.
In those days, the young earth

Protected life from such extremes.
How fitting is the name "Mother Earth,"
For she gave birth to humankind,
As well as the beasts of the mountains
And the birds of the skies.
But, like any mother,
Her ability to give life diminished with age.
Time changes the nature of all things,
And nothing remains the same forever.
All things come and go.
Nature transforms everything:
Some things decay and wither,
While others rise and flourish.
Thus, as time passes,
The earth takes on new roles.
What she once created,
She can no longer produce,
And what she never bore before,
She may bring forth today.
In those ancient times,
The earth also gave rise to strange creatures—
Monsters with bizarre forms and limbs.
There were beings that were neither male nor female,
Lacking characteristics of either sex.
Some had no feet, others no hands.
Some were dumb horrors without mouths,
Or blind creatures with no eyes.
Some were so malformed
That their limbs were fused to their bodies,
Preventing them from moving,
Escaping harm, or seeking what they needed.
Earth produced such monsters in vain.
Nature refused to let them thrive.
They could not mature, find food,
Or reproduce.

For life requires certain conditions:
There must be food,
A way for reproductive seeds
To move through the body,
And the physical means for male and female
To unite and propagate life.
And after monsters passed away,
Many creatures could not stay, unable
To survive or grow a lasting line.
For every creature that you see,
Living, breathing, as they be,
Has, from earliest days, survived,
By clever tricks, or strength, or flight.
Many kinds are still alive today
Because they serve in some helpful way,
Entrusted now to human care.
Strength has kept fierce lions alive
And other beasts that inspire fear;
Foxes live by clever schemes,
While stags are saved by speed and grace.
Faithful dogs, with hearts alert,
And animals bred for strength and work,
The woolly sheep and horned cattle too,
All are guarded under human watch.
For they fled from savage beasts,
Seeking peace and food in rest,
A life where they need not labor hard,
A reward for their service true.
But beasts without these gifts to give—
Those that could not thrive alone
Or serve in ways that made them safe—
Were left exposed to harsher fates,
Chained by nature to doom's hold,
As prey and prize for others' needs,
Until their kind met utter end.

No Centaurs were, nor could there be,
Creatures made of double form,
Mixed with limbs not built alike,
Yet somehow strong in every way—
For even if your mind is slow,
You'll see that horses, by year three,
Stand in the peak of strength and speed;
A child, by then, is still so small,
Sometimes seeking his mother's care,
An infant yet. And later on,
When strong and sturdy horse limbs fail,
Youth is only then taking root
In boys, with down upon their cheeks.
So never think that human kind
And horse could join to make Centaurs,
Or Scyllas, half-dog and half-fish—
Or others mixed in strange design,
For their parts could never blend;
Their ages, needs, and growth don't match.
They wouldn't share one lust or taste,
For just as goats can eat the plant
That poisons men, each kind is set.
Flame burns lions just the same
As it scorches any flesh or blood.
So how could Chimaera's form—
With lion front, dragon tail, and goat between—
Breathe fire from its body so?
And those who claim such beings were born
When earth was young and sky was fresh
Base their words on tales alone.
They say that rivers of gold once flowed
Through lands and trees bore gems as fruit,
Or that humans walked as giants tall,
Able to wade through oceans deep
Or spin the heavens in their hands.

But even though, in ancient times,
Earth held seeds of every life,
This is not proof that creatures mixed,
With parts of all kinds bound as one.
Even now, each plant and tree
Sprouts from the earth in its own way;
They cannot join into one kind—
Each follows its own nature true,
Bound by nature's fixed decree.

ORIGINS AND SAVAGE PERIOD OF MANKIND

But mortal man
Was hardier then, in the old plains,
As well he should be, born from earth
That was stronger too; he was built
With bigger, sturdier bones within,
And flesh bound tight with solid sinews,
Unaffected by heat or cold,
Or strange foods, or aches and pains.
And as many suns rolled by,
They lived a roaming life like beasts.
No one then guided curved plows,
Or tilled the soil with iron tools,
Or planted shoots in the turned-up earth,
Or trimmed the old branches from trees.
What the sun and rains brought forth,
What earth itself created freely,
Was enough to please their simple hearts.
Among the oak trees full of acorns
They refreshed themselves for a time;
The wild berries of the arbutus,
Now ripening red in winter's chill,
The old earth yielded then more full.
And many coarse foods, back then,
The fresh, young world provided,
Enough for those poor, early folk.

Rivers and springs summoned them
To quench their thirst, as now the hills
Call down to the creatures of the wild
With water rushing far and wide.
They also sought the Nymphs' grottos—
Woodland shelters they found while roaming—
From which they knew that streams slid out,
Splashing, soaking rocks with moss,
And bursting forth across the plains.
They didn't yet know how to make fire
To guard against the cold, nor use
The furry skins of beasts as clothes;
They huddled in groves, in caves, in woods,
Or hid in thickets to shield their backs,
Driven to flee the sting of wind
And pounding rains. Nor could they yet
Understand the common good,
Or share any customs, any laws:
Whatever fortune brought to each
They kept alone, trained by instinct
Only to survive and thrive.
And in the woods, Venus joined
The lovers' bodies; the woman gave
Either from a shared desire,
Or from the man's wild, insistent urge,
Or from a gift—perhaps acorns, ripe pears,
Or berries from the arbutus tree.
And trusting strength in hands and legs,
They'd chase the beasts that roamed the forests;
They caught many, but a few escaped,
Fleeing into their hiding places...
With thrown stones and heavy branches
Twisted and gnarled. When night arrived,
They'd lie down, like bristly boars,
Their wild bodies on the bare earth,

Rolling themselves in leaves and boughs.
They did not call out to the sun
Or the fields in loud lament,
Quaking in the night's shadows;
But, silent and buried in sleep,
They waited until dawn brought light
And the sun's rosy flames. From youth,
Seeing the dark and light come back
In turns, they had no fear at all
That night would last forever, that light
Of the sun would vanish for good.
Their worries instead were more of beasts,
The savage animals that often
Turned their sleep to frightful scenes,
Forcing them to leave their caves
As boars with foaming mouths or strong lions
Pushed them from beds of scattered leaves.
Yet even then, much as today,
They left the fading light of life.
In those times, a person might be seized
By beasts, devoured alive,
Echoing in the forests as he watched
His living flesh become a grave;
While those who escaped would scream,
Pressing hands to their wounded flesh,
Begging for eternal rest,
Till, lacking any help at hand
To ease their pain, they died from it.
But not in those early days would war
Destroy great armies in a day,
Nor did raging seas then crash
Entire ships upon the rocks.
The ocean raged in vain,
Its fury ending empty, and with ease
It let go of its threats;

Nor did the calm sea's gentle waves
Tempt men toward disaster:
The bold skill of ship-sailing
Was unknown in those early days.
Again, back then a lack of food
Would drain men's strength to death; today
It's excess that overwhelms.
Unknowing, they once poured poison
For themselves; now, with more skill,
They pass the drink to others.

Beginnings of Civilization

Afterwards,
When they had gained huts, pelts, and fire,
And when the woman joined the man,
Withdrew with him to share one home,
And children born from them were known,
Then humankind began to soften.
For now fire warmed their shivering frames,
And made them less strong to bear the cold
Under the open sky; and Love
Softened their rough and shaggy ways.
Children's chatter and gentle kisses
Soon broke their proud, wild nature down.
Then neighbors began to join as friends,
No longer wanting to harm or suffer,
And urged for women and children, too,
Mercy from fathers, while they showed
With cries and gestures how it was fit
To show compassion for the weak. And still,
Though full harmony was not yet found,
A good part of men kept their faith—
For otherwise, mankind would long ago
Have perished utterly, and none

Would have survived the passing years.
Lest perhaps,
You ponder this in silent thought,
Let me say that lightning first brought fire
To earth for mortals, spreading flames
Across the lands. For even now we see
So many things flash into flame,
Struck by lightning's celestial power.
And also, when a tree with many branches,
Swaying from winds, rubs to and fro
Against the branches of a nearby tree,
There, by the power of rub and rub,
Fire is created; at times outbursts
The scorching heat of flames, when boughs
Chafe against tree trunks. Either cause
Could well have given fire to mortal men.
Next, food to cook and soften in flame,
The sun taught them, as they often saw
How warmth could mellow things it touched
With its bright and fiery rays
Across the fields.
And day by day
The stronger, wiser men would teach
Them to change their old way of life
With fire and new devices. Kings began
To found cities and to build strongholds
For protection, places safe for themselves,
Dividing flocks and fields for each
According to beauty, strength, and mind—
For beauty was prized then, and strength
Held supreme rights. After that, wealth
Was discovered, and gold revealed,
Which soon stripped honour from the strong and fair,
For men, however fair in form
Or brave, would mostly choose the rich.

But if men lived by better reason,
They'd find great wealth in a simple life,
Content with what they have; for I believe
There's never a lack of little in the world.
But men desired power and fame
So they could lay firm foundations
And live quietly in wealth—
In vain, in vain; for, in the race to climb
To the heights of honour, they make
Their path so terrible; and once they reach
The top, envy, like a thunderbolt,
Will strike, hurling them headlong down
Into darkest Tartarus with scorn; for all
Summits and highest regions
Smoke as if scorched by envy's flames;
So it is far better to obey in peace
Than to seek mastery of affairs
And possession of empires. Let it be;
And let the weary exhaust themselves,
All to no end, fighting on
The narrow path of human ambition;
Since all they know is from others' words,
All they seek is from what they hear,
And not from what they think. And this folly
Is no greater today, nor will it grow,
Than it was long ago
And thus, kings were slain,
And the ancient majesty of golden thrones
And haughty scepters lay cast down in dust;
Crowns, once splendid on royal heads,
Became bloody beneath common feet,
Groaning for their lost glories—for once feared,
They were now trampled under with greedy zeal
By the crowd. So, down to the dregs,
All things fell to the brawling mobs,

As each man sought to rule alone. Then some
Wiser minds taught men to form
The magistrates' office and to frame
Laws that all might choose to follow.
For humankind, weary of a life
Ruled by brute force, was tired of feuds;
And so it soon, of its own free will,
Gave way to laws and strictest codes. Since then,
Each man, in anger, no longer took
A vengeance harsher than what fair laws
Would now allow, they loathed the life
Led by force alone. From this arose
The fear of punishments that taints each gain
Of wickedness, for force and deceit
Circle back on the one who used them.
Not easy is it for a person
Who breaks the peace to live a calm,
Composed life. For though he may escape
The wrath of gods and men, he must still fear
That it will not stay hidden—for indeed,
Many, often babbling in dreams,
Or raving in sickness, have let slip
Their secrets and confessed their sins.
But nature itself
Urged men to speak in different sounds,
And need and use shaped the names of things,
Just as speechless years compel young children
To make gestures with their hands,
Pointing here and there at what's before them.
For each creature knows, by instinct,
How best to use its powers. Before
The bull-calf's horns have barely budded,
He starts to butt and fiercely thrust.
Panther cubs and lion whelps,
With claws and teeth not fully formed,

Already begin to fight and claw.
We see all young birds use their wings
And seek to fly with early flutters.
Thus, to think that, in those days, one man
Gave things their names, teaching others
First words, is foolishness. For why would he
Name each thing by words while others, too,
Could have made such sounds? And if others
Had not already used such words,
How did he know their use himself,
Or alone have this power to name things?
One man could scarcely make
A whole crowd remember his names.
It is not easy to persuade
The deaf on what they need to do.
They would not accept nor endure
Endless strange sounds in their ears. And why,
In the end, would it seem so strange
That humans (who had voice and tongue)
Should use various words for things,
Led by their differing senses?—
For even speechless herds, and even
The beasts of the wild, send forth different sounds
When in fear, in pain, or in joy.
You can know this from simple facts:
When great-jowled hounds, maddened, begin
To bare their teeth and snarl, they make
A sound far different from their barks
That echo through the fields.
And when they lick their young with love,
Or play with gentle, snapping bites,
They whimper softly, far different from
The sounds they make when, alone in the house,
They howl or cringe from blows.
Or take the neighing of the horse—

Is it not different when the stallion
In his prime, driven by Love,
Raves among the mares, or snorts
A call to battle, or whinnies
In fright with trembling limbs?
Finally, the dappled birds,
The hawks, ospreys, and sea-gulls,
Searching for food along the waves,
Cry differently at different times—
When they fight for food, or struggle
With prey in their grasp. There are birds
That change their calls with the weather—
The ancient crows or flocks of rooks
Are said to cry out for rain,
Or to call for winds and storms. Thus, if moods
Move the speechless beasts to make
Different sounds, then surely much more
Would mortal men, even then,
Use many sounds to name each thing..
And now what cause
Has spread belief in gods abroad
Through mighty nations, and filled cities full
Of high altars, leading to the practice
Of solemn rites in due season—rites which still
Flourish amid the great affairs of state
And at the heart of civic life,
Rites that plant a trembling awe in humankind,
Raising new temples to the gods from land to land
And drawing crowds to them on holy days—
It's not so hard to explain. For even then
People saw, with minds awake,
Visions of gods in mighty forms; and more,
In their sleep, they saw bodies of wondrous size.
Thus, they attributed to these beings
Awareness and life, as they seemed to move,

To speak grand words befitting their power.
Men believed they had eternal life,
For their images appeared constantly
And did not change; and mainly because men thought
That beings of such mighty power
Could not be overcome by any force.
They thought them full of happiness,
For the fear of death troubled them not,
And in dreams men saw them do great things
Without suffering or weariness. Besides,
They saw how the heavens followed a set course,
How seasons changed in steady cycles,
But did not understand the causes. So,
They took refuge in the idea that all
Was guided by the gods' will, and believed
The heavens were the gods' dwelling place, for there
The night, the moon, and all the stars
Are seen to move—moon, day, and night, and night's
Ancient constellations and bright fires,
The shooting stars, clouds, sun, rain,
Snow, winds, lightning, hail,
The rumblings and the hollow roar
Of thunder's mighty threats forevermore.
O humankind unhappy!—when it assigned
Such deeds to the gods, adding fierce wrath!
What pain did men on that sad day bring
To themselves, and what wounds for us,
What tears for generations yet to come!
O humankind, this is not true piety:
To approach altars with veiled head,
To bow before a stone,
To fall to earth, arms outstretched,
Before shrines of the gods, nor to stain
Altars with blood from four-footed beasts,
Nor to link one vow to another. But rather this:

To look on all things with a calm mind
And clear understanding. For when we look up
At the sky's vault, and the vast world beyond,
And ether high over the twinkling stars,
And think of the sun's and moon's paths,
Then into our already burdened hearts
Rises a new fear: whether, perhaps,
The gods' mighty powers turn round and round
The far-off constellations. For lack
Of knowledge troubles the puzzled mind:
Did the world have a beginning,
And will there be an end? How long can
The world's walls withstand this constant strain
Of movement, or will they, blessed forever,
Glide through endless ages untouched
By the vast powers of immeasurable time?
What man, fearing the gods,
Does not shrink, whose limbs do not tremble,
When the dry earth quakes under the force
Of thunderbolts, and rumbling shakes the sky?
Do not all people tremble, and kings,
Even the proudest, hold themselves tight,
Afraid that something done or said in folly
Is now to be repaid? When fierce winds
Sweep a fleet across the sea,
Dashing it along with soldiers and beasts,
Does not the leader seek the gods' peace,
And beg for calm winds and friendly seas?—in vain,
For often, swept up in raging storms,
He is borne helpless to a fatal shore.
Yes, it seems that some hidden power
Always tramples on the affairs of men,
Grinding down the highest honors,
Mocking their rods and axes with scorn.
And when the earth shakes from end to end,

And cities collapse, or are on the brink,
What wonder then that mortals bow low
And give the gods, in earthly matters,
Almighty powers to govern all?
Now for the rest: copper, gold, and iron
Were discovered, with silver's weight
And lead's power, when the burning heat
Of great fires devoured the forest trees
Upon the mighty mountains, struck
By lightning from the sky, or perhaps because
Men, fighting in the woods, threw flames
To frighten and confuse their foes,
Or because they sought to clear rich fields
For pasture, or to hunt for game
And thrive on the spoils they gained.
(For hunting by pitfall or by fire came first,
Before the art of encircling the coverts
With nets or chasing with trained dogs.)
Whatever the cause, when fire's crackling heat
Had devoured the forest roots below,
And baked the earth with blazing flames,
Then from deep veins began to flow
Rivulets of silver and of gold,
Of lead and copper, pooling soon
In hollow places on the ground.
And when men saw the cooled lumps shining
With a splendid gleam upon the earth,
Moved by that smooth, bright delight,
They dug them out and saw how each
Held the shape of its earthen mold.
Then came the thought that these same lumps,
If melted by heat, could take any form,
Or be drawn into points or sharpened edges,
Yielding tools that could chop down forests,
Carve beams and planks, bore holes,

And drill through wood. They began to work
With tools of silver and gold at first,
Alongside copper's impetuous strength;
But in vain—for silver and gold,
Too soft, could not endure the strain
Like copper in that hard labor. Back then,
Copper was prized, while gold lay dull,
Blunt-edged and useless. Now copper lies low,
And gold is raised to loftiest honors.
Thus do the ages roll, changing the worth
Of things: what once was prized
Becomes of little value, while something
Rises from contempt to glory,
Treasured more each day, and praised
As a wondrous honor.
Now, Memmius,
How iron was discovered, you may
Easily imagine. Man's earliest arms
Were hands, nails, teeth, stones and branches—
Broken from forest trees—and flame and fire
As soon as they were known. Then came
The discovery of iron and copper;
Copper was used before iron, since
It was more abundant and easier to shape.
With copper they began to till the soil,
To rouse the waves of war,
To inflict great wounds, and seize
Another's flocks and fields. Thus armed,
They conquered all that lay defenseless.
Then, slowly, the iron sword replaced
The bronze one, and the copper sickle
Fell to scorn. With iron they cleaved
The earth, and warfare became equal.
And soon men learned
To ride horses armed, guiding them with reins,

With free right hands, long before they tried
The chariot's dangers; yokes of two horses came
Before the yokes of four, or chariots
With scythes where men-at-arms would stand.
Then the Punic folk trained elephants—
Those monstrous Lucanian beasts, terrifying,
With serpent-like trunks and towers on their backs—
To withstand the wounds of war, to strike fear
Into the mighty ranks of Mars. Thus sad Discord
Brought forth one terror after another,
Spreading horror among the nations,
And day by day adding to the grim art of war.
They even tried
Bulls in battle, and sent wild boars
Against their foes. Some sent forth
Mighty lions, with armed trainers
To guide and hold them, but in vain—
For once in a frenzy of slaughter,
They would fly wildly through the ranks,
Their dreadful crests shaking on their heads,
Leaping here and there. No rider could calm
His panicked horse or rein it back to face the foe.
The infuriated lionesses would leap,
Rending those who met them face to face,
Or from behind would drag down others,
Wrapping their powerful claws around them,
Until, defeated by wounds, they fell to earth.
Bulls would toss their allies,
Goring horses with their horns,
And pressing threatening heads to the ground;
Boars would strike with sharp tusks,
Splashing blood on spears shattered in their flesh,
Felling infantry and horse in chaos.
There you might see beasts rearing up,
Hooves pawing the air in vain—

Until, with tendons cut, they'd fall heavily,
Strewn across the ground. Even those well-trained
Foamed with fury amidst wounds, cries,
Flight, and panic; men could not
Rally their numbers. All types of beasts
Fled apart, just as in today's battles
The wounded Lucanian oxen do,
Having caused so many deaths among their friends.
(If, indeed, they did this at all—
I can hardly believe men didn't foresee
The foul disaster this would bring.
But this we may hold as true, happening
In diverse worlds created in different ways,
More likely somewhere far from here.)
But men did this less in hopes of winning
Than to give their foes cause for woe,
Even if it led to their own ruin,
For they were few in number and lacked arms.
Now, rough clothes made of twisted strands
Came long before woven coverings;
And weaving came later than iron itself,
Since iron is needed for weaving's craft,
And without it, none could make the polished tools—
The treadles, spindles, shuttles,
And yarn beams sounding as they work.
And nature first compelled men
To work the wool before women's hands:
For the male of the species excels in skill,
Far cleverer in such things—until at last
The rugged farmers scorned these tasks
And soon were eager to hand them down
To women's hands, while they grew strong
In the hard labor of the fields.
But nature herself,
Mother of all, was the first sower,

The first to graft; for berries and acorns,
Falling from trees, would sprout below
With swarms of tiny shoots in season.
Thus men grew fond of grafting slips
Onto branches, and planting shrubs
In the fields. Then they would try
New ways of tilling the soil they loved,
And notice how the earth improved
The taste of wild fruits under care.
Day by day they cleared the woods,
Moving higher up the mountain slopes
And leaving the plains below for crops—
There, on flatlands and hills, they grew
Meadows, cisterns, crops of grain,
And joyful vineyards, and laid out belts
Of silvery-green olive trees,
Marking the landscape far and wide,
As you see today with lovely rows
Of fruit trees that men plant and ring
With thriving hedges.
And by the mouth,
Imitating birds' liquid notes,
Men learned to make sounds long before
The measured songs and verses
That delight the ears. The whistling wind
Through hollow reeds first taught
The peasants how to blow through stalks
Of hollow hemlock. Then, bit by bit,
They learned sweet melodies, like those
Played on pipes by singing fingers,
Echoing through deep, untrodden groves,
In forest meadows and the stillness
Of shepherd's fields. Thus, time brings forth
Each thing little by little among men,
And reason raises it to light.

These tunes soothed and gladdened mortals
When they were full from meals—for songs
Are sweetest then. And often, lying
With friends on soft grass beside a river,
Underneath a tree's wide branches,
They refreshed themselves with ease,
Especially when the weather smiled,
And flowers painted the green grass around.
Then came laughter, jokes, and talk,
For the rustic muse was in her prime;
Then lively Mirth would prompt them all
To crown their heads and shoulders with
Chaplets of flowers and leafy vines,
To dance along with swaying limbs,
Clownishly stamping the earth,
Which brought forth laughter and joy—
Such merry acts in their glory then,
Being new and strange. And wakeful men
Found comfort for sleepless hours
In drawing forth varied notes,
Modulating melodies, running lips
Along the tuned reeds, which even now
The watchmen guard in faithful measure,
Honoring old traditions. Yet they find
No greater joy than the woodland folk
In ancient times. For whatever we have
Seems best, if sweeter things are unknown—
Until some later, better find
Changes our desires anew,
And dims the worth of yesterday.
And thus
Began the loathing of the acorn; thus
Were beds of grass abandoned, and leaves
Scattered for rest were left behind.
Thus, too, the pelts of beasts fell from grace—

Once a robe of honor, which, I suppose,
Stirred up such fierce envy then
That the first wearer met his end,
Ambushed by foes; and that prize, torn
To shreds by greedy hands, stained with blood,
Was ruined beyond all use or gain.
In olden days it was pelts, and today
It's purple and gold that burden men's lives,
With cares and weary struggles for wealth.
Wherefore, I think, the greater blame
Rests on us today: the earth's bare sons,
Without pelts, would shiver from the cold;
But we could well live without
Our purple robes embroidered with gold,
And still manage with simple clothes.
Thus, man toils on in vanities,
Wasting his years in idle cares—
For truly, he has not learned
The true end of gathering wealth, nor knows
How far pleasure may grow.
Desire for better and for more
Has carried men to the depths,
And stirred the mighty waves of war.
The sun and moon, those watchmen of the world,
With their bright lamps circling round
The vast, revolving sky, have taught
Mankind that seasons come again,
And that all follows a fixed order.
Already men lived surrounded
By strong towers; they tilled the land
Marked by boundaries; already
The sea bloomed with sail-winged ships;
Already men, through treaties and pacts,
Had allies and confederates, when poets
First began to record heroic deeds in verse.

And not long before this, letters were devised—
Thus, our age is unable to look back
Except by reason's trace of what came before.
Sailing the seas, tilling fields,
Building walls, making laws, forging arms, roads,
Clothing and such, all prizes and delights
Of finer life, poems, paintings, sculptures
Of polished beauty—all these arts were learned
Through practice and the mind's experience,
As men advanced step by step.
Thus time brings forth each thing
Little by little into the world of men,
And reason lifts it to the shores of light.
For one thing after another, men saw
Grow clear by intellect, till now,
Through their arts, they've reached the peak.

Book VI

Proem

'Twas Athens first, renowned in name,
That once gave humankind the harvest's sheaves,
Reordered life, decreed the laws,
And first brought comforts to the world,
When she gave birth to a man so wise,
Who poured out wisdom from his truthful lips.
His glory, though he's dead, lives on,
For those divine discoveries of old
Raised his fame high up to the sky.
For when he saw that almost everything
Which mortals most urgently require
Was close at hand, that life was safe
And men had wealth, honor, and praise,
And noble fame for worthy sons,

Yet still, within their homes, they bore
Anxious hearts that vexed their lives,
And raved with cries of endless pain,
Then he, the master, understood
That it was the vessel, cracked and flawed,
Which spoiled all good it took within—
Partly because it was leaky,
And could not ever be filled to the brim,
And partly because it stained with bitter taste
Whatever entered it. So he, the master,
Through his words of truth, did cleanse
The hearts of men and set clear bounds
To lust and fear, and showed the way
To the highest good we seek,
Guiding us by a straight-cut path,
And showing from which gates each ill
Might enter human life, whether by chance or fate,
Since nature destined it so. And he proved
That most of human suffering rolls in vain
Within the breast, grim waves of care.
For just as children tremble in the dark
And fear all things unseen, so we,
In the light, dread many things no more
Fearsome than the fantasies children fear
In darkness. This terror, this shadow of the mind,
Is not dispelled by sunlight's fiery beams
Or arrows of the morning, but only by
Nature's aspect and her laws.
Therefore, I will continue now to weave
In verse this task I've undertaken.
And since I've taught you that the world's great vault
Is mortal, and that the sky was formed
In time, and that all within it moves
By need and must go on,
The most I have unraveled; what remains,

Take now as well; for once we rise
To mount the winds' chariot,
The storms calm, and all things once raging
Are changed now, with fury stilled;
Other movements through earth and sky
Which mortals see (often with anxious,
Quaking thoughts) abase their minds
With dread of gods, pressing them down,
For in ignorance they yield all things
To gods' rule, believing them to reign.
For even those who know that gods live free
From care, still wonder by what means
Things can proceed (especially those things
In the sky above). And thus they fall back
To the old fears and again submit
To harsh masters, thinking them almighty—
Wretched, not knowing what can be and what cannot,
Nor by what law each thing has limits set,
Its bounds so deeply rooted in Time.
And so they wander, led astray
By blind reasoning. And, Memmius, unless
You cast out of your mind these thoughts,
Unworthy of gods, alien to their peace,
Then often will the majesty of gods
Seem harmful to you, as your thoughts degrade them—
Not because gods would be outraged
Or thirst for vengeance, but because
You torment yourself, thinking the gods,
Serene and calm, roll waves of wrath;
And you will never approach their shrines
With a tranquil mind, nor will you receive
Those images that from their holy forms
Are carried into human minds,
Reflecting their divine nature.
What kind of life would follow, you can see;

But that pure reason may drive away
Such a life far from us, much remains
To polish in my verse, though much has poured
Already from me. Behold, the law and form
Of the sky are to be grasped by reason;
There are the tempests and bright lightnings—
Why they happen and from what cause
They move—that you may no longer tremble,
Dividing the sky in anxious thoughts
For auguries, and wondering whence comes
The flying flame or to which side of heaven
It turns, or how it finds its way
Through walls, or how, after its force is shown,
It speeds forth again—
Men do not know these causes,
And think divinities are at work.
Do thou, Calliope, ingenious Muse,
Delight of mortals, joy of gods,
Show me the path as I press on
To the white line of my goal,
That I may win the crown,
With you, my guide!

Great Meteorological Phenomena, Etc.

And first of all,
Thunder shakes the blue depths of heaven,
When the ethereal clouds, racing high,
Clash together as winds battle fiercely.
For no sound ever comes from the serene
Regions of the sky; but wherever dense clouds
Gather in force, there more often comes
A crash with mighty rumbling. And again,
Clouds cannot be as dense as stones and wood,
Nor as fine as mist or drifting smoke,

For if they were, they'd either fall, pulled down
By sheer weight, like stones, or be too weak,
Like smoke, to hold their mass together,
To retain within them snow and hailstorms.
And they send forth, across the open sky,
A sound above, like a linen awning stretched
Over mighty theaters, which gives a crack
When struck by gusts between poles and beams.
Sometimes, too, when torn by playful winds,
It raves, making sounds like tearing sheets
Of paper; even this noise you can hear
In thunder, or the sound as when winds
Whip and buffet in the air a cloth
Or sheets of paper flying loose.
For sometimes the clouds do not crash head-on,
But move side-by-side, brushing each other's sides
With motions slow and contrary,
Creating that dry sound that grates
On our ears, drawn out until the clouds
Have passed from their close embrace.
And again,
It often seems as though all things shake
At the shock of heavy thunder, and the high walls
Of the wide heavens suddenly split apart,
Riven asunder, when a fierce blast
Of hurricane wind has all at once
Twisted into a cloud mass, and enclosed,
Spins tighter and tighter, forcing the cloud
To grow hollow with a thickening crust.
For when the power and force of wind
Weakens that crust, then the cloud, split in two,
Bursts with a hideous crash and boom.
No wonder, for a small bladder filled with air,
When it suddenly bursts, can make a sound as loud.
There's reason, too,

Why clouds make sounds as winds blow through them:
We often see clouds with rough, jagged edges,
Or branching into many forked shapes,
Much like when sudden gusts of wind
Sweep through dense forests, making leaves rustle
And branches crash. It happens too at times
That the fierce force of a hurricane
Tears through a cloud, breaking it apart with a blow.
For what a blast of wind can do above
Is clear from what we see on earth,
When a lesser wind twists tall trees
And tears them madly from their roots.
Besides, within the clouds are waves that crash,
Giving off a rumbling roar,
Like the loud surf breaking along deep streams
Or upon the great sea. It happens, too, when
A thunderbolt's fiery energy
Falls from one cloud into another;
If the cloud is full of moisture, it quenches
The fire with a mighty noise,
Just as hot iron plunged into cold water
Sizzles and cools. But if a drier cloud
Receives the fire, it will suddenly ignite,
Burning with monstrous sound,
As if flames driven by whirling winds
Raced across laurel-crowned mountains,
Setting the trees ablaze with a fierce assault.
There is nothing that crackles in flame
With sound more fearsome to man
Than Apollo's sacred laurel.
Often, too, the crashing of ice
And the swift downpour of hail send out a sound
Among the mighty clouds above; for when
The wind has packed them tight, each towering
Rain-cloud, frozen and mingled with hail,

Breaks and booms...
Likewise, it lightens when clouds collide,
Striking forth seeds of fire with their clash,
As if stone struck stone or steel;
Then, too, light leaps out, and sparks
Of fire scatter in shining bursts.
But we hear the thunder after we see the flash,
For sound forever reaches our ears
More slowly than sight meets our eyes—
As you can see from this example:
When you see someone far away
Chopping a tree with a two-edged ax,
You'll see the swing of the blow before
The sound reaches your ears; so too,
We see the lightning flash before
We hear the thunder, even though both
Are born together from the same clash
And by the same cause.
Thus,
The clouds light up the lands with their flashes,
And the storm trembles with bursts of flame.
When the wind has swept into a cloud
And, whirling within, has twisted it hollow
With a thick crust, it heats up quickly
From its swift motion—just as you see
How movement itself can overheat
And ignite objects: even a leaden ball,
Hurtling through space, can melt.
Therefore, when the fiery wind splits
The black cloud, it scatters seeds of fire,
Pressed out by force, bursting forth in flames;
Then follows the detonation, reaching our ears
After the sight meets our eyes.
This happens when clouds are piled high,
Layered upon one another with great force—

And do not be deceived by the view below,
Where we see only their broad base,
Not how high they tower. Watch when
The winds drive clouds across the horizon,
Like mountain ranges moving along,
Or see them massed around tall peaks,
Anchored in calm, winds stilled around:
Then you may know their mighty masses,
And view their caverns, as if built of cliffs;
When the storms have filled them utterly,
Prisoned in clouds, they roar around,
Blustering like savage beasts, sending
Growls through the clouds from side to side,
Whirling within to find an outlet,
Gathering seeds of fire until they burst
In forked flashes from the broken clouds.
Again, from this cause it comes to pass
That swift, golden streams of fire
Plunge downward to the earth: for clouds
Hold abundant seeds of fire;
When clouds are dry, they appear mostly
Flame-colored, resplendent in hue.
And indeed, they must take to themselves
Many seeds from sunlight, glowing bright.
So, when the wind has thrust these clouds together,
It presses forth the seeds of fire,
Making flames flash with colors bright.
Likewise, it lightens when clouds grow thin;
When the wind gently unravels them,
The seeds of light must naturally fall,
Lighting the sky without the dreadful roar
And crashing terror of storms.
To continue,
What nature thunderbolts possess
Is made clear by the marks they leave,

The scorched brands of their fiery heat,
And the fumes of sulfur rising around.
All these are marks not of wind or rain, but fire.
They often ignite the roofs of houses
And, inside rooms, hold fierce dominion
With swift flames. Know that nature fashioned
This fire subtler than all other fires,
With minute and darting bodies—a fire
That nothing can withstand:
The thunderbolt, so mighty, passes through
Walls and barriers as easily as voices pass through air,
Piercing stones and bronze, melting them
Instantly, melting bronze and gold,
And causing wine to vanish suddenly
From jars left intact. Its heat makes porous
The sides of the earthen wine jars,
Seeping within and scattering the elements
Of the wine in a quick dissolution—
A feat which even the sun's fiery rays,
For all their strength, could not accomplish.
So much more agile and overpowering is this force.
Now, in what way are these forces formed,
With such fierce strength as to split towers apart,
To topple houses, wrench beams and timbers,
And cast down monuments of heroes' past,
To take breath forever from men,
And to lay cattle low across the fields—
Yes, by what power lightnings do all this,
All this and more, I'll now reveal,
And keep you no longer with mere promises.
Thunderbolts must be conceived as born
In those thicker clouds piled high above;
For from the clear sky and lighter clouds
They never strike. This fact is clear:
When dense clouds gather across the sky,

So thick we might think the darkness of Acheron
Had risen and filled the vault of heaven—
So heavy do those storm clouds loom,
When tempests begin to forge their thunderbolts.
And often, far out at sea,
A black thunderhead, like a pitch-dark cataract
Falling from heaven, bulges thick
And drops with a mighty roar on the waves,
Bringing tempests heavy with thunder
And hurricanes; crammed so full with fire
And wind, that even those on land shudder
And seek cover. Therefore, as I said,
These storms must be thought to rise far above us,
For clouds would not cast such heavy dark
Unless built high, towering heap on heap,
To block out the sun. Nor could they bring
So much rain to flood rivers and fields,
If ether weren't crowded with clouds stacked high.
Then, here we find winds and fires combined—
Thus come the long lightning bolts and loud thunder.
For, as I've shown before, cavernous clouds
Hold countless fiery seeds, and they must
Draw many more from sunlight's heat.
So, when wind gathers clouds in one region
And presses out fiery seeds, mingling with fire,
That wind becomes a whirlwind in the cloud's
Deep belly, spinning tightly within
And sharpening the thunderbolt in fiery furnaces.
For the wind ignites in two ways:
Its own swift motion heats it, and the fire's
Repeated touch makes it burn. Then,
When wind's energy is fully heated,
And fierce fire moves deep within, the bolt,
Now ripened, bursts the cloud apart,
And flashes forth, illuminating with forking light

All around. Then follows a clap so heavy,
The vaults of the sky seem to burst apart,
Engulfing the earth. A quake spreads fearfully
Across the land, and far through the skies
Run the long rumbles. For in that moment
The whole tempest quakes, shaken through,
And roaring echoes fill the air. From this shock
Falls such resounding rain that all dark ether
Seems to turn to water, flooding fields
Back to their primal state, as rain pours down
From bursting clouds and hurricanes,
When the thunder, from a burning bolt,
Cracks through the sky. At times,
A force of wind from outside strikes
Into a cloud already hot with fire,
And when it bursts that cloud, down comes
That coil of flame we still call,
With our forebears' word, a thunderbolt.
The same thing happens on any side
Where that force sweeps forth. Sometimes, too,
A wind, though hurled forth without flame,
Ignites in flight, gathering heat as it goes,
Losing larger particles that can't pass
Through the air's bulk as swiftly as others—
And gathering smaller ones from the air,
Which, mingling, create fire as they fly:
Just as a leaden ball can grow hot in flight,
Losing cold particles and gaining warmth
From the air. Sometimes the force of a blow
Creates fire, when a cold wind strikes forth
Without flame. No wonder, for with a fierce blow
It releases fiery elements, streaming out
From the wind itself and from whatever
Receives the strike, as when fire springs forth
From steel striking stone. Though the steel is cold,

Its seeds of heat speed out swiftly.
And so, an object struck by a thunderbolt
Can catch flame, if it is suited to burn.
Yet we shouldn't think the force of wind
Entirely cold—this power sent from high
With such strength; and if not kindled by fire
On its course, it still arrives mixed with heat.
And now, the speed and stroke of thunderbolt
Is so tremendous, and with glide so swift
These thunderbolts descend, because their force
First gathers itself within the clouds,
Building up for their powerful release.
Then, when the cloud can no longer hold
The intense force pressing within, it bursts,
And so the bolt flies forth with such fierce power,
Much like a shot from Roman catapults.
Know too, this force is made of elements
Both small and smooth, so nothing resists it easily;
It darts between and penetrates the pores of things,
Without delay from countless collisions,
Flying onward with a swift, unstoppable surge.
Next, since every weight by nature falls downward,
The bolt's speed doubles, and the rush grows wild,
As the weight joins with the blow, shaking to pieces
All that blocks its path as it travels on.
And, because it moves along in one continuous surge,
It gains new speed as it goes,
And this constant momentum adds power,
Driving all the fiery seeds of thunder
Into a single, straight course,
Casting them onward, one by one.
And sometimes, it pulls from the air around
Certain bodies, which by their own blows
Further spark its velocity. And, behold,
It passes through objects unharmed,

Moving through many things without breaking them,
For the liquid fire flies through their pores.
Yet it pierces what it strikes when the bolt's atoms
Meet just where the atoms of other things
Are tightly joined. Further, it easily melts brass
And quickly fuses gold, because its force
Is made of such minute, smooth parts
That it winds its way within with ease,
And, once inside, quickly loosens all bonds
And unties every knot holding them together.
And most often in autumn, the heavens shake,
The star-studded vaults, and all the earth below—
And again in spring, when flowers unfold:
For in the cold season, there is little fire,
And winds are sparse in summer, while clouds
Have less bulk. But in those seasons in between,
The diverse causes of thunderbolts unite;
For then, cold and heat cross paths,
Raising discord in the air, which billows
In furious tumult with fire and wind—
Both of which the clouds need to form thunderbolts.
For spring brings the first touch of warmth and the last of cold,
So elements that oppose must clash,
And, when mixed, rage with chaotic fury.
And when the year brings summer's last warmth
Mixed with the earliest chill, in autumn's time,
Then, too, fierce cold and heat wrestle hard.
These seasons are called "cross-seas"—and no wonder
That thunderbolts prevail and storms rise then,
Since both sides rage in dubious war,
One with flame, the other with winds and rain mixed in.
This, O Memmius, is to see through
The true nature of fire-filled thunderbolts;
O this is to know by what blind force
Each effect is made, and not to unwind

Etrurian scrolls for tokens of gods' will,
Asking whence the flaming bolt has come,
Or to which part of heaven it turns,
Or how it winds through walls,
Or, after proving its force there,
How it speeds forth again, or what ill
It brings from high heaven. For if Jupiter
And the gods shake the shining vaults
With dread, and hurl fire where they will,
Why strike not the wicked in punishment,
So they may breathe forth flames in pain,
A warning for all? Why instead is he,
Guiltless, yet caught in the fiery storm,
Lifted by a whirlwind, though innocent?
Why then do bolts strike barren places,
Wasting their force? Do they practice their aim,
Strengthening their arms? Why let the Father's spear
Strike earth in vain? Why, too, does he allow it,
Nor keep it for his enemies? Why often
Aim at high places? Why do we find
Marks of lightning on mountain tops?
Why then does he strike the sea—
What guilt have waves or the vast deep
Of foam and spray? And if he wishes
To make us cautious of the bolt, why not
Give us the sight to see it come?
Or, if he seeks to catch us unawares,
Why thunder first in a distant sky,
So we may flee? Why rouse the dark air
With rumblings from afar? And how
Can one believe he strikes in many ways?
Do you think it never happens that
Thunderbolts strike in more than one place?
Yet it often has, and will again, as rain
Falls over many regions, so too do bolts

Fall at the same time across different lands.
Why does Jupiter never cast a bolt
When skies are clear? Does he descend
With the clouds to decide the shot himself?
And why, with his destructive bolt,
Does he break apart the holy shrines of gods,
Destroy his splendid thrones, and shatter
The images of his own divinities,
Robbing them of glory with violent wounds?
But to return apace,
It's easy now to see how those "bellows" fall,
As the Greeks have called them, discharged from above
Onto the seas. For at times from the sky,
A column descends upon the waters, pushed down,
Around which waves seethe in furious turmoil,
Stirred by powerful gusts; and any ship caught
Within that churning is placed in grave danger,
Thrown by the tempest. This happens when the force
Of the wind cannot burst through the cloud it strikes,
And instead pushes the cloud down in a column
Upon the sea, like a fist pressing down,
Stretching toward the waves. When the wind finally
Rips through the cloud, it pours down upon the sea,
Stirring up wondrous waves with swirling whirl,
Dragging the cloud's soft body downward.
And when it reaches the surface of the deep,
The whirl plunges itself into the water
With monstrous roar, forcing it to seethe.
At times, too, that vortex of wind enfolds
Itself in clouds, gathering particles from the air,
Forming a "bellows" descending from the sky.
When it bursts on land, it releases an immense
Force of whirlwind and blast. But since it forms
Rarely on land, where hills break its path,
It's seen more often out on the open sea,

Across the free horizons.
The clouds take shape
When in the upper regions of the sky,
Particles gather suddenly as they fly—
Rougher ones that, though loosely linked,
Hold each other firm. These form small clouds
That join and swell, drawn by the winds,
Until a storm's fury forms. It happens, too,
That mountains close to the sky smoke more often
With dark clouds, for as the mists begin to form,
The winds drive them upward before the eyes
Can see them, until they reach the peaks;
Then they gather in thicker mass,
Rising from the mountain's peak up to the sky.
Indeed, as we climb high mountains, we see
How windy those upper regions are.
Clothes hung out along the shore, when wet,
Show that nature lifts from the sea below
Unnumbered particles. Thus it is clear
That many particles rise from the salt waves
To build the bulk of clouds, for sea moisture
Is akin to that of clouds. From rivers, too,
And from the land itself, mists and steam
Rise like breath, covering the sky in a murk
That slowly gathers to form clouds.
Additionally, the heat from the starry ether
Weighs down upon them, condensing them
Under the blue sky into clouds. Sometimes,
Particles even come from far Beyond
To form the clouds and flying thunderheads.
For I have shown that particles are infinite
And fly with tremendous speed, passing through
Space beyond our grasp. It's no wonder, then,
That darkness and storms swiftly cover
The oceans and lands, bulking thunderheads

Hanging above, for everywhere through
The ether's narrow channels, or the "breathing-holes"
Of the upper world, the elemental particles
Have exits and entrances.
Now come,
And I'll tell how rain condenses in clouds
And pours upon the land in heavy showers.
First, I'll persuade you that water's seeds
Rise together with the clouds, growing alike—
Both clouds and water increase proportionately,
As our bodies grow with blood and sweat
And moisture within us. Clouds also draw
Moisture from the broad sea as winds
Carry them, like floating fleeces of wool.
Thus, rivers also lift moisture into the clouds.
When water's seeds gather in abundance,
The crowded clouds struggle to release rain
For two reasons: wind presses them together,
And the great mass of storm clouds urges rain
To pour. And when the winds winnow the clouds,
Or the sun strikes them, they release
Their rainy moisture, distilling drops
Like wax that melts under a fire's heat.
Heavy rains fall when clouds are weighed down
By their mass and the force of wind. Rains
Continue when water's seeds are stirred,
And clouds pile layer on layer,
While the earth exhales its moisture.
When the sun shines amid dark storms,
Its rays strike the blackened rains, and there,
In the dark clouds, the bright bow appears.
And now, as to things
Not yet mentioned here, which grow by themselves
Or form within the clouds—
Snow and wind, hail and hoarfrost, chill with ice,

And the freezing power that hardens lakes and pools,
Binding rivers in winter's icy grip—
It's easy still to see and understand
How these all happen and how they are born,
Once you understand the functions given
To the procreating atoms of the world.
Now come, and hear the law of earthquakes;
First, know that under the earth, as above,
Are caverns full of wind, dark pools,
Deep abysses, cliffs, and jagged rocks,
And rivers rolling rapidly below,
With waves and crashing stones. For it's clear
That earth must be of like form in every part.
Thus, with these things set underneath,
The earth above trembles with big tumblings,
When time erodes the huge, underground caves.
Whole mountains fall, and from the spot
Of that massive jolt, tremors quiver out wide.
For houses shake when jarred by a cart
Of little weight, and furniture leaps
When wheels hit a block in the street.
Sometimes, too, when heavy soil rolls down
From mountain slopes into dark pools,
The land rocks from the water's swell,
Just as a basin rocks until the liquid
Within settles still, with no undulation.
And besides,
When winds gather in the hollow depths,
Pressing mightily from one spot,
They push against high caverns until
The earth bulges in that direction;
Then buildings above lean ominously,
And beams hang forward, ready to fall.
Yet people still doubt that a time may come
For the world's end, though they see

Such bulging and breaking of the ground!
If not for the winds blowing back again,
Nothing could halt the collapse. But because
Winds alternate, charge, and retreat,
Earth more often threatens than brings about
A complete collapse. She leans to one side,
Then sways back; after teetering forward,
She returns to her seat of balance.
This is why buildings rock, with roofs
Shaking more than middle floors,
Middle more than the lowest,
And lowest least of all.
This same great quaking
Arises when wind and fierce air,
Either from outside or deep below,
Force themselves into the earth's caves,
Churning wildly until their stirred-up power
Breaks out, ripping deep chasms in the ground—
As happened once in Syrian Sidon,
And once in Aegium of the Peloponnese,
When the wild force of air burst forth,
Overthrowing those cities with earth's convulsion.
Many a walled town has fallen this way,
And many cities have sunk below the sea,
Engulfed with all their people. If the air
Does not break forth, then its wild rush
Disperses through the earth's countless pores,
Shaking her whole form—just as a chill,
Seeping to our bones, makes us shake.
Therefore, people run through cities in fear,
Dreading the roofs above, fearing the caverns below,
Lest the earth split open suddenly,
Gaping wide with a tremendous maw,
Swallowing everything in ruin.
Let people go on believing that earth and sky

Will remain secure forever; yet at times,
Danger forces a goad of fear—
One fear among many—that the earth might slip,
Suddenly vanishing beneath their feet,
Hurried down into the abyss,
Dragging all of existence in a world's wreckage.

Extraordinary and Paradoxical Telluric Phenomena

Firstly, men marvel why the ocean's bulk
Grows not bigger and bigger, though vast waters
Pour down into it, and every river flows
From every realm to the sea;
Add the random rains and gusty storms
That sprinkle every sea and land,
And add the springs themselves:
Yet all these added to the ocean's sum
Are but the increase of a single drop.
So it's less a wonder that the sea,
The mighty ocean, does not rise.
Besides, the sun draws off a mighty part—
We see its burning rays dry clothes wet with rain;
And we behold the sun over seas far outspread,
Drying the waters bit by bit.
So even though the sun takes a small part from any spot,
Across the vast waves it removes much.
Then, too, winds sweeping over the waters
Bear away much moisture—
We often see highways dry overnight,
And soft mud crusted over by dawn.
I've told you that clouds carry off moisture too,
Lifted from the vast ocean, sprinkling it about
Over all lands when rain falls,
Driven by winds that carry misty vapors.
Lastly, since the earth is porous, and lies

Near the seas, touching their shores,
Water must seep from briny ocean into the lands
Just as it flows from land to sea.
For brine is filtered out, and fresh water
Seeps back again, reappearing at river sources,
Returning to the land in flowing streams
Through channels cut long ago.
Now, the cause
For why vast fires blow forth from Aetna's mouth,
I will unfold; for with no small force
The fiery storms rose there, reigning over
Sicilian fields, drawing the upturned faces
Of nearby peoples, who saw the sky afar
A-smoke and sparking, filling their hearts with dread
Of what new thing nature was creating.
In such matters,
It's wise to look far and wide, to see how vast
The universe is, and to recognize
How small a part of it is this sky of ours—
No larger, truly, than one man compared
To the entire earth. If you understand
This cosmic truth, you will cease to wonder
At many things. Who among us marvels
When a fever gathers heat in a man's joints,
Or other painful ailments attack his limbs?
For soon the foot swells blue and sore,
Or sharp pain seizes teeth and eyes;
The sacred fire breaks out, burning all it touches
And creeping over the body. No wonder here,
Since earth and sky bring forth enough seeds of harm
To fuel countless diseases.
Thus, we must suppose that earth and sky, too,
Receive from the infinite enough of all things—
Enough for earthquakes, typhoons over land and sea,
Aetna's fires overflowing, or a blaze in heaven.

For that happens too; the vaults of the sky
Glow with fire, and heavier rains pour,
When seeds of water gather from infinity.
"But such fires are massive!" you may say.
True, but many a river seems huge to one
Who has never seen a larger.
Thus, trees and men seem large,
And whatever we see as biggest in each kind
We think is "huge"; yet all these, along with land,
Sea, and sky, are nothing to the all-encompassing
Universe.
Now, I will explain at last
How that fierce flame bursts forth from Aetna.
First, the mountain's nature is hollow,
Propped by basaltic caverns, and in these
Caverns are air and wind.
Wind forms when air is stirred
By violent agitation; when this air
Heats up and rages, it makes the earth
And rocks hot, striking off
Swift flames that lift themselves,
Hurtling upwards through the mountain's throat
Into the sky, scattering burning blasts,
Ashes, and pitch-black smoke,
While heaving up boulders of wondrous weight—
Leaving no doubt it's the air's
Tumultuous force. Besides, the sea
At the mountain's roots breaks its waves,
Sucking back its surf.
Grottoes run from the sea below
Into the mountain's base,
And from here you must believe they travel…
Conditions force both water and air
To penetrate deeply from the open sea,
Then blow outward, lifting flames on high,

Casting boulders up from the depths,
And raising clouds of sand. At the top
Are "bowls," as people there call them,
What we in Rome would name the throats or mouths.
There are some things for which one cause alone
Is not enough—there may be several,
And one among them must be true.
For if you saw someone lying dead from afar,
You'd have to consider all causes of death
To name his true end; for he may not have died
By steel or poison, nor from cold or disease,
Yet something of this sort must have happened—
And we must reason the same in many cases.
Toward summer, the Nile swells up,
Overflowing the plains—a singular river,
Watering Egypt alone. In the mid-summer heat,
It often floods the land, either because
The Etesian winds blow northward that season,
Forcing back its waves, swelling its waters,
And halting its flow. These winds from the icy north
Drive straight up the river. That river flows
From sultry lands to the far south,
Where sun-darkened people live with sun-baked skin.
Or perhaps sandbanks pile against its mouths,
Blocked by winds driving sand inland,
So the river's outlet becomes less free,
And its floods less swift. Or it may be that rains
Fall more abundantly at its source,
Since the Etesian blasts drive clouds inland.
When clouds gather in the central heat of day,
They're pressed against high mountains, forced to mass.
Or, perhaps, its waters grow far away
In the Ethiopian mountains, when the sun's
Warming rays melt the white snows down into the valleys.
Now come, and I'll explain the Birdless spots

And Birdless lakes, and what nature they hold.
First, they're called "birdless" because they're harmful
To all birds. When birds fly above these places,
They lose their strength and fold their wings,
Drooping their necks as they fall,
Plummeting to the earth if such is the nature
Of the spot, or into water if Birdless lake lies below.
At Cumae, there is such a place, where mountains smoke,
Filled with the scent of sulfur, steaming springs rising.
And there is one within Athens' walls,
On the Acropolis' summit, beside
The temple of Tritonian Pallas, where crows
Will not fly, even when smoke rises from offerings—
They flee not from the goddess's wrath,
As Greek poets once told the tale,
But from the nature of the place itself.
In Syria, too, they say there's a spot
Where four-footed animals collapse
Once they step within, as if struck down
For the gods below. All these wonders work
By natural law, their causes clear to see.
Let no one think these places are gateways to Orcus,
Or imagine gods of the underworld
Drawing souls to Acheron's dark shores—
As stags, it's said, use their scent
To draw hidden snakes from shadowed lairs.
How far from reason such ideas stray!
Now I'll try to explain the truth.
Firstly, as I've often said,
The earth holds atoms of every kind;
All things rise from it—
Many life-giving, fit for food,
And many which bring disease and hasten death;
Many seeds of many kinds, in many forms,
Since earth mingles and releases them all.

We've shown that some things suit certain creatures,
Based on nature, texture, and shape.
You see how many things are oppressive, foul,
And harmful to us in many ways:
Some irritate the ears,
Some fill the nostrils with harsh scents,
Or poison the breath we draw.
Some are loathsome to touch or see,
Others disgusting to taste.
Some weaken the limbs
Or drain the soul within.
Some trees cast a shade so noxious
That they bring headaches to those resting below.
On Helicon's hills, a tree grows that kills
By the stench of its flowers.
The sharp smell of a freshly snuffed lamp
Can put to sleep a person
Afflicted with convulsions.
The scent of castor makes a woman drowsy,
Her handiwork slipping from her fingers,
If she inhales it at certain times.
If you linger too long in hot baths,
Over-full, you might faint suddenly;
And the heavy fumes of charcoal
Can cloud the brain without a drink of water.
When fever seizes the limbs,
Even the smell of wine is unbearable.
Have you not seen how earth itself produces sulfur
And thickens bitumen with its stench?
What noxious odors rise from Scaptensula below,
Where men dig for silver and gold,
Or from the deadly air in gold mines?
What pale, ghastly look it gives them!
Many die quickly, the life drained from them,
Forced by grim necessity to work there.

Thus, this earth releases many toxic fumes,
Breathing them into the visible world.
Thus, Birdless places release
A fatal essence to flying creatures,
Rising from the earth to poison the air.
When birds fly into this unseen danger,
They're struck down, losing control,
And fall to where the fumes arose.
Once down, this poison drains life from every limb,
First striking them with dizzying weakness,
Then, once they've fallen to the source,
They release their souls, the toxic fumes too thick.
At times, the power of Birdless places
Displaces the air between birds and the ground,
Leaving nearly a void. When birds enter,
Their wings lose lift, falling useless.
Unable to hold themselves up,
They're forced by nature's weight to fall,
Prostrate upon the near-empty space,
Their life seeping out from every pore.
Further, well water is colder in summer
Because the earth, heated, releases into the air
Whatever fiery seeds it may hold within.
The more the ground loses heat,
The colder the water stays deep below.
Yet in winter, when the earth contracts
Under cold's grip and grows dense and solid,
It presses its own heat down into the wells.
They say at the shrine of Hammon there's a spring
That's cold in daylight but warms by night.
Men wonder at this and claim it heats
From a hidden sun beneath the ground,
Covered by night's dark shroud—
A notion far from reason. For when the sun,
Beaming on open waters, has no power

To warm their surface with his scorching light,
How, then, can he, hidden beneath the earth,
Boil water to make it burn with heat?
Especially since he can't even send his warmth
Through the walls of houses with ease.
What's the true cause? Here's the likely answer:
The earth around that spring is porous, more so
Than usual ground, and many seeds of fire
Lie close by. When night's dewy shades
Chill the earth, it contracts and squeezes out
These fiery seeds into the spring,
Which heat the water's steam and touch.
Then, when the sun rises and his rays warm the soil,
The seeds of fire return to their hidden places,
And the warmth retreats, leaving the spring cold.
Moreover, the sun's rays strike the water,
Making it thinner as dawn arrives;
Thus, it releases any fiery seeds it holds,
Just as it sheds frost and melts its ice.
There is also a cold spring that lights
Tow from a distance, making it flame.
Even a pitch torch flares when held near its waves,
As it floats before the breeze. This marvel is
No wonder, for within this water, many seeds
Of heat must rise from the earth's depths,
Flowing up through the spring and into the air—
Yet not in numbers enough to warm the water.
These seeds gather, though scattered through the liquid,
And ignite into flame above.
Much like a spring near Aradus, amid the sea,
Where sweet water bubbles out,
Surrounded by salt waves. Elsewhere, the vast ocean
Gives sailors fresh water in their time of need,
Issuing sweet streams among the salt waves.
In this way, seeds of fire may rise

Through this spring and kindle on the tow;
As they gather and cling to the torch,
They ignite readily, since tow and torches themselves
Hold many hidden seeds of fire.
Have you not seen, when you hold
A wick close to a lamp, it catches flame
Before it touches the fire? The same with a torch.
Many things, touched only by heat,
Flare from a distance before reaching true flame.
This we must suppose also happens in this spring.
Now to other matters!
I'll explain why iron is drawn by the stone
The Greeks call "magnet" from the land of Magnesia,
Where its origin lies. This stone is wondrous—
It can hold a chain of rings hanging down,
Swaying in the wind, one linked to another,
Each feeling the stone's power to bind,
Its strength flowing down.
In such things, much must be known
Before we can explain this power;
We must examine it from every side.
So I urge you to listen closely.
First, from everything we see,
Particles flow out constantly,
Touching the eyes to bring sight,
Odors to the nose, warmth from the sun,
Spray from waves that eat away
The coastlines. And echoes flow
Through the air. At the sea,
A salty taste comes to the mouth,
And when we watch wormwood mixed,
Its bitterness stings us.
So from everything flows something,
Spreading all around us without rest,
For we constantly see, smell,

And hear all things at hand.
Now let me remind you how porous
All things are. In my first verse,
I proved this truth—it's essential
To understand that all is body and void.
In caves, rocks above drip moisture;
Our bodies sweat, hair grows, and veins
Carry food down to the nails.
Cold and heat move through bronze,
Silver, and gold goblets we hold.
Sounds pass through walls of stone;
Odors, cold, and fire's heat penetrate iron.
And so, at times, harmful influences
Enter our world from afar. Tempests gather
From both earth and sky, only to return there—
For all things must be porous, designed to absorb.
Furthermore, not all particles from things around
Have the same qualities we can perceive,
Nor do they suit every substance alike.
For instance: the sun scorches the earth,
Melts ice, and softens snow on mountain tops.
Wax under heat turns to liquid; fire will melt
Copper and fuse gold, but shrivels hides and flesh.
Water hardens iron fresh from fire, yet softens
The same hides and flesh, which heat had hardened.
Wild olive trees seem like ambrosia to goats,
Though their leaves are bitter food for humans.
Pigs recoil from marjoram and scented oils,
Which seem like poison to them but refresh us.
While mud disgusts us, it delights pigs,
Who roll from belly to back, contented.
Now, one more thing to clarify before
Explaining what's at hand. Different things
Contain different kinds of pores in unique shapes,
Sized and shaped specifically for their purpose.

In creatures, we see this through the senses,
Each capturing its own unique quality:
Sounds travel to one place, flavors to another,
Scents to a third. Some things seep through rock,
Others through wood or gold or glass. Some
Bring heat, others color or form, moving through
Various paths according to their nature.
With these ideas established,
It's easier to explain why a magnet attracts iron.
First, the magnet emits a stream of particles
That displaces the air between the stone and iron.
As that space empties, the iron's own particles
Rush to fill the void, pulling the iron ring with them,
Since iron holds its parts so tightly bound.
This force draws the ring until it connects,
Bound by an invisible link to the magnet.
The air behind helps to push it along,
Moving through iron's tiny pores like wind through sails.
When the iron reaches the void, it continues,
Driven by the surrounding air's constant motion.
Sometimes, iron even resists the magnet,
Repelled as if it alternates between fleeing and following.
I've seen Samothracian rings leap and iron filings
Bubble and froth in brass bowls above the magnet.
This happens because the brass obstructs the flow,
And the magnetic current, finding no path,
Pushes iron away, stirring it as it struggles
Against the obstruction. While other metals,
Like gold, remain unmoved, iron is uniquely suited
To the magnet's force, as its structure complements
The magnet's particles.
Now, turning to diseases, their spread, and origin:
We know life-giving particles exist alongside
Particles that bring decay. When these gather,
They corrupt the air, spreading a pestilence

That falls upon humans and animals alike.
It can descend from above, like clouds or fog,
Or rise from the earth, which, after heavy rains
Or intense heat, can emit decay.
Notice how travelers often fall ill in foreign lands,
Affected by the unfamiliar air and water.
Each region has a unique climate:
The Britons differ from Egypt's people,
Or the Pontic coast from sunny Gades,
As each area shapes its inhabitants.
Each disease, too, is bound to a place:
Elephantiasis near the Nile,
Affects the feet in Attica, and the eyes in Achaea.
These afflictions arise from the nature of the air,
Which, when it shifts or grows tainted, moves like a cloud,
Creeping across the land, altering what it touches.
When such a foreign atmosphere mingles with ours,
It infects and corrupts it. The blight settles
On crops and livestock or hangs in the air,
Waiting for us to inhale. So, like us,
Cattle and sheep suffer pestilence too,
Whether we journey to strange lands or they bring
A poisoned air to us, disrupting our health.

The Plague Athens

It was this kind of disease, this deadly plague,
That once swept through Cecropian lands,
Turning plains into fields of bones, emptying roads,
Draining Athens of its people. It came from afar,
Rising out of Egypt, crossing air and sea,
Until it descended on all of Pandion's folk.
Soon, many were struck by the sickness and death.
At first, they felt their heads burning with fever,
Their eyes blazing red, throats blackened inside,

Oozing blood, and their voices choked
By ulcers. The tongue, weakened and sore,
Dripped blood, rough and slow to speak.
When that sickness spread through their throats,
Down into their chests and to their hearts,
Every part of life began to collapse.
Their breath grew foul, like rotting corpses,
And soon, every ounce of strength faded,
And every power of the mind, too.
Pain and despair, with endless groans,
Were constant companions to their suffering.
Day and night, they vomited in waves,
Their exhausted bodies breaking down.
Their skin wasn't fever-hot to the touch;
Instead, it felt warm, covered in red sores,
Branded with blisters like "sacred fires"
Burned into their skin. Inside, their bodies
Burned down to the bone, as if a furnace
Raged in their stomachs. No relief was enough—
They craved cool air and breezes, always.
Some even threw themselves into icy rivers,
Diving in with mouths open wide, desperate,
But a shower of water seemed like mere drops.
Their thirst was unquenchable. They lay, drained,
Silent, while doctors, helpless, muttered low,
Seeing their patients stare with open, sleepless eyes,
Already marked for death.
In those days, death brought many signs:
The mind twisted by dread and despair,
The face fierce and delirious, tormented ears
Ringing, breaths short or labored,
Sweat soaking the neck, the spit turning thick
And bitter, the throat rattling with a cough.
The fingers curled, the body shook,
The cold crept from feet upward.

Near the end, their faces hollowed,
The eyes sunken, temples drawn,
Skin cold and stiff, twisted into a grimace,
Muscles swollen around the brows—
And soon after, they would lie rigid in death.
By about the eighth or ninth day,
They'd give up the struggle for life.
If anyone survived that bout of death,
Still they'd be plagued by sores and sickness,
Their bellies releasing black, foul fluids,
Or blood seeping from their noses,
While pain throbbed in their heads, draining
All strength and flesh from their bodies.
If they managed to outlast this bleeding sickness,
It still attacked their muscles, their joints,
Even their private parts.
Some, so terrified of death, lived on
But only after surgeons removed their limbs.
Others, though lopped of hands and feet,
Held on to life, and some lost their eyes—
Such was their fierce fear of dying.
And some, besides, lost all memory,
Forgetting even themselves.
Bodies lay unburied, piling up,
And birds and animals would shy away,
Fleeing the deadly stench; or, if they fed,
They'd soon fall sick and die. Through those days,
Hardly a bird appeared, and the wild beasts
Were seldom seen, overcome by disease.
Most often, the loyal dogs lay dying in the streets,
Breath leaving their bodies painfully—
Such was the plague's grip. No single cure
Could work for all: what saved one
Might doom another, and what let one
Breathe freely might bring death to the next.

But worst of all, the most pitiful part,
Was this: once someone felt themselves
Trapped by the disease, they lost all hope,
Their hearts heavy with dread, as if they already
Saw their own funeral. They'd give up the fight.
People infected each other constantly,
Like flocks of sheep or herds of cattle,
And this made the dead pile up faster.
Some, fearing death, avoided their sick friends,
Choosing to flee rather than risk their lives.
But this only brought its own punishment,
For soon after, they too fell to the same neglect,
Abandoned and alone, and they died.
Yet those who stayed to care for their sick,
Compelled by duty, fell ill too, worn out
By the infection and by the unending cries
Of the dying. This kind of death
Was the price of nobility.
Funerals were hurried, neglected,
Rushed along as families competed
To bury their dead as quickly as they could.
And people, struggling to bury their dead,
Piled body upon body in heaps.
Weary from sorrow and tears, they would return home,
Only to fall ill themselves from grief.
There was no one left untouched—no one
Escaped those dreadful times without
Facing sickness, death, or heartbreak.
Even the shepherds, cattle herders,
And strong plowmen grew weak,
Their bodies huddled in dark corners of huts,
Succumbing to squalor and disease.
Often, you could have seen lifeless children
Clinging to their parents' bodies,
Or children lying beside the corpses

Of mothers and fathers, giving up life.
And from the countryside, floods of sick,
Sick farmers streamed into the city,
Carrying their misery with them, crowding
Every space. More and more, death
Filled the packed city, claiming lives in droves.
Bodies lay strewn along the streets,
Dragged and rolled by thirst to die beside
Fountains, their last breaths choked
By a desperate need for water.
Everywhere, in the city squares,
On roads, you could see half-dead bodies,
Covered in grime, barely more than bones,
Dying from sheer neglect, clothed in rags,
Skin stretched over bones, already like
Corpses rotting in filth and vile sores.
The temples, too, were full of bodies,
Crowded with corpses, once holy places
Now filled with death, each shrine packed
With the dead—sacred spaces that had once
Welcomed worshipers now overwhelmed by plague.
People no longer honored the gods;
The suffering was too great to think of worship.
In the city, the usual burial rites were gone,
And those devout customs of the past
Were abandoned in a frenzy of fear.
Each person buried their dead in haste,
Doing whatever they could manage.
The chaos and poverty drove people
To desperate acts. In a panic, they'd place
Their loved ones on strangers' funeral pyres,
Setting the torch beneath, fighting each other
With cries and bloody brawls,
Desperate to lay to rest those they'd loved in life.

Translated by Tim Zengerink

Fear And Trembling

Søren Kierkegaard

Preface

Not merely in the realm of commerce but in the world of ideas as well our age is organizing a regular clearance sale. Everything is to be had at such a bargain that it is questionable whether in the end there is anybody who will want to bid. Every speculative price-fixer who conscientiously directs attention to the significant march of modern philosophy, every Privatdocent, tutor, and student, every crofter and cottar in philosophy, is not content with doubting everything but goes further. Perhaps it would be untimely and ill-timed to ask them where they are going, but surely it is courteous and unobtrusive to regard it as certain that they have doubted everything, since otherwise it would be a queer thing for them to be going further. This preliminary movement they have therefore all of them made, and presumably with such ease that they do not find it necessary to let drop a word about the how; for not even he who anxiously and with deep concern sought a little enlightenment was able to find any such thing, any guiding sign, any little dietetic prescription, as to how one was to comport oneself in supporting this prodigious task. "But Descartes3 did it." Descartes, a venerable, humble and honest thinker, whose writings surely no one can read without the deepest emotion, did what he said and said what he did. Alas, alack, that is a great rarity in our times! Descartes, as he repeatedly affirmed, did not doubt in matters of faith.

What those ancient Greeks (who also had some understanding of philosophy) regarded as a task for a whole lifetime, seeing that dexterity in doubting is not acquired in a few days or weeks, what the veteran combatant attained when he had preserved the equilibrium of doubt through all the pitfalls he encountered, who intrepidly denied the certainty of sense-perception and the certainty of the processes of thought, incorruptibly defied the apprehensions of self-love and the insinuations of sympathy—that is where everybody begins in our time. In our time nobody is content to stop with faith but wants to go further. It would perhaps be rash to ask where these people are going, but it is surely a sign of breeding and culture for me to assume that everybody has faith, for otherwise it would be queer for them to be … going further. In those old days it was different, then faith was a task for a whole lifetime, because it was assumed that dexterity in faith is not acquired in a few days or weeks. When the tried oldster drew near to his last hour, having fought the good fight and kept the faith, his heart was still young enough not to have forgotten that fear and trembling which chastened the youth, which the man indeed held in check, but which no man quite outgrows … except as he might succeed at the earliest opportunity in going further. Where these revered figures arrived, that is the point where everybody in our day begins to go further. The present writer is nothing of a philosopher, he has not understood the System, does not know whether it actually exists, whether it is completed; already he has enough for his weak head in the thought of what a prodigious head everybody in our day must have, since everybody has such a prodigious thought. Even though one were capable of converting the whole content of faith into the form of a concept, it does not follow that one has adequately conceived faith and understands how one got into it, or how it got into one. The present writer is nothing of a philosopher; he is, poetice et eleganter, an amateur writer who neither writes the System nor promises6 of the System, who neither subscribes to the System nor ascribes anything to it. He writes because for him it is a luxury which becomes the more agreeable and more evident, the fewer there are who buy and read what he writes. He can easily foresee his fate in an age when passion has been obliterated in favor of learning, in an age when an author who wants to have readers must take care to write in such a way that the book can easily be perused during the afternoon nap, and take care to fashion his outward deportment in likeness to the picture of that polite young gardener in the advertisement sheet,7 who with hat in hand, and with a good certificate from the place where he last served, recommends himself to the esteemed public. He foresees his fate—that he will be entirely ignored. He has a presentiment of the dreadful event, that a jealous criticism will many a time let him feel the birch; he trembles at the still more dreadful thought that one or another enterprising scribe, a gulper of paragraphs, who to rescue learning is always willing to do with other peoples' writings what Trop8 "to preserve good taste" magnanimously resolved to do with a book called The Destruction of the Human Race–that is, he will slice the author into paragraphs, and will do it with the same inflexibility as the man who in the interest of the science of punctuation divided his discourse by counting the words, so that there were fifty words for a period and thirty-five for a semicolon. I prostrate myself with the profoundest deference before every systematic "bag-peerer" at the custom house, protesting, "This is not the System, it has nothing whatever to do with the System." I call down every blessing upon the System and upon the Danish shareholders in this omnibus9–for a tower it is hardly likely to become. I wish them all and sundry good luck and all prosperity.

Respectfully,

Johannes DE SILENTIO

Fear and Trembling

PRELUDE10 Once upon a time there was a man who as a child had heard the beautiful story11 about how God tempted Abraham, and how he endured temptation, kept the faith, and a second time received again a son contrary to expectation. When the child became older he read the same story with even greater admiration, for life had separated what was united in the pious simplicity of the child. The older he became, the more frequently his mind reverted to that story, his enthusiasm became greater and greater, and yet he was less and less able to understand the story. At last in his interest for that he forgot everything else; his soul had only one wish, to see Abraham, one longing, to have been witness to that event. His desire was not to behold the beautiful countries of the Orient, or the earthly glory of the Promised Land, or that godfearing couple whose old age God had blessed, or the venerable figure of the aged patriarch, or the vigorous young manhood of Isaac whom God had bestowed upon Abraham— he saw no reason why the same thing might not have taken place on a barren heath in Denmark. His yearning was to accompany them on the three days' journey when Abraham rode with sorrow before him and with Isaac by his side. His only wish was to be present at the time when Abraham lifted up his eyes and saw Mount Moriah afar off, at the time when he left the asses behind and went alone with Isaac up unto the mountain; for what his mind was intent upon was not the ingenious web of imagination but the shudder of thought. That man was not a thinker, he felt no need of getting beyond faith; he deemed it the most glorious thing to be remembered as the father of it, an enviable lot to possess it, even though no one else were to know it. That man was not a learned exegete, he didn't know Hebrew, if he had known Hebrew, he perhaps would easily have understood the story and Abraham. I "And God tempted Abraham and said unto him, Take Isaac, shine only son, whom thou lovest, and get thee into the land of Moriah, and offer him there for a burnt offering upon the mountain which I will show thee." It was early in the morning, Abraham arose betimes, he had the asses saddled, left his tent, and Isaac with him, but Sarah looked out of the window after them until they had passed down the valley and she could see them no more.12 They rode in silence for three days. On the morning of the fourth day Abraham said never a word, but he lifted up his eyes and saw Mount Moriah afar off. He left the young men behind and went on alone with Isaac beside him up to the mountain. But Abraham said to himself, "I will not conceal from Isaac whither this course leads him." He stood still, he laid his hand upon the head of Isaac in benediction, and Isaac bowed to receive the blessing. And Abraham's face was fatherliness, his look was mild, his speech encouraging. But Isaac was unable to understand him, his soul could not be exalted; he embraced Abraham's knees, he fell at his feet imploringly, he begged for his young life, for the fair hope of his future, he called to mind the joy in Abraham's house, he called to mind the sorrow and loneliness. Then Abraham lifted up the boy, he walked with him by his side, and his talk was full of comfort and exhortation. But Isaac could not understand him. He climbed Mount Moriah, but Isaac understood him not. Then for an instant he turned away from him, and when

Isaac again saw Abraham's face it was changed, his glance was wild, his form was horror. He seized Isaac by the throat, threw him to the ground, and said, "Stupid boy, dost thou then suppose that I am thy father? I am an idolater. Dost thou suppose that this is God's bidding? No, it is my desire." Then Isaac trembled and cried out in his terror, "O God in heaven, have compassion upon me. God of Abraham, have compassion upon me. If I have no father upon earth, be Thou my father!" But Abraham in a low voice said to himself, "O Lord in heaven, I thank Thee. After all it is better for him to believe that I am a monster, rather than that he should lose faith in Thee." When the child must be weaned, the mother blackens her breast, it would indeed be a shame that the breast should look delicious when the child must not have it. So the child believes that the breast has changed, but the mother is the same, her glance is as loving and tender as ever. Happy the person who had no need of more dreadful expedients for weaning the child! II It was early in the morning, Abraham arose betimes, he embraced Sarah, the bride of his old age, and Sarah kissed Isaac, who had taken away her reproach, who was her pride, her hope for all time. So they rode on in silence along the way, and Abraham's glance was fixed upon the ground until the fourth day when he lifted up his eyes and saw afar off Mount Moriah, but his glance turned again to the ground. Silently he laid the wood in order, he bound Isaac, in silence he drew the knife—then he saw the ram which God had prepared. Then he offered that and returned home. ... From that time on Abraham became old, he could not forget that God had required this of him. Isaac throve as before, but Abraham's eyes were darkened, and he knew joy no more. When the child has grown big and must be weaned, the mother virginally hides her breast, so the child has no more a mother. Happy the child which did not in another way lose its mother. III It was early in the morning, Abraham arose betimes, he kissed Sarah, the young mother, and Sarah kissed Isaac, her delight, her joy at all times. And Abraham rode pensively along the way, he thought of Hagar and of the son whom he drove out into the wilderness, he climbed Mount Moriah, he drew the knife. It was a quiet evening when Abraham rode out alone, and he rode to Mount

Moriah; he threw himself upon his face, he prayed God to forgive him his sin, that he had been willing to offer Isaac, that the father had forgotten his duty toward the son. Often he rode his lonely way, but he found no rest. He could not comprehend that it was a sin to be willing to offer to God the best thing he possessed, that for which he would many times have given his life; and if it was a sin, if he had not loved Isaac as he did, then he could not understand that it might be forgiven. For what sin could be more dreadful? When the child must be weaned, the mother too is not without sorrow at the thought that she and the child are separated more and more, that the child which first lay under her heart and later reposed upon her breast will be so near to her no more. So they mourn together for the brief period of mourning. Happy the person who has kept the child as near and needed not to sorrow any more! IV It was early in the morning, everything was prepared for the journey in Abraham's house. He bade Sarah farewell, and Eleazar, the faithful servant, followed him along the way, until he turned back. They rode together in harmony, Abraham and Isaac, until they came to Mount Moriah. But Abraham prepared everything for the sacrifice, calmly and quietly; but when he turned and drew the knife, Isaac saw that his left hand was clenched in despair, that a tremor passed through his body—but Abraham drew the knife. Then they returned again home, and Sarah hastened to meet them, but Isaac had lost his faith. No word of this had ever been spoken in the world, and Isaac never talked to anyone about what he had seen, and Abraham did not suspect that anyone had seen it. When the child must be weaned, the mother has stronger food in readiness, lest the child should perish. Happy the person who has stronger food in readiness! Thus and in many like ways that man of whom we are speaking thought concerning this event. Every time he returned home after wandering to Mount Moriah, he sank down with weariness, he folded his hands and said, "No one is so great as Abraham! Who is capable of understanding him?" A PANEGYRIC UPON ABRAHAM If there were no eternal consciousness in a man, if at the foundation of all there lay only a wildly seething power which writhing with obscure passions produced everything that is great and everything that is insignificant, if a bottomless void never satiated lay hidden beneath all– what then would life be but despair? If such were the case, if there were no sacred bond which united mankind, if one generation arose after another like the leafage in the forest, if the one generation replaced the other like the song of birds in the forest, if the human race passed through the world as the ship goes through the sea, like the wind through the desert, a thoughtless and fruitless activity, if an eternal oblivion were always lurking hungrily for its prey and there was no power strong enough to wrest it from its maw–how empty then and comfortless life would be! But therefore it is not thus, but as God created man and woman, so too He fashioned the hero and the poet or orator. The poet cannot do what that other does, he can only admire, love and rejoice in the hero. Yet he too is happy, and not less so, for the hero is as it were his better nature, with which he is in love, rejoicing in the fact that this after all is not himself, that his love can be admiration. He is the genius of recollection, can do nothing except call to mind what has been done, do nothing but admire what has been done; he contributes nothing of his own, but is jealous of the intrusted treasure. He follows the option of his heart, but when he has found what he sought, he wanders before every man's door with his song and with his oration, that all may admire the hero as he does, be proud of the hero as he is. This is his achievement, his humble work, this is his faithful service in the house of the hero. If he thus remains true to his love, he strives day and night against the cunning of oblivion which would trick him out of his hero, then he has completed his work, then he is gathered to the hero, who has loved him just as faithfully, for the poet is as it were the hero's better nature, powerless it may be as a memory is, but also transfigured as a memory is. Hence no one shall be forgotten who was great, and though time tarries long, though a cloud13 of misunderstanding takes the hero away, his lover comes nevertheless, and the longer the time that has passed, the more faithfully will he cling to him. No, not one shall be forgotten who was great in the world. But each was great in his own way, and each in proportion to the greatness of that which he loved. For he who loved himself became great by himself, and he who loved other men became great by his selfless devotion, but he who loved God became greater than all. Everyone shall be remembered, but each became great in proportion to his expectation. One became great by expecting the possible, another by expecting the eternal, but he who expected the impossible became greater than all. Everyone shall be remembered, but each was great in proportion to the greatness of that with which he strove. For he who strove with the world became great by overcoming the world, and he who strove with himself became great by overcoming himself, but he who strove with God became greater than all. So there was strife in the world, man against man, one against a thousand, but he who strove with God was greater than all. So there was strife upon earth: there was one who overcame all by his power, and there was one who overcame God by his impotence. There was one who relied upon himself and gained all, there was one who secure in his strength sacrificed all, but he who believed God was greater than all. There was one who was great by reason of his power, and one who was great by reason of his wisdom, and one who was great by reason of his hope, and one who was great by reason of his love; but Abraham was greater than all, great by reason of his power whose strength is impotence, great by reason of his wisdom whose secret is foolishness, great by reason of his hope whose form is madness, great by reason of the love which is hatred of oneself. By faith Abraham went out from the land of his fathers and became a sojourner in the land of promise. He left one thing behind, took one thing with him: he left his earthly understanding behind and took faith with him– otherwise he would not have wandered forth but would have thought this unreasonable. By faith he was a stranger in the land of promise, and there was nothing to recall what was dear to him, but by its novelty everything tempted his soul to melancholy yearning–and yet he was God's elect, in whom the Lord was well pleased! Yea, if he had been disowned, cast off from God's grace, he could have comprehended it better; but now it was like a mockery of him and of his faith. There was in the world one too who lived in banishment14 from the fatherland he loved. He is not forgotten, nor his Lamentations when he sorrowfully sought and found what he had lost. There is no song of Lamentations by Abraham. It is human to lament, human to weep with them that weep, but it is greater to believe, more blessed to contemplate the believer. By faith Abraham received the promise that in his seed all races of the world would be blessed. Time passed, the possibility was there, Abraham believed; time passed, it became unreasonable, Abraham believed. There was in the world one who had an expectation, time passed, the evening drew nigh, he was not paltry enough to have forgotten his expectation, therefore he too shall not be forgotten. Then he sorrowed, and sorrow did not deceive him as life had done, it did for him all it could, in the sweetness of sorrow he possessed his delusive expectation. It is human to sorrow, human to sorrow with them that sorrow, but it is greater to believe, more blessed to contemplate the believer. There is no song of Lamentations by Abraham. He did not mournfully count the days while time passed, he did not look at Sarah with a suspicious glance, wondering whether she were growing old, he did not arrest the course of the sun, that Sarah might not grow old, and his expectation with her. He did not sing lullingly before Sarah his mournful lay. Abraham became old, Sarah became a laughingstock in the land, and yet he was God's elect and inheritor of the promise that in his seed all the races of the world would be blessed. So were it not better if he had not been God's elect? What is it to be God's elect? It is to be denied in youth the wishes of youth, so as with great pains to get them fulfilled in old age. But Abraham believed and held fast the expectation. If Abraham had wavered, he would have given it up. If he had said to God, "Then perhaps it is not after all Thy will that it should come to pass, so I will give up the wish. It was my only wish, it was my bliss. My soul is sincere, I hide no secret malice because Thou didst deny it to me"—he would not have been forgotten, he would have saved many by his example, yet he would not be the father of faith. For it is great to give up one's wish, but it is greater to hold it fast after having given it up, it is great to grasp the eternal, but it is greater to hold fast to the temporal after having given it up.15 Then came the fulness of time. If Abraham had not believed, Sarah surely would have been dead of sorrow, and Abraham, dulled by grief, would not have understood the fulfilment but would have smiled at it as at a dream of youth. But Abraham believed, therefore he was young; for he who always hopes for the best becomes old, and he who is always prepared for the worst grows old early, but he who believes preserves an eternal youth. Praise therefore to that story! For Sarah, though stricken in years, was young enough to desire the pleasure of motherhood, and Abraham, though gray-haired, was young enough to wish to be a father. In an outward respect the marvel consists in the fact that it came to pass according to their expectation, in a deeper sense the miracle of faith consists in the fact that Abraham and Sarah were young enough to wish, and that faith had preserved their wish and therewith their youth. He accepted the fulfilment of the promise, he accepted it by faith, and it came to pass according to the promise and according to his faith–for Moses smote the rock with his rod, but he did not believe. Then there was joy in Abraham's house, when Sarah became a bride on the day of their golden wedding. But it was not to remain thus. Still once more Abraham was to be tried. He had fought with that cunning power which invents everything, with that alert enemy which never slumbers, with that old man who outlives all things–he had fought with Time and preserved his faith. Now all the terror of the strife was concentrated in one instant. "And God tempted Abraham and said unto him, Take Isaac, thine only son, whom thou lovest, and get thee into the land of Moriah, and offer him there for a burnt offering upon the mountain which I will show thee." So all was lost–more dreadfully than if it had never come to pass! So the Lord was only making sport of Abraham! He made miraculously the preposterous actual, and now in turn He would annihilate it. It was indeed foolishness, but Abraham did not laugh at it like Sarah when the promise was announced. All was lost! Seventy years of faithful expectation, the brief joy at the fulfilment of faith. Who then is he that plucks away the old man's staff, who is it that requires that he himself shall break it? Who is he that would make a man's gray hairs comfortless, who is it that requires that he himself shall do it? Is there no compassion for the venerable oldling, none for the innocent child? And yet Abraham was God's elect, and it was the Lord who imposed the trial. All would now be lost. The glorious memory to be preserved by the human race, the promise in Abraham's seed–this was only a whim, a fleeting thought which the Lord had had, which Abraham should now obliterate. That glorious treasure which was just as old as faith in Abraham's heart, many, many years older than Isaac, the fruit of Abraham's life, sanctified by prayers, matured in conflict–the blessing upon Abraham's lips, this fruit was now to be plucked prematurely and remain without significance. For what significance had it when Isaac was to be sacrificed? That sad and yet blissful hour when Abraham was to take leave of all that was dear to him, when yet once more he was to lift up his head, when his countenance would shine like that of the Lord, when he would concentrate his whole soul in a blessing which was potent to make Isaac blessed all his days–this time would not come! For he would indeed take leave of Isaac, but in such a way that he himself would remain behind; death would separate them, but in such a way that Isaac remained its prey. The old man would not be joyful in death as he laid his hands in blessing upon Isaac, but he would be weary of life as he laid violent hands upon Isaac. And it was God who tried him. Yea, woe, woe unto the messenger who had come before Abraham with such tidings! Who would have ventured to be the emissary of this srrow? But it was God who tried Abraham. Yet Abraham believed, and believed for this life. Yea, if his faith had been only for a future life, he surely would have cast everything away in order to hasten out of this world to which he did not belong. But Abraham's faith was not of this sort, if there be such a faith; for really this is not faith but the furthest possibility of faith which has a presentiment of its object at the extremest limit of the horizon, yet is separated from it by a yawning abyss within which despair carries on its game. But Abraham believed precisely for this life, that he was to grow old in the land, honored by the people, blessed in his generation, remembered forever in Isaac, his dearest thing in life, whom he embraced with a love for which it would be a poor expression to say that he loyally fulfilled the father's duty of loving the son, as indeed is evinced in the words of the summons, "the son whom thou lovest."

Jacob had twelve sons, and one of them he loved; Abraham had only one, the son whom he loved. Yet Abraham believed and did not doubt, he believed the preposterous. If Abraham had doubted—then he would have done something else, something glorious; for how could Abraham do anything but what is great and glorious! He would have marched up to Mount Moriah, he would have cleft the fire-wood, lit the pyre, drawn the knife—he would have cried out to God, "Despise not this sacrifice, it is not the best thing I possess, that I know well, for what is an old man in comparison with the child of promise; but it is the best I am able to give Thee. Let Isaac never come to know this, that he may console himself with his youth." He would have plunged the knife into his own breast. He would have been admired in the world, and his name would not have been forgotten; but it is one thing to be admired, and another to be the guiding star which saves the anguished. But Abraham believed. He did not pray for himself, with the hope of moving the Lord—it was only when the righteous punishment was decreed upon Sodom and Gomorrha that Abraham came forward with his prayers. We read in those holy books: "And God tempted Abraham, and said unto him, Abraham, Abraham, where art thou? And he said, Here am I." Thou to whom my speech is addressed, was such the case with thee? When afar off thou didst see the heavy dispensation of providence approaching thee, didst thou not say to the mountains, Fall on me, and to the hills, Cover me? Or if thou wast stronger, did not thy foot move slowly along the way, longing as it were for the old path? When a call was issued to thee, didst thou answer, or didst thou not answer perhaps in a low voice, whisperingly? Not so Abraham: joyfully, buoyantly, confidently, with a loud voice, he answered, "Here am I." We read further: "And Abraham rose early in the morning"—as though it were to a festival, so he hastened, and early in the morning he had come to the place spoken of, to Mount Moriah. He said nothing to Sarah, nothing to Eleazar. Indeed who could understand him? Had not the temptation by its very nature exacted of him an oath of silence? He cleft the wood, he bound Isaac, he lit the pyre, he drew the knife. My hearer, there was many a father who believed that with his son he lost everything that was dearest to him in the world, that he was deprived of every hope for the future, but yet there was none that was the child of promise in the sense that Isaac was for Abraham. There was many a father who lost his child; but then it was God, it was the unalterable, the unsearchable will of the Almighty, it was His hand took the child. Not so with Abraham. For him was reserved a harder trial, and Isaac's fate was laid along with the knife in Abraham's hand. And there he stood, the old man, with his only hope! But he did not doubt, he did not look anxiously to the right or to the left, he did not challenge heaven with his prayers. He knew that it was God the Almighty who was trying him, he knew that it was the hardest sacrifice that could be required of him; but he knew also that no sacrifice was too hard when God required it—and he drew the knife. Who gave strength to Abraham's arm? Who held his right hand up so that it did not fall limp at his side? He who gazes at this becomes paralyzed. Who gave strength to Abraham's soul, so that his eyes did not grow dim, so that he saw neither Isaac nor the ram? He who gazes at this becomes blind.—And yet rare enough perhaps is the man who becomes paralyzed and blind, still more rare one who worthily recounts what happened. We all know it—it was only a trial. If Abraham when he stood upon Mount Moriah had doubted, if he had gazed about him irresolutely, if before he drew the knife he had by chance discovered the ram, if God had permitted him to offer it instead of Isaac— then he would have betaken himself home, everything would have been the same, he has Sarah, he retained Isaac, and yet how changed! For his retreat would have been a flight, his salvation an accident, his reward dishonor, his future perhaps perdition. Then he would have borne witness neither to his faith nor to God's grace, but would have testified only how dreadful it is to march out to Mount Moriah. Then Abraham would not have been forgotten, nor would Mount Moriah, this mountain would then be mentioned, not like Ararat where the Ark landed, but would be spoken of as a consternation, because it was here that Abraham doubted. Venerable Father Abraham! In marching home from Mount Moriah thou hadst no need of a panegyric which might console thee for thy loss; for thou didst gain all and didst retain

Isaac. Was it not so? Never again did the Lord take him from thee, but thou didst sit at table joyfully with him in thy tent, as thou cost in the beyond to all eternity. Venerable Father Abraham! Thousands of years have run their course since those days, but thou hast need of no tardy lover to snatch the memorial of thee from the power of oblivion, for every language calls thee to remembrance—and yet thou cost reward thy lover more gloriously than does any other; hereafter thou cost make him blessed in thy bosom; here thou cost enthral his eyes and his heart by the marvel of thy deed. Venerable Father Abraham! Second Father of the human race! Thou who first wast sensible of and didst first bear witness to that prodigious passion which disdains the dreadful conflict with the rage of the elements and with the powers of creation in order to strive with God; thou who first didst know that highest passion, the holy, pure and humble expression of the divine madness16 which the pagans admired—forgive him who would speak in praise of thee, if he does not do it fittingly. He spoke humbly, as if it were the desire of his own heart, he spoke briefly, as it becomes him to do, but he will never forget that thou hadst need of a hundred years to obtain a son of old age against expectation, that thou didst have to draw the knife before retaining Isaac; he will never forget that in a hundred and thirty years thou didst not get further than to faith. PROBLEMATA: PRELIMINARY EXPECTORATION An old proverb fetched from the outward and visible world says: "Only the man that works gets the bread." Strangely enough this proverb does not aptly apply in that world to which it expressly belongs. For the outward world is subjected to the law of imperfection, and again and again the experience is repeated that he too who does not work gets the bread, and that he who sleeps gets it more abundantly than the man who works. In the outward world everything is made payable to the bearer, this world is in bondage to the law of indifference, and to him who has the ring, the spirit of the ring is obedient, whether he be Noureddin or Aladdin,17 and he who has the world's treasure, has it, however he got it. It is different in the world of spirit. Here an eternal divine order prevails, here it does not rain both upon the just and upon the unjust, here the sun does not shine both upon the good and upon the evil, here it holds good that only he who works gets the bread, only he who was in anguish finds repose, only he who descends into the underworld rescues the beloved, only he who draws the knife gets Isaac. He who will not work does not get the bread but remains deluded, as the gods deluded Orpheus with an airy figure in place of the loved one, deluded him because he was effeminate, not courageous, because he was a cithara-player, not a man. Here it is of no use to have Abraham for one's father, nor to have seventeen ancestors—he who will not work must take note of what is written about the maidens of Israel,18 for he gives birth to wind, but he who is willing to work gives birth to his own father. There is a knowledge which would presumptuously introduce into the world of spirit the same law of indifference under which the external world sighs. It counts it enough to think the great—other work is not necessary. But therefore it doesn't get the bread, it perishes of hunger, while everything is transformed into gold. And what does it really know? There were many thousands of Greek contemporaries, and countless numbers in subsequent generations, who knew all the triumphs of Miltiades, but only one19 was made sleepless by them. There were countless generations which knew by rote, word for word, the story of Abraham—how many were made sleepless by it? Now the story of Abraham has the remarkable property that it is always glorious, however poorly one may understand it; yet here again the proverb applies, that all depends upon whether one is willing to labor and be heavy laden. But they will not labor, and yet they would understand the story. They exalt Abraham—but how? They express the whole thing in perfectly general terms: "The great thing was that he loved God so much that he was willing to sacrifice to Him the best." That is very true, but "the best" is an indefinite expression. In the course of thought, as the tongue wags on, Isaac and "the best" are confidently identified, and he who meditates can very well smoke his pipe during the meditation, and the auditor can very well stretch out his legs in comfort. In case that rich young man whom Christ encountered on the road had sold all his goods and given to the poor, we should extol him, as we do all that is great, though without labor we would not understand him—and yet he would not have become an Abraham, in spite of the fact that he offered his best. What they leave out of Abraham's history is dread;20 for to money I have no ethical obligation, but to the son the father has the highest and most sacred obligation. Dread, however, is a perilous thing for effeminate natures, hence they forget it, and in spite of that they want to talk about Abraham. So they talk—in the course of the oration they use indifferently the two terms, Isaac and "the best." All goes famously. However, if it chanced that among the auditors there was one who suffered from insomnia—then the most dreadful, the profoundest tragic and comic misunderstanding lies very close. He went home, he would do as Abraham did, for the son is indeed "the best." If the orator got to know of it, he perhaps went to him, he summoned all his clerical dignity, he shouted, "O abominable man, offscouring of society, what devil possessed thee to want to murder thy son?" And the parson, who had not been conscious of warmth or perspiration in preaching about Abraham, is astonished at himself, at the earnest wrath which he thundered down upon that poor man. He was delighted with himself, for he had never spoken with such verve and unction. He said to himself and to his wife, "I am an orator. What I lacked was the occasion. When I talked about Abraham on Sunday I did not feel moved in the least." In case the same orator had a little superabundance of reason which might be lost, I think he would have lost it if the sinner were to say calmly and with dignity, "That in fact is what you yourself preached on Sunday." How could the parson be able to get into his head such a consequence? And yet it was so, and the mistake was merely that he didn't know what he was saying. Would there were a poet who might resolve to prefer such situations, rather than the stuff and nonsense with which comedies and novels are filled! The comic and the tragic here touch one another at the absolute point of infinity. The parson's speech was perhaps in itself ludicrous enough, but it became infinitely ludicrous by its effect, and yet this consequence was quite natural. Or if the sinner, without raising any objection, were to be converted by the parson's severe lecture, if the zealous clergyman were to go joyfully home, rejoicing in the consciousness that he not only was effective in the pulpit, but above all by his irresistible power as a pastor of souls, who on Sunday roused the congregation to enthusiasm, and on Monday like a cherub with a flaming sword placed himself before the man who by his action wanted to put to shame the old proverb, that "things don't go on in the world as the parson preaches."* *In the old days they said, "What a pity things don't go on in the world as the parson preaches"–perhaps the time is coming, especially with the help of philosophy, when they will say, "Fortunately things don't go on as the parson preaches; for after all there is some sense in life, but none at all in his preaching." If on the other hand the sinner was not convinced, his situation is pretty tragic. Presumably he would be executed or sent to the lunatic asylum, in short, he would have become unhappy in relation to so-called reality–in another sense I can well think that Abraham made him happy, for he that labors does not perish. How is one to explain the contradichon illustrated by that orator? Is it because Abraham had a prescriptive right to be a great man, so that what he did is great, and when another does the same it is sin, a heinous sin? In that case I do not wish to participate in such thoughtless eulogy. If faith does not make it a holy act to be willing to murder one's son, then let the same condemnation be pronounced upon Abraham as upon every other man. If a man perhaps lacks courage to carry his thought through, and to say that Abraham was a murderer, then it is surely better to acquire this courage, rather than waste time upon undeserved eulogies. The ethical expression for what Abraham did is, that he would murder Isaac; the religious expression is, that he would sacrifice Isaac; but precisely in this contradiction consists the dread which can well make a man sleepless, and yet Abraham is not what he is without this dread. Or perhaps he did not do at all what is related, but something altogether different, which is accounted for by the circumstances of his times–then let us forget him, for it is not worth while to remember that past which cannot become a present. Or had perhaps that orator forgotten something which corresponds to the ethical forgetfulness of the fact that Isaac was the son? For when faith is eliminated by becoming null or nothing, then there only remains the crude fact that Abraham wanted to murder Isaac–which is easy enough for anyone to imitate who has not faith, the faith, that is to say, which makes it hard for him. For my part I do not lack the courage to think a thought whole. Hitherto there has been no thought I have been afraid of; if I should run across such a thought, I hope that I have at least the sincerity to say, "I am afraid of this thought, it stirs up something else in me, and therefore I will not think it. If in this I do wrong, the punishment will not fail to follow." If I had recognized that it was the verdict of truth that Abraham was a murderer, I do not know whether I would have been able to silence my pious veneration for him. However, if I had thought that, I presumably would have kept silent about it, for one should not initiate others into such thoughts. But Abraham is no dazzling illusion, he did not sleep into renown, it was not a whim of fate. Can one then speak plainly about Abraham without incurring the danger that an individual might in bewilderment go ahead and do likewise? If I do not dare to speak freely, I will be completely silent about Abraham, above all I will not disparage him in such a way that precisely thereby he becomes a pitfall for the weak. For if one makes faith everything, that is, makes it what it is, then, according to my way of thinking, one may speak of it without danger in our age, which hardly extravagates in the matter of faith, and it is only by faith one attains likeness to Abraham, not by murder. If one makes love a transitory mood, a voluptuous emotion in a man, then one only lays pitfalls for the weak when one would talk about the exploits of love. Transient emotions every man surely has, but if as a consequence of such emotions one would do the terrible thing which love has sanctified as an immortal exploit, then all is lost, including the exploit and the bewildered doer of it. So one surely can talk about Abraham, for the great can never do harm when it is apprehended in its greatness; it is like a two-edged sword which slays and saves. If it should fall to my lot to talk on the subject, I would begin by showing what a pious and God-fearing man Abraham was, worthy to be called God's elect. Only upon such a man is imposed such a test. But where is there such a man? Next I would describe how Abraham loved Isaac.

To this end I would pray all good spirits to come to my aid, that my speech might be as glowing as paternal love is. I hope that I should be able to describe it in such a way that there would not be many a father in the realms and territories of the King who would dare to affirm that he loved his son in such a way. But if he does not love like Abraham, then every thought of offering Isaac would be not a trial but a base temptation [Anfechtung]. On this theme one could talk for several Sundays, one need be in no haste. The consequence would be that, if one spoke rightly, some few of the fathers would not require to hear more, but for the time being they would be joyful if they really succeeded in loving their sons as Abraham loved. If there was one who, after having heard about the greatness, but also about the dreadfulness of Abraham's deed, ventured to go forth upon that road, I would saddle my horse and ride with him. At every stopping place till we came to Mount Moriah I would explain to him that he still could turn back, could repent the misunderstanding that he was called to be tried in such a conflict, that he could confess his lack of courage, so that God Himself must take Isaac, if He would have him. It is my conviction that such a man is not repudiated but may become blessed like all the others. But in time he does not become blessed. Would they not, even in the great ages of faith, have passed this judgment upon such a man? I knew a person who on one occasion could have saved my life if he21 had been magnanimous. He said, "I see well enough what I could do, but I do not dare to. I am afraid that later I might lack strength and that I should regret it." He was not magnanimous, but who for this cause would not continue to love him? Having spoken thus and moved the audience so that at least they had sensed the dialectical conflict of faith and its gigantic passion, I would not give rise to the error on the part of the audience that "he then has faith in such a high degree that it is enough for us to hold on to his skirts." For I would add, "I have no faith at all, I am by nature a shrewd pate, and every such person always has great difficulty in making the movements of faith– not that I attach, however, in and for itself, any value to this difficulty which through the overcoming of it brought the clever head further than the point which the simplest and most ordinary man reaches more easily." After all, in the poets love has its priests, and sometimes one hears a voice which knows how to defend it; but of faith one hears never a word. Who speaks in honor of this passion? Philosophy goes further. Theology sits rouged at the window and courts its favor, offering to sell her charms to philosophy. It is supposed to be difficult to understand Hegel, but to understand Abraham is a trifle. To go beyond Hegel22 is a miracle, but to get beyond Abraham is the easiest thing of all. I for my part have devoted a good deal of time to the understanding of the Hegelian philosophy, I believe also that I understand it tolerably well, but when in spite of the trouble I have taken there are certain passages I cannot understand, I am foolhardy enough to think that he himself has not been quite clear. All this I do easily and naturally, my head does not suffer from it. But on the other hand when I have to think of Abraham, I am as though annihilated. I catch sight every moment of that enormous paradox which is the substance of Abraham's life, every moment I am repelled, and my thought in spite of all its passion cannot get a hairs-breadth further. I strain every muscle to get a view of it—that very instant I am paralyzed. I am not unacquainted with what has been admired as great and noble in the world, my soul feels affinity with it, being convinced in all humility that it was in my cause the hero contended, and the instant I contemplate his deed I cry out to myself, jam tua res agitur. 23 I think myself into the hero, but into Abraham I cannot think myself; when I reach the height I fall down, for what I encounter there is the paradox. I do not however mean in any sense to say that faith is something lowly, but on the contrary that it is the highest thing, and that it is dishonest of philosophy to give something else instead of it and to make light of faith. Philosophy cannot and should not give faith, but it should understand itself and know what it has to offer and take nothing away, and least of all should fool people out of something as if it were nothing. I am not unacquainted with the perplexities and dangers of life, I do not fear them, and I encounter them buoyantly. I am not unacquainted with the dreadful, my memory is a faithful wife, and my imagination is (as I myself am not) a diligent little maiden who all day sits quietly at her work, and in the evening knows how to chat to me about it so prettily that I must look at it, though not always, I must say, is it landscapes, or flowers, or pastoral idyls she paints. I have seen the dreadful before my own eyes, I do not flee from it timorously, but I know very well that, although I advance to meet it, my courage is not the courage of faith, nor anything comparable to it. I am unable to make the movements of faith, I cannot shut my eyes and plunge confidently into the absurd, for me that is an impossibility ... but I do not boast of it. I am convinced that God is love,24 this thought has for me a primitive lyrical validity. When it is present to me, I am unspeakably blissful, when it is absent, I long for it more vehemently than does the lover for his object; but I do not believe, this courage I lack. For me the love of God is, both in a direct and in an inverse sense, incommensurable with the whole of reality. I am not cowardly enough to whimper and complain, but neither am I deceitful enough to deny that faith is something much higher. I can well endure living in my way, I am joyful and content, but my joy is not that of faith, and in comparison with that it is unhappy. I do not trouble God with my petty sorrows, the particular does not trouble me, I gaze only at my love, and I keep its virginal flame pure and clear. Faith is convinced that God is concerned about the least things. I am content in this life with being married to the left hand, faith is humble enough to demand the right hand—for that this is humility I do not deny and shall never deny. But really is everyone in my generation capable of making the movements of faith, I wonder? Unless I am very much mistaken, this generation is rather inclined to be proud of making what they do not even believe I am capable of making, viz. incomplete movements. It is repugnant to me to do as so often is done, namely, to speak inhumanly about a great deed, as though some thousands of years were an immense distance; I would rather speak humanly about it, as though it had occurred yesterday, letting only the greatness be the distance, which either exalts or condemns. So if (in the quality of a tragic hero, for I can get no higher) I had been summoned to undertake such a royal progress to Mount Moriah, I know well what I would have done. I would not have been cowardly enough to stay at home, neither would I have laid down or sauntered along the way, nor have forgotten the knife, so that there might be a little delay—I am pretty well convinced that I would have been there on the stroke of the clock and would have had everything in order, perhaps I would have arrived too early in order to get through with it sooner. But I also know what else I would have done. The very instant I mounted the horse I would have said to myself, "Now all is lost. God requires Isaac, I sacrifice him, and with him my joy—yet God is love and continues to be that for me; for in the temporal world God and I cannot talk together, we have no language in common." Perhaps one or another in our age will be foolish enough, or envious enough of the great, to want to make himself and me believe that if I really had done this, I would have done even a greater deed than Abraham; for my prodigious resignation was far more ideal and poetic than Abraham's narrow-mindedness. And yet this is the greatest falsehood, for my prodigious resignation was the surrogate for faith, nor could I do more than make the infinite movement, in order to find myself and again repose in myself. In that case I would not have loved Isaac as Abraham loved. That I was resolute in making the movement might prove my courage, humanly speaking; that I loved him with all my soul is the presumption apart from which the whole thing becomes a crime, but yet I did not love like Abraham, for in that case I would have held back even at the last minute, though not for this would I have arrived too late at Mount Moriah. Besides, by my behavior I would have spoiled the whole story; for if I had got Isaac back again, I would have been in embarrassment. What Abraham found easiest, I would have found hard, namely to be joyful again with Isaac; for he who with all the infinity of his soul, propio motu et propiis auspiciis [by his own power and on his own responsibility], has performed the infinite movement [of resignation] and cannot do more, only retains Isaac with pain. But what did Abraham do? He arrived neither too soon nor too late. He mounted the ass, he rode slowly along the way. All that time he believed— he believed that God would not require Isaac of him, whereas he was willing nevertheless to sacrifice him if it was required. He believed by virtue of the absurd;

for there could be no question of human calculation, and it was indeed the absurd that God who required it of him should the next instant recall the requirement. He climbed the mountain, even at the instant when the knife glittered he believed ... that God would not require Isaac. He was indeed astonished at the outcome, but by a doublemovement he had reached his first position, and therefore he received Isaac more gladly than the first time. Let us go further. We let Isaac be really sacrificed. Abraham believed. He did not believe that some day he would be blessed in the beyond, but that he would be happy here in the world. God could give him a new Isaac, could recall to life him who had been sacrificed. He believed by virtue of the absurd; for all human reckoning had long since ceased to function. That sorrow can derange a man's mind, that we see, and it is sad enough. That there is such a thing as strength of will which is able to haul up so exceedingly close to the wind that it saves a man's reason, even though he remains a little queer,25 that too one sees. I have no intention of disparaging this; but to be able to lose one's reason, and therefore the whole of finiteness of which reason is the broker, and then by virtue of the absurd to gain precisely the same finiteness—that appalls my soul, but I do not for this cause say that it is something lowly, since on the contrary it is the only prodigy. Generally people are of the opinion that what faith produces is not a work of art, that it is coarse and common work, only for the more clumsy natures; but in fact this is far from the truth. The dialectic of faith is the finest and most remarkable of all; it possesses an elevation, of which indeed I can form a conception, but nothing more. I am able to make from the springboard the great leap whereby I pass into infinity, my back is like that of a tight-rope dancer, having been twisted in my childhood,26 hence I find this easy; with a one-two-three! I can walk about existence on my head; but the next thing I cannot do, for I cannot perform the miraculous, but can only be astonished by it. Yes, if Abraham the instant he swung his leg over the ass's back had said to himself, "Now, since Isaac is lost, I might just as well sacrifice him here at home, rather than ride the long way to Moriah"– then I should have no need of Abraham, whereas now I bow seven times before his name and seventy times before his deed. For this indeed he did not do, as I can prove by the fact that he was glad at receiving Isaac, heartily glad, that he needed no preparation, no time to concentrate upon the finite and its joy. If this had not been the case with Abraham, then perhaps he might have loved God but not believed; for he who loves God without faith reflects upon himself, he who loves God believingly reflects upon God. Upon this pinnacle stands Abraham. The last stage he loses sight of is the infinite resignation. He really goes further, and reaches faith; for all these caricatures of faith, the miserable lukewarm indolence which thinks, "There surely is no instant need, it is not worth while sorrowing before the time," the pitiful hope which says, "One cannot know what is going to happen … it might possibly be after all"–these caricatures of faith are part and parcel of life's wretchedness, and the infinite resignation has already consigned them to infinite contempt. Abraham I cannot understand,27 in a certain sense there is nothing I can learn from him but astonishment. If people fancy that by considering the outcome of this story they might let themselves be moved to believe, they deceive themselves and want to swindle God out of the first movement of faith, the infinite resignation. They would suck worldly wisdom out of the paradox. Perhaps one or another may succeed in that, for our age is not willing to stop with faith, with its miracle of turning water into wine, it goes further, it turns wine into water. Would it not be better to stop with faith, and is it not revolting that everybody wants to go further? When in our age (as indeed is proclaimed in various ways) they will not stop with love, where then are they going? To earthy wisdom, to petty calculation, to paltriness and wretchedness, to everything which can make man's divine origin doubtful. Would it not be better that they should stand still at faith, and that he who stands should take heed lest he fall? For the movements of faith must constantly be made by virtue of the absurd, yet in such a way, be it observed, that one does not lose the finite but gains it every inch. For my part I can well describe the movements of faith, but I cannot make them. When one would learn to make the motions of swimming one can let oneself be hung by a swimming-belt from the ceiling and go through the motions (describe them, so to speak, as we speak of describing a circle), but one is not swimming. In that way I can describe the movements of faith, but when I am thrown into the water, I swim, it is true (for I don't belong to the beach-waders), but I make other movements, I make the movements of infinity, whereas faith does the opposite: after having made the movements of infinity, it makes those of finiteness. Hail to him who can make those movements, he performs the marvellous, and I shall never grow tired of admiring him, whether he be Abraham or a slave in Abraham's house; whether he be a professor of philosophy or a servantgirl, I look only at the movements. But at them I do look, and do not let myself be fooled, either by myself or by any other man. The knights of the infinite resignation are easily recognized: their gait is gliding and assured. Those on the other hand who carry the jewel of faith are likely to be delusive, because their outward appearance bears a striking resemblance to that which both the infinite resignation and faith profoundly despise ... to Philistinism. I candidly admit that in my practice I have not found any reliable example of the knight of faith, though I would not therefore deny that every second man may be such an example. I have been trying, however, for several years to get on the track of this, and all in vain. People commonly travel around the world to see rivers and mountains, new stars, birds of rare plumage, queerly deformed fishes, ridiculous breeds of men—they abandon themselves to the bestial stupor which gapes at existence, and they think they have seen something. This does not interest me. But if I knew where there was such a knight of faith, I would make a pilgrimage to him on foot, for this prodigy interests me absolutely. I would not let go of him for an instant, every moment I would watch to see how he managed to make the movements, I would regard myself as secured for life, and would divide my time between looking at him and practicing the exercises myself, and thus would spend all my time admiring him. As was said, I have not found any such person, but I can well think him. Here he is. Acquaintance made, I am introduced to him. The moment I set eyes on him I instantly push him from me, I myself leap backwards, I clasp my hands and say half aloud, "Good Lord, is this the man? Is it really he? Why, he looks like a taxcollector!" However, it is the man after all. I draw closer to him, watching his least movements to see whether there might not be visible a little heterogeneous fractional telegraphic message from the infinite, a glance, a look, a gesture, a note of sadness, a smile, which betrayed the infinite in its heterogeneity with the finite. No! I examine his figure from tip to toe to see if there might not be a cranny through which the infinite was peeping. No! He is solid through and through. His tread? It is vigorous, belongingentirely to finiteness; no smartly dressed townsman who walksout to Fresberg on a Sunday afternoon treads the ground more firmly, he belongs entirely to the world, no Philistine more so. One can discover nothing of that aloof and superior nature whereby one recognizes the knight of the infinite. He takes delight in everything, and whenever one sees him taking part in a particular pleasure, he does it with the persistence which is the mark of the earthly man whose soul is absorbed in such things. He tends to his work. So when one looks at him one might suppose that he was a clerk who had lost his soul in an intricate system of book-keeping, so precise is he. He takes a holiday on Sunday. He goes to church. No heavenly glance or any other token of the incommensurable betrays him; if one did not know him, it would be impossible to distinguish him from the rest of the congregation, for his healthy and vigorous hymnsinging proves at the most that he has a good chest. In the afternoon he walks to the forest. He takes delight in everything he sees, in the human swarm, in the new omnibuses,25 in the water of the Sound; when one meets him on the Beach Road one might suppose he was a shopkeeper taking his fling, that's just the way he disports himself, for he is not a poet, and I have sought in vain to detect in him the poetic incommensurability. Toward evening he walks home, his gait is as indefatigable as that of the postman. On his way he reflects that his wife has surely a special little warm dish prepared for him, e.g. a calf's head roasted, garnished with vegetables. If he were to meet a man like-minded, he could continue as far as East Gate to discourse with him about that dish, with a passion befitting a hotel chef. As it happens, he hasn't four pence to his name, and yet he fully and firmly believes that his wife has that dainty dish for him. If she had it, it would then be an invidious sight for superior people and an inspiring one for the plain man, to see him eat; for his appetite is greater than Esau's. His wife hasn't it—strangely enough, it is quite the same to him. On the way he comes past a building site and runs across another man. They talk together for a moment. In the twinkling of an eye he erects a new building, he has at his disposition all the powers necessary for it. The stranger leaves him with the thought that he certainly was a capitalist, while my admired knight thinks, "Yes, if the money were needed, I dare say I could get it." He lounges at an open window and looks out on the square on which he lives; he is interested in everything that goes on, in a rat which slips under the curb, in the children's play, and this with the nonchalance of a girl of sixteen. And yet he is no genius, for in vain I have sought in him the incommensurability of genius. In the evening he smokes his pipe; to look at him one would swear that it was the grocer over the way vegetating in the twilight. He lives as carefree as a ne'er-do-well, and yet he buys up the acceptable time at the dearest price, for he does not do the least thing except by virtue of the absurd. And yet, and yet—actually I could become furious over it, for envy if for no other reason—this man has made and every instant is making the movements of infinity. With infinite resignation he has drained the cup of life's profound sadness, he knows the bliss of the infinite, he senses the pain of renouncing everything, the dearest things he possesses in the world, and yet finiteness tastes to him just as good as to one who never knew anything higher, for his continuance in the finite did not bear a trace of the cowed and fearful spirit produced by the process of training; and yet he has this sense of security in enjoying it, as though the finite life were the surest thing of all. And yet, and yet the whole earthly form he exhibits is a new creation by virtue of the absurd. He resigned everything infinitely, and then he grasped everything again by virtue of the absurd. He constantly makes the movements of infinity, but he does this with such correctness and assurance that he constantly gets the finite out of it, and there is not a second when one has a notion of anything else. It is supposed to be the most difficult task for a dancer to leap into a definite posture in such a way that there is not a second when he is grasping after the posture, but by the leap itself he stands fixed in that posture. Perhaps no dancer can do it—that is what this knight does. Most people live dejectedly in worldly sorrow and joy; they are the ones who sit along the wall and do not join in the dance. The knights of infinity are dancers and possess elevation. They make the movements upward, and fall down again; and this too is no mean pastime, nor ungraceful to behold. But whenever they fall down they are not able at once to assume the posture, they vacillate an instant, and this vacillation shows that after all they are strangers in the world. This is more or less strikingly evident in proportion to the art they possess, but even the most artistic knights cannot altogether conceal this vacillation. One need not look at them when they are up in the air, but only the instant they touch or have touched the ground—then one recognizes them. But to be able to fall down in such a way that the same second it looks as if one were standing and walking, to transform the leap of life into a walk, absolutely to express the sublime in the pedestrian—that only the knight of faith can do—and this is the one and only prodigy. But since the prodigy is so likely to be delusive, I will describe the movements in a definite instance which will serve to illustrate their relation to reality, for upon this everything turns. A young swain falls in love with a princess,29 and the whole content of his life consists in this love, and yet the situation is such that it is impossible for it to be realized, impossible for it to be translated from ideality into reality.*

Of course any other instance whatsoever in which the individual finds that for him the whole reality of actual existence is concentrated, may, when it is seen to be unrealizable, be an occasion for the movement of resignation. However, I have chosen a love experience to make the movement visible, because this interest is doubtless easier to understand, and so relieves me from the necessity of making preliminary observations which in a deeper sense could be of interest only to a few. The slaves of paltriness, the frogs in life's swamp, will naturally cry out, "Such a love is foolishness. The rich brewer's widow is a match fully as good and respectable." Let them croak in the swamp undisturbed. It is not so with the knight of infinite resignation, he does not give up his love, not for all the glory of the world. He is no fool. First he makes sure that this really is the content of his life, and his soul is too healthy and too proud to squander the least thing upon an inebriation. He is not cowardly, he is not afraid of letting love creep into his most secret, his most hidden thoughts, to let it twine in innumerable coils about every ligament of his consciousness—if the love becomes an unhappy love, he will never be able to tear himself loose from it. He feels a blissful rapture in letting love tingle through every nerve, and yet his soul is as solemn as that of the man who has drained the poisoned goblet and feels how the juice permeates every drop of blood—for this instant is life and death.30 So when he has thus sucked into himself the whole of love and absorbed himself in it, he does not lack courage to make trial of everything and to venture everything. He surveys the situation of his life, he convokes the swift thoughts, which like tame doves obey his every bidding, he waves his wand over them, and they dart off in all directions. But when they all return, all as messengers of sorrow, and declare to him that it is an impossibility, then he becomes quiet, he dismisses them, he remains alone, and then he performs the movements. If what I am saying is to have any significance, it is requisite that the movement come about normally. *To this end passion is necessary. Every movement of infinity comes about by passion, and no reflection can bring a movement about. This is the continual leap in existence which explains the movement, whereas mediation is a chimera which according to Hegel is supposed to explain everything, and at the same time this is the only thing he has never tried to explain. Even to make the well-known Socratic distinction between what one understands and what one does not understand, passion is required, and of course even more to make the characteristic Socratic movement, the movement, namely, of ignorance. What our age lacks, however, is not reflection but passion. Hence in a sense our age is too tenacious of life to die, for dying is one of the most remarkable leaps, and a little verse of a poet has always attracted me much, because, after having expressed prettily and simply in five or six preceding lines his wish for good things in life, he concludes thus:31 Ein seliger Sprung in die Ewigkeit. So for the first thing, the knight will have power to concentrate the whole content of life and the whole significance of reality in one single wish. If a man lacks this concentration, this intensity, if his soul from the beginning is dispersed in the multifarious, he never comes to the point of making the movement, he will deal shrewdly in life like the capitalists who invest their money in all sorts of securities, so as to gain on the one what they lose on the other–in short, he is not a knight. In the next place the knight will have the power to concentrate the whole result of the operations of thought in one act of consciousness. If he lacks this intensity, if his soul from the beginning is dispersed in the multifarious, he will never get time to make the movements, he will be constantly running errands in life, never enter into eternity, for even at the instant when he is closest to it he will suddenly discover that he has forgotten something for which he must go back. He will think that to enter eternity is possible the next instant, and that also is perfectly true, but by such considerations one never reaches the point of making the movements, but by their aid one sinks deeper and deeper into the mire. So the knight makes the movement–but what movement? Will he forget the whole thing? (For in this too there is indeed a kind of concentration.) No! For the knight does not contradict himself, and it is a contradiction to forget the whole content of one's life and yet remain the same man. To become another man he feels no inclination, nor does he by any means regard this as greatness. Only the lower natures forget themselves and become something new. Thus the butterfly has entirely forgotten that it was a caterpillar, perhaps it may in turn so entirely forget it was a butterfly that it becomes a fish. The deeper natures never forget themselves and never become anything else than what they were. So the knight remembers everything, but precisely this remembrance is pain, and yet by the infinite resignation he is reconciled with existence. Love for that princess became for him the expression for an eternal love, assumed a religious character, was transfigured into a love for the Eternal Being, which did to be sure deny him the fulfilment of his love, yet reconciled him again by the eternal consciousness of its validity in the form of eternity, which no reality can take from him. Fools and young men prate about everything being possible for a man. That, however, is a great error. Spiritually speaking, everything is possible, but in the world of the finite there is much which is not possible. This impossible, however, the knight makes possible by expressing it spiritually, but he expresses it spiritually by waiving his claim to it. The wish which would carry him out into reality, but was wrecked upon the impossibility, is now bent inward, but it is not therefore lost, neither is it forgotten. At one moment it is the obscure emotion of the wish within him which awakens recollections, at another moment he awakens them himself; for he is too proud to be willing that what was the whole content of his life should be the thing of a fleeting moment. He keeps this love young, and along with him it increases in years and in beauty. On the other hand, he has no need of the intervention of the finite for the further growth of his love. From the instant he made the movement the princess is lost to him. He has no need of those erotic tinglings in the nerves at the sight of the beloved etc., nor does he need to be constantly taking leave of her in a finite sense, because he recollects her in an eternal sense,32 and he knows very well that the lovers who are so bent upon seeing "her" yet once again, to say farefell for the last time, are right in being bent upon it, are right in thinking that it is the last time, for they forget one another the soonest. He has comprehended the deep secret that also in loving another person one must be sufficient unto oneself. He no longer takes a finite interest in what the princess is doing, and precisely this is proof that he has made the movement infinitely. Here one may have an opportunity to see whether the movement on the part of a particular person is true or fictitious. There was one who also believed that he had made the movement; but lo, time passed, the princess did something else, she married33–a prince, let us say–then his soul lost the elasticity of resignation. Thereby he knew that he had not made the movement rightly; for he who has made the act of resignation infinitely is sufficient unto himself. The knight does not annul his resignation, he preserves his love just as young as it was in its first moment, he never lets it go from him, precisely because he makes the movements infinitely. What the princess does, cannot disturb him, it is only the lower natures which find in other people the law for their actions, which find the premises for their actions outside themselves. If on the other hand the princess is like-minded, the beautiful consequence will be apparent. She will introduce herself into that order of knighthood into which one is not received by balloting, but of which everyone is a member who has courage to introduce himself, that order of knighthood which proves its immortality by the fact that it makes no distinction between man and woman. The two will preserve their love young and sound, she also will have triumphed over her pains, even though she does not, as it is said in the ballad, "lie every night beside her lord." These two will to all eternity remain in agreement with one another, with a well-timed harmonia praestabilita, 34 so that if ever the moment were to come, the moment which does not, however, concern them finitely (for then they would be growing older), if ever the moment were to come which offered to give love its expression in time, then they will be capable of beginning precisely at the point where they would have begun if originally they had been united. He who understands this, be he man or woman, can never be deceived, for it is only the lower natures which imagine they were deceived. No girl who is not so proud really knows how to love; but if she is so proud, then the cunning and shrewdness of all the world cannot deceive her. In the infinite resignation there is peace and rest; every man who wills it, who has not abased himself by scorning himself (which is still more dreadful than being proud), can train himself to make this movement which in its pain reconciles one with existence. Infinite resignation is that shirt we read about in the old fable.35 The thread is spun under tears, the cloth bleached with tears, the shirt sewn with tears; but then too it is a better protection than iron and steel. The imperfection in the fable is that a third party can manufacture this shirt. The secret in life is that everyone must sew it for himself, and the astonishing thing is that a man can sew it fully as well as a woman. In the infinite resignation there is peace and rest and comfort in sorrow—that is, if the movement is made normally. It would not be difficult for me, however, to write a whole book, were I to examine the various misunderstandings, the preposterous attitudes, the deceptive movements, which I have encountered in my brief practice. People believe very little in spirit, and yet making this movement depends upon spirit, it depends upon whether this is or is not a one-sided result of a dira necessitas, and if this is present, the more dubious it always is whether the movement is normal. If one means by this that the cold, unfruitful necessity must necessarily be present, one thereby affirms that no one can experience death before he actually dies, and that appears to me a crass materialism. However, in our time people concern themselves rather little about making pure movements. In case one who was about to learn to dance were to say, "For centuries now one generation after another has been learning positions, it is high time I drew some advantage out of this and began straightway with the French dances"–then people would laugh at him; but in the world of spirit they find this exceedingly plausible. What is education? I should suppose that education was the curriculum one had to run through in order to catch up with oneself, and he who will not pass through this curriculum is helped very little by the fact that he was born in the most enlightened age. The infinite resignation is the last stage prior to faith, so that one who has not made this movement has not faith; for only in the infinite resignation do I become clear to myself with respect to my eternal validity, and only then can there be any question of grasping existence by virtue of faith. Now we will let the knight of faith appear in the role just described. He makes exactly the same movements as the other knight, infinitely renounces claim to the love which is the content of his life, he is reconciled in pain; but then occurs the prodigy, he makes still another movement more wonderful than all, for he says, "I believe nevertheless that I shall get her, in virtue, that is, of the absurd, in virtue of the fact that with God all things are possible."36 The absurd is not one of the factors which can be discriminated within the proper compass of the understanding: it is not identical with the improbable, the unexpected, the unforeseen. At the moment when the knight made the act of resignation37 he was convinced, humanly speaking, of the impossibility. This was the result reached by the understanding, and he had sufficient energy to think it. On the other hand, in an infinite sense it was possible, namely, by renouncing it; but this sort of possessing is at the same time a relinquishing, and yet there is no absurdity in this for the understanding, for the understanding continued to be in the right in affirming that in the world of the finite where it holds sway this was and remained an impossibility. This is quite as clear to the knight of faith, so the only thing that can save him is the absurd, and this he grasps by faith. So he recognizes the impossibility, and that very instant he believes the absurd; for, if without recognizing the impossibility with all the passion of his soul and with all his heart, he should wish to imagine that he has faith, he deceives himself, and his testimony has no bearing, since he has not even reached the infinite resignation. Faith therefore is not an aesthetic emotion but something far higher, precisely because it has resignation as its presupposition; it is not an immediate instinct of the heart, but is the paradox of life and existence. So when in spite of all difficulties a young girl still remains convinced that her wish will surely be fulfilled, this conviction is not the assurance of faith, even if she was brought up by Christian parents, and for a whole year perhaps has been catechized by the parson. She is convinced in all her childish naïveté and innocence, this conviction also ennobles her nature and imparts to her a preternatural greatness, so that like a thaumaturge she is able to conjure the finite powers of existence and make the very stones weep, while on the other hand in her flurry she may just as well run to Herod as to Pilate and move the whole world by her tears. Her convichon is very lovable, and one can learn much from her, but one thing is not to be learned from her, one does not learn the movements, for her conviction does not dare in the pain of resignation to face the impossibility. So I can perceive that it requires strength and energy and freedom of spirit to make the infinite movement of resignation, I can also perceive that it is feasible. But the next thing astonishes me, it makes my head swim, for after having made the movement of resignation, then by virtue of the absurd to get everything, to get the wish whole and uncurtailed—that is beyond human power, it is a prodigy. But this I can perceive, that the young girl's conviction is mere levity in comparison with the firmness faith displays notwithstanding it has perceived the impossibility. Whenever I essay to make this movement, I turn giddy, the very instant I am admiring it absolutely a prodigious dread grips my soul—for what is it to tempt God? And yet this movement is the movement of faith and remains such, even though philosophy, in order to confuse the concepts, would make us believe that it has faith, and even though theology would sell out faith at a bargain price. For the act of resignation faith is not required, for what I gain by resignation is my eternal consciousness, and this is a purely philosophical movement which I dare say I am able to make if it is required, and which I can train myself to make, for whenever any finiteness would get the mastery over me, I starve myself until I can make the movement, for my eternal consciousness is my love to God, and for me this is higher than everything. For the act of resignation faith is not required, but it is needed when it is the case of acquiring the very least thing more than my eternal consciousness, for this is the paradoxical. The movements are frequently confounded, for it is said that one needs faith to renounce the claim to everything, yea, a stranger thing than this may be heard, when a man laments the loss of his faith, and when one looks at the scale to see where he is, one sees, strangely enough, that he has only reached the point where he should make the infinite movement of resignation. In resignation I make renunciation of everything, this movement I make by myself, and if I do not make it, it is because I am cowardly and effeminate and without enthusiasm and do not feel the significance of the lofty dignity which is assigned to every man, that of being his own censor, which is a far prouder title than that of Censor General to the whole Roman Republic. This movement I make by myself, and what I gain is myself in my eternal consciousness, in blissful agreement with my love for the Eternal Being. By faith I make renunciation of nothing, on the contrary, by faith I acquire everything, precisely in the sense in which it is said that he who has faith like a grain of mustard can remove mountains. A purely human courage is required to renounce the whole of the temporal to gain the eternal; but this I gain, and to all eternity I cannot renounce it—that is a selfcontradiction. But a paradoxical and humble courage is required to grasp the whole of the temporal by virtue of the absurd, and this is the courage of faith. By faith Abraham did not renounce his claim upon Isaac, but by faith he got Isaac. By virtue of resignation that rich young man should have given away everything, but then when he had done that, the knight of faith should have said to him, "By virtue of the absurd thou shalt get every penny back again. Canst thou believe that?" And this speech ought by no means to have been indifferent to the aforesaid rich young man, for in case he gave away his goods because he was tired of them, his resignation was not much to boast of. It is about the temporal, the finite, everything turns in this case. I am able by my own strength to renounce everything, and then to find peace and repose in pain. I can stand everything—even though that horrible demon, more dreadful than death, the king of terrors, even though madness were to hold up before my eyes the motley of the fool, and I understood by its look that it was I who must put it on, I still am able to save my soul, if only it is more to me than my earthly happiness that my love to God should triumph in me. A man may still be able at the last instant to concentrate his whole soul in a single glance toward that heaven from which cometh every good gift, and his glance will be intelligible to himself and also to Him whom it seeks as a sign that he nevertheless remained true to his love. Then he will calmly put on the motley garb. He whose soul has not this romantic enthusiasm has sold his soul, whether he got a kingdom for it or a paltry piece of silver. But by my own strength I am not able to get the least of the things which belong to finiteness, for I am constantly using my strength to renounce everything. By my own strength I am able to give up the princess, and I shall not become a grumbler, but shall find joy and repose in my pain; but by my own strength I am not able to get her again, for I am employing all my strength to be resigned. But by faith, says that marvellous knight, by faith I shall get her in virtue of the absurd. So this movement I am unable to make. As soon as I would begin to make it everything turns around dizzily, and I flee back to the pain of resignation. I can swim in existence, but for this mystical soaring I am too heavy. To exist in such a way that my opposition to existence is expressed as the most beautiful and assured harmony with it, is something I cannot do. And yet it must be glorious to get the princess, that is what I say every instant, and the knight of resignation who does not say it is a deceiver, he has not had one only wish, and he has not kept the wish young by his pain. Perhaps there was one who thought it fitting enough that the wish was no longer vivid, that the barb of pain was dulled, but such a man is no knight. A free-born soul who caught himself entertaining such thoughts would despise himself and begin over again, above all he would not permit his soul to be deceived by itself. And yet it must be glorious to get the princess, and yet the knight of faith is the only happy one, the heir apparent to the finite, whereas the knight of resignation is a stranger and a foreigner. Thus to get the princess, to live with her joyfully and happily day in and day out (for it is also conceivable that the knight of resignation might get the princess, but that his soul had discerned the impossibility of their future happiness), thus to live joyfully and happily every instant by virtue of the absurd, every instant to see the sword hanging over the head of the beloved, and yet not to find repose in the pain of resignation, but joy by virtue of the absurd—this is marvellous. He who does it is great, the only great man. The thought of it stirs my soul, which never was niggardly in the admiration of greatness. In case then everyone in my generation who will not stop at faith is really a man who has comprehended life's horror, who has understood what Daub38 means when he says that a soldier who stands alone at his post with a loaded gun in a stormy night beside a powder-magazine … will get strange thoughts into his head—in case then everyone who will not stop at faith is a man who had strength of soul to comprehend that the wish was an impossibility, and thereupon gave himself time to remain alone with this thought, in case everyone who will not stop at faith is a man who is reconciled in pain and is reconciled to pain, in case everyone who will not stop at faith is a man who in the next place (and if he has not done all the foregoing, there is no need of his troubling himself about faith)—in the next place did the marvellous thing, grasped the whole of existence by virtue of the absurd … then what I write is the highest eulogy of my contemporaries by one of the lowliest among them, who was able only to make the movement of resignation. But why will they not stop at faith, why does one sometimes hear that people are ashamed to acknowledge that they have faith? This I cannot comprehend. If ever I contrive to be able to make this movement, I shall in the future ride in a coach and four. If it is really true that all the Philistinism I behold in life (which I do not permit my word but my actions to condemn) is not what it seems to be–is it the miracle? That is conceivable, for the hero of faith had in fact a striking resemblance to it–for that hero of faith was not so much an ironist or a humorist, but something far higher. Much is said in our age about irony and humor, especially by people who have never been capable of engaging in the practice of these arts, but who neverthless know how to explain everything. I am not entirely unacquainted with these two passions,39 I know a little more about them than what is to be found in German and German-Danish compendiums. I know therefore that these two passions are essentially different from the passion of faith. Irony and humor reflect also upon themselves, and therefore belong within the sphere of the infinite resignation, their elasticity is due to the fact that the individual is incommensurable with reality. The last movement, the paradoxical movement of faith, I cannot make (be that a duty or whatever it may be), in spite of the fact that I would do it more than gladly. Whether a man has a right to make this affirmation, must be left to him, it is a question between him and the Eternal Being who is the object of faith whether in this respect he can hit upon an amicable compromise. What every man can do is to make the movement of infinite resignation, and I for my part would not hesitate to pronounce everyone cowardly who wishes to make himself believe he can not do it. With faith it is a different matter. But what every man has not a right to do, is to make others believe that faith is something lowly, or that it is an easy thing, whereas it is the greatest and the hardest. People construe the story of Abraham in another way. They extol God's grace in bestowing Isaac upon him again–the whole thing was only a trial. A trial–that word may say much or little, and yet the whole thing is over as quickly as it is said. One mounts a winged horse, the same instant one is at Mount Moriah, the same instant one sees the ram; one forgets that Abraham rode only upon an ass, which walks slowly along the road, that he had a journey of three days, that he needed some time to cleave the wood, to bind Isaac, and to sharpen the knife. And yet they extol Abraham. He who is to deliver the discourse can very well sleep till a quarter of an hour before he has to preach, the auditor can well take a nap during the discourse, for all goes smoothly, without the least trouble from any quarter. If there was a man present who suffered from insomnia, perhaps he then went home and sat in a corner and thought: "It's an affair of a moment, this whole thing; if only you wait a minute, you see the ram, and the trial is over." If the orator were to encounter him in this condition, he would, I think, confront him with all his dignity and say, "Wretched man, that thou couldst let thy soul sink into such foolishness! No miracle occurs. The whole of life is a trial." In proportion as the orator proceeds with his outpouring, he would get more and more excited, would become more and more delighted with himself, and whereas he had noticed no congestion of the blood while he talked about Abraham, he now felt how the vein swelled in his forehead. Perhaps he would have lost his breath as well as his tongue if the sinner had answered calmly and with dignity, "But it was about this you preached last Sunday." Let us then either consign Abraham to oblivion, or let us learn to be dismayed by the tremendous paradox which constitutes the significance of Abraham's life, that we may understand that our age, like every age, can be joyful if it has faith. In case Abraham is not a nullity, a phantom, a show one employs for a pastime, then the fault can never consist in the fact that the sinner wants to do likewise, but the point is to see how great a thing it was that Abraham did, in order that man may judge for himself whether he has the call and the courage to be subjected to such a test. The comic contradiction in the behavior of the orator is that he reduced Abraham to an insignificance, and yet would admonish the other to behave in the same way. Should not one dare then to talk about Abraham? I think one should. If I were to talk about him, I would first depict the pain of his trial. To that end I would like a leech suck all the dread and distress and torture out of a father's sufferings, so that I might describe what Abraham suffered, whereas all the while he nevertheless believed. I would remind the audience that the journey lasted three days and a good part of the fourth, yea, that these three and a half days were infinitely longer than the few thousand years which separate me from Abraham. Then I would remind them that, in my opinion, every man dare still turn around ere he begins such an undertaking, and every instant he can repentantly turn back. If one does this, I fear no danger, nor am I afraid of awakening in people an inclination to be tried like Abraham. But if one would dispose of a cheap edition of Abraham, and yet admonish everyone to do likewise, then it is ludicrous. It is now my intention to draw out from the story of Abraham the dialectical consequences inherent in it, expressing them in the form of problemata, in order to see what a tremendous paradox faith is, a paradox which is capable of transforming a murder into a holy act well-pleasing to God, a paradox which gives Isaac back to Abraham, which no thought can master, because faith begins precisely there where thinking leaves off. PROBLEM I Is there such a thing as a teleological suspension of the ethical? The ethical as such is the universal, and as the universal it applies to everyone, which may be expressed from another point of view by saying that it applies every instant. It reposes immanently in itself, it has nothing without itself which is its telos, 40 but is itself telos for everything outside it, and when this has been incorporated by the ethical it can go no further. Conceived immediately as physical and psychical, the particular individual is the individual who has his telos in the universal, and his ethical task is to express himself constantly in it, to abolish his particularity in order to become the universal. As soon as the individual would assert himself in his particularity over against the universal he sins, and only by recognizing this can he again reconcile himself with the universal. Whenever the individual after he has entered the universal feels an impulse to assert himself as the particular, he is in temptation (Anfechtung), and he can labor himself out of this only by penitently abandoning himself as the particular in the universal. If this be the highest thing that can be said of man and of his existence, then the ethical has the same character as man's eternal blessedness, which to all eternity and at every instant is his telos, since it would be a contradiction to say that this might be abandoned (i.e. teleologically suspended), inasmuch as this is no sooner suspended than it is forfeited, whereas in other cases what is suspended is not forfeited but is preserved precisely in that higher thing which is its telos. 41 If such be the case, then Hegel is right when in his chapter on "The Good and the Conscience," 42 he characterizes man merely as the particular and regards this character as "a moral form of evil" which is to be annulled in the teleology of the moral, so that the individual who remains in this stage is either sinning or subjected to temptation (Anfechtung). On the other hand, Hegel is wrong in talking of faith, wrong in not protesting loudly and clearly against the fact that Abraham enjoys honor and glory as the father of faith, whereas he ought to be prosecuted and convicted of murder. For faith is this paradox, that the particular is higher than the universal— yet in such a way, be it observed, that the movement repeats itself, and that consequently the individual, after having been in the universal, now as the particular isolates himself as higher than the universal. If this be not faith, then Abraham is lost, then faith has never existed in the world … because it has always existed. For if the ethical (i.e. the moral) is the highest thing, and if nothing incommensurable remains in man in any other way but as the evil (i.e. the particular which has to be expressed in the universal), then one needs no other categories besides those which the Greeks possessed or which by consistent thinking can be derived from them. This fact Hegel ought not to have concealed, for after all he was acquainted with Greek thought. One not infrequently hears it said by men who for lack of losing themselves in studies are absorbed in phrases that a light shines upon the Christian world whereas a darkness broods over paganism. This utterance has always seemed strange to me, inasmuch as every profound thinker and every serious artist is even in our day rejuvenated by the eternal youth of the Greek race. Such an utterance may be explained by the consideration that people do not know what they ought to say but only that they must say something. It is quite right for one to say that paganism did not possess faith, but if with this one is to have said something, one must be a little clearer about what one understands by faith, since otherwise one falls back into such phrases. To explain the whole of existence and faith along with it, without having a conception of what faith is, is easy, and that man does not make the poorest calculation in life who reckons upon admiration when he possesses such an explanation; for, as Boileau says, "un sot trouve toujours un plus sot qui l'admire." Faith is precisely this paradox, that the individual as the particular is higher than the universal, is justified over against it, is not subordinate but superior—yet in such a way, be it observed, that it is the particular individual who, after he has been subordinated as the particular to the universal, now through the universal becomes the individual who as the particular is superior to the universal, for the fact that the individual as the particular stands in an absolute relation to the absolute. This position cannot be mediated, for all mediation comes about precisely by virtue of the universal; it is and remains to all eternity a paradox, inaccessible to thought. And yet faith is this paradox—or else (these are the logical deductions which I would beg the reader to have in mente at every point, though it would be too prolix for me to reiterate them on every occasion)— or else there never has been faith ... precisely because it always has been. In other words, Abraham is lost. That for the particular individual this paradox may easily be mistaken for a temptation (Anfechtung) is indeed true, but one ought not for this reason to conceal it. That the whole constitution of many persons may be such that this paradox repels them is indeed true, but one ought not for this reason to make faith something different in order to be able to possess it, but ought rather to admit that one does not possess it, whereas those who possess faith should take care to set up certain criteria so that one might distinguish the paradox from a temptation (Anfechtung). Now the story of Abraham contains such a teleological suspension of the ethical. There have not been lacking clever pates and profound investigators who have found analogies to it. Their wisdom is derived from the pretty proposition that at bottom everything is the same. If one will look a little more closely, I have not much doubt that in the whole world one will not find a single analogy (except a later instance which proves nothing), if it stands fast that Abraham is the representative of faith, and that faith is normally expressed in him whose life is not merely the most paradoxical that can be thought but so paradoxical that it cannot be thought at all. He acts by virtue of the absurd, for it is precisely absurd that he as the particular is higher than the universal. This paradox cannot be mediated; for as soon as he begins to do this he has to admit that he was in temptation (Anfechtung), and if such was the case, he never gets to the point of sacrificing Isaac, or, if he has sacrificed Isaac, he must turn back repentantly to the universal. By virtue of the absurd he gets Isaac again. Abraham is therefore at no instant a tragic hero but something quite different, either a murderer or a believer. The middle term which saves the tragic hero, Abraham has not. Hence it is that I can understand the tragic hero but cannot understand Abraham, though in a certain crazy sense I admire him more than all other men. Abraham's relation to Isaac, ethically speaking, is quite simply expressed by saying that a father shall love his son more dearly than himself. Yet within its own compass the ethical has various gradations. Let us see whether in this story there is to be found any higher expression for the ethical such as would ethically explain his conduct, ethically justify him in suspending the ethical obligation toward his son, without in this search going beyond the teleology of the ethical. When an undertaking in which a whole nation is concerned is hindered,43 when such an enterprise is brought to a standshll by the disfavor of heaven, when the angry deity sends a calm which mocks all efforts, when the seer performs his heavy task and proclaims that the deity demands a young maiden as a sacrifice—then will the father heroically make the sacrifice. He will magnanimously conceal his pain, even though he might wish that he were "the lowly man who dares to weep," 44 not the king who must act royally. And though solitary pain forces its way into his breast, he has only three confidants among the people, yet soon the whole nation will be cognizant of his pain, but also cognizant of his exploit, that for the welfare of the whole he was willing to sacrifice her, his daughter, the lovely young maiden. O charming bosom! O beautiful cheeks! O bright golden hair! (v. 687). And the daughter will affect him by her tears, and the father will turn his face away, but the hero will raise the knife.–When the report of this reaches the ancestral home, then will the beautiful maidens of Greece blush with enthusiasm, and if the daughter was betrothed, her true love will not be angry but be proud of sharing in the father's deed, because the maiden belonged to him more feelingly than to the father. When the intrepid judge45 who saved Israel in the hour of need in one breath binds himself and God by the same vow, then heroically the young maiden's jubilation, the beloved daughter's joy, he will turn to sorrow, and with her all Israel will lament her maiden youth; but every free-born man will understand, and every stout-hearted woman will admire Jephtha, and every maiden in Israel will wish to act as did his daughter. For what good would it do if Jephtha were victorious by reason of his vow if he did not keep it? Would not the victory again be taken from the nation? When a son is forgetful of his duty,46 when the state entrusts the father with the sword of justice, when the laws require punishment at the hand of the father, then will the father heroically forget that the guilty one is his son, he will magnanimously conceal his pain, but there will not be a single one among the people, not even the son, who will not admire the father, and whenever the law of Rome is interpreted, it will be remembered that many interpreted it more learnedly, but none so gloriously as Brutus. If, on the other hand, while a favorable wind bore the fleet on with swelling sails to its goal, Agamemnon had sent that messenger who fetched Iphigenia in order to be sacrificed; if Jephtha, without being bound by any vow which decided the fate of the nahon, had said to his daughter, "Bewail now thy virginity for the space of two months, for I will sacrifice thee"; if Brutus had had a righteous son and yet would have ordered the lictors to execute him–who would have understood them? If these three men had replied to the query why they did it by saying, "It is a trial in which we are tested," would people have understood them better? When Agamemnon, Jephtha, Brutus at the decisive moment heroically overcome their pain, have heroically lost the beloved and have merely to accomplish the outward sacrifice, then there never will be a noble soul in the world who will not shed tears of compassion for their pain and of admiration for their exploit. If, on the other hand, these three men at the decisive moment were to adjoin to their heroic conduct this little word, "But for all that it will not come to pass," who then would understand them? If as an explanation they added, "This we believe by virtue of the absurd," who would understand them better? For who would not easily understand that it was absurd, but who would understand that one could then believe it? The difference between the tragic hero and Abraham is clearly evident. The tragic hero still remains within the ethical. He lets one expression of the ethical find its telos in a higher expression of the ethical; the ethical relation between father and son, or daughter and father, he reduces to a sentiment which has its dialectic in its relation to the idea of morality. Here there can be no question of a teleological suspension of the ethical itself. With Abraham the situation was different. By his act he overstepped the ethical entirely and possessed a higher telos outside of it, in relation to which he suspended the former. For I should very much like to know how one would bring Abraham's act into relation with the universal, and whether it is possible to discover any connection whatever between what Abraham did and the universal ... except the fact that he transgressed it. It was not for the sake of saving a people, not to maintain the idea of the state, that Abraham did this, and not in order to reconcile angry deities. If there could be a question of the deity being angry, he was angry only with Abraham, and Abraham's whole action stands in no relation to the universal, is a purely private undertaking. Therefore, whereas the tragic hero is great by reason of his moral virtue, Abraham is great by reason of a purely personal virtue. In Abraham's life there is no higher expression for the ethical than this, that the father shall love his son. Of the ethical in the sense of morality there can be no question in this instance. In so far as the universal was present, it was indeed cryptically present in Isaac, hidden as it were in Isaac's loins, and must therefore cry out with Isaac's mouth, "Do it not! Thou art bringing everything to naught." Why then did Abraham do it? For God's sake, and (in complete identity with this) for his own sake. He did it for God's sake because God required this proof of his faith; for his own sake he did it in order that he might furnish the proof. The unity of these two points of view is perfectly expressed by the word which has always been used to characterize this situation: it is a trial, a temptation (Fristelse).47 A temptation—but what does that mean? What ordinarily tempts a man is that which would keep him from doing his duty, but in this case the temptation is itself the ethical ... which would keep him from doing God's will. But what then is duty? Duty is precisely the expression for God's will. Here is evident the necessity of a new category if one would understand Abraham. Such a relationship to the deity paganism did not know. The tragic hero does not enter into any private relationship with the deity, but for him the ethical is the divine, hence the paradox implied in his situation can be mediated in the universal. Abraham cannot be mediated, and the same thing can be expressed also by saying that he cannot talk. So soon as I talk I express the universal, and if I do not do so, no one can understand me. Therefore if Abraham would express himself in terms of the universal, he must say that his situation is a temptation (Anfechtung), for he has no higher expression for that universal which stands above the universal which he transgresses. Therefore, though Abraham arouses my admiration, he at the same time appalls me. He who denies himself and sacrifices himself for duty gives up the finite in order to grasp the infinite, and that man is secure enough. The tragic hero gives up the certain for the still more certain, and the eye of the beholder rests upon him confidently. But he who gives up the universal in order to grasp something still higher which is not the universal—what is he doing? Is it possible that this can be anything else but a temptation (Anfechtung)? And if it be possible ... but the individual was mistaken—what can save him? He suffers all the pain of the tragic hero, he brings to naught his joy in the world, he renounces everything ... and perhaps at the same instant debars himself from the sublime joy which to him was so precious that he would purchase it at any price. Him the beholder cannot understand nor let his eye rest confidently upon him. Perhaps it is not possible to do what the believer proposes, since it is indeed unthinkable. Or if it could be done, but if the individual had misunderstood the deity– what can save him? The tragic hero has need of tears and claims them, and where is the envious eye which would be so barren that it could not weep with Agamemnon; but where is the man with a soul so bewildered that he would have the presumption to weep for Abraham? The tragic hero accomplishes his act at a definite instant in time, but in the course of time he does something not less significant, he visits the man whose soul is beset with sorrow, whose breast for stifled sobs cannot draw breath, whose thoughts pregnant with tears weigh heavily upon him, to him he makes his appearance, dissolves the sorcery of sorrow, loosens his corslet, coaxes forth his tears by the fact that in his sufferings the sufferer forgets his own. One cannot weep over Abraham. One approaches him with a horror religiosus, as Israel approached Mount Sinai.–If then the solitary man who ascends Mount Moriah, which with its peak rises heaven-high above the plain of Aulis, if he be not a somnambulist who walks securely above the abyss while he who is stationed at the foot of the mountain and is looking on trembles with fear and out of reverence and dread dare not even call to him–if this man is disordered in his mind, if he had made a mistake! Thanks and thanks again to him who proffers to the man whom the sorrows of life have assaulted and left naked–proffers to him the figleaf of the word with which he can cover his wretchedness. Thanks be to thee, great Shakespeare, who art able to express everything, absolutely everything, precisely as it is–and yet why didst thou never pronounce this pang? Didst thou perhaps reserve it to thyself–like the loved one whose name one cannot endure that the world should mention? For the poet purchases the power of words, the power of uttering all the dread secrets of others, at the price of a little secret he is unable to utter … and a poet is not an apostle, he casts out devils only by the power of the devil. But now when the ethical is thus teleologically suspended, how does the individual exist in whom it is suspended? He exists as the particular in opposition to the universal. Does he then sin? For this is the form of sin, as seen in the idea. Just as the infant, though it does not sin, because it is not as such yet conscious of its existence, yet its existence is sin, as seen in the idea, and the ethical makes its demands upon it every instant. If one denies that this form can be repeated [in the adult] in such a way that it is not sin, then the sentence of condemnation is pronounced upon Abraham. How then did Abraham exist? He believed. This is the paradox which keeps him upon the sheer edge and which he cannot make clear to any other man, for the paradox is that he as the individual puts himself in an absolute relation to the absolute. Is he justified in doing this? His justification is once more the paradox; for if he is justified, it is not by virtue of anything universal, but by virtue of being the particular individual. How then does the individual assure himself that he is justified? It is easy enough to level down the whole of existence to the idea of the state or the idea of society. If one does this, one can also mediate easily enough, for then one does not encounter at all the paradox that the individual as the individual is higher than the universal–which I can aptly express also by the thesis of Pythagoras, that the uneven numbers are more perfect than the even. If in our age one occasionally hears a rejoinder which is pertinent to the paradox, it is likely to be to the following effect: "It is to be judged by the result." A hero who has become a skándalon48 to his contemporaries because they are conscious that he is a paradox who cannot make himself intelligible, will cry out defiantly to his generation, "The result will surely prove that I am justified." In our age we hear this cry rather seldom, for as our age, to its disadvantage, does not produce heroes, it has also the advantage of producing few caricatures. When in our age one hears this saying, "It is to be judged according to the result," a man is at once clear as to who it is he has the honor of talking with. Those who talk thus are a numerous tribe, whom I will denominate by the common name of Docents. 49 In their thoughts they live secure in existence, they have a solid position and sure prospects in a well-ordered state, they have centuries and even millenniums between them and the concussions of existence, they do not fear that such things could recur–for what would the police say to that! and the newspapers! Their lifework is to judge the great, and to judge them according to the result. Such behavior toward the great betrays a strange mixture of arrogance and misery: of arrogance because they think they are called to be judges; of misery because they do not feel that their lives are even in the remotest degree akin to the great. Surely a man who possesses even a little erectioris ingenii [of the higher way of thinking] has not become entirely a cold and clammy mollusk, and when he approaches what is great it can never escape his mind that from the creation of the world it has been customary for the result to come last, and that, if one would truly learn anything from great actions, one must pay attention precisely to the beginning. In case he who should act were to judge himself according to the result, he would never get to the point of beginning. Even though the result may give joy to the whole world, it cannot help the hero, for he would get to know the result only when the whole thing was over, and it was not by this he became a hero, but he was such for the fact that he began. Moreover, the result (inasmuch as it is the answer of finiteness to the infinite query) is in its dialectic entirely heterogeneous with the existence of the hero. Or is it possible to prove that Abraham was justified in assuming the position of the individual with relation to the universal ... for the fact that he got Isaac by miracle? If Abraham had actually sacrificed Isaac, would he then have been less justified? But people are curious about the result, as they are about the result in a book—they want to know nothing about dread, distress, the paradox. They flirt aesthetically with the result, it comes just as unexpectedly but also just as easily as a prize in the lottery; and when they have heard the result they are edified. And yet no robber of temples condemned to hard labor behind iron bars, is so base a criminal as the man who pillages the holy, and even Judas who sold his Master for thirty pieces of silver is not more despicable than the man who sells greatness. It is abhorrent to my soul to talk inhumanly about greatness, to let it loom darkly at a distance in an indefinite form, to make out that it is great without making the human character of it evident—wherewith it ceases to be great. For it is not what happens to me that makes me great, but it is what I do, and there is surely no one who thinks that a man became great because he won the great prize in the lottery. Even if a man were born in humble circumstances, I would require of him nevertheless that he should not be so inhuman toward himself as not to be able to think of the King's castle except at a remote distance, dreaming vaguely of its greatness and wanting at the same time to exalt it and also to abolish it by the fact that he exalted it meanly. I require of him that he should be man enough to step forward confidently and worthily even in that place. He should not be unmanly enough to desire impudently to offend everybody by rushing straight from the street into the King's hall. By that he loses more than the King. On the contrary, he should find joy in observing every rule of propriety with a glad and confident enthusiasm which will make him frank and fearless. This is only a symbol, for the difference here remarked upon is only a very imperfect expression for spiritual distance. I require of every man that he should not think so inhumanly of himself as not to dare to enter those palaces where not merely the memory of the elect abides but where the elect themselves abide. He should not press forward impudently and impute to them kinship with himself; on the contrary, he should be blissful every time he bows before them, but he should be frank and confident and always be something more than a charwoman, for if he will not be more, he will never gain entrance. And what will help him is precisely the dread and distress by which the great are tried, for otherwise, if he has a bit of pith in him, they will merely arouse his justified envy. And what distance alone makes great, what people would make great by empty and hollow phrases, that they themselves reduce to naught. Who was ever so great as that blessed woman, the Mother of God, the Virgin Mary? And yet how do we speak of her? We say that she was highly favored among women. And if it did not happen strangely that those who hear are able to think as inhumanly as those who talk, every young girl might well ask, "Why was not I too the highly favored?" And if I had nothing else to say, I would not dismiss such a question as stupid, for when it is a matter of favor, abstractly considered, everyone is equally entitled to it. What they leave out is the distress, the dread, the paradox. My thought is as pure as that of anyone, and the thought of the man who is able to think such things will surely become pure—and if this be not so, he may expect the dreadful; for he who once has evoked these images cannot be rid of them again, and if he sins against them, they avenge themselves with quiet wrath, more terrible than the vociferousness of ten ferocious reviewers. To be sure, Mary bore the child miraculously, but it came to pass with her after the manner of women, and that season is one of dread, distress and paradox. To be sure, the angel was a ministering spirit, but it was not a servile spirit which obliged her by saying to the other young maidens of Israel, "Despise not Mary. What befalls her is the extraordinary." But the Angel came only to Mary, and no one could understand her. After all, what woman was so mortified as Mary? And is it not true in this instance also that one whom God blesses He curses in the same breath? This is the spirit's interpretation of Mary, and she is not (as it shocks me to say, but shocks me still more to think that they have thoughtlessly and coquettishly interpreted her thus)—she is not a fine lady who sits in state and plays with an infant god. Nevertheless, when she says, "Behold the handmaid of the Lord"—then she is great, and I think it will not be found difficult to explain why she became the Mother of God. She has no need of worldly admiration, any more than Abraham has need of tears, for she was not a heroine, and he was not a hero, but both of them became greater than such, not at all because they were exempted from distress and torment and paradox, but they became great through these.50 It is great when the poet, presenting his tragic hero before the admiration of men, dares to say, "Weep for him, for he deserves it." For it is great to deserve the tears of those who are worthy to shed tears. It is great that the poet dares to hold the crowd in check, dares to castigate men, requiring that every man examine himself whether he be worthy to weep for the hero. For the waste-water of blubberers is a degradation of the holy.— But greater than all this it is that the knight of faith dares to say even to the noble man who would weep for him, "Weep not for me, but weep for thyself." One is deeply moved, one longs to be back in those beautiful times, a sweet yearning conducts one to the desired goal, to see Christ wandering in the promised land. One forgets the dread, the distress, the paradox. Was it so easy a matter not to be mistaken? Was it not dreadful that this man who walks among the others—was it not dreadful that He was God? Was it not dreadful to sit at table with Him? Was it so easy a matter to become an Apostle? But the result, eighteen hundred years—that is a help, it helps to the shabby deceit wherewith one deceives oneself and others. I do not feel the courage to wish to be contemporary with such events, but hence I do not judge severely those who were mistaken, nor think meanly of those who saw aright. I return, however, to Abraham. Before the result, either Abraham was every minute a murderer, or we are confronted by a paradox which is higher than all mediation. The story of Abraham contains therefore a teleological suspension of the ethical. As the individual he became higher than the universal. This is the paradox which does not permit of mediation. It is just as inexplicable how he got into it as it is inexplicable how he remained in it. If such is not the position of Abraham, then he is not even a tragic hero but a murderer. To want to continue to call him the father of faith, to talk of this to people who do not concern themselves with anything but words, is thoughtless. A man can become a tragic hero by his own powers—but not a knight of faith. When a man enters upon the way, in a certain sense the hard way of the tragic hero, many will be able to give him counsel; to him who follows the narrow way of faith no one can give counsel, him no one can understand. Faith is a miracle, and yet no man is excluded from it; for that in which all human life is unified is passion,* and faith is a passion. *Lessing has somewhere given expression to a similar thought from a purely aesthetic point of view. What he would show expressly in this passage is that sorrow too can find a witty expression. To this end he quotes a rejoinder of the unhappy English king, Edward II. In contrast to this he quotes from Diderot a story of a peasant woman and a rejoinder of hers. Then he continues: "That too was wit, and the wit of a peasant at that; but the situation made it inevitable. Consequently one must not seek to kind the excuse for the witty expressions of pain and of sorrow in the fact that the person who uttered them was a superior person, well educated, intelligent, and witty withal, for the passions make all men again equal—but the explanation is to be found in the fact that in all probability everyone would have said the same thing in the same situation. The thought of a peasant woman a queen could have had and must have had, just as what the king said in that instance a peasant too would have been able to say and doubtless would have said." Cf. Sämtliche Werke, XXX. p. 223.51 PROBLEM II Is there such a thing as an absolute duty toward God? The ethical is the universal, and as such it is again the divine. One has therefore a right to say that fundamentally every duty is a duty toward God; but if one cannot say more, then one affirms at the same time that properly I have no duty toward God. Duty becomes duty by being referred to God, but in duty itself I do not come into relation with God. Thus it is a duty to love one's neighbor, but in performing this duty I do not come into relation with God but with the neighbor whom I love. If I say then in this connection that it is my duty to love God, I am really uttering only a tautology, inasmuch as "God" is in this instance used in an entirely abstract sense as the divine, i.e. the universal, i.e. duty. So the whole existence of the human race is rounded off completely like a sphere, and the ethical is at once its limit and its content. God becomes an invisible vanishing point, a powerless thought, His power being only in the ethical which is the content of existence. If in any way it might occur to any man to want to love God in any other sense than that here indicated, he is romantic, he loves a phantom which, if it had merely the power of being able to speak, would say to him, "I do not require your love. Stay where you belong." If in any way it might occur to a man to want to love God otherwise, this love would be open to suspicion, like that of which Rousseau speaks, referring to people who love the Kaffirs instead of their neighbors. So in case what has been expounded here is correct, in case there is no incommensurability in a human life, and what there is of the incommensurable is only such by an accident from which no consequences can be drawn, in so far as existence is regarded in terms of the idea, Hegel is right; but he is not right in talking about faith or in allowing Abraham to be regarded as the father of it; for by the latter he has pronounced judgment both upon Abraham and upon faith. In the Hegelian philosophy52 das Äussere (die Entäusserung) is higher than das Innere. This is frequently illustrated by an example. The child is das Innere, the man das Äussere. Hence it is that the child is defined by the outward, and conversely, the man, as das Äussere, is defined precisely by das Innere. Faith, on the contrary, is the paradox that inwardness is higher than outwardness—or, to recall an expression used above, the uneven number is higher than the even. In the ethical way of regarding life it is therefore the task of the individual to divest himself of the inward determinants and express them in an outward way. Whenever he shrinks from this, whenever he is inclined to persist in or to slip back again into the inward determinants of feeling, mood, etc., he sins, he is in a temptation (Anfechtung). The paradox of faith is this, that there is an inwardness which is incommensurable for the outward, an inwardness, be it observed, which is not identical with the first but is a new inwardness. This must not be overlooked. Modern philosophy53 has permitted itself without further ado to substitute in place of "faith" the immediate. When one does that it is ridiculous to deny that faith has existed in all ages. In that way faith comes into rather simple company along with feeling, mood, idiosyncrasy, vapors, etc. To this extent philosophy may be right in saying that one ought not to stop there. But there is nothing to justify philosophy in using this phrase with regard to faith. Before faith there goes a movement of infinity, and only then, necopinate, 54 by virtue of the absurd, faith enters upon the scene. This I can well understand without maintaining on that account that I have faith. If faith is nothing but what philosophy makes it out to be, then Socrates already went further, much further, whereas the contrary is true, that he never reached it. In an intellectual respect he made the movement of infinity. His ignorance is infinite resignation. This task in itself is a match for human powers, even though people in our time disdain it; but only after it is done, only when the individual has evacuated himself in the infinite, only then is the point attained where faith can break forth. The paradox of faith is this, that the individual is higher than the universal, that the individual (to recall a dogmatic distinction now rather seldom heard) determines his relation to the universal by his relation to the absolute, not his relation to the absolute by his relation to the universal. The paradox can also be expressed by saying that there is an absolute duty toward God; for in this relationship of duty the individual as an individual stands related absolutely to the absolute. So when in this connection it is said that it is a duty to love God, something different is said from that in the foregoing; for if this duty is absolute, the ethical is reduced to a position of relativity. From this, however, it does not follow that the ethical is to be abolished, but it acquires an entirely different expression, the paradoxical expression—that, for example, love to God may cause the knight of faith to give his love to his neighbor the opposite expression to that which, ethically speaking, is required by duty. If such is not the case, then faith has no proper place in existence, then faith is a temptation (Anfechtung), and Abraham is lost, since he gave in to it. This paradox does not permit of mediation, for it is founded precisely upon the fact that the individual is only the individual. As soon as this individual [who is aware of a direct command from God] wishes to express his absolute duty in [terms of] the universal [i.e. the ethical, and] is sure of his duty in that [i.e. the universal or ethical precept], he recognizes that he is in temptation [i.e. a trial of faith], and, if in fact he resists [the direct indication of God's will], he ends by not fulfilling the absolute duty so called [i.e. what here has been called the absolute duty]; and, if he doesn't do this, [i.e. doesn't put up a resistance to the direct intimation of God's will], he sins, even though realiter his deed were that which it was his absolute duty to do.* *The translator has ventured to render this muddy sentence very liberally (though he has bracketed his explanatory additions), in order to bring out the meaning this sentence must have if it is to express the anguishing paradox of a "teleological suspension of the ethical." This is the meaning Niels Thulstrup gets out of it, and he tells me that this is the translation of Emanuel Hirsch. As S.K.'s sentence stands, without explanatory additions, it reminds me of a rigmarole I have often recited to the mystification of my hearers: "If a man were to signify, which he were not, if he had the power, which being denied him, he were to endeavor anyhow—merely because he don't, would you?"

Much as I love Kierkegaard, I sometimes hate him for keeping me awake at night. Only between sleeping and waking am I able to unravel some of his most complicated sentences. So what should Abraham do? If he would say to another person, "Isaac I love more dearly than everything in the world, and hence it is so hard for me to sacrifice him"; then surely the other would have shaken his head and said, "Why will you sacrifice him then?"—or if the other had been a sly fellow, he surely would have seen through Abraham and perceived that he was making a show of feelings which were in strident contradiction to his act. In the story of Abraham we find such a paradox. His relation to Isaac, ethically expressed, is this, that the father should love the son. This ethical relation is reduced to a relative position in contrast with the absolute relation to God. To the question, "Why?" Abraham has no answer except that it is a trial, a temptation (Fristelse)—terms which, as was remarked above, express the unity of the two points of view: that it is for God's sake and for his own sake. In common usage these two ways of regarding the matter are mutually exclusive. Thus when we see a man do something which does not comport with the universal, we say that he scarcely can be doing it for God's sake, and by that we imply that he does it for his own sake. The paradox of faith has lost the intermediate term, i.e. the universal. On the one side it has the expression for the extremest egoism (doing the dreadful thing it does for one's own sake); on the other side the expression for the most absolute self-sacrifice (doing it for God's sake). Faith itself cannot be mediated into the universal, for it would thereby be destroyed. Faith is this paradox, and the individual absolutely cannot make himself intelligible to anybody. People imagine maybe that the individual can make himself intelligible to another individual in the same case. Such a notion would be unthinkable if in our time people did not in so many ways seek to creep slyly into greatness. The one knight of faith can render no aid to the other. Either the individual becomes a knight of faith by assuming the burden of the paradox, or he never becomes one. In these regions partnership is unthinkable. Every more precise explication of what is to be understood by Isaac the individual can give only to himself. And even if one were able, generally speaking,55 to define ever so precisely what should be intended by Isaac (which moreover would be the most ludicrous self-contradiction, i.e. that the particular individual who definitely stands outside the universal is subsumed under universal categories precisely when he has to act as the individual who stands outside the universal), the individual nevertheless will never be able to assure himself by the aid of others that this application is appropriate, but he can do so only by himself as the individual. Hence even if a man were cowardly and paltry enough to wish to become a knight of faith on the responsibility of an outsider, he will never become one; for only the individual becomes a knight of faith as the particular individual, and this is the greatness of this knighthood, as I can well understand without entering the order, since I lack courage; but this is also its terror, as I can comprehend even better. In Luke 14:26, as everybody knows, there is a striking doctrine taught about the absolute duty toward God: "If any man cometh unto me and hateth not his own father and mother and wife and children and brethren and sisters, yea, and his own life also, he cannot be my disciple." This is a hard saying, who can bear to hear it? For this reason it is heard very seldom. This silence, however, is only an evasion which is of no avail. Nevertheless, the student of theology learns to know that these words occur in the New Testament, and in one or another exegetical aid56 he finds the explanation that miseîn in this passage and a few others is used in the sense of meísein, signifying minus diligo, posthabeo, non colo, nihili facio. However, the context in which these words occur does not seem to strengthen this tasteful explanation. In the verse immediately following there is a story about a man who desired to build a tower but first sat down to calculate whether he was capable of doing it, lest people might laugh at him afterwards. The close connection of this story with the verse here cited seems precisely to indicate that the words are to be taken in as terrible a sense as possible, to the end that everyone may examine himself as to whether he is able to erect the building. In case this pious and kindly exegete, who by abating the price thought he could smuggle Christianity into the world, were fortunate enough to convince a man that grammatically, linguistically and kat' a'nalogían [analogically] this was the meaning of that passage, it is to be hoped that the same moment he will be fortunate enough to convince the same man that Christianity is one of the most pitiable things in the world. For the doctrine which in one of its most lyrical outbursts, where the consciousness of its eternal validity swells in it most strongly, has nothing else to say but a noisy word which means nothing but only signifies that one is to be less kindly, less attentive, more indifferent; the doctrine which at the moment when it makes as if it would give utterance to the terrible ends by driveling instead of terrifying–that doctrine is not worth taking off my hat to. The words are terrible, yet I fully believe that one can understand them without implying that he who understands them has courage to do them. One must at all events be honest enough to acknowledge what stands written and to admit that it is great, even though one has not the courage for it. He who behaves thus will not find himself excluded from having part in that beautiful story which follows, for after all it contains consolation of a sort for the man who had not courage to begin the tower. But we must be honest, and not interpret this lack of courage as humility, since it is really pride, whereas the courage of faith is the only humble courage. One can easily perceive that if there is to be any sense in this passage, it must be understood literally. God it is who requires absolute love. But he who in demanding a person's love thinks that this love should be proved also by becoming lukewarm to everything which hitherto was dear–that man is not only an egoist but stupid as well, and he who would demand such love signs at the same moment his own death-warrant, supposing that his life was bound up with this coveted love. Thus a husband demands that his wife shall leave father and mother, but if he were to regard it as a proof of her extraordinary love for him that she for his sake became an indolent, lukewarm daughter etc., then he is the stupidest of the stupid. If he had any notion of what love is, he would wish to discover that as daughter and sister she was perfect in love, and would see therein the proof that she would love him more than anyone else in the realm. What therefore in the case of a man one would regard as a sign of egoism and stupidity, that one is to regard by the help of an exegete as a worthy conception of the Deity. But how hate them? I will not recall here the human distinction between loving and hating—not because I have much to object to in it (for after all it is passionate), but because it is egoistic and is not in place here. However, if I regard the problem as a paradox, then I understand it, that is, I understand it in such a way as one can understand a paradox. The absolute duty may cause one to do what ethics would forbid, but by no means can it cause the knight of faith to cease to love. This is shown by Abraham. The instant he is ready to sacrifice Isaac the ethical expression for what he does is this: he hates Isaac. But if he really hates Isaac, he can be sure that God does not require this, for Cain and Abraham are not identical. Isaac he must love with his whole soul; when God requires Isaac he must love him if possible even more dearly, and only on this condition can he sacrifice him; for in fact it is this love for Isaac which, by its paradoxical opposition to his love for God, makes his act a sacrifice. But the distress and dread in this paradox is that, humanly speaking, he is entirely unable to make himself intelligible. Only at the moment when his act is in absolute contradiction to his feeling is his act a sacrifice, but the reality of his act is the factor by which he belongs to the universal, and in that aspect he is and remains a murderer. Moreover, the passage in Luke must be understood in such a way as to make it clearly evident that the knight of faith has no higher expression of the universal (i.e. the ethical) by which he can save himself. Thus, for example, if we suppose that the Church requires such a sacrifice of one of its members, we have in this case only a tragic hero. For the idea of the Church is not qualitatively different from that of the State, in so far as the individual comes into it by a simple mediation, and in so far as the individual comes into the paradox he does not reach the idea of the Church; he does not come out of the paradox, but in it he must find either his blessedness or his perdition. Such an ecclesiastical hero expresses in his act the universal, and there will be no one in the Church—not even his father and mother etc.—who fails to understand him. On the other hand, he is not a knight of faith, and he has also a different answer from that of Abraham: he does not say that it is a trial or a temptation in which he is tested. People commonly refrain from quoting such a text as this in Luke. They are afraid of giving men a free rein, are afraid that the worst will happen as soon as the individual takes it into his head to comport himself as the individual. Moreover, they think that to exist as the individual is the easiest thing of all, and that therefore people have to be compelled to become the universal. I cannot share either this fear or this opinion, and both for the same reason. He who has learned that to exist as the individual is the most terrible thing of all will not be fearful of saying that it is great, but then too he will say this in such a way that his words will scarcely be a snare for the bewildered man, but rather will help him into the universal, even though his words do to some extent make room for the great. The man who does not dare to mention such texts will not dare to mention Abraham either, and his notion that it is easy enough to exist as the individual implies a very suspicious admission with regard to himself; for he who has a real respect for himself and concern for his soul is convinced that the man who lives under his own supervision, alone in the whole world, lives more strictly and more secluded than a maiden in her lady's bower. That there may be some who need compulsion, some who, if they were free-footed, would riot in selfish pleasures like unruly beasts, is doubtless true; but a man must prove precisely that he is not of this number by the fact that he knows how to speak with dread and trembling; and out of reverence for the great one is bound to speak, lest it be forgotten for fear of the ill effect, which surely will fail to eventuate when a man talks in such a way that one knows it for the great, knows its terror—and apart from the terror one does not know the great at all. Let us consider a little more closely the distress and dread in the paradox of faith. The tragic hero renounces himself in order to express the universal, the knight of faith renounces the universal in order to become the individual. As has been said, everything depends upon how one is placed. He who believes that it is easy enough to be the individual can always be sure that he is not a knight of faith, for vagabonds and roving geniuses are not men of faith. The knight of faith knows, on the other hand, that it is glorious to belong to the universal. He knows that it is beautiful and salutary to be the individual who translates himself into the universal, who edits as it were a pure and elegant edition of himself, as free from errors as possible and which everyone can read. He knows that it is refreshing to become intelligible to oneself in the universal so that he understands it and so that every individual who understands him understands through him in turn the universal, and both rejoice in the security of the universal. He knows that it is beautiful to be born as the individual who has the universal as his home, his friendly abiding-place, which at once welcomes him with open arms when he would tarry in it. But he knows also that higher than this there winds a solitary path, narrow and steep; he knows that it is terrible to be born outside the universal, to walk without meeting a single traveller. He knows very well where he is and how he is related to men. Humanly speaking, he is crazy and cannot make himself intelligible to anyone. And yet it is the mildest expression, to say that he is crazy. If he is not supposed to be that, then he is a hypocrite, and the higher he climbs on this path, the more dreadful a hypocrite he is. The knight of faith knows that to give up oneself for the universal inspires enthusiasm, and that it requires courage, but he also knows that security is to be found in this, precisely because it is for the universal. He knows that it is glorious to be understood by every noble mind, so glorious that the beholder is ennobled by it, and he feels as if he were bound; he could wish it were this task that had been allotted to him. Thus Abraham could surely have wished now and then that the task were to love Isaac as becomes a father, in a way intelligible to all, memorable throughout all ages; he could wish that the task were to sacrifice Isaac for the universal, that he might incite the fathers to illustrious deeds—and he is almost terrified by the thought that for him such wishes are only temptations and must be dealt with as such, for he knows that it is a solitary path he treads and that he accomplishes nothing for the universal but only himself is tried and examined. Or what did Abraham accomplish for the universal? Let me speak humanly about it, quite humanly. He spent seventy years in getting a son of his old age. What other men get quickly enough and enjoy for a long time he spent seventy years in accomplishing. And why? Because he was tried and put to the test. Is not that crazy? But Abraham believed, and Sarah wavered and got him to take Hagar as a concubine—but therefore he also had to drive her away. He gets Isaac, then he has to be tried again. He knew that it is glorious to express the universal, glorious to live with Isaac. But this is not the task. He knew that it is a kingly thing to sacrifice such a son for the universal, he himself would have found repose in that, and all would have reposed in the commendation of his deed, as a vowel reposes in its consonant,57 but that is not the task—he is tried. That Roman general who is celebrated by his name of Cunctator58 checked the foe by procrastination—but what a procrastinator Abraham is in comparison with him! ... yet he did not save the state. This is the content of one hundred and thirty years. Who can bear it? Would not his contemporary age, if we can speak of such a thing, have said of him, "Abraham is eternally procrastinating. Finally he gets a son. That took long enough. Now he wants to sacrifice him. So is he not mad? And if at least he could explain why he wants to do it—but he always says that it is a trial." Nor could Abraham explain more, for his life is like a book placed under a divine attachment and which never becomes publici juris. 59 This is the terrible thing. He who does not see it can always be sure that he is no knight of faith, but he who sees it will not deny that even the most tried of tragic heroes walks with a dancing step compared with the knight of faith, who comes slowly creeping forward. And if he has perceived this and assured himself that he has not courage to understand it, he will at least have a presentiment of the marvellous glory this knight attains in the fact that he becomes God's intimate acquaintance, the Lord's friend, and (to speak quite humanly) that he says "Thou" to God in heaven, whereas even the tragic hero only addresses Him in the third person. The tragic hero is soon ready and has soon finished the fight, he makes the infinite movement and then is secure in the universal. The knight of faith, on the other hand, is kept sleepless, for he is constantly tried, and every instant there is the possibility of being able to return repentantly to

the universal, and this possibility can just as well be a temptation as the truth. He can derive evidence from no man which it is, for with that query he is outside the paradox. So the knight of faith has first and foremost the requisite passion to concentrate upon a single factor the whole of the ethical which he transgresses, so that he can give himself the assurance that he really loves Isaac with his whole soul.*
*I would elucidate yet once more the difference between the collisions which are encountered by the tragic hero and by the knight of faith. The tragic hero assures himself that the ethical obligation [i.e., the lower ethical obligation, which he puts aside for the higher in the present case, accordingly, it is the obligation to spare his daughter's life] is totally present in him by the fact that he transforms it into a wish. Thus Agamemnon can say, "The proof that I do not offend against my parental duty is that my duty is my only wish." So here we have wish and duty face to face with one another. The fortunate chance in life is that the two correspond, that my wish is my duty and vice versa, and the task of most men in life is precisely to remain within their duty and by their enthusiasm to transform it into their wish. The tragic hero gives up his wish in order to accomplish his duty. For the knight of faith wish and duty are also identical, but he is required to give up both. Therefore when he would resign himself to giving up his wish he does not find repose, for that is after all his duty. If he would remain within his duty and his wish he is not a knight of faith, for the absolute duty requires precisely that he should give them up. The tragic hero apprehended a higher expression of duty but not an absolute duty. If he cannot do that, he is in temptation (Anfechtung). In the next place, he has enough passion to make this assurance available in the twinkling of an eye and in such a way that it is as completely valid as it was in the first instance. If he is unable to do this, he can never budge from the spot, for he constantly has to begin all over again. The tragic hero also concentrated in one factor the ethical which he teleologically surpassed, but in this respect he had support in the universal. The knight of faith has only himself alone, and this constitutes the dreadfulness of the situation. Most men live in such a way under an ethical obligation that they can let the sorrow

be sufficient for the day, but they never reach this passionate concentration, this energetic consciousness. The universal may in a certain sense help the tragic hero to attain this, but the knight of faith is left all to himself. The hero does the deed and finds repose in the universal, the knight of faith is kept in constant tension. Agamemnon gives up Iphigenia and thereby has found repose in the universal, then he takes the step of sacrificing her. If Agamemnon does not make the infinite movement, if his soul at the decisive instant, instead of having passionate concentration, is absorbed by the common twaddle that he had several daughters and vielleicht [perhaps] the Ausserordentliche [extraordinary] might occur– then he is of course not a hero but a hospital-case. The hero's concentration Abraham also has, even though in his case it is far more difficult, since he has no support in the universal; but he makes one more movement by which he concentrates his soul upon the miracle. If Abraham did not do that, he is only an Agamemnon–if in any way it is possible to explain how he can be justified in sacrificing Isaac when thereby no profit accrues to the universal. Whether the individual is in temptation (Anfechtung) or is a knight of faith only the individual can decide. Nevertheless it is possible to construct from the paradox several criteria which he too can understand who is not within the paradox. The true knight of faith is always absolute isolation, the false knight is sectarian. This sectarianism is an attempt to leap away from the narrow path of the paradox and become a tragic hero at a cheap price. The tragic hero expresses the universal and sacrifices himself for it. The sectarian punchinello, instead of that, has a private theatre, i.e. several good friends and comrades who represent the universal just about as well as the beadles in The Golden Snuffbox60 represent justice. The knight of faith, on the contrary, is the paradox, is the individual, absolutely nothing but the individual, without connections or pretensions. This is the terrible thing which the sectarian manikin cannot endure. For instead of learning from this terror that he is not capable of performing the great deed and then plainly admitting it (an act which I cannot but approve, because it is what I do) the manikin thinks that by uniting with several other manikins he will be able to do it. But that is quite out of the question. In the world of spirit no swindling is tolerated. A dozen sectaries join arms with one another, they know nothing whatever of the lonely temptations which await the knight of faith and which he dares not shun precisely because it would be still more dreadful if he were to press forward presumptuously. The sectaries deafen one another by their noise and racket, hold the dread off by their shrieks, and such a hallooing company of sportsmen think they are storming heaven and think they are on the same path as the kight of faith who in the solitude of the universe never hears any human voice but walks alone with his dreadful responsibility. The knight of faith is obliged to rely upon himself alone, he feels the pain of not being able to make himself intelligible to others, but he feels no vain desire to guide others. The pain is his assurance that he is in the right way, this vain desire he does not know, he is too serious for that. The false knight of faith readily betrays himself by this proficiency in guiding which he has acquired in an instant. He does not comprehend what it is all about, that if another individual is to take the same path, he must become entirely in the same way the individual and have no need of any man's guidance, least of all the guidance of a man who would obtrude himself. At this point men leap aside, they cannot bear the martyrdom of being uncomprehended, and instead of this they choose conveniently enough the worldly admiration of their proficiency. The true knight of faith is a witness, never a teacher, and therein lies his deep humanity, which is worth a good deal more than this silly participation in others' weal and woe which is honored by the name of sympathy, whereas in fact it is nothing but vanity. He who would only be a witness thereby avows that no man, not even the lowliest, needs another man's sympathy or should be abased that another may be exalted. But since he did not win what he won at a cheap price, neither does he sell it out at a cheap price, he is not petty enough to take men's admiration and give them in return his silent contempt, he knows that what is truly great is equally accessible to all. Either there is an absolute duty toward God, and if so it is the paradox here described, that the individual as the individual is higher than the universal and as the individual stands in an absolute relation to the absolute/or else faith never existed, because it has always existed, or, to put it differently, Abraham is lost, or one must explain the passage in the fourteenth chapter of Luke as did that tasteful exegete, and explain in the same way the corresponding passages and similar ones.61 PROBLEM III Was Abraham ethically defensible in keeping silent about his purpose before Sarah, before Eleazar, before Isaac? The ethical as such is the universal, again, as the universal it is the manifest, the revealed. The individual regarded as he is immediately, that is, as a physical and psychical being, is the hidden, the concealed. So his ethical task is to develop out of this concealment and to reveal himself in the universal. Hence whenever he wills to remain in concealment he sins and lies in temptation (Anfechtung), out of which he can come only by revealing himself. With this we are back again at the same point. If there is not a concealment which has its ground in the fact that the individual as the individual is higher than the universal, then Abraham's conduct is indefensible, for he paid no heed to the intermediate ethical determinants. If on the other hand there is such a concealment, we are in the presence of the paradox which cannot be mediated inasmuch as it rests upon the consideration that the individual as the individual is higher than the universal, but it is the universal precisely which is mediation. The Hegelian philosophy holds that there is no justified concealment, no justified incommensurability. So it is self-consistent when it requires revelation, but it is not warranted in regarding Abraham as the father of faith and in talking about faith. For faith is not the first immediacy but a subsequent immediacy. The first immediacy is the aesthetical, and about this the Hegelian philosophy may be in the right. But faith is not the aesthetical—or else faith has never existed because it has always existed. It will be best to regard the whole matter from a purely aesthetical point of view, and with that intent to embark upon an aesthetic deliberation, to which I beg the reader to abandon himself completely for the moment, while I, to contribute my share, will modify my presentation in conformity with the subject. The category I would consider a little more closely is the interesting, a category which especially in our age (precisely because our age lives in discrimine rerum) [at a turning point in history] has acquired great importance, for it is properly the category of the turning-point. Therefore we, after having loved this category pro virili [with all our power], should not scorn it as some do because we have outgrown it, but neither should we be too greedy to attain it, for certain it is that to be interesting or to have an interesting life is not a task for industrial art but a fateful privilege, which like every privilege in the world of spirit is bought only by deep pain. Thus, for example, Socrates was the most interesting man that ever lived, his life the most interesting that has been recorded, but this existence was allotted to him by the Deity, and in so far as he himself had to acquire it he was not unacquainted with trouble and pain. To take such a life in vain does not beseem a man who takes life seriously, and yet it is not rare to see in our age examples of such an endeavor. Moreover the interesting is a border-category, a boundary between aesthetics and ethics. For this reason our deliberation must constantly glance over into the field of ethics, while in order to be able to acquire significance it must grasp the problem with aesthetic intensity and concupiscence. With such matters ethics seldom deals in our age. The reason is supposed to be that there is no appropriate place for it in the System. Then surely one might do it in a monograph, and moreover, if one would not do it prolixly, one might do it briefly and yet attain the same end–if, that is to say, a man has the predicate in his power, for one or two predicates can betray a whole world. Might there not be some place in the System for a little word like the predicate? In his immortal Poetics (Chapter 11) Aristotle says,62 dúo mèn oûn toû múqou mérh perì taût' e'stí, peripéteia kaì a'nagnw'risiv. I am of course concerned here only with the second factor, a'nagnw'risiv, recognition. Where there can be question of a recognition there is implied eo ipso a previous concealment. So just as recognition is the relieving, the relaxing factor in the dramatic life, so is concealment the factor of tension. What Aristotle has to say in the same chapter about the merits of tragedy which are variously appraised in proportion as peripéteia and a'nagnw'risiv impinge63 upon one another, and also what he says about the "individual" and the "double recognition," I cannot take into consideration here, although by its inwardness and quiet concentration what he says is peculiarly tempting to one who is weary of the superficial omniscience of encyclopedic scholars. A more general observation may be appropriate here. In Greek tragedy concealment (and consequently recognition) is an epic survival grounded upon a fate in which the dramatic action disappears from view and from which it derives its obscure and enigmatic origin. Hence it is that the effect produced by a Greek tragedy is like the impression of a marble statue which lacks the power of the eye. Greek tragedy is blind. Hence a certain abstraction is necessary in order to appreciate it properly. A son64 murders his father, but only afterwards does he learn that it was his father. A sister65 wants to sacrifice her brother, but at the decisive moment she learns who he is. This dramatic motive is not so apt to interest our reflective age. Modern drama has given up fate, has emancipated itself dramatically, sees with its eyes, scrutinizes itself, resolves fate in its dramatic consciousness. Concealment and revelation are in this case the hero's free act for which he is responsible. Recognition and concealment are also present as an essential element in modern drama. To adduce examples of this would be too prolix. I am courteous enough to assume that everybody in our age, which is so aesthetically wanton, so potent and so enflamed that the act of conception comes as easy to it as to the partridge hen, which, according to Aristotle's affirmation,66 needs only to hear the voice of the cock or the sound of its flight overhead— I assume that everyone, merely upon hearing the word "concealment" will be able to shake half a score of romances and comedies out of his sleeve. Wherefore I express myself briefly and so will throw out at once a general observation. In case one who plays hide and seek (and thereby introduces into the play the dramatic ferment) hides something nonsensical, we get a comedy; if on the other hand he stands in relation to the idea, he may come near being a tragic hero. I give here merely an example of the comic. A man rouges his face and wears a periwig. The same man is eager to try his fortune with the fair sex, he is perfectly sure of conquering by the aid of the rouge and the periwig which make him absolutely irresistible. He captures a girl and is at the acme of happiness. Now comes the gist of the matter: if he is able to admit this embellishment, he does not lose all of his infatuating power; when he reveals himself as a plain ordinary man, and bald at that, he does not thereby lose the loved one.–Concealment is his free act, for which aesthetics also holds him responsible. This science is no friend of bald hypocrites, it abandons him to the mercy of laughter. This must suffice as a mere hint of what I mean–the comical cannot be a subject of interest for this investigation. It is incumbent upon me to examine dialectically the part played by concealment in aesthetics and ethics, for the point is to show the absolute difference between the aesthetic concealment and the paradox. A couple of examples. A girl is secretly in love with a man, although they have not definitely avowed their love to one another. Her parents compel her to marry another (there may be moreover a consideration of filial piety which determines her), she obeys her parents, she conceals her love, "so as not to make the other unhappy, and no one will ever know what she suffers."–A young man is able by a single word to get possession of the object of his longings and his restless dreams. This little word, however, will compromise, yea, perhaps (who knows?) bring to ruin a whole family, he resolves magnanimously to remain in his concealment, "the girl shall never get to know it, so that she may perhaps become happy by giving her hand to another." What a pity that these two persons, both of whom were concealed from their respective beloveds, were also concealed from one another, otherwise a remarkable higher unity might have been brought about.–Their concealment is a free act, for which they are responsible also to aesthetics. Aesthetics, however, is a courteous and sentimental science which knows of more expedients than a pawnbroker. So what does it do? It makes everything possible for the lovers. By the help of a chance the partners to the projected marriage get a hint of the magnanimous resolution of the other part, it comes to an explanation, they get one another and at the same time attain rank with real heroes. For in spite of the fact that they did not even get time to sleep over their resolution, aesthetics treats them nevertheless as if they had courageously fought for their resolution during many years. For aesthetics does not trouble itself greatly about time, whether in jest or seriousness time flies equally fast for it. But ethics knows nothing about that chance or about that sentimentality, nor has it so speedy a concept of time. Thereby the matter receives a different aspect. It is no good arguing with ethics for it has pure categories. It does not appeal to experience, which of all ludicrous things is the most ludicrous, and which so far from making a man wise rather makes him mad if he knows nothing higher than this. Ethics has in its possession no chance, and so matters do not come to an explanation, it does not jest with dignities, it lays a prodigious responsibility upon the shoulders of the puny hero, it denounces as presumption his wanting to play providence by his actions, but it also denounces him for wanting to do it by his suffering. It bids a man believe in reality and have courage to fight against all the afflictions of reality, and still more against the bloodless sufferings he has assumed on his own responsibility. It warns against believing the calculations of the understanding, which are more perfidious than the oracles of ancient times. It warns agtunst every untimely magnanimity. Let reality decide—then is the time to show courage, but then ethics itself offers all possible assistance. If, however, there was something deeper which moved in these two, if there was seriousness to see the task, seriousness to commence it, then something will come of them; but ethics cannot help, it is offended, for they keep a secret from it, a secret they hold at their own peril. So aesthetics required concealment and rewarded it, ethics required revelation and punished concealment. At times, however, even aesthetics requires revelation. When the hero ensnared in the aesthetic illusion thinks by his silence to save another man, then it requires silence and rewards it. On the other hand, when the hero by his action intervenes disturbingly in another man's life, then it requires revelation. I am now on the subject of the tragic hero. I would consider for a moment Euripides' Iphigenia in Aulis. Agamemnon must sacrifice Iphigenia. Now aesthetics requires silence of Agamemnon inasmuch as it would be unworthy of the hero to seek comfort from any other man, and out of solicitude for the women too he ought to conceal this from them as long as possible. On the other hand, the hero, precisely in order to be a hero, must be tried by dreadful temptations which the tears of Clytemnestra and Iphigenia provide for him. What does aesthetics do? It has an expedient, it has in readiness an old servant who reveals everything to Clytemnestra. Then all is as it should be. Ethics, however, has at hand no chance and no old servant. The aesthetical idea contradicts itself as soon as it must be carried out in reality. Hence ethics requires revelation. The tragic hero displays his ethical courage precisely by the fact that it is he who, without being ensnared in any aesthetic illusion, himself announces to Iphigenia her fate. If the tragic hero does this, then he is the beloved son of ethics in whom it is well pleased. If he keeps silent, it may be because he thinks thereby to make it easier for others, but it may also be because thereby he makes it easier for himself. However, he knows that he is not influenced by this latter motive. If he keeps silent, he assumes as the individual a serious responsibility inasmuch as he ignores an argument which may come from without. As a tragic hero he cannot do this, for ethics loves him precisely because he constantly expresses the universal. His heroic action demands courage, but it belongs to this courage that he shall shun no argumentation. Now it is certain that tears are a dreadful argumentum ad hominem, and doubtless there are those who are moved by nothing yet are touched by tears. In the play Iphigenia had leave to weep, really she ought to have been allowed like Jephthah's daughter two months for weeping, not in solitude but at her father's feet, allowed to employ all her art "which is but tears," and to twine about his knees instead of presenting the olive branch of the suppliant. Aesthetics required revelation but helped itself out by a chance; ethics required revelation and found in the tragic hero its satisfaction. In spite of the severity with which ethics requires revelation, it cannot be denied that secrecy and silence really make a man great precisely because they are characteristics of inwardness. When Amor leaves Psyche he says to her, "Thou shalt give birth to a child which will be a divine infant if thou dost keep silence, but a human being if thou dost reveal the secret." The tragic hero who is the favorite of ethics is the purely human, and him I can understand, and all he does is in the light of the revealed. If I go further, then I stumble upon the paradox, either the divine or the demoniac, for silence is both. Silence is the snare of the demon, and the more one keeps silent, the more terrifying the demon becomes; but silence is also the mutual understanding between the Deity and the individual. Before going on to the story of Abraham, however, I would call before the curtain several poetic personages. By the power of dialectic I keep them upon tiptoe, and by wielding over them the scourge of despair I shall surely keep them from standing still, in order that in their dread they may reveal one thing and another.* *These movements and attitudes might well be a subject for further aesthetic treatment. However, I leave it undecided to what extent faith and the whole life of faith might be a fit subject for such treatment. Only, because it is always a joy to me to thank him to whom I am indebted, I would thank Lessing for some hints of a Christian drama which is found in his Hamburgische Dramaturgie. 69 He, however, fixed his glance upon the purely divine side of the Christian life (the consummated victory) and hence he had misgivings; perhaps he would have expressed a different judgment if he had paid more attention to the purely human side (theologia viatorum).70 Doubtless what he says is very brief, in part evasive, but since I am always glad to have the company of Lessing, I seize it at once. Lessing was not merely one of the most comprehensive minds Germany has had, he not only was possessed of rare exactitude in his learning (for which reason one can securely rely upon him and upon his autopsy without fear of being duped by inaccurate quotations which can be traced nowhere, by half-understood phrases which are drawn from untrustworthy compendiums, or to be disoriented by a foolish trumpeting of novelties which the ancients have expounded far better) but he possessed at the same time an exceedingly uncommon gift of explaining what he himself had understood. There he stopped. In our age people go further and explain more than they have understood. In his Poetics67 Aristotle relates a story of a political disturbance at Delphi which was provoked by a question of marriage. The bridegroom, when the augurs68 foretell to him that a misfortune would follow his marriage, suddenly changes his plan at the decisive moment when he comes to fetch the bride—he will not celebrate the wedding. I have no need of more.* *According to Aristotle the historic catastrophe was as follows. To avenge themselves the family of the bride introduced a temple-vessel among his household goods, and he is sentenced as a temple-robber. This, however, is of no consequence, for the question is not whether the family is shrewd or stupid in taking revenge. The family has an ideal significance only in so far as it is drawn into the dialectic of the hero. Besides it is fateful enough that he, when he would shun danger by not marrying, plunges into it, and also that his life comes into contact with the divine in a double way: first by the saying of the augurs, and then by being condemned for sacrilege. In Delphi this event hardly passed without tears; if a poet were to have adopted it as his theme, he might have dared to count very surely upon sympathy. Is it not dreadful that love, which in human life often enough was cast into exile, is now deprived of the support of heaven? Is not the old proverb that "marriages are made in heaven" here put to shame? Usually it is all the afflictions and difficulties of the finite which like evil spirits separate the lovers, but love has heaven on its side, and therefore this holy alliance overcomes all enemies. In this case it is heaven itself which separates what heaven itself has joined together. And who would have guessed such a thing? The young bride least of all. Only a moment before she was sitting in her chamber in all her beauty, and the lovely maidens had conscientiously adorned her so that they could justify before all the world what they had done, so that they not merely derived joy from it but envy, yea, joy for the fact that it was not possible for them to become more envious, because it was not possible for her to become more beautiful. She sat alone in her chamber and was transformed from beauty unto beauty, for every means was employed that feminine art was capable of to adorn worthily the worthy. But there still was lacking something which the young maidens had not dreamed of: a veil finer, lighter and yet more impenetrable than that in which the young maidens had enveloped her, a bridal dress which no young maiden knew of or could help her to obtain, yea, even the bride herself did not know how to obtain it. It was an invisible, a friendly power, taking pleasure in adorning a bride, which enveloped her in it without her knowledge; for she saw only how the bridegroom passed by and went up to the temple. She saw the door shut behind him, and she became even more calm and blissful, for she only knew that he now belonged to her more than ever. The door of the temple opened, he stepped out, but maidenly she cast down her eyes and therefore did not see that his countenance was troubled, but he saw that heaven was jealous of the bride's loveliness and of his good fortune. The door of the temple opened, and the young maidens saw the bridegroom step out, but they did not see that his countenance was troubled, they were busy fetching the bride. Then forth she stepped in all her maidenly modesty and yet like a queen surrounded by her maids of honor, who bowed before her as the young maiden always bows before a bride. Thus she stood at the head of her lovely band and waited–it was only an instant, for the temple was near at hand–and the bridegroom came … but he passed by her door. But here I break off–I am not a poet, I go about things only dialectically. It must be remembered first of all that it is at the decisive instant the hero gets this elucidation, so he is pure and blameless, has not light-mindedly tied himself to the fiancée. In the next place, he has a divine utterance for him, or rather against him,71 he is therefore not guided like those puny lovers by his own conceit. Moreover, it goes without saying that this utterance makes him just as unhappy as the bride, yea, a little more so, since he after all is the occasion of her unhappiness. It is true enough that the augurs only foretold a misfortune to him, but the question is whether this misfortune is not of such a sort that in injuring him it would also affect injuriously their conjugal happiness. What then is he to do? (1) Shall he preserve silence and celebrate the wedding?–with the thought that "perhaps the misfortune will not come at once, at any rate I have upheld love and have not feared to make myself unhappy. But keep silent I must, for otherwise even the short moment is wasted." This seems plausible, but it is not so by any means, for in doing this he has insulted the girl. He has in a way made the girl guilty by his silence, for in case she had known the truth she never would have consented to such a union. So in the hour of need he would not only have to bear the misfortune but also the responsibility for having kept silent and her justified indignation that he had kept silent. Or (2) shall he keep silent and give up celebrating the wedding? In this case he must embroil himself in a mystifictition by which he reduces himself to naught in relation to her. Aesthetics would perhaps approve of this. The catastrophe might then be fashioned like that of the real story, except that at the last instant an explanation would be forthcoming—however, that would be after it was all over, since aesthetically viewed it is a necessity to let him die ... unless this science should see its way to annul the fateful prophecy. Still, this behavior, magnanimous as it is, implies an offense against the girl and against the reality of her love. Or (3) shall he speak? One of course must not forget that our hero is a little too poetical for us to suppose that to sign away his love might not have for him a significance very different from the result of an unsuccessful business speculation. If he speaks, the whole thing becomes a story of unhappy love in the style of Axel and Valborg.* *Moreover, from this point one might conduct the dialectical movements in another direction. Heaven foretells a misfortune consequent upon his marriage, so in fact he might give up the wedding but not for this reason give up the girl, rather live with her in a romantic union which for the lovers would be more than satisfactory. This implies, however, an offense against the girl because in his love for her he does not express the universal. However, this would be a theme both for a poet and for an ethicist who would defend marriage. On the whole, if poetry were to pay attention to the religious and to the inwardness of personalities, it would find themes of far greater importance than those with which it now busies itself. In poetry one hears again and again this story: a man is bound to a girl whom he once loved—or perhaps never sincerely loved, for now he has seen another girl who is the ideal. A man makes a mistake in life, it was in the right street but it was in the wrong house, for opposite, on the second floor, dwells the ideal—this people think a theme for poetry. A lover has made a mistake, he saw his fiancée by lamplight and thought she had dark hair, but, lo, on closer inspection she is blonde—but her sister, she is the ideal! This they think is a theme for poetry! My opinion is that every such man is a lout who may be intolerable enough in real life but ought instantly to be hissed off the stage when he would give himself airs in poetry. Only passion against passion provides a poetic collision, not the rumpus of these particulars within the same passion. If, for example, a girl in the Middle Ages, after having fallen in love, convinces herself that all earthly love is a sin and prefers a heavenly, here is a poetic collision, and the girl is poetic, for her life is in the idea. This is a pair which heaven itself separates.72 However, in the present case the separation is to be conceived somewhat differently since it results at the same time from the free act of the individuals. What is so very difficult in the dialectic of this case is that the misfortune is to fall only upon him. So the two lovers do not find like Axel and Valborg a common expression for their suffering, inasmuch as heaven levels its decree equally against Axel and Valborg because they are equally near of kin to one another. If this were the case here, a way out would be thinkable. For since heaven does not employ any visible power to separate them but leaves this to them, it is thinkable that they might resolve between them to defy heaven and its misfortune too. Ethics, however, will require him to speak. His heroism then is essentially to be found in the fact that he gives up aesthetic magnanimity, which in this case, however, could not easily be thought to have any admixture of the vanity which consists in being hidden, for it must indeed be clear to him that he makes the girl unhappy. The reality of this heroism depends, however, upon the fact that he had had his opportunity [for a genuine love] and annulled it; for if such heroism could be acquired without this, we should have plenty of heroes in our age, in our age which has attained an unparalleled proficiency in forgery and does the highest things by leaping over the intermediate steps. But then why this sketch, since I get no further after all than the tragic hero? Well, because it is at least possible that it might throw light upon the paradox. Everything depends upon how this man stands related to the utterance of the augurs which is in one way or another decisive for his life. Is this utterance publici juris, or is it a privatissimum? The scene is laid in Greece, the utterance of the augur is intelligible to all. I do not mean merely that the ordinary man is able to understand its content lexically, but that the ordinary man can understand that an augur announces to the individual the decision of heaven. So the utterance of the augur is not intelligible only to the hero but to all, and no private relationship to the deity results from it. Do what he will, that which is foretold will come to pass, and neither by doing nor by leaving undone does he come into closer relationship with the deity, or become either the object of its grace or of its wrath. The result foretold is a thing which any ordinary man will be just as well able as the hero to understand, and there is no secret writing which is legible to the hero only. Inasmuch as he would speak, he can do so perfectly well, for he is able to make himself intelligible; inasmuch as he would keep silent, it is because by virtue of being the individual he would be higher than the universal, would delude himself with all sorts of fantastic notions about how she will soon forget the sorrow, etc. On the other hand, in case the will of heaven had not been announced to him by an augur, in case it had come to his knowledge in an entirely private way, in case it had put itself into an entirely private relationship with him, then we encounter the paradox (supposing there is such a thing–for my reflection takes the form of a dilemma), then he could not speak, however much he might wish to.73 He did not then enjoy himself in the silence but suffered pain–but this precisely was to him the assurance that he was justified. So the reason for his silence is not that he as the individual would place himself in an absolute relation to the universal, but that he as the individual was placed in an absolute relation to the absolute. In this then he would also be able to find repose (as well as I am able to figure it to myself), whereas his magnanimous silence would constantly have been disquieted by the requirements of the ethical. It is very much to be desired that aesthetics would for once essay to begin at the point where for so many years it has ended, with the illusory magnanimity. Once it were to do this it would work directly in the interest of the religious, for religion is the only power which can deliver the aesthetical out of its conflict with the ethical. Queen

Elizabeth74 sacrificed to the State her love for Essex by signing his death-warrant. This was a heroic act, even if there was involved a little personal grievance for the fact that he had not sent her the ring. He had in fact sent it, as we know, but it was kept back by the malice of a lady of the court. Elizabeth received intelligence of this (so it is related, ni fallor), thereupon she sat for ten days with one finger in her mouth and bit it without saying a word, and thereupon she died. This would be a theme for a poet who knew how to wrench the mouth open—without this condition it is at the most serviceable to a conductor of the ballet, with whom in our time the poet too often confuses himself. I will follow this with a sketch which involves the demoniacal. The legend of Agnes and the Merman will serve my purpose. The merman is a seducer who shoots up from his hiding-place in the abyss, with wild lust grasps and breaks the innocent flower which stood in all its grace on the seashore and pensively inclined its head to listen to the howling of the ocean. This is what the poets hitherto have meant by it. Let us make an alteration. The merman was a seducer. He had called to Agnes, had by his smooth speech enticed from her the hidden sentiments, she has found in the merman what she sought, what she was gazing after down at the bottom of the sea. Agnes would like to follow him. The merman has lifted her up in his arms, Agnes twines about his neck, with her whole soul she trustingly abandons herself to the stronger one; he already stands upon the brink, he leans over the sea, about to plunge into it with his prey—then Agnes looks at him once more, not timidly, not doubtingly, not proud of her good fortune, not intoxicated by pleasure, but with absolute faith in him, with absolute humility, like the lowly flower she conceived herself to be; by this look she entrusts to him with absolute confidence her whole fate.75 And, behold, the sea roars no more, its voice is mute, nature's passion which is the merman's strength leaves him in the lurch, a dead calm ensues—and still Agnes continues to look at him thus. Then the merman collapses, he is not able to resist the power of innocence, his native element is unfaithful to him, he cannot seduce Agnes. He leads her back again, he explains to her that he only wanted to show her how beautiful the sea is when it is calm, and

Agnes believes him.–Then he turns back alone and the sea rages, but despair in the merman rages more wildly. He is able to seduce Agnes, he is able to seduce a hundred Agneses, he is able to infatuate every girl–but Agnes has conquered, and the merman has lost her. Only as a prey can she become his, he cannot belong faithfully to any girl, for in fact he is only a merman. Here I have taken the liberty of making a little alteration* in the merman; substantially I have also altered Agnes a little, for in the legend Agnes is not entirely without fault–and generally speaking it is nonsense and coquetry and an insult to the feminine sex to imagine a case of seduction where the girl is not the least bit to blame. *One might also treat this legend in another way. The merman does not want to seduce Agnes, although previously he had seduced many. He is no longer a merman, or, if one so will, he is a miserable merman who already has long been sitting on the floor of the sea and sorrowing. However, he knows (as the legend in fact teaches),76 that he can be delivered by the love of an innocent girl. But he has a bad conscience with respect to girls and does not dare to approach them. Then he sees Agnes. Already many a time when he was hidden in the reeds he had seen her walking on the shore.77 Her beauty, her quiet occupation with herself, fixes his attention upon her; but only sadness prevails in his soul, no wild desire stirs in it. And so when the merman mingles his sighs with the soughing of the reeds she turns her ear thither, and then stands still and falls to dreaming, more charming than any woman and yet beautiful as a liberating angel which inspires the merman with confidence. The merman plucks up courage, he approaches Agnes, he wins her love, he hopes for his deliverance. But Agnes was no quiet maiden, she was fond of the roar of the sea, and the sad sighing beside the inland lake pleased her only because then she seethed more strongly within. She would be off and away, she would rush wildly out into the infinite with the merman whom she loved–so she incites the memman. She disdained his humility, now pride awakens. And the sea roars and the waves foam and the merman embraces Agnes and plunges with her into the deep. Never had he been so wild, never so full of desire, for he had hoped by this girl to find deliverance. He soon became tired of Agnes, yet no one ever found her corpse, for she became a mermaid who tempted men by her songs. In the legend Agnes is (to modernize my expression a little) a woman who craves "the interesting," and every such woman can always be sure that there is a merman in the offing, for with half an eye mermen discover the like of that and steer for it like a shark after its prey. It is therefore very stupid to suppose (or is it a rumor which a merman has spread abroad?) that the so-called culture protects a girl against seduction. No, existence is more righteous and fair: there is only one protection, and that is innocence. We will now bestow upon the merman a human consciousness and suppose that the fact of his being a merman indicates a human preexistence in the consequences of which his life is entangled. There is nothing to prevent him from becoming a hero, for the step he now takes is one of reconciliation. He is saved by Agnes, the seducer is crushed, he has bowed to the power of innocence, he can never seduce again. But at the same instant two powers are striving for possession of him: repentance; and Agnes and repentance. If repentance alone takes possession of him, then he is hidden; if Agnes and repentance take possession of him, then he is revealed. Now in case repentance grips the merman and he remains concealed, he has clearly made Agnes unhappy, for Agnes loved him in all her innocence, she believed that at the instant when even to her he seemed changed, however well he hid it, he was telling the truth in saying that he only wanted to show her the beautiful calmness of the sea. However, with respect to passion the merman himself becomes still more unhappy, for he loved Agnes with a multiplicity of passions and had besides a new guilt to bear. The demoniacal element in repentance will now explain to him that this is precisely his punishment [for the faults of his pre-existent state], and that the more it tortures him the better. If he abandons himself to this demoniacal influence, he then perhaps makes still another attempt to save Agnes, in such a way as one can, in a certain sense, save a person by means of the evil. He knows that Agnes loves him. If he could wrest from Agnes this love, then in a way she is saved. But how? The merman has too much sense to depend upon the notion that an open-hearted confession would awaken her disgust. He will therefore try perhaps to incite in her all dark passions, will scorn her, mock her, hold up her love to ridicule, if possible he will stir up her pride. He will not spare himself any torment; for this is the profound contradiction in the demoniacal, and in a certain sense there dwells infinitely more good in a demoniac than in a trivial person. The more selfish Agnes is, the easier the deceit will prove for him (for it is only very inexperienced people who suppose that it is easy to deceive innocence; existence is very profound, and it is in fact the easiest thing for the shrewd to fool the shrewd)—but all the more terrible will be the merman's sufferings. The more cunningly his deceit is planned, the less will Agnes bashfully hide from him her suffering; she will resort to every means, nor will they be without effect—not to shake his resolution, I mean, but to torture him. So by help of the demoniacal the merman desires to be the individual who as the individual is higher than the universal. The demoniacal has the same characteristic as the divine inasmuch as the individual can enter into an absolute relation to it. This is the analogy, the counterpart, to that paradox of which we are talking. It has therefore a certain resemblance which may deceive one. Thus the merman has apparently the proof that his silence is justified for the fact that by it he suffers all his pain. However, there is no doubt that he can talk. He can thus become a tragic hero, to my mind a grandiose tragic hero, if he talks. Some, perhaps, will only understand wherein this is grandiose.* *Aesthetics sometimes treats a similar subject with its customary coquetry. The merman is saved by Agnes, and the whole thing ends in a happy marriage. A happy marriage! That's easy enough. On the other hand, if ethics were to deliver the address at the wedding service, it would be quite another thing, I imagine. Aesthetics throws the cloak of love over the merman, and so everything is forgotten. It is also careless enough to suppose that at a wedding things go as they do at an auction where everything is sold in the state it is in when the hammer falls. All it cares for is that the lovers get one another, it doesn't trouble about the rest. If only it could see what happens afterwards—but for that it has no time, it is at once in full swing with the business of clapping together a new pair of lovers. Aesthetics is the most faithless of all sciences. Everyone who has deeply loved it becomes in a certain sense unhappy, but he who has never loved it is and remains a pecus. He will then be able to wrest from his mind every self-deceit about his being able to make Agnes happy by his trick, he will have courage, humanly speaking, to crush Agnes. Here I would make in conclusion only one psychological observation. The more selfishly Agnes has been developed, the more dazzling will the self-deception be, indeed it is not inconceivable that in reality it might come to pass that a merman by his demoniac shrewdness has, humanly speaking, not only saved an Agnes but brought something extraordinary out of her; for a demon knows how to torture powers out of even the weakest person, and in his way he may have the best intentions toward a human being. The merman stands at the dialectical turning-point. If he is delivered out of the demoniacal into repentance there are two paths open to him. He may hold back, remain in his concealment, but not rely upon his shrewdness. He does not come as the individual into an absolute relationship with the demoniacal but finds repose in the counter-paradox that the deity will save Agnes. (So it is the Middle Ages would perform the movement, for according to its conception the merman is absolutely dedicated to the cloister.) Or else he may be saved along with Agnes. Now this is not to be understood to mean that by the love of Agnes for him he might be saved from being henceforth a deceiver (this is the aesthetic way of performing a rescue, which always goes around the main point, which is the continuity of the merman's life); for so far as that goes he is already saved, he is saved inasmuch as he becomes revealed. Then he marries Agnes. But still he must have recourse to the paradox. For when the individual by his guilt has gone outside the universal he can return to it only by virtue of having come as the individual into an absolute relationship with the absolute. Here I will make an observation by which I say more than was said at any point in the foregoing discussion.* *In the foregoing discussion I have intentionally refrained from any consideration of sin and its reality. The whole discussion points to Abraham, and him I can still approach by immediate categories—in so far, that is to say, as I am able to understand him. As soon as sin makes its appearance ethics comes to grief precisely upon repentance; for repentance is the highest ethical expression, but precisely as such it is the deepest ethical selfcontradiction. Sin is not the first immediacy, sin is a later immediacy. By sin the individual is already higher (in the direction of the demoniacal paradox) than the universal, because it is a contradiction on the part of the universal to impose itself upon a man who lacks the conditio sine qua non. If philosophy among other vagaries were also to have the notion that it could occur to a man to act in accordance with its teaching, one might make out of that a queer comedy. An ethics which disregards sin is a perfectly idle science; but if it asserts sin, it is eo ipso well beyond itself. Philosophy teaches that the immediate must be annulled (aufgehoben). That is true enough; but what is not true in this is that sin is as a matter of course the immediate, for that is no more true than that faith as a matter of course is the immediate. As long as I move in these spheres everything goes smoothly, but what is said here does not by any means explain Abraham; for it was not by sin Abraham became the individual, on the contrary, he was a righteous man, he is God's elect. So the analogy to Abraham will not appear until after the individual has been brought to the point of being able to accomplish the universal, and then the paradox repeats itself. The movements of the merman I can understand, whereas I cannot understand Abraham; for it is precisely through the paradox that the merman comes to the point of realizing the universal. For if he remains hidden and initiates himself into all the torments of repentance, then he becomes a demon and as such is brought to naught. If he remains concealed but does not think cunningly that being himself tormented in the bondage of repentance he could work Agnes loose, then he finds peace indeed but is lost for this world. If he becomes revealed and allows himself to be saved by Agnes, then he is the greatest man I can picture to myself; for it is only the aesthetic writer who thinks lightmindedly that he extols the power of love by letting the lost man be loved by an innocent girl and thereby saved, it is only the aesthetic writer who sees amiss and believes that the girl is the heroine, instead of the man being the hero.

So the merman cannot belong to Agnes unless, after having made the infinite movement, the movement of repentance, he makes still one more movement by virtue of the absurd. By his own strength he can make the movement of repentance, but for that he uses up absolutely all his strength and hence he cannot by his own strength return and grasp reality. If a man has not enough passion to make either the one movement or the other, if he loiters through life, repenting a little, and thinks that the rest will take care of itself, he has once for all renounced the effort to live in the idea—and then he can very easily reach and help others to reach the highest attainments, i.e. delude himself and others with the notion that in the world of spirit everything goes as in a well-known game of cards where everything depends on haphazard. One can therefore divert oneself by reflecting how strange it is that precisely in our age when everyone is able to accomplish the highest things doubt about the immortality of the soul could be so widespread, for the man who has really made even so much as the movement of infinity is hardly a doubter. The conclusions of passion are the only reliable ones, that is, the only convincing conclusions. Fortunately existence is in this instance more kindly and more faithful than the wise maintain, for it excludes no man, not even the lowliest, it fools no one, for in the world of spirit only he is fooled who fools himself. It is the opinion of all, and so far as I dare permit myself to pass judgment it is also my opinion, that it is not the highest thing to enter the monastery; but for all that it is by no means my opinion that in our age when nobody enters the monastery everybody is greater than the deep and earnest souls who found repose in a monastery. How many are there in our age who have passion enough to think this thought and then to judge themselves honestly? This mere thought of taking time upon one's conscience, of giving it time to explore with its sleepless vigilance every secret thought, with such effect that, if even, instant one does not make the movement by virtue of the highest and holiest there is in a man, one is able with dread and horror to discover* and by dread itself, if in no other way, to lure forth the obscure libido78 which is concealed after all in even, human life, whereas on the contrary, when one lives in society with others one so easily forgets, is let off so easily, is sustained in so many ways, gets opportunity to start afresh–this mere thought, conceived with proper re spect, I would suppose, must chasten many an individual in our age which imagines it has already reached the highest attainment. *People do not believe this in our serious age, and yet it is remarkable that even in paganism, more easy-going and less given to redection, the two outstanding representatives of the Greek gnôqi sautón [know thyself] as a conception of existence intimated each in his way that by delving deep into oneself one would first of all discover the disposition to evil. I surely do not need to say that I am thinking of Pythagoras and Socrates. But about this people concern themselves very little in our age which has reached the highest attainment, whereas in truth no age has so fallen victim to the comic as this has, and it is incomprehensible that this age has not already by a generatio acquivoca [breeding without mating] given birth to its hero, the demon who would remorselessly produce the dreadful spectacle of making the whole age laugh and making it forget that it was laughing at itself. Or what is existence for but to be laughed at if men in their twenties have already attained the utmost? And for all that, what loftier emotion has the age found since men gave up entering the monastery? Is it not a pitiable prudence, shrewdness, faintheartedness, it has found, which sits in high places and cravenly makes men believe they have accomplished the greatest things and insidiously withholds them from attempting to do even the lesser things? The man who has performed the cloister-movement has only one movement more to make, that is, the movement of the absurd. How many in our age understand what the absurd is? How many of our contemporaries so live that they have renounced all or have gained all? How many are even so honest with themselves that they know what they can do and what they cannot? And is it not true that in so far as one finds such people one finds them rather among the less cultured and in part among women? The age in a kind of clairvoyance reveals its weak point, as a demoniac always reveals himself without understanding himself, for over and over again it is demanding the comic. If it really were this the age needed, the theater might perhaps need a new play in which it was made a subject of laughter that a person died of love—or would it not rather be salutary for this age if such a thing were to happen among us, if the age were to witness such an occurrence, in order that for once it might acquire courage to believe in the power of spirit, courage to stop quenching cravenly the better impulses in oneself and quenching enviously the better impulses in others ... by laughter? Does the age really need a ridiculous exhibition by a religious enthusiast in order to get something to laugh at, or does it not need rather that such an enthusiastic figure should remind it of that which has been forgotten? If one would like to have a story written on a similar theme but more touching for the fact that the passion of repentance was not awakened, one might use to this effect a tale which is narrated in the book of Tobit. The young Tobias wanted to marry Sarah the daughter of Raguel and Edna. But a sad fatality hung over this young girl. She had been given to seven husbands, all of whom had perished in the bride-chamber. With a view to my plan this feature is a blemish in the narrative, for almost irresistibly a comic effect is produced by the thought of seven fruitless attempts to get married notwithstanding she was very near to it—just as near as a student who seven times failed to get his diploma. In the book of Tobit the accent falls on a different spot, therefore the high figure is significant and in a certain sense is contributary to the tragic effect, for it enhances the courage of Tobias, which was the more notable because he was the only son of his parents (6:14) and because the deterrent was so striking. So this feature must be left out. Sarah is a maiden who has never been in love, who treasures still a young maiden's bliss, her enormous first mortgage upon life, her Vollmachtbrief zum Glücke, 79 the privilege of loving a man with her whole heart. And yet she is the most unhappy maiden, for she knows that the evil demon who loves her will kill the bridegroom the night of the wedding. I have read of many a sorrow, but I doubt if there is anywhere to be found so deep a sorrow as that which we discover in the life of this girl. However, if the misfortune comes from without, there is some consolation to be found after all. Although existence did not bring one that which might have made one happy, there is still consolation in the thought that one would have been able to receive it. But the unfathomable sorrow which time can never divert, which time can never heal: To be aware that it was of no avail though existence were to do everything! A Greek writer conceals so infinitely much by his simple naïveté when he says: pántov gàr ou'deís erota efugen h feúxetai, mécriv an kállov h kaì o'fqalmoì bléposin (cf. Longi Pastoralia).80 There has been many a girl who became unhappy in love, but after all she became so, Sarah was so before she became so. It is hard not to find the man to whom one can surrender oneself devotedly, but it is unspeakably hard not to be able to surrender oneself. A young girl surrenders herself, and then they say, "Now she is no longer free"; but Sarah was never free, and yet she had never surrendered herself. It is hard if a girl surrendered herself and then was cheated,81 but Sarah was cheated before she surrendered herself. What a world of sorrow is implied in what follows, when finally Tobias wishes to marry Sarah! What wedding ceremonies! What preparations! No maiden has ever been so cheated as Sarah, for she was cheated out of the most sacred thing of all, the absolute wealth which even the poorest girl possesses, cheated out of the secure, boundless, unrestrained, unbridled devotion of surrender— for first there had to be a fumigation by laying the heart of the fish and its liver upon glowing coals. And think of how the mother had to take leave of her daughter, who having herself been cheated out of all, in continuity with this must cheat the mother out of her most beautiful possession. Just read the narrative. "Edna prepared the chamber and brought Sarah thither and wept and received the tears of her daughter. And she said unto her, Be of good comfort, my child, the Lord of heaven and earth give thee joy for this thy sorrow! Be of good courage, my daughter." And then the moment of the nuptials! Let one read it if one can for tears. "But after they were both shut in together Tobias rose up from the bed and said, Sister, arise, and let us pray that the Lord may have mercy upon us" (8:4). In case a poet were to read this narrative, in case he were to make use of it, I wager a hundred to one that he would lay all the emphasis upon the young Tobias. His heroic courage in being willing to risk his life in such evident danger—which the narrative recalls once again, for the morning after the nuptials Raguel says to Edna, "Send one of the maidservants and let her see whether he be alive; but if not, that we may bury him and no man know of it" (8:12)—this heroic courage would be the poet's theme. I take the liberty of proposing another. Tobias acted bravely, stoutheartedly and chivalrously, but any man who has not the courage for this is a mollycoddle who does not know what love is, or what it is to be a man, or what is worth living for; he had not even comprehended the little mystery, that it is better to give than to receive, and has no inkling of the great one, that it is far more difficult to receive than to give—that is, if one has had courage to do without and in the hour of need did not become cowardly. No, it is Sarah that is the heroine. I desire to draw near to her as I never have drawn near to any girl or felt tempted in thought to draw near to any girl I have read about. For what love to God it requires to be willing to let oneself be healed when from the beginning one has been thus bungled without one's fault, from the beginning has been an abortive specimen of humanity!82 What ethical maturity was required for assuming the responsibility of allowing the loved one to do such a daring deed! What humility before the face of another personl What faith in God to believe that the next instant she would not hate the husband to whom she owed everything! Let Sarah be a man, and with that the demoniacal is close at hand. The proud and noble nature can endure everything, but one thing it cannot endure, it cannot endure pity. In that there is implied an indignity which can only be inflicted upon one by a higher power, for by oneself one can never become an object of pity. If a man has sinned, he can bear the punishment for it without despairing; but without blame to be singled out from his mother's womb as a sacrifice to pity, as a sweet-smelling savor in its nostrils, that he cannot put up with. Pity has a strange dialectic, at one moment it requires guilt, the next moment it will not have it, and so it is that to be predestinated to pity is more and more dreadful the more the individual's misfortune is in the direction of the spiritual. But Sarah had no blame attaching to her, she is cast forth as a prey to every suffering and in addition to this has to endure the torture of pity—for even I who admire her more than Tobias loved her, even I cannot mention her name without saying, "Poor girl." Put a man in Sarah's place, let him know that in case he were to love a girl a spirit of hell would come and murder his loved one—it might well be possible that he would choose the demoniacal part, that he would shut himself up within himself and say in the way a demoniacal nature talks in secret, "Many thanks, I am no friend of courteous and prolix phrases, I do not absolutely need the pleasure of love, I can become a Blue Beard, finding my delight in seeing maidens perish during the night of their nuptials." Commonly one hears little about the demoniacal, notwithstanding that this field, particularly in our time, has a valid claim to be explored, and notwithstanding that the observer, in case he knows how to get a little in rapport with the demon, can, at least occasionally, make use of almost every man for this purpose. As such an explorer Shakespeare is and constantly remains a hero. That horrible demon, the most demoniacal figure Shakespeare has depicted and depicted incomparably, the Duke of Gloucester (afterwards to become Richard III)—what made him a demon? Evidently the fact that he could not bear the pity he had been subjected to since childhood. His monologue in the first act of Richard III is worth more than all the moral systems which have no inkling of the terrors of existence or of the explanation of them. I, that am rudely stamped, and want love's majesty To strut before a wanton ambling nymph; I, that am curtail'd of this fair proportion, Cheated of feature by dissembling nature, Deformed, unfinished, sent before my time Into this breathing world, scarse half made up, And that so lamely and unfashionable That dogs bark at me as I halt by them. Such natures as that of Gloucester one cannot save by mediating them into an idea of society. Ethics in fact only makes game of them, just as it would be a mockery of Sarah if ethics were to say to her, "Why dost thou not express the universal and get married?" Essentially such natures are in the paradox and are no more imperfect than other men, but are either lost in the demoniacal paradox or saved in the divine. Now from time out of mind people have been pleased to think that witches, hobgoblins, gnomes etc. were deformed, and undeniably every man on seeing a deformed person has at once an inclination to associate this with the notion of moral depravity. What a monstrous injustice! For the situation must rather be inverted, in the sense that existence itself has corrupted them, in the same way that a stepmother makes the children wicked. The fact of being originally set outside of the universal, by nature or by a historical circumstance, is the beginning of the demoniacal, for which the individual himself however is not to blame. Thus Cumberland's Jew83 is also a demon notwithstanding he does what is good. Thus too the demoniacal may express itself as contempt for men–a contempt, be it observed, which does not cause a man to behave contemptibly, since on the contrary he counts it his forte that he is better than all who condemn him.–In view of such cases the poets ought to lose no time in sounding the alarm. God knows what books are read now by the younger generation of verse makers! Their study likely consists in learning rhymes by rote. God knows what significance in existence these men have! At this moment I do not know what use they are except to furnish an edifying proof of the immortality of the soul, for the fact that one can say of them as Baggesen says84 of the poet of our town, Kildevalle, "If he is immortal, then we all are."–What has here been said about Sarah, almost as a sort of poetic production and therefore with a fantastic presupposition, acquires its full significance if one with psychological interest will delve deep into the meaning of the old saying: Nullum unquam exstitit magnum ingenium sine aliqua dementia. 85 For this dementia is the suffering allotted to genius in existence, it is the expression, if I may say so, of the divine jealousy, whereas the gift of genius is the expression of the divine favor. So from the start the genius is disoriented in relation to the universal and is brought into relation with the paradox–whether it be that in despair at his limitation (which in his eyes transforms his omnipotence into impotence) he seeks a demoniacal reassurance and therefore will not admit such limitation either before God or men, or whether he reassures himself religiously by love to the Deity. Here are implied psychological topics to which, it seems to me, one might gladly sacrifice a whole life–and yet one so seldom hears a word about them.86 What relation has madness to genius? Can we construct the one out of the other? In what sense and how far is the genius master of his madness? For it goes without saying that to a certain degree he is master of it, since otherwise he would be actually a madman. For such observations, however, ingenuity in a high degree is requisite, and love; for to make observation upon a superior mind is very difficult. If with due attention to this difficulty one were to read through the works of particular authors most celebrated for their genius, it might in barely a single instance perhaps be possible, though with much pains, to discover a little. I would consider skill another case, that of an individual who by being hidden and by his silence would save the universal. To this end I make use of the legend of Faust.87 Faust is a doubter,* an apostate against the spirit, who takes the path of the flesh. *If one would prefer not to make use of a doubter, one might choose a similar figure, an ironist, for example, whose sharp sight has discovered fundamentally the ludicrousness of existence, who by a secret understanding with the forces of life ascertains what the patient wishes. He knows that he possesses the power of laughter if he would use it, he is sure of his victory, yea, also of his good fortune. He knows that an individual voice will be raised in resistance, but he knows that he is stronger, he knows that for an instant one still can cause men to seem serious, but he knows also that privately they long to laugh with him; he knows that for an instant one can still cause a woman to hold a fan before her eyes when he talks, but he knows that she is laughing behind the fan, that the fan is not absolutely impervious to vision, he knows that one can write on it an invisible inscription, he knows that when a woman strikes at him with her fan it is because she has understood him, he knows without the least danger of deception how laughter sneaks in, and how when once it has taken up its lodging it lies in ambush and waits. Let us imagine such an Aristophanes, such a Voltaire, a little altered, for he is at the same time a sympathetic nature, he loves existence, he loves men, and he knows that even though the reproof of laughter will perhaps educate a saved young race, yet in the contemporary generation a multitude of men will be ruined. So he keeps silent and as far as possible forgets how to laugh. But dare he keep silent? Perhaps there are sundry persons who do not in the least understand the difficulty I have in mind. They are likely of the opinion that it is an admirable act of magnanimity to keep silent. That is not at all my opinion, for I think that every such character, if he has not had the magnanimity to keep silent, is a traitor against existence. So I require of him this magnanimity, but when he possesses it, dare he then keep silent? Ethics is a dangerous science and it might be possible that Aristophanes was determined by purely ethical considerations in resolving to reprove by laughter his misguided age. Aesthetical magnanimity does not help [to solve the question whether one ought to keep silent], for on the credit of that one does not take such a risk. If he is to keep silent, then into the paradox he must go.–I will suggest still another plan for a story. Suppose e.g. that a man possessed a explanation of a heroic life which explained it in a sorry way, and yet a whole generation reposes securely in an absolute belief in this hero, without suspecting anything of the sort. This is what the poets mean by it, and whereas again and again it is repeated that every age has its Faust, yet one poet after another follows indefatigably the same beaten track. Let us make a little alteration. Faust is the doubter par excellence, but he is a sympathetic nature. Even in Goethe's interpretation of Faust I sense the lack of a deeper psychological insight into the secret conversations of doubt with itself. In our age, when indeed all have experienced doubt, no poet has yet made a step in this direction. So I think I might well offer them Royal Securities88 to write on, so that they could write down all they have experienced in this respect– they would hardly write more than there is room for on the left hand margin. Only when one thus deflects Faust back into himself, only then can doubt appear poetic, only then too does he himself discover in reality all its sufferings. He knows that it is spirit which sustains existence, but he knows then too that the security and joy in which men live is not founded upon the power of spirit but is easily explicable as an unreflected happiness. As a doubter, as the doubter, he is higher than all this, and if anyone would deceive him by making him believe that he has passed through a course of training in doubt, he readily sees through the deception; for the man who has made a movement in the world of spirit, hence an infinite movement, can at once hear through the spoken word whether it is a tried and experienced man who is speaking or a Münchhausen. What a Tamberlane is able to accomplish by means of his Huns, that Faust is able to accomplish by means of his doubt: to frighten men up in dismay, to cause existence to quake beneath their feet, to disperse men abroad, to cause the shriek of dread to be heard on all sides. And if he does it, he is nevertheless no Tamberlane, he is in a certain sense warranted and has the warranty of thought. But Faust is a sympathetic nature, he loves existence, his soul is acquainted with no envy, he perceives that he is unable to check the raging he is well able to arouse, he desires no Herostratic honor89–he keeps silent, he hides the doubt in his soul more carefully than the girl who hides under her heart the fruit of a sinful love, he endeavors as well as he can to walk in step with other men, but what goes on within him he consumes within himself, and thus he offers himself a sacrifice for the universal. When an eccentric pate raises a whirlwind of doubt one may sometimes hear people say, "Would that he had kept silent." Faust realizes this idea. He who has a conception of what it means to live upon spirit knows also what the hunger of doubt is, and that the doubter hungers just as much for the daily bread of life as for the nutriment of the spirit. Although all the pain Faust suffers may be a fairly good argument that is was not pride possessed him, yet to test this further I will employ a little precautionary expedient which I invent with great ease. For as Gregory of Rimini was called tortor infantium90 because he espoused the view of the damnation of infants, so I might be tempted to call myself tortor heroum; for I am very inventive when it is a question of putting heroes to the torture. Faust sees Marguerite–not after he had made the choice of pleasure, for my Faust does not choose pleasure– he sees Marguerite, not in the concave mirror of Mephistopheles but in all her lovable innocence, and as his soul has preserved love for mankind he can perfectly well fall in love with her. But he is a doubter, his doubt has annihilated reality for him; for so ideal is my Faust that he does not belong to these scientific doubters who doubt one hour every semester in the professorial chair, but at other times are able to do everything else, as indeed they do this, without the support of spirit or by virtue of spirit. He is a doubter, and the doubter hungers just as much for the daily bread of joy as for the food of the spirit. He remains, however, true to his resolution and keeps silent, and he talks to no man of his doubt, nor to Marguerite of his love. It goes without saying that Faust is too ideal a figure to be content with the tattle that if he were to talk he would give occasion to an ordinary discussion and the whole thing would pass off without any consequences— or perhaps, and perhaps. ... (Here, as every poet will easily see, the comic is latent in the plan, threatening to bring Faust into an ironical relation to these fools of low comedy who in our age run after doubt, produce an external argument, e.g. a doctor's diploma, to prove that they really have doubted, or take their oath that they have doubted everything, or prove it by the fact that on a journey they met a doubter—these expressmessengers and foot-racers in the world of spirit, who in the greatest haste get from one man a little hint of doubt, from another a little hint of faith, and then turn it to account as best they can, according as the congregation wants to have fine sand or coarse sand.)91 Faust is too ideal a figure to go about in carpet-slippers. He who has not an infinite passion is not the ideal, and he who has an infinite passion has long ago saved his soul out of such nonsense. He keeps silent and sacrifices himself/or he talks with the consciousness that he will confound everything. If he keeps silent, ethics condemns him, for it says, "Thou shalt acknowledge the universal, and it is precisely by speaking thou dost acknowledge it, and thou must not have compassion upon the universal." One ought not to forget this consideration when sometimes one judges a doubter severely for talking. I am not inclined to judge such conduct leniently, but in this case as everywhere all depends upon whether the movements occur normally. If worse comes to worst, a doubter, even though by talking he were to bring down all possible misfortune upon the world, is much to be preferred to these miserable sweet-tooths who taste a little of everything, and who would heal doubt without being acquainted with it, and who are therefore usually the proximate cause of it when doubt breaks out wildly and with ungovernable rage.–If he speaks, then he confounds everything–for though this does not actually occur, he does not get to know it till afterwards, and the upshot cannot help a man either at the moment of action or with regard to his responsibility. If he keeps silent on his own responsibility, he may indeed be acting magnanimously, but to his other pains he adds a little temptation (Anfechtung), for the universal will constantly torture him and say, "You ought to have talked. Where will you find the certainty that it was not after all a hidden pride which governed your resolution?" If on the other hand the doubter is able to become the particular individual who as the individual stands in an absolute relation to the absolute, then he can get a warrant for his silence. In this case he must transform his doubt into guilt. In this case he is within the paradox, but in this case his doubt is cured, even though he may get another doubt. Even the New Testament would approve of such a silence. There are even passages in the New Testament which commend irony–if only it is used to conceal something good. This movement, however, is as properly a movement of irony as is any other which has its ground in the fact that subjectivity is higher than reality. In our age people want to hear nothing about this, generally they want to know no more about irony than Hegel has said about it92–who strangely enough had not much understanding of it, and bore a grudge against it, which our age has good reason not to give up, for it had better beware of irony. In the Sermon on the Mount it is said, "When thou fastest, anoint thy head and wash thy face, that thou be not seen of men to fast." This passage bears witness directly to the truth that subjectivity is incommensurable with reality, yea, that it has leave to deceive. If only the people who in our age go gadding about with vague talk about the congregational idea93 were to read the New Testament, they would perhaps get other ideas into their heads. But now as for Abraham–how did he act? For I have not forgotten, and the reader will perhaps be kind enough to remember, that it was with the aim of reaching this point I entered into the whole foregoing discussion–not as though Abraham would thereby become more intelligible, but in order that the unintelligibility might become more desultory.94 For, as I have said, Abraham I cannot understand, I can only admire him. It was also observed that the stages I have described do none of them contain an analogy to Abraham. The examples were simply educed in order that while they were shown in their own proper sphere they might at the moment of variation [from Abraham's case] indicate as it were the boundary of the unknown land. If there might be any analogy, this must be found in the paradox of sin, but this again lies in another sphere and cannot explain Abraham and is itself far easier to explain than Abraham. So then, Abraham did not speak, he did not speak to Sarah, nor to Eleazar, nor to Isaac, he passed over three ethical authorities; for the ethical had for Abraham no higher expression than the family life. Aesthetics permitted, yea, required of the individual silence, when he knew that by keeping silent he could save another. This is already sufficient proof that Abraham does not lie within the circumference of aesthetics. His silence has by no means the intention of saving Isaac, and in general his whole task of sacrificing Isaac for his own sake and for God's sake is an offense to aesthetics, for aesthetics can well understand that I sacrifice myself, but not that I sacrifice another for my own sake. The aesthetic hero was silent. Ethics condemned him, however, because he was silent by virtue of his accidental particularity. His human foreknowledge was what determined him to keep silent. This ethics cannot forgive, every such human knowledge is only an illusion, ethics requires an infinite movement, it requires revelation. So the aesthetic hero can speak but will not. The genuine tragic hero sacrifices himself and all that is his for the universal, his deed and every emotion with him belong to the universal, he is revealed, and in this self-revelation he is the beloved son of ethics. This does not fit the case of Abraham: he does nothing for the universal, and he is concealed. Now we reach the paradox. Either the individual as the individual is able to stand in an absolute relation to the absolute (and then the ethical is not the highest)/or Abraham is lost—he is neither a tragic hero, nor an aesthetic hero. Here again it may seem as if the paradox were the easiest and most convenient thing of all. However, I must repeat that he who counts himself convinced of this is not a knight of faith, for distress and anguish are the only legitimations that can be thought of, and they cannot be thought in general terms, for with that the paradox is annulled. Abraham keeps silent—but he cannot speak. Therein lies the distress and anguish. For if I when I speak am unable to make myself intelligible, then I am not speaking—even though I were to talk uninterruptedly day and night. Such is the case with Abraham. He is able to utter everything, but one thing he cannot say, i.e. say it in such a way that another understands it, and so he is not speaking. The relief of speech is that it translates me into the universal. Now Abraham is able to say the most beautiful things any language can express about how he loves Isaac. But it is not this he has at heart to say, it is the profounder thought that he would sacrifice him because it is a trial. This latter thought no one can understand, and hence everyone can only misunderstand the former. This distress the tragic hero does not know. He has first of all the comfort that every counter-argument has received due consideration, that he has been able to give to Clytemnestra, to Iphigenia, to Achilles, to the chorus, to every living being, to every voice from the heart of humanity, to every cunning, every alarming, every accusing, every compassionate thought, opportunity to stand up against him. He can be sure that everything that can be said against him has been said, unsparingly, mercilessly— and to strive against the whole world is a comfort, to strive with oneself is dreadful. He has no reason to fear that he has overlooked anything, so that afterwards he must cry out as did King Edward the Fourth at the news of the death of Clarence:95 Who su'd to me for him? who, in my wrath, Kneel'd at my feet and bade me be advised? Who spoke of brotherhood? who spoke of love? The tragic hero does not know the terrible responsibility of solitude. In the next place he has the comfort that he can weep and lament with Clytemnestra and Iphigenia—and tears and cries are assuaging, but unutterable sighs are torture. Agamemnon can quickly collect his soul into the certainty that he will act, and then he still has time to comfort and exhort. This Abraham is unable to do. When his heart is moved, when his words would contain a blessed comfort for the whole world, he does not dare to offer comfort, for would not Sarah, would not Eleazar, would not Isaac say, "Why wilt thou do it? Thou canst refrain?" And if in his distress he would give vent to his feelings and would embrace all his dear ones before taking the final step, this might perhaps bring about the dreadful consequence that Sarah, that Eleazar, that Isaac would be offended in him and would believe he was a hypocrite. He is unable to speak, he speaks no human language. Though he himself understood all the tongues of the world, though his loved ones also understood them, he nevertheless cannot speak—he speaks a divine language ... he "speaks with tongues." This distress I can well understand, I can admire Abraham, I am not afraid that anyone might be tempted by this narrative light-heartedly to want to be the individual, but I admit also that I have not the courage for it, and that I renounce gladly any prospect of getting further—if only it were possible that in any way, however late, I might get so far. Every instant Abraham is able to break off, he can repent the whole thing as a temptation (Anfechtung), then he can speak, then all could understand him—but then he is no longer Abraham. Abraham cannot speak, for he cannot utter the word which explains all (that is, not so that it is intelligible), he cannot say that it is a test, and a test of such a sort, be it noted, that the ethical is the temptation (Versuchung). He who is so situated is an emigrant from the sphere of the universal. But the next word he is still less able to utter. For, as was sufficiently set forth earlier, Abraham makes two movements: he makes the infinite movement of resignahon and gives up Isaac (this no one can understand because it is a private venture); but in the next place, he makes the movement of faith every instant. This is his comfort, for he says: "But yet this will not come to pass, or, if it does come to pass, then the Lord will give me a new Isaac, by virtue viz. of the absurd." The tragic hero does at last get to the end of the story. Iphigenia bows to her father's resolution, she herself makes the infinite movement of resignation, and now they are on good terms with one another. She can understand Agamemnon because his undertaking expresses the universal. If on the other hand Agamemnon were to say to her, "In spite of the fact that the deity demands thee as a sacrifice, it might yet be possible that he did not demand it—by virtue viz. of the absurd," he would that very instant become unintelligible to Iphigenia. If he could say this by virtue of human calculation, Iphigenia would surely understand him, but from that it would follow that Agamemnon had not made the infinite movement of resignation, and so he is not a hero, and so the utterance of the seer is a sea-captain's tale and the whole occurrence a vaudeville. Abraham did not speak. Only one word of his has been preserved, the only reply to Isaac, which also is sufficient proof that he had not spoken previously. Isaac asks Abraham where the lamb is for the burnt offering. "And Abraham said, God will provide Himself the lamb for the burnt offering, my son." This last word of Abraham I shall consider a little more closely. If there were not this word, the whole event would have lacked something; if it were to another effect, everything perhaps would be resolved into confusion. I have often reflected upon the question whether a tragic hero, be the culmination of his tragedy a suffering or an action, ought to have a last rejoicer. In my opinion it depends upon the life-sphere to which he belongs, whether his life has intellectual significance, whether his suffering or his action stands in relation to spirit. It goes without saying that the tragic hero, like every other man who is not deprived of the power of speech, can at the instant of his culmination utter a few words, perhaps a few appropriate words, but the question is whether it is appropriate for him to utter them. If the significance of his life consists in an outward act, then he has nothing to say, since all he says is essentially chatter whereby he only weakens the impression he makes, whereas the ceremonial of tragedy requires that he perform his task in silence, whether this consists in action or in suffering. Not to go too far afield, I will take an example which lies nearest to our discussion. If Agamemnon himself and not Calchas had had to draw the knife against Iphigenia, then he would have only demeaned himself by wanting at the last moment to say a few words, for the significance of his act was notorious, the juridical procedure of piety, of compassion, of emotion, of tears was completed, and moreover his life had no relation to spirit, he was not a teacher or a witness to the spirit. On the other hand, if the significance of a hero's life is in the direction of spirit, then the lack of a rejoinder would weaken the impression he makes. What he has to say is not a few appropriate words, a little piece of declamation, but the significance of his rejoinder is that in the decisive moment he carries himself through. Such an intellectual tragic hero ought to have what in other circumstances is too often striven for in ludicrous ways, he ought to have and he ought to keep the last word. One requires of him the same exalted bearing which is seemly in every tragic hero, but in addition to this there is required of him one word. So when such an intellectual tragic hero has his culmination in suffering (in death), then by his last word he becomes immortal before he dies, whereas the ordinary tragic hero on the other hand does not become immortal till after his death. One may take Socrates as an example. He was an intellectual tragic hero. His death sentence was announced to him. That instant he dies—for one who does not understand that the whole power of the spirit is required for dying, and that the hero always dies before he dies, that man will not get so very far with his conception of life. So as a hero it is required of Socrates that he repose tranquilly in himself, but as an intellectual tragic hero it is required of him that he at the last moment have spiritual strength sufficient to carry himself through. So he cannot like the ordinary tragic hero concentrate upon keeping himself face to face with death, but he must make this movement so quickly that at the same instant he is consciously well over and beyond this strife and asserts himself. If Socrates had been silent in the crisis of death, he would have weakened the effect of his life and aroused the suspicion that in him the elasticity of irony was not an elemental power but a game, the flexibility of which he had to employ at the decisive moment to sustain him emotionally.* *Opinions may be divided as to which rejoinder of Socrates is to be regarded as the decisive one, inasmuch as Socrates has been in so many ways volatilized by Plato. I propose the following. The sentence of death is announced to him, the same instant he dies, the same instant he overcomes death and carries himself through in the famous reply which expresses surprise that he had been condemned by a majority of three votes.96 With no vague and idle talk in the marketplace, with no foolish remark of an idiot, could he have jested more ironically than with the sentence which condemned him to death. What is briefly suggested here has to be sure no application to Abraham in case one might think it possible to find out by analogy an appropriate word for Abraham to end with, but it does apply to this extent, that one thereby perceives how necessary it is that Abraham at the last moment must carry himself through, must not silently draw the knife, but must have a word to say, since as the father of faith he has absolute significance in a spiritual sense. As to what he must say, I can form no conception beforehand; after he has said it I can maybe understand it, maybe in a certain sense can understand Abraham in what he says, though without getting any closer to him than I have been in the foregoing discussion. In case no last rejoinder of Socrates had existed, I should have been able to think myself into him and formulate such a word; if I were unable to do it, a poet could, but no poet can catch up with Abraham. Before I go on to consider Abraham's last word more closely I would call attention to the difficulty Abraham had in saying anything at all. The distress and anguish in the paradox consisted (as was set forth above) in silence–Abraham cannot speak.* *If there can be any question of an analogy, the circumstance of the death of Pythagoras furnishes it, for the silence which he had always maintained he had to carry through in his last moment, and therefore [being compelled to speak] he said, "It is better to be put to death than to speak" (cf. Diogenes Laertius, viii. 39). So in view of this fact it is a contradiction to require him to speak, unless one would have him out of the paradox again, in such a sense that at the last moment he suspends it, whereby he ceases to be Abraham and annuls all that went before. So then if Abraham at the last moment were to say to Isaac, "To thee it applies," this would only have been a weakness. For if he could speak at all, he ought to have spoken long before, and the weakness in this case would consist in the fact that he did not possess the maturity of spirit and the concentration to think in advance the whole pain but had thrust something away from him, so that the actual pain contained a plus over and above the thought pain. Moreover, by such a speech he would fall out of the role of the paradox, and if he really wanted to speak to Isaac, he must transform his situation into a temptation (Anfechtung), for otherwise he could say nothing, and if he were to do that, then he is not even so much as a tragic hero. However, a last word of Abraham has been preserved, and in so far as I can understand the paradox I can also apprehend the total presence of Abraham in this word. First and foremost, he does not say anything, and it is in this form he says what he has to say. His reply to Isaac has the form of irony, for it always is irony when I say something and do not say anything. Isaac interrogates Abraham on the supposition that Abraham knows. So then if Abraham were to have replied, "I know nothing," he would have uttered an untruth. He cannot say anything, for what he knows he cannot say. So he replies, "God will provide Himself the lamb for the burnt offering, my son." Here the double movement in Abraham's soul is evident, as it was described in the foregoing discussion. If Abraham had merely renounced his claim to Isaac and had done no more, he would in this last word be saying an untruth, for he knows that God demands Isaac as a sacrifice, and he knows that he himself at that instant precisely is ready to sacrifice him. We see then that after making this movement he made every instant the next movement, the movement of faith by virtue of the absurd. Because of this he utters no falsehood, for in virtue of the absurd it is of course possible that God could do something entirely different. Hence he is speaking no untruth, but neither is he saying anything, for he speaks a foreign language. This becomes still more evident when we consider that it was Abraham himself who must perform the sacrifice of Isaac. Had the task been a different one, had the Lord commanded Abraham to bring Isaac out to Mount Moriah and then would Himself have Isaac struck by lightning and in this way receive him as a sacrifice, then, taking his words in a plain sense, Abraham might have been right in speaking enigmatically as he did, for he could not himself know what would occur. But in the way the task was prescribed to Abraham he himself had to act, and at the decisive moment he must know what he himself would do, he must know that Isaac will be sacrificed. In case he did not know this definitely, then he has not made the infinite movement of resignation, then, though his word is not indeed an untruth, he is very far from being Abraham, he has less significance than the tragic hero, yea, he is an irresolute man who is unable to resolve either on one thing or another, and for this reason will always be uttering riddles. But such a hesitator is a sheer parody of a knight of faith. Here again it appears that one may have an understanding of Abraham, but can understand him only in the same way as one understands the paradox. For my part I can in a way understand Abraham, but at the same time I apprehend that I have not the courage to speak, and still less to act as he did—but by this I do not by any means intend to say that what he did was insignificant, for on the contrary it is the one only marvel. And what did the contemporary age think of the tragic hero? They thought that he was great, and they admired him. And that honorable assembly of nobles, the jury which every generation impanels to pass judgment upon the foregoing generation, passed the same judgment upon him. But as for Abraham there was no one who could understand him. And yet think what he attained! He remained true to his love. But he who loves God has no need of tears, no need of admiration, in his love he forgets his suffering, yea, so completely has he forgotten it that afterwards there would not even be the least inkling of his pain if God Himself did not recall it, for God sees in secret and knows the distress and counts the tears and forgets nothing. So either there is a paradox, that the individual as the individual stands in an absolute relation to the absolute/or Abraham is lost. EPILOGUE One time in Holland when the market was rather dull for spices the merchants had several cargoes dumped into the sea to peg up prices. This was a pardonable, perhaps a necessary device for deluding people. Is it something like that we need now in the world of spirit? Are we so thoroughly convinced that we have attained the highest point that there is nothing left for us but to make ourselves believe piously that we have not got so far—just for the sake of having something left to occupy our time? Is it such a self-deception the present generation has need of, does it need to be trained to virtuosity in self-deception, or is it not rather sufficiently perfected already in the art of deceiving itself? Or rather is not the thing most needed an honest seriousness which dauntlessly and incorruptibly points to the tasks, an honest seriousness which lovingly watches over the tasks, which does not frighten men into being over hasty in getting the highest tasks accomplished, but keeps the tasks young and beautiful and charming to look upon and yet difficult withal and appealing to noble minds. For the enthusiasm of noble natures is aroused only by difficulties. Whatever the one generation may learn from the other, that which is genuinely human no generation learns from the foregoing. In this respect every generation begins primitively, has no different task from that of every previous generation, nor does it get further, except in so far as the preceding generation shirked its task and deluded itself. This authentically human factor is passion, in which also the one generation perfectly understands the other and understands itself. Thus no generation has learned from another to love, no generation begins at any other point than at the beginning, no generation has a shorter task assigned to it than had the preceding generation, and if here one is not willing like the previous generations to stop with love but would go further, this is but idle and foolish talk. But the highest passion in a man is faith, and here no generation begins at any other point than did the preceding generation, every generation begins all over again, the subsequent generation gets no further than the foregoing—in so far as this remained faithful to its task and did not leave it in the lurch. That this should be wearisome is of course something the generation cannot say, for the generation has in fact the task to perform and has nothing to do with the consideration that the foregoing generation had the same task—unless the particular generation or the particular individuals within it were presumptuous enough to assume the place which belongs by right only to the Spirit which governs the world and has patience enough not to grow weary. If the generation begins that sort of thing, it is upside down, and what wonder then that the whole of existence seems to it upside down, for there surely is no one who has found the world so upside down as did the tailor in the fairy tale97 who went up in his lifetime to heaven and from that standpoint contemplated the world. If the generation would only concern itself about its task, which is the highest thing it can do, it cannot grow weary, for the task is always sufficient for a human life. When the children on a holiday have already got through playing all their games before the clock strikes twelve and say impatiently, "Is there nobody can think of a new game?" does this prove that these children are more developed and more advanced than the children of the same generation or of a previous one who could stretch out the familiar games, to last the whole day long? Or does it not prove rather that these children lack what I would call the lovable seriousness which belongs essentially to play? Faith is the highest passion in a man. There are perhaps many in every generation who do not even reach it, but no one gets further. Whether there be many in our age who do not discover it, I will not decide, I dare only appeal to myself as a witness who makes no secret that the prospects for him are not the best, without for all that wanting to delude himself and to betray the great thing which is faith by reducing it to an insignificance, to an ailment of childhood which one must wish to get over as soon as possible. But for the man also who does not so much as reach faith life has tasks enough, and if one loves them sincerely, life will by no means be wasted, even though it never is comparable to the life of those who sensed and grasped the highest. But he who reached faith (it makes no difference whether he be a man of distinguished talents or a simple man) does not remain standing at faith, yea, he would be offended if anyone were to say this of him, just as the lover would be indignant if one said that he remained standing at love, for he would reply, "I do not remain standing by any means, my whole life is in this." Nevertheless he does not get further, does not reach anything different, for if he discovers this, he has a different explanation for it. "One must go further, one must go further." This impulse to go further is an ancient thing in the world. Heraclitus the obscure, who deposited his thoughts in his writings and his writings in the Temple of Diana (for his thoughts had been his armor during his life, and therefore he hung them up in the temple of the goddess),98 Heraclitus the obscure said, "One cannot pass twice through the same stream." [Plato's Cratyllus, §402.] Heraclitus the obscure had a disciple who did not stop with that, he went further and added, "One cannot do it even once." [Cf. Tennemann, Geschichte der Philosophie, I, p. 220.] Poor Heraclitus, to have such a disciple! By this amendment the thesis of Heraclitus was so improved that it became an Eleatic thesis which denies movement, and yet that disciple desired only to be a disciple of Heraclitus ... and to go further–not back to the position Heraclitus had abandoned

Translated by Tim Zengerink

The Genealogy of Morals

Friedrich Nietzsche

Prologue

We don't truly know ourselves—we who try to understand so much. And there's a good reason for that. We've never really looked for ourselves, so how could we possibly expect to find ourselves? It's been wisely said, "Where your treasure is, there your heart will be also." Our treasure lies in the things we strive to understand. It's like a beehive for us, filled with the knowledge we're always working to gather. As creatures of the air, born to roam, we're like bees gathering honey for our hive. Deep down, we care about one thing: bringing something valuable back home to that hive.

When it comes to the rest of life—what people call "experiences"— how many of us really care about them deeply? Who even has the time or the focus? We rarely engage seriously with those moments. To be honest, our hearts aren't truly in it, and neither are our ears. It's like someone lost in a dream, so absorbed in their thoughts that they don't even notice the loud tolling of the clock. Then, when the clock has finished striking twelve, they suddenly snap out of it and wonder, "Wait, what just happened?" That's how we often feel. We rub our ears afterward, confused, and ask ourselves in complete surprise, "What exactly have we just been through? Who are we, really?"

When we try to make sense of our experiences—those twelve striking moments of our life and being—we always miscount. We get it wrong every time. We remain strangers to ourselves, unable to truly understand who we are. For us, the saying is eternally true: "Each of us is furthest from knowing ourselves." When it comes to understanding ourselves, we are not "knowers."

The thoughts I have about the origins of our moral beliefs—because that's what this argument is all about—were first put into words in my book Human,

All- Too- Human: A Book for Free Spirits. I began writing it in Sorrento during the winter of 1876-77, a time when I could look back on the wide and challenging journey my mind had traveled up to that point. But these ideas aren't new; they're older.

The thoughts I share here are essentially the same as those I explored in that earlier book. Over the years, I hope they've become sharper, clearer, stronger, and more complete. The fact that I still hold onto them today—that they've grown and evolved together—gives me confidence. It makes me believe that these ideas didn't come about by accident or in isolation. Instead, they must have a common source, rooted in a deep and fundamental desire for knowledge. That desire has grown stronger and more focused over time, becoming clearer in its demands. For a philosopher, that's exactly how things should be.

We have no right to be disconnected. Our thoughts must not err separately, nor should we stumble upon truth by chance or in isolation. Like the fruit that a tree bears out of necessity, our thoughts, values, affirmations, denials, questions, and doubts must grow in connection with one another. They are all interrelated, bearing witness to one will, one health, one unity, one guiding light. As for whether you, the observer, find these fruits pleasing to your taste—does that matter to the tree? Should it matter to us, the philosophers?

I must reluctantly admit to a peculiar and deeply ingrained scrupulousness within myself, one that revolves around morality. This trait, evident in me from an early age, appeared so naturally, so persistently, and with such strong resistance to the influences of my environment, time, traditions, and ancestry that I might almost call it my a priori. From a young age, my curiosity and skepticism forced me to confront the question of the true origin of our ideas of "Good" and "Evil." At just thirteen years old, when most children are divided between playing games and contemplating God, I was already haunted by the problem of the origin of Evil. It was at that age that I wrote my first philosophical essay, a naïve and childlike attempt to tackle the question. My solution, as you might expect, attributed the creation of evil to God Himself— I named Him its father. Was that conclusion driven by my own a prior i? That new, immoral—or at least "amoral"—instinct, that inner imperative so far removed from Kant's ideals and yet so full of its own challenges? This imperative has since become the focus of not just my attention but something far greater.

Fortunately, I soon learned to separate theological prejudices from moral ones. I gave up the search for a supernatural origin of evil. Through a combination of historical and philological study—and an innate talent for psychological insight—I was able to shift my original question into a new and more precise form: under what conditions did humanity create these value judgments of "Good" and "Evil"? What inherent worth do they possess? Have these values up to now helped or hindered human flourishing? Are they signs of humanity's suffering, decline, and impoverishment? Or are they, instead, manifestations of life's fullness, strength, and determination—its courage, its self-assurance, its will to face the future?

To these questions, I entertained a variety of answers. I explored distinctions across different periods, cultures, and social classes. I became a specialist in my chosen problem, and each answer led to further questions, deeper investigations, new theories, and fresh possibilities. Gradually, I found myself with my own domain, my own fertile ground, a hidden world filled with growing and blooming ideas—secret gardens that no one could have suspected existed. How happy we are, we seekers of knowledge, as long as we know how to remain silent for long enough!

My initial urge to publish some of my ideas about the origins of morality came from a small, clear, well-written book— precocious even—in which a twisted and flawed kind of moral philosophy (a quintessentially English kind) was laid out plainly for the first time. This book intrigued me, pulling me in with that irresistible attraction that comes from encountering something fundamentally opposed to one's own beliefs. The book was titled The Origin of the Moral Emotions, authored by Dr. Paul Rée, and it was published in 1877.

I can almost say that I've never read anything where every argument and conclusion inspired such a strong, unequivocal rejection from me as this book did. Yet my rejection was free of irritation or intolerance. In fact, I often referred to its arguments in my own writings of that time—not to refute them (for I see no point in mere refutations), but rather to replace improbable theories with ones I found more plausible. Occasionally, of course, I might have substituted one philosophical error with another.

It was during that early phase that I began publicly expressing the theories of origin that these essays now explore, though I did so with a clumsiness I could not ignore. I lacked a specialized language for these particular topics and often found myself vacillating or falling back into old patterns.

For specific examples, one might compare what I wrote in Human, All- Too- Human, Part I, Aphorism 45, about the parallel early histories of Good and Evil—how they originated from the castes of aristocrats and slaves. Or Aphorisms 136 and following, on the birth and value of ascetic morality. Similarly, Aphorisms 96 and 99 in Volume II, and Aphorism 89, regarding the Morality of Custom—a much older and more fundamental form of morality, completely distinct from the altruistic ethics that Dr. Rée and other English moral philosophers mistake for the "essence" of ethics. Finally, see Aphorism 92.

Likewise, consider Aphorism 26 in Human, All- Too- Human, Part II, or Aphorism 112 in The Dawn of Day, where I discuss the origin of Justice as a balance of power between individuals of roughly equal strength. This equilibrium serves as the foundation for all agreements and thus for all law. Similarly, my thoughts on the origin of Punishment in Human, All- Too- Human, Part II, Aphorisms 22 and 23, challenge Dr. Rée's view. Contrary to his belief that the primary purpose of punishment is deterrence, I argue that this purpose is neither original nor essential but is instead a secondary addition that arises under specific conditions.

At that time, my focus was not so much on the theories—my own or others'—about the origins of morality. The real purpose of those theories, in my view, was to serve as a means to a greater end. My true concern was the value of morality itself. To approach this question, I had to place myself in a state of detachment, almost as though I were entirely alone with my great teacher, Schopenhauer. It was to him that my work, with all its passion and inherent contradictions (for it, too, was a polemic), turned for guidance, as if he were still alive.

The issue I grappled with was, oddly enough, the value of "unegoistic" instincts—the instincts of pity, self-denial, and self-sacrifice. Schopenhauer had persistently celebrated these instincts, portraying them in golden hues, exalting and idealizing them until they appeared to him as ultimate, intrinsic values. It was on the basis of these instincts that he pronounced his negation of both Life and himself. Yet, within me, a deep and growing mistrust arose toward these very instincts. My skepticism dug deeper and deeper, and I came to see in these instincts a profound danger to humanity. They seemed to me humanity's most sublime temptation, its greatest seduction. But seduction to what? To nothingness?

In these unegoistic instincts, I saw the seeds of humanity's decline—the beginning of its end. I saw stagnation, exhaustion, a longing to retreat, and the will turning against Life itself. These instincts appeared to me as the heralds of humanity's last illness, signaling their arrival with a delicate, sorrowful melancholy. I realized that the morality of pity, spreading ever wider and infecting even philosophers with its sickness, was the darkest symptom of modern European civilization. It was the path along which this civilization was sliding—toward what? A new Buddhism? A European Buddhism? Nihilism?

This overvaluation of pity by modern philosophers is a completely new phenomenon. Until then, philosophers were unanimous in their disdain for pity. I need only mention Plato, Spinoza, La Rochefoucauld, and Kant—four thinkers as vastly different as one could imagine, yet united on this one point: their contempt for pity.

This question about the value of pity and the morality it represents (I am deeply opposed to the modern, disgraceful softening of our emotions) might at first seem like an isolated issue—a problem standing on its own. But anyone who pauses to examine it, as I did, and learns to ask the right questions will experience what I experienced: a vast and immense new perspective unfolds before them. A sense of limitless possibilities overtakes them, almost like vertigo. Doubts, mistrust, and fears spring up everywhere. Belief in morality—indeed, in all morality—begins to waver. Finally, a new demand makes itself heard.

Let us state this demand clearly: we need a critique of moral values. The worth of these values themselves must, for the first time, be called into question. To do this, we need to understand the conditions and circumstances under which these values arose, evolved, and were distorted. Morality must be examined as both a result and a symptom, as a mask, as hypocrisy, as disease, and as misunderstanding—but also as a cause, as a remedy, as a stimulant, as a restraint, and as a drug. Such an investigation has never existed before, nor has it even been desired. Up until now, the value of these "values" has been taken as self-evident, beyond any question. No one has ever doubted or hesitated in judging the "good man" to be of higher worth than the "evil man," particularly regarding human progress, utility, and general well-being, including the future.

But what if the opposite were true? What if the "good man" turned out to be a symptom of decline—a danger, a temptation, a poison, a narcotic that allows the present to feed off the future? What if this morality is more comfortable and less risky than its opposite, but also smaller, meaner? What if morality itself is to blame for preventing humanity from reaching its highest potential for power and greatness? What if morality is, in fact, the greatest danger of all dangers?

Once this perspective opened up to me, I had every reason to search for colleagues—scholarly, bold, and diligent companions to help explore this immense, distant, and entirely uncharted territory of morality. This search continues even today. To question morality with such fresh and pressing inquiries, to see it with entirely new eyes, is practically equivalent to discovering morality for the first time. This is a morality that has actually existed, one that has been lived! And isn't discovering it for the first time like uncovering a new land?

When I thought of Dr. Paul Rée in this context, it was because I believed that his questions would eventually force him to adopt a more accurate method to arrive at his answers. Was I wrong to think so? In any case, I wanted to guide his sharp and impartial vision toward a better path. I wanted to point him toward the real history of morality and to warn him, while there was still time, against the world of English theories, which lead ultimately to the empty blue vacuum of heaven. Other colors, more grounded and powerful than blue, are far better suited for the genealogy of morals. Grey, for example, represents hard, provable facts, things that truly happened. It stands for that long, intricate script—the history of human morality—which is so difficult to decipher.

This script was unknown to Dr. Rée. What he had read was Darwin. And so, in his philosophy, the Darwinian beast and the refined, modern weakling— the polite dilettante who "bites no longer"—join hands in a way that, at least, provides an interesting lesson. The latter wears an expression of refined laziness, good-natured indifference, tinged with pessimism and exhaustion, as though it were hardly worth taking moral problems seriously.

I, on the other hand, believe there is no subject more deserving of serious attention. One of the rewards for taking these issues seriously is that, eventually, they may allow us to approach them with a light heart. This light-heartedness— or, to use my own term, this joyful wisdom—is a reward for long, courageous, and painstaking effort, a reward for digging deep. Such effort, of course, is the province of only a few. But the day will come when we can say, with full hearts, "Forward! Even our old morality is fit for comedy!" Then we will have discovered a new plot, a new possibility for the Dionysian drama of The Soul's Fate. And who better to make use of it than the ancient, eternal playwright of the grand comedy of existence?

If anyone finds this writing unclear or discordant, I do not believe the fault necessarily lies with me. My assumption is that the reader has already gone through my earlier works and has invested the effort required to grasp their essence—an effort that is far from simple. Take, for example, my Zarathustra. I do not consider anyone to truly understand that book unless every word in it has, at some point, deeply wounded them and, at another point, profoundly enchanted them. Only then can they earn the privilege of partaking reverently in the tranquil, radiant realm from which that work emerged—a realm of sunlight, vast horizons, clarity, and certainty.

In many cases, difficulty arises from the aphoristic form itself, though this is often because it is approached too superficially. A well-crafted aphorism, carefully formed and cast into its final shape, is far from being "understood" merely upon reading. On the contrary, it is only after being read that it demands interpretation and explanation—and this requires a true art of exposition. An example of what I mean by this can be found in the third essay of this book. That essay begins with an aphorism, and the essay itself serves as its commentary.

There is, however, one quality that has been largely forgotten in our time— a quality necessary to practice reading as an art. It is, in fact, why my writings will require time before they become widely readable. This quality demands, above all else, the patience of a cow— an ability completely foreign to the modern man. That quality is rumination.

Sils-Maria, Upper Engadine,
July, 1887.

Chapter 1
Good and Evil, Good and Bad

The English psychologists, who so far are the only philosophers to have made any real attempt at tracing the history of morality's origins, present us with an intriguing puzzle—not a minor one, either. To be completely honest, their personalities as living riddles are often more fascinating than their books.

They themselves are interesting! But what do these English psychologists truly aim to achieve?

We find them, consciously or unconsciously, always engaged in the same endeavor: bringing to the forefront the partie honteuse—the "shameful part"—of our inner world. They seek the driving, governing, and decisive principles of human behavior in precisely the places where intellectual pride would least want to look. They point to things like the inertia of habit, forgetfulness, blind chance, mechanical associations of ideas, or passive, reflexive, molecular, and fundamentally senseless processes. Why do these psychologists feel compelled to search in such degrading and uncomfortable corners?

Is it a dark instinct for disparagement—a sinister, vulgar, and malicious impulse, perhaps not even understood by themselves?

Or is it a residue of pessimistic jealousy, the bitterness of disillusioned idealists who have become grim and poisoned? Could it be an unspoken, subconscious grudge against Christianity (and perhaps Plato), never fully acknowledged in their minds? Or might it simply reflect a strange fascination with the grotesque, the painfully paradoxical, the mystical, and the illogical elements of life? Perhaps the answer lies in a mix of all these motives—a little vulgarity, a touch of gloominess, a sprinkle of anti-Christian sentiment, and a craving for the bizarre and provocative.

Some would say these psychologists are nothing more than cold, tiresome frogs, hopping and crawling inside people as if they were as much at home in human minds as they are in a swamp. But I reject this idea; I cannot believe it. If, in the absence of certain knowledge, one is permitted to wish, then I sincerely hope the opposite is true.

I hope that these analysts with their psychological microscopes are, at their core, brave, proud, and magnanimous beings. I wish they are individuals who know how to restrain both their hearts and their pains and have trained themselves to sacrifice what is desirable for the sake of what is true. Any truth— even the bitter, ugly, unpleasant, unchristian, and immoral truths—for such truths do exist.

All honor, then, to the noble minds who strive to surpass these historians of morality. Yet it is truly unfortunate that they lack a historical sense themselves, that they are utterly abandoned by the guiding spirits of history. Their entire mode of thinking follows the pattern of old-fashioned philosophers: thoroughly unhistorical. There can be no doubt about this. The glaring inadequacy of their genealogy of morals becomes evident the moment they try to determine the origin of the concept and judgment of "good."

Their theory declares, "Originally, humans praised and called 'good' those altruistic acts that benefited others, specifically those who received the acts' advantages. Over time, people forgot the origin of this praise, and altruistic acts came to be regarded as good in themselves, as if they contained an inherent goodness." This explanation is typical of English psychologists and contains all their signature elements: "utility," "forgetting," "habit," and finally "error." These elements combine to form a foundation for a system of values—a system upon which higher humanity has prided itself as if it were a unique and universal privilege of humankind. But this pride must be humbled; this system of values must be dismantled. Does their theory achieve that?

The first objection that comes to mind is that they have sought and located the true home of the concept of "good" in entirely the wrong place. The idea of "good" did not originate among those to whom goodness was shown. Rather, it was the good themselves—

the aristocratic, the powerful, the high-ranking, and the noble-minded—who felt that they themselves wer e good, along with their actions. Their "goodness" was of the first rank, standing in stark contrast to everything low, common, vulgar, and plebeian. From this sense of superiority—the pathos of distance—they claimed for themselves the right to define values, to name them, and to create a moral hierarchy that served their own nature. What concern did they have for utility?

The perspective of utility is utterly foreign and irrelevant when we consider such an explosive outpouring of supreme values— values that create and delineate their own hierarchies. This creative force stands in stark contrast to the lukewarm conditions that underpin worldly wisdom and calculations of practical expediency, conditions that are not just occasional but perpetual. The pathos of nobility and distance, as I have said—the persistent and commanding esprit de corps of a dominant higher race in contact with a subordinate or lower race—this is the true origin of the contrast between "good" and "bad."

(The masters' right to name things extends so far that language itself can be viewed as an expression of their power: they declare, "This is this," and "That is that," sealing every object and event with a sound, and in doing so, they claim possession of it.) Because of this origin, the word "good" has no necessary connection to altruistic acts, despite the superstitious assumptions of moral philosophers. On the contrary, it is only during the decline of aristocratic values that the contrast between "egoistic" and "altruistic" begins to weigh heavily on the human conscience. To use my own terminology, this contrast is an expression of the herd instinct, which eventually embeds itself in many forms of morality. Even then, it takes considerable time for this instinct to dominate so thoroughly that moral valuations become inseparable from this contrast, as we see in contemporary Europe. Today, the prejudice persists—obsessive and ingrained, like a mental affliction—that equates "moral," "altruistic," and désintéressé (selfless) as interchangeable concepts.

In addition to the historical inaccuracy of this hypothesis about the origin of "good," it suffers from a fundamental psychological

ontradiction. The theory suggests that the utility of altruistic acts led to their being praised and that this origin was subsequently forgotten. But how, exactly, could such forgetting occur? Did the utility of altruistic acts suddenly vanish at some point? Clearly not. Quite the opposite: their utility is experienced constantly, every day, and is therefore continually reinforced. This utility does not fade from memory; instead, it becomes ever more deeply imprinted on human consciousness. Far from being forgotten, it should, by all logic, grow increasingly prominent and undeniable with time.

A more coherent—though not necessarily more correct—theory is that proposed by Herbert Spencer, who equates the concept of "good" with "useful" or "purposeful." According to this perspective, judgments of "good" and "bad" are humanity's way of summarizing and formalizing its unforgettable and continually reinforced experiences of what is "useful-purposeful" and "harmful- non-purposeful." In this view, "good" is attributed to whatever has repeatedly proven to be useful and, therefore, comes to be regarded as "valuable in the highest degree," even "valuable in itself."

While I maintain that this explanation is also flawed, it at least has the merit of being internally consistent and psychologically plausible.

The key insight that set me on the right path came from asking this question: What is the true etymological meaning of the symbols for the concept of "good" across different languages? I discovered that they all traced back to the same evolution of an idea: universally, the root meaning of "good" is tied to "aristocrat" or "noble" (in the social sense). From this root developed the meanings of "good" as "possessing an aristocratic soul," "noble" as "possessing a high-caliber soul," or "having a privileged soul." This evolution consistently parallels another: the transformation of terms like "vulgar," "plebeian," or "low" into their eventual meaning of "bad."

One of the most striking examples of this is the German word schlecht. Originally, schlecht was identical in meaning to schlicht— (consider expressions like schlechtweg and schlechterdings)—which, at first, carried no negative connotation. It simply referred to someone of plebeian origin, as opposed to someone of aristocratic standing. It was only much later, around the time of the Thirty Years' War, that schlecht came to mean what it does today.

From the perspective of the Genealogy of Mor als, this discovery is significant. The delay in recognizing it can be attributed to the influence of democratic prejudice, which has long distorted questions of origin in the modern era. This bias, as I will soon demonstrate, extends even into fields like natural science and physiology, which are ostensibly the most objective of disciplines. The harm caused by this prejudice—particularly in the fields of ethics and history—is considerable once it breaks free from constraints and acts purely out of malice.

The notorious example of Buckle illustrates this point. In Buckle, the plebeianism of the modern spirit—rooted in English culture— erupted once again from its foul soil, as violent and uncontrolled as a slimy volcano. This eruption came with the same coarse, overblown, and vulgar rhetoric that has always accompanied such phenomena, mirroring the crude eloquence with which all volcanoes seem to speak.

Regarding our subject, which is undoubtedly an intimate one and appeals only to a select few, it is significant to note that in the words and roots associated with "good," we glimpse the defining traits by which aristocrats perceive themselves as beings of a higher order. Often, they name themselves based on their power and superiority, referring to themselves as "the powerful," "the lords," or "the commanders." Similarly, they might draw upon visible markers of their status, such as wealth, naming themselves "the rich" or "the possessors"—a meaning reflected in words like arya in Sanskrit, as well as parallels in Iranian and Slavic languages.

But they also name themselves according to their unique qualities, which is particularly relevant to our inquiry. For instance, they call themselves "the truthful," a designation originating with the Greek nobility, voiced through Theognis, the poet of Megara. The Greek word ἐσθλός, crafted for this purpose, etymologically means "one who is," someone real, someone true. Later, it takes on a more subjective sense as "truthful." At this stage, the concept evolves into the motto and rallying cry of the nobility, distinguishing them from the "lying," vulgar man, as Theognis describes. Over time, as the nobility decays, the term ἐσθλός comes to represent a psychological nobility, maturing into a more abstract notion of "noble."

On the other hand, words like κακ ός and δειλ ός (contrasting with ἀγαθός, the noble) emphasize cowardice. This provides a clue about the etymological origin of the ambiguous ἀγαθός, which likely developed along similar lines. The Latin word malus (possibly related to μέλας, meaning "black") reflects a similar distinction: the vulgar man was often characterized as dark-complexioned or black-haired, in contrast to the lighter- haired Aryan conquerors who subjugated them. The pre-Aryan inhabitants of Italy, marked by their darker features, became the visual antithesis of the blonde ruling class. Gaelic offers a striking parallel, with the word Fin—as in Fin- Gal—being a term of nobility that originally denoted blonde-haired individuals as opposed to dark-haired aboriginals.

The Celts, I should note, were largely a blonde-haired people. It is a mistake, as Virchow and others have suggested, to associate the dark-haired populations mapped in certain regions of Germany with Celtic ancestry. Instead, these populations are remnants of the pre-Aryan inhabitants of Europe. This phenomenon is not limited to Germany; throughout Europe, the characteristics of the older subject races—darker complexions, shorter skulls—have resurfaced, even becoming dominant. One might speculate whether modern democracy, anarchism, or the widespread socialist push for communal structures— primitive societal forms—represents a regression to this earlier state. Could it signify that the once-dominant Aryan "master race" is now in physiological decline?

As for the Latin word bonus, I propose that it originally meant "the warrior." My hypothesis derives bonus from an earlier form, duonus, as seen in the word duellum (an older form of bellum, "war"), where duonus seems embedded. Bonus, then, would signify "the man of discord," "one who divides" (duo), the warrior. This sheds light on what "the good" meant in ancient Rome: a man of battle.

Finally, consider our German word gut. Could it mean "the godlike," referring to "a man of godlike race"? Might it even share origins with the national name of the Goths, originally a noble designation? The evidence for this hypothesis lies outside the scope of this work.

Above all, there are no exceptions—though there are opportunities for exceptions—to the rule that the idea of political superiority ultimately transforms into the idea of psychological superiority. This is particularly evident when the highest caste also serves as the priestly caste, and in line with its defining traits, claims titles that specifically refer to its priestly role. In such cases, the concepts of "clean" and "unclean" emerge as markers of class distinction for the first time. Here, the notions of "good" and "bad" take on meanings that go beyond mere social distinctions.

It is important, however, not to interpret these concepts of "clean" and "unclean" too broadly, seriously, or symbolically. On the contrary, the ideas of ancient humanity must be understood in their most rudimentary and literal sense—crude, coarse, physical, and narrowly practical, without symbolic undertones. The "clean man," at the start, is simply someone who washes himself, avoids foods that might cause skin diseases, abstains from contact with lower-class women deemed "unclean," and feels a revulsion toward blood. Nothing more—at least not much more.

The nature of a priestly aristocracy itself explains why such societies are prone to dangerously intensifying opposing values at an early stage. These oppositions carve deep divisions into the social fabric, creating chasms that even the boldest free thinkers might hesitate to cross. From the beginning, there is something inherently diseased about priestly aristocracies, and this affliction permeates their way of life. Their aversion to direct action fosters a peculiar blend of introspection and intense emotional volatility. This results in a kind of introspective morbidity and nervous exhaustion—neurasthenia—that seems to cling inevitably to priests across all times and places.

As for the remedies these priestly societies devised for their own maladies, the philosopher can only observe that these so-called cures have often proven far more harmful than the original disease they sought to treat. Humanity still bears the scars of the naïve "cures" of priestly societies. Consider their dietary restrictions (such as abstaining from meat), their fasting, their insistence on sexual continence, and their withdrawal into wilderness isolation—a form of treatment reminiscent of the Weir - Mitchell rest cure, though without the system of excessive feeding and strengthening that effectively counters the hysteria of the ascetic ideal.

Reflect also on the metaphysical systems created by priests, with their war on the senses, their weakening effects, and their obsessive attention to minute details. Consider their practices of self-hypnosis, modeled on the principles of the fakir and Brahman (using metaphysical concepts like Brahman as a kind of fixation device). And finally, note the culmination of this path in an overwhelming desire for annihilation—disguised as a union with God. The longing for unio mystica with God mirrors the Buddhist's yearning for nothingness: Nirvana—and nothing else.

In priestly societies, everything operates on a more dangerous scale—not only their remedies but also their pride, vengeance, cunning, ecstasy, love, ambition, virtue, and even their morbidity. It is fair to say that on the soil of this inherently perilous form of human society, the priestly society, humanity first became an interesting animal. It was within this framework that the human soul reached new depths and developed its capacity for evil. These two traits—depth and evil—remain the fundamental markers of humanity's superiority over every other animal.

The reader will likely have already guessed how easily the priestly mode of valuation could diverge from the knightly-aristocratic mode and develop into its direct opposite. This opposition is further fueled in situations where the priestly and warrior castes confront each other with mutual jealousy, unable to agree on who should hold the highest status.

The knightly-aristocratic values are rooted in a careful cultivation of physical strength and vitality—a flourishing, rich, and exuberant health that exceeds mere survival. These values celebrate war, adventure, hunting, dancing, tournaments, and all forms of bold, free, and joyous action. In contrast, the priestly- aristocratic mode of valuation, as we have seen, rests on entirely different assumptions. For this caste, war itself is an undesirable affair! And yet, as is well known, priests are the most dangerous of enemies—why? Because they are the weakest.

Their weakness fuels a hatred that grows into something vast and sinister— subtle, cunning, and venomous. Throughout history, the greatest haters have always been priests, who are also the most intelligent haters. Compared to the ingenuity of priestly revenge, all other forms of cleverness pale into insignificance. Without the cleverness of the weak, human history would be unbearably dull. Consider the most striking example of this: all the efforts directed against the aristocrats, the powerful, the masters, and the rulers of society are insignificant compared to what the Jews—a priestly nation— achieved in their struggle.

The Jews, that priestly people, discovered that their ultimate weapon against their enemies and oppressors was a radical transvaluation of values, which was simultaneously the most ingenious act of revenge. This strategy was uniquely suited to a nation of priests, deeply steeped in the jealousy and resourcefulness of priestly vengeance. Opposing the aristocratic equation of "good = noble = beautiful = happy = loved by the gods," the Jews had the audacity to propose and fiercely uphold the opposite equation. With a terrifying logic and the deepest hatred—the hatred born of weakness—they asserted:

"The wretched are the only ones who are good. The poor, the weak, the lowly—they alone are good. The suffering, the needy, the sick, and the loathsome—they are the pious, the blessed, and only they shall be saved. But you, aristocrats, you men of power, you are evil for all eternity! You are the horrible, the greedy, the insatiable, the godless! Eternally cursed and damned shall you be!"

We know who inherited this Jewish transvaluation. In the context of the monumental and far-reaching consequences of the Jews' initiative—arguably the most fundamental declaration of war in history—I am reminded of something I wrote elsewhere (Beyond Good and Evil, Aphorism 195): that it was with the Jews that the slave revolt in morality began. This revolt, with its roots two millennia deep, has endured through history and, in our present age, has simply disappeared from view—because it has triumphed.

But you do not understand this? You cannot see the power that took two thousand years to achieve its victory? There is no surprise in that: all long processes are difficult to perceive and even harder to grasp. Yet this is what happened: from the trunk of that tree of revenge and hatred—Jewish hatred, the most profound and sublime hatred, capable of creating ideals and transforming old values into something entirely new and unparalleled on earth— there emerged a phenomenon just as incomparable: a new kind of love, the deepest and most sublime form of love ever known. And from what other trunk could such a love have grown?

But do not mistake this love as a negation of the thirst for revenge, as an opposition to Jewish hatred. Quite the opposite! This love grew out of that hatred, becoming its ultimate crown, its victorious crown. It expanded ever outward, basking in the light and fullness of the sun, while still pursuing the goals of hatred— its victory, its spoils, its cunning strategies—with the same fervor as the roots of that tree of hatred drove deeper and deeper into the dark and evil depths of existence, growing ever more stable, ever more insatiable.

Consider Jesus of Nazareth, the living embodiment of the gospel of love, this "Redeemer" who brought salvation and victory to the poor, the sick, and the sinful. Was he not, in truth, the most sinister and irresistible form of temptation? A temptation to adopt the tortuous path toward precisely those Jewish values and ideals? Did Israel not, through this "Redeemer," achieve the ultimate goal of its sublime revenge, despite his appearance as Israel's opponent and destroyer?

Could it be that this extraordinary outcome—Israel's triumph— was the result of the dark genius of a truly great policy of revenge? A revenge that was slow, far-seeing, and methodical, digging deeply into the fabric of time and history? Is it not possible that Israel had to renounce and condemn, before the eyes of the world, the very instrument of its revenge—nailing it to the cross—so that the world, all of Israel's enemies, might unsuspectingly take the bait?

Could any human mind, with all its ingenuity, have devised a bait more dangerous, more insidious? Could anything else rival the seductive, intoxicating, corrupting power of the symbol of the holy cross? This terrifying paradox of "a god on the cross," this unfathomable mystery of a god's self-crucifixion for the salvation of humanity—does it not represent the ultimate, supreme horror, a horror so profound that it defies comprehension?

It is certain, at least, that sub hoc signo—under this sign—Israel, through its revenge and its transvaluation of all values, has consistently triumphed over all other ideals, including the more aristocratic ones.

"But why speak of nobler ideals? Let us face the facts: the people have triumphed—whether you call them the slaves, the masses, the herd, or whatever other name suits you. If this triumph came through the Jews, so be it! In that case, no nation has ever had a greater mission in the history of the world. The 'masters' have been overthrown, and the morality of the common man has prevailed. This victory may be likened to a kind of blood-poisoning, as it has blended the races together—I do not deny this—but it cannot be disputed that this intoxication has succeeded. The 'redemption' of humanity (that is, its liberation from the masters) is proceeding smoothly. Everything is clearly becoming Judaised, Christianised, or vulgarised—what difference does the label make? The poisoning seems unstoppable as it spreads through the entire body politic of humanity.

However, perhaps from this point forward, its tempo can be slowed, its progress made more refined, more subtle, quieter, and more restrained—there is no rush. In this context, one might ask: does the Church still serve a necessary purpose? Does it even have a right to exist? Could humanity now do without it? Quaeritur. It seems that the Church hinders and slows this process instead of accelerating it. Perhaps that is precisely its utility.

Certainly, the Church remains a crude and clumsy institution, offensive to any mind with even a hint of delicacy or to anyone with genuinely modern tastes. Should it not, at the very least, learn to refine itself a little? Today, it repels more people than it attracts. Which of us would even bother to be a freethinker if not for the Church? It is the Church that drives us away, not its poison— because, apart from the Church, we actually like the poison."

These are the parting words of a freethinker responding to my argument— a respectable man by his own standards (as he has often demonstrated) and a democrat as well. He had listened to me patiently but could not endure my silence on this matter. As for me, there is indeed much on this subject about which I prefer to remain silent.

The revolt of the slaves in morality begins with the principle of resentment becoming creative and giving rise to values. This resentment is experienced by those who, unable to act directly, are forced to channel their frustrations into an imagined revenge. While aristocratic morality originates in a triumphant affirmation of its own existence and values, slave morality begins by saying "no"—a rejection of everything "outside itself," "different from itself," and "not itself." This "no" is its creative act.

This reversal of the valuing process—a shift from affirming the self to focusing on the external—is characteristic of resentment. Slave morality depends on an external, objective world as a condition for its very existence. To use a physiological metaphor, it requires external stimuli to activate itself; its essence is reaction, not action. It lacks the spontaneous, self-generating energy of aristocratic morality.

In the case of aristocratic values, action and growth occur naturally and independently. The aristocratic morality does not need an adversary to define itself but instead seeks an antithesis only to enhance its joyful and emphatic "yes" to itself. Its negative concepts—"low," "vulgar," "bad"—are mere afterthoughts, secondary contrasts to its primary, life-affirming essence. This essence is rich with vitality and passion, grounded in the aristocrat's self-perception: "We aristocrats, we good ones, we beautiful ones, we happy ones."

When the aristocratic morality goes astray and violates reality, this misstep is confined to the particular sphere with which it is not sufficiently familiar—a sphere that it deliberately avoids understanding and disdains to engage with. It often misjudges, in certain instances, the sphere it holds in contempt: that of the common, vulgar man and the lower classes. However, it is important to note that even if its disdain falsely represents the object of its contempt, this misrepresentation will always be far less egregious than the fabrications and grotesque distortions born of the vindictive hatred and vengefulness of the weak when they attack their enemies. Contempt inherently carries too much nonchalance, casualness, boredom, impatience, and even personal exhilaration to ever transform its object into a complete caricature or monstrosity.

Attention should be drawn to the almost benevolent nuances infused by the Greek nobility into the terms they used to distinguish the common people from themselves. Observe how, in such words, there often lingers a kind of pity, care, and consideration that softens their tone. Eventually, many of these terms evolved into expressions meaning "unhappy" or "worthy of pity." For example, words like δειλός, δείλαιος, πονηρός, and μοχθηρός, initially used to describe the vulgar man as a laborer or beast of burden, ultimately acquired connotations of misfortune. Similarly, terms for "bad," "low," and "unhappy" in Greek carried a resonance in which "unhappy" was the dominant note. This linguistic inheritance from noble morality reflects how, even in scorn, it remained consistent with its values.

The "well-born" naturally felt themselves to be the happy ones. They did not need to manufacture their happiness artificially by focusing on their enemies or delude themselves into happiness through false narratives, as is common among resentful men. Their happiness arose organically, as an outpouring of their strength and energy. To them, happiness and action were inseparable concepts; to act was to be happy. This is reflected in the etymology of the Greek phrase εὖ πράττειν ("to fare well"), which originally meant "to act well." In contrast, the happiness of the weak and oppressed is fundamentally passive—it is a sedative, a tranquilizing state of rest, peace, and quiet, akin to a Sabbath for the soul, a relaxation of the body and mind.

The aristocratic man, confident and at ease with himself, exemplified sincerity and straightforwardness. The Greek term γεννα ῖος ("noble-born") emphasizes this quality of being candid and perhaps even naïve. By contrast, the resentful man is neither sincere nor honest with himself. His soul is crooked; his mind thrives in hidden corners, on secret paths, and in backdoor dealings. For him, the concealed and indirect are his refuge, his safety, and his comfort. He is a master of silence, grudge-holding, waiting, and self-deprecation.

Over time, a race of resentful individuals necessarily becomes more prudent than any aristocratic race. For them, prudence is not a luxury or refinement, as it is for the aristocrats, but a critical necessity for survival. Among aristocratic men, prudence carries an air of indulgence and refinement. It plays a secondary role compared to the reliable functioning of their instincts and unconscious drives, or even a certain recklessness in their actions. They might charge boldly into danger or battle or exhibit bursts of passionate emotion—whether in love, reverence, or gratitude. Such displays of vitality and spirit have always been the hallmarks of noble souls.

When the aristocratic man experiences resentment, it expresses itself immediately and exhausts itself in the reaction, leaving no lingering venom. In many situations, aristocratic resentment does not even arise, where in weaker individuals it would be unavoidable. Their inability to dwell on their enemies, injuries, or misfortunes signals the fullness of their nature. Their excess of energy heals wounds and fosters forgetfulness. Mirabeau provides a modern example of this disposition; he bore no memory of the insults and petty wrongs committed against him. His inability to forgive was simply a byproduct of his tendency to forget. Such men shrug off insults like worms that would otherwise burrow into others.

In these individuals, we see the possibility—if it exists at all—of a true "love of one's enemies." An aristocratic man respects his enemies, and this respect can act as a bridge to love. He demands that his enemies be worthy adversaries—men he can admire, whose character holds much to honor and nothing to despise. He tolerates no enemy who is beneath his contempt.

In contrast, consider how the resentful man conceives of his enemy. It is here that his creativity emerges. He imagines the "evil enemy," the "wicked one," and from this fabricated figure, he derives a contrasting and corresponding idea: the "good one." This "good one" is none other than himself. Through this inversion, the resentful man defines his identity by vilifying those he opposes.

The method of the resentful man is entirely opposite to that of the aristocratic man. The aristocratic man forms the concept of "good" spontaneously and directly—arising naturally from his own being. From this starting point, he then creates the idea of "bad," which serves as a secondary concept, an afterthought. In contrast, the resentful man's concept of "evil" emerges from the cauldron of unfulfilled hatred. The aristocratic "bad" is merely a nuance, an imitation, an addition; the resentful "evil," however, is original, foundational, the central act in the creation of slave morality.

These two words—"bad" and "evil"—mark an immense difference, even though they share a common opposition in the idea of "good." But the idea of "good" itself is not the same in the two systems. Let us ask instead: Who is truly evil according to the morality of resentment? The answer, given with full seriousness, is this: precisely the good man of the aristocratic morality—the noble, the powerful, the ruler—transfigured and distorted through the venomous lens of resentment into something entirely different, into a figure of malevolence.

This much must be admitted: the man who came to know these "good" ones only as enemies also came to know them only as evil enemies. Those same aristocratic men, who among their equals were bound by strict conventions, respect, customs, and gratitude—and even more by mutual vigilance and jealousy—these same men, who within their circle displayed countless forms of courtesy, self-restraint, refinement, loyalty, pride, and friendship, behaved in entirely different ways outside their group. Toward those beyond their circle, where the foreign begins, they were little better than beasts of prey set loose.

In the wilderness, freed from the constraints of societal control, they released the pent-up tension created by their confinement in the order and peace of their own society. There, they returned to the innocence of the predator's conscience, reveling like jubilant monsters in their wild freedom. Emerging from acts of murder, arson, rape, and torture, they carried themselves with a moral ease, even a sense of playfulness, as if these horrors were nothing more than a rowdy prank from students on a spree—utterly convinced that poets would celebrate their deeds in song and story.

It is impossible to overlook the beast of prey that lies at the core of all aristocratic races. This magnificent, blonde brute, driven by a relentless hunger for plunder and victory, is a defining feature of these noble classes. This primal force demands an outlet; the beast must occasionally break free, returning to the wilderness. We see this need in the Romans, Arabs, Germans, and Japanese nobility, in the Homeric heroes, and in the Scandinavian Vikings. All these groups share this essential trait: the need to unleash their inner beast and revel in the unrestrained innocence of their savage nature.

It is the aristocratic races that have left the imprint of the word "barbarian" along every path they have traveled. Indeed, an awareness of this very barbarism, and even a pride in it, is evident even in their most advanced civilizations. For example,

Pericles, in his famous funeral oration, declares to the Athenians, "Our audacity has forced a way over every land and sea, rearing everywhere imperishable memorials of itself for good and for evil."

This audacity of aristocratic races, however reckless, absurd, and spasmodic its manifestations may seem, reflects the unpredictable and extravagant nature of their endeavors. Pericles especially highlights the $\varrho\alpha\ \vartheta\upsilon\mu\iota\alpha$ of the Athenians—their nonchalance, their disregard for safety, bodily well-being, life, and comfort. He celebrates their terrifying joy and intense delight in destruction, in the ecstasies of victory, and even in cruelty. These traits— when viewed by those who have suffered at their hands—become crystallized into the image of the "barbarian," the "evil enemy," or figures like the "Goth" and the "Vandal."

The profound, icy mistrust that the German provokes as soon as he attains power—even today—is a lingering echo of the inextinguishable horror with which Europe regarded the wrath of the blonde Teutonic beast for centuries. This mistrust persists despite the fact that there is now barely any psychological, let alone physical, continuity between the ancient Germans and modern ones. I have previously pointed out Hesiod's difficulty when he attempted to describe the series of social ages in terms of gold, silver, and bronze. Hesiod faced a contradiction when trying to reconcile the Homeric world, which aristocratic families remembered as a glorious age filled with their heroic ancestors, with its simultaneously dreadful and violent reality. He resolved this by splitting one age into two: the heroic age of demigods, as it was remembered by the aristocracy, and the bronze age, as it appeared to the descendants of the oppressed, the enslaved, and the exiled. To them, it was a brutal and merciless era—a true age of bronze—hard, cold, and unfeeling, crushing everything and staining all it touched with blood.

If we accept the modern theory, now widely believed, that the very essence of civilization lies in taming humanity's beastly instincts and transforming humans into domesticated and civil animals, then it follows that the real tools of civilization must include the instincts of reaction and resentment. These are the very instincts by which aristocratic races, along with their ideals, were eventually degraded and defeated. However, this does not imply that the bearers of these tools of civilization were themselves representatives of civilization. On the contrary—this is not merely probable but evident even today.

These bearers of vindictive instincts, compelled to repress their vengeance and resentment, are the descendants of all European and non-European slaves, particularly the pre-Aryan populations. These people, I assert, represent not the advancement of humanity but its decline.

These "tools of civilization" are a disgrace to humanity and, in truth, provide more reason to question and distrust civilization than to defend it. While it is perfectly reasonable to be wary of the blonde beast that lies at the heart of all aristocratic races and to remain vigilant against it, who would not prefer to live with fear—and at the same time, admiration—than to endure the constant, revolting sight of the deformed, the dwarfed, the stunted, and the poisoned? Is that not our current condition? What drives our disgust with "man" today? For it is clear that we suffer from man—there is no denying it.

It is not fear that troubles us. Rather, it is that there is nothing left to fear from men. The worm that is "man" now crawls to the forefront, multiplying endlessly. The "tame man," the pitiful, mediocre, uninspiring creature, has come to see himself as the goal, the pinnacle, the meaning, the historic principle—the "higher man." Worse still, he may even be right to see himself this way. Compared to the overwhelming deformity, sickness, exhaustion, and decay that now pollutes Europe, he may indeed represent a kind of relative success. At least he still says yes to life.

At this point, I cannot help but express a sigh and one last hope. What is it that I find so intolerable? What chokes me, suffocates me, and makes me faint? Bad air! Bad air! The stench of something misshapen, the foul odor of the insides of a malformed soul near me—that is what I cannot endure. Beyond that, what hardship could not be borne? What privation, bad weather, illness, toil, or solitude would be insurmountable? In truth, one can endure anything, being born to dig, to battle, to survive. One always finds the light again, always experiences life's golden moment of triumph, and stands again as one was born: unbroken, tense, and ready for something more challenging, something more distant. Like a bow, stretched tauter by every strain, one prepares for the next shot.

But I beg—if there are goddesses beyond good and evil who can grant such things—grant me, from time to time, just one glimpse. Just one glimpse of something perfect, fully realized, mighty, triumphant. Grant me the sight of something that still inspires fear! Let me see a man who justifies humanity's existence. A man whose happiness, realized and embodied, redeems the idea of mankind. A man for whom one might cling to belief in humanity!

The reality, however, is bleak. The dwarfing and flattening of European man is our greatest danger. It is this trend that wears us down, for we see nothing today that strives to grow greater. The trajectory appears to move ever backward—toward something smaller, more insipid, more calculating, more comfortable, more mediocre, more indifferent, more Chinese, more Christian. There is no doubt: man is becoming "better." And it is precisely this process—this loss of fear of man—that has also robbed us of hope in man, even of the will to be man.

The sight of man now wearies us. What is modern nihilism, if not this? We are tired of man.

But let us return to the subject. The problem of a differ ent origin of "good"—as it has been imagined by the resentful man—requires an answer. It's no surprise that lambs might hold a grudge against the great birds of prey. But this doesn't mean we should blame the birds of prey for hunting the lambs. When the lambs say among themselves, "These birds of prey are evil, and anyone who is the opposite of them, who is not a bird of prey but a lamb—such a person is good," there's nothing particularly objectionable about this view. It is natural for the lambs to create such an ideal. At the same time, however, the birds of prey might mockingly say to themselves, "We don't bear any grudge against these good lambs. In fact, we like them—there's nothing tastier than a tender lamb."

To demand that strength should not show itself as strength—that it should not seek to dominate, to overcome, to rule, to thirst for challenges, opponents, and victories—is just as absurd as expecting weakness to behave like strength. A force is simply what it is: movement, will, and action—it cannot be separated from these expressions. Force is not something separate from what it does. Yet language (and the flawed reasoning built into it) misleads us. It tempts us to see every action as requiring a subject behind it, a "doer" behind the deed.

For example, people separate lightning from its flash. They think of the flash as something done by the lightning, as if lightning itself were a kind of being or subject that causes the flash to happen. In the same way, popular morality separates strength from its actions, imagining that there is some neutral, independent force behind a strong person, one that can choose whether or not to act with strength. But this is a false idea. There is no "being" behind the doing, no "doer" behind the act. The action itself is everything. The so-called "doer" is just a shadow of the action, a label we attach to it.

This is like saying the lightning "flashes," as though the flash were something separate from the lightning itself. It's a kind of doubling of the same event— making the lightning both the cause and the effect of its own flash. Scientists, too, fall into this trap when they say things like, "Force moves," or "Force causes." Even modern science, despite its cold objectivity, remains ensnared by the tricks of language. It cannot let go of the old superstition of the "subject." The atom, for instance, is one such imaginary subject, just like Kant's "Thing-in-itself."

Is it any wonder, then, that suppressed feelings of revenge and hatred seize upon this belief for their own purposes? Nothing fuels these emotions more than the idea that "the strong have the choice to be weak, and the bird of prey has the option to be a lamb." This belief gives the oppressed and downtrodden a way to hold the birds of prey accountable for being what they are. The weak and powerless, driven by their resentment, convince themselves that the strong are to blame for their strength, and that the predators are at fault for being predators.

"Let us be different from evil, let us be good! And good is anyone who does not oppress, who does not harm others, who does not attack, who does not seek revenge, who leaves vengeance to God, who keeps himself hidden as we do, who avoids evil, and who asks little from life; in short, someone like us—patient, meek, and just." Yet, when this sentiment is stripped of its pretenses and interpreted coldly and without bias, it means little more than, "The weak are weak, and it is good to avoid doing anything beyond our strength."

This grim prudence, this lowest form of survival instinct, is no different from what insects demonstrate when they feign death in the face of great danger, avoiding any action that could cost them too much. Yet this basic instinct, through the self-deception and trickery of weakness, has been dressed up in the grandeur of an ascetic, silent, and expectant virtue. It pretends, as if by choice, that the weakness of the weak—their very nature, their being, their actions, their inescapable reality—is a deliberate decision, a conscious act of will, a merit, a virtue.

Such individuals rely on the belief in a neutral, free-choosing "subject"—or, in simpler terms, the soul. This belief is essential for their self-preservation and self-assertion, where every lie about themselves can be sanctified. The notion of the subject, or soul, has perhaps been the most effective dogma ever devised because it enables the weak, the oppressed, and the frail masses to engage in the ultimate self-deception: interpreting their weakness as a form of freedom, seeing their condition—whether being one thing or another—not as necessity but as merit.

Who dares to peer into the secret of how ideals are created in this world?

Who has the courage to confront it? Come forward!

Here, a glimpse is granted into these dark and grimy workshops. But wait! Just a moment, curious and reckless soul—your eyes must first adjust to this strange, shifting light. Now, look carefully! Enough! Speak! What is happening down there, in the depths? Tell us what you see, you with the most dangerous curiosity—for now I will listen.

"I see nothing, but I hear much more. It is a careful, spiteful, soft whispering and murmuring from every corner and crevice. It seems to me they are lying; every sound is coated with a sugary sweetness. Weakness is being turned into merit—there's no question about it. It is exactly as you say."

Go on!

"And the inability to retaliate is being called 'goodness.' Cowardly baseness is being rebranded as meekness. Submission to those they hate is renamed obedience—obedience, they say, to someone who supposedly commanded this submission, whom they call God. The harmlessness of the weak, their abundance of cowardice, their standing at the door and waiting because they have no other choice—these things are given noble labels like 'patience,' which they even call a virtue. Their inability to take revenge is transformed into not wanting revenge, perhaps even forgiveness (as if they know not what they do— though we know well enough what they do). They speak of 'love for their enemies' and sweat as they say it."

Go on!

"They are wretched, without a doubt—all these whisperers and forgers in the corners, though they huddle together for warmth. And yet they tell me their misery is a special favor and distinction granted to them by God, much like one beats the dogs one loves most. They even say this misery is a preparation, a test, a form of training. Perhaps, they say, it is more than that—it might one day be repaid with immense interest, in gold or in happiness. This they call 'blessedness.'"

Go on!

"Now they are trying to convince me that not only are they better people than the mighty, than the lords of the earth—whose spittle they are forced to lick (not out of fear, of course, oh no, not out of fear! But because God commands that all authority must be honored)—but also that they have a 'better time.' If not now, then one day they will surely have a 'better time.' But enough! Enough! I can bear no more. Bad air! Bad air! These workshops where ideals are created—they reek of the rankest lies!"

Wait, hold on! You're not mentioning the masterpieces crafted by these virtuosos of black magic, these masters who can transform blackness into whiteness, guilt into innocence, and darkness into light. Have you not noticed the level of refinement they achieve in their ultimate work, their most daring, subtle, ingenious, and deceitful trick?

Be careful! These creatures of the cellar, filled with revenge and hatred—what do they make out of that revenge and hatred? Do you hear their words? Would you ever guess, if you trusted only their words, that you are among people seething with resentment and nothing else?

"I understand now—I prick up my ears (ah! ah! ah!—and hold my nose). Now, for the first time, I truly hear what they have always said: 'We are the good, we are the righteous.' What they demand is not called revenge; they call it 'the triumph of righteousness.' What they hate is not their enemies; no, they claim to hate 'unrighteousness' and 'godlessness.' What they believe in and hope for is not the joy of revenge, not the intoxicating sweetness of revenge (did not Homer call it 'sweeter than honey'?), but rather the victory of God—the righteous God— over the 'godless.' What is left for them to love in this world? Not their brothers in hate, but their 'brothers in love,' as they say: all the good and righteous people of the earth."

And what do they call that vision that comforts them through the hardships of life—their grand illusion of future blessedness?

"What? Am I hearing this correctly? They call it 'the Last Judgment,' the coming of their kingdom, 'the Kingdom of God.' But for now, they say they live 'in faith,' 'in love,' and 'in hope.'"

Enough! Enough!

Faith in what? Love for what? Hope for what? These weaklings! It is clear they also wish to be strong one day. There is no doubt about it—their kingdom must come someday. They call it "the Kingdom of God," as already mentioned. They are so meek in everything, so patient! Yet to experience that kingdom, they must live long—beyond death itself. Yes, eternal life is required to finally compensate for this earthly life of "faith," "love," and "hope."

Compensate for what? Compensate with what?

Dante, I believe, made a glaring error when, with terrifying brilliance, he inscribed over the gates of his Hell, "Me too made eternal love." Surely, the following inscription would be far more fitting over the gates of the Christian Paradise and its so-called "eternal blessedness." "Me too made eternal hate." That is, of course, assuming one is willing to put a truth above the entrance to a lie.

What is this "blessedness" of Paradise, exactly? Perhaps we could guess, but it's better to let an authority explicitly state it— someone whose expertise in such matters is beyond question: Thomas Aquinas, the great teacher and saint.

"Beati in regno celesti," says Thomas Aquinas, as softly as a lamb, "videbunt paenas damnatorum, ut beatitudo illis magis complaceat." ("The blessed in the heavenly kingdom will witness the punishment of the damned, so that their bliss will be all the greater.")

Or, if you wish to hear a stronger tone, let us take the words of a triumphant early Church Father, warning his followers against the cruel pleasures of public spectacles. Why? Because, he explains, faith offers something far greater. De Spectaculis (Chapter 29 and following) lays it out plainly: thanks to redemption, we have access to joys of an entirely different kind. Instead of athletes, we have martyrs. Do we crave blood? Then we have the blood of Christ. But what will await us on the day of His return, on the day of His triumph?

Then this enraptured visionary continues:

"But indeed, other spectacles await us—that final and eternal day of judgment, that day unexpected by the nations, that day scorned by them, when the vast age of the world and all its generations will be consumed in one fir e. What a spectacle will that be! What shall I marvel at? What shall I laugh at? Where shall I rejoice? Where shall I exult, as I watch so many mighty kings, who were once proclaimed to be taken into heaven, groaning in the deepest darkness along with Jupiter himself and their own witnesses! Then, too, the governors, those persecutors of the name of the Lord, being consumed in fir es more savage than the flames with which they tormented Christians! And what about those wise philosopher s, ashamed as they burn alongside their disciples, those same philosophers who taught that nothing pertained to God, who declared that souls either did not exist or would not return to their bodies! What of the poets, trembling not before Rhadamanthus or Minos but before the unexpected tribunal of Christ! Then, truly, the tragedies will be heard again, with voices much louder and screams far more violent in their own calamities. Then, the actors will be seen, more unrestrained in their movements through the flames. Then, the charioteer s will be on fiery wheels, their whole bodies blazing red. Then, the athletes will be thrown not in the gymnasiums, but into fire.

Unless, of course, I prefer not to see them alive even then, for I would rather direct my insatiable gaze to those who were most cruel against the Lord. 'Her e he is,' I will say, 'the carpenter 's son or the child of a prostitute' (as the following passages and especially the description of Mary in the Talmud make clear , Tertullian is here refer ring to the Jews). 'Her e he is, the break er of the Sabbath, the Samaritan possessed by a demon. Her e he is, the one whom you purchased from Judas, the one who was beaten with a reed and struck with fists, who was defiled with spit, given gall and vinegar to dr ink. Her e he is, the one whose body his disciples supposedly stole to claim he had risen—or per haps the gardener took it, to prevent visitors from trampling his lettuce!' To witness such things, to revel in such spectacles—what praetor, what consul, what priest could offer you such gifts from their generosity? And yet we already have a foretaste of these things, in a way, through faith, as the Spirit brings them to us in vivid imagination. But how much more magnificent are those things that eye has not seen, nor ear heard, nor the heart of man imagined (1 Corinthians 2 :9). I believe they will be far more pleasing than any arena or stage, whether comedic or tragic."

And so it is written: Perfidem—by faith.

Let us come to a conclusion. The two opposing value systems—"good and bad" versus "good and evil"—have waged a terrible battle across the centuries. This thousand-year struggle has shaped the world, and though the "good and evil" morality has long held the upper hand, there are still places where the outcome remains undecided. It could even be said that this conflict continues to escalate, reaching ever higher levels of complexity and intensity. It has become increasingly psychological, so much so that one might argue there is no greater mark of a higher or more psychological nature than to embody this very contradiction—to still serve as a battlefield for these opposing values.

The symbol of this struggle, etched into history in a script still worth reading, is encapsulated in the phrase: Rome against Judea, Judea against Rome. This conflict, this confrontation, this antagonism remains unparalleled in significance. There has been no greater event in history than this fight, no more profound question than the one it poses.

To Rome, the Jew represented the embodiment of the unnatural, a being utterly monstrous in its opposition to the Roman way of life. The Romans saw in the Jews a race consumed by hatred for all of humanity—and they were right, insofar as the well-being and future of humanity were tied to the unconditional dominance of aristocratic values, the values of Rome. Conversely, what did the Jews feel toward Rome? This can be gleaned from countless hints, but it is enough to turn to the Book of Revelation (the Johannine Apocalypse), which stands as perhaps the most obscene of written outbursts, a text steeped in the spirit of vengeance.

And yet, consider the profound irony—and the cunning logic—of the Christian instinct, which labeled this very book of hate with the name of the "Disciple of Love." This is the same disciple to whom the ecstatic and passionate Gospel was attributed. There is a fragment of truth in this association, even if it required considerable literary forgery to make it plausible.

The Romans were a strong and aristocratic people—perhaps the strongest and most aristocratic the world has ever known, or even imagined. Every relic of their civilization, every inscription, inspires awe, provided one can perceive the spirit behind the words. In contrast, the Jews were the quintessential priestly nation of resentment, endowed with a singular genius for shaping popular morality. To fully appreciate their exceptionalism, compare the Jews to other nations with similar tendencies, such as the Chinese or the Germans. It is only after such a comparison that one can grasp what is truly first-rate and what is merely fifth-rate.

Which of the two has been provisionally victorious, Rome or Judea? There can be no doubt. Just look at whom, even today, people bow to in Rome itself, as though before the embodiment of the highest values. And not only in Rome, but across nearly half the world—everywhere humanity has been tamed or is in the process of being tamed—people bow before three Jews and one Jewess: Jesus of Nazareth, Peter the fisherman, Paul the tent- maker, and Mary, the mother of Jesus. This fact is extraordinary. Rome has undoubtedly been defeated.

At least, that is the case for now. During the Renaissance, there was a brilliantly sinister resurgence of the classical ideal, the aristocratic valuation of all things. Rome, like a man shaking off a deep sleep, seemed to stir under the weight of the Judaised Rome that had been built over it—a Rome that had become an ecumenical synagogue and called itself the "Church." But just as quickly, Judea triumphed again, this time through that fundamentally popular (German and English) movement of revenge called the Reformation. Along with it came the inevitable restoration of the Church and, with it, the return of the graveyard peace of classical Rome.

Judea triumphed once more, and even more decisively, during the French Revolution. Here, the victory was deeper and more profound than ever. The last political aristocracy in Europe—the French aristocracy of the seventeenth and eighteenth centuries— was shattered by the instincts of a resentful populace. Never before had the world heard such jubilant celebration, such uproarious enthusiasm. And in the midst of it all, something monstrous and unexpected occurred: the ancient ideal itself was revived, parading before the conscience of humanity with unprecedented brilliance and vitality.

Against the cry of resentment—the call for equality, abasement, and the levelling of humanity, for regression into mediocrity— there resounded a counter-cry, terrible and seductive: the prer ogative of the few.

As though marking a final crossroads, there appeared Napoleon, the most singular and violent anachronism to have ever lived. In Napoleon was embodied the very problem of the aristocratic ideal itself—an ideal both magnificent and monstrous. Napoleon was a synthesis of the Monster and the Superman. Consider carefully what a profound problem he represents.

Was that the end? Was the greatest of all conflicts between ideals thereby laid to rest forever? Or was it merely postponed— postponed for a long time? Might there not come a day when the old fire reignites, more terrifying and more deliberately prepared than ever before? And further—should one not wish for such a culmination with all their strength? Should one not will it, demand it, strive for it with every fiber of their being?

For those who, like my readers, begin to reflect and think more deeply on these questions, it will not be easy to arrive quickly at a conclusion. This is reason enough for me to bring my own reflections to a close here, trusting that my meaning has by now become sufficiently clear. Surely it is evident what I mean by the dangerous motto inscribed on the body of my last book: Beyond Good and Evil. At the very least, it should be understood that this is not synonymous with "Beyond Good and Bad."

Note. I take this opportunity afforded by this treatise to express openly and formally a wish that I have, until now, shared only in casual conversations with scholars. I hope that some Faculty of Philosophy might earn the honor of advancing the study of the history of morals by initiating a series of prize essays on the subject. Perhaps this book may serve as a compelling impetus for such an endeavor.

In connection with this possibility, the following question deserves thoughtful consideration. It merits the attention not only of philologists and historians but also of professional philosophers:

"What can philology, and particularly the study of etymology, tell us about the historical evolution of moral ideas?"

At the same time, it is equally crucial to encourage physiologists and doctors to take an interest in these problems—specifically, the value of the valuations that have prevailed throughout history. In this effort, professional philosophers should act as spokesmen and intermediaries. But this requires first transforming the traditionally cold and suspicious relationship between philosophy, physiology, and medicine into one of mutual respect and productive collaboration.

Indeed, every historical and cultural "table of values"—every "thou shalt" known to history and ethnology—needs to be examined and interpreted primarily from a physiological perspective, rather than exclusively a psychological one. Additionally, all these values demand critique from the standpoint of medical science. The question, "What is the value of this or that table of values or morality?" must be examined from a variety of perspectives. For instance, the question "valuable for what?" cannot be analyzed too carefully or in too much detail.

What might have value for one purpose—such as promoting a race's capacity for endurance, its adaptability to a particular climate, or even the survival of the greatest number—might have far less value if the goal is the evolution of a stronger species. In evaluating values, the interests of the majority and those of the minority represent fundamentally opposing perspectives. It is left to the naïveté of English biologists to assume that the former perspective— the good of the majority—is inherently superior.

All the sciences must now work to prepare the ground for the philosopher's future task: to solve the problem of value. This task requires the philosopher to establish and define a hierarchy of values.

Chapter 2
Guilt, Bad Conscience, and The Like

The cultivation of an animal capable of making promises—is this not the paradoxical task that nature has set for itself in regard to humanity? Is this not the very essence of the problem of man? The fact that this problem has been largely solved is extraordinary, especially to those who recognize the immense power of forgetfulness that works against it. Forgetfulness is not simply a passive inertia, as many superficial thinkers assume. Rather, it is an active force—a positive and deliberate function. It prevents what we have lived through, experienced, and absorbed from constantly intruding upon our consciousness, just as the processes of physical digestion and assimilation operate without entering our awareness.

Forgetfulness provides a temporary closing of the doors and windows of consciousness, offering relief from the ceaseless activity of the subconscious organs working together in harmony or conflict. It allows a moment of quiet, a clean slate, so to speak—a tabula rasa— to make space for new experiences and, more importantly, for higher functions like governance, planning, and decision-making. The human organism, like an oligarchy, requires this order to function properly. Active forgetfulness, therefore, is the guardian and nurturer of mental order, peace, and proper conduct. Without it, there can be no happiness, joy, hope, pride, or even a sense of the present.

A person in whom this preventive apparatus of forgetfulness is damaged is like a dyspeptic who cannot "digest" anything, and this comparison is not merely figurative. Such a person cannot "let go" of anything. Yet this same human animal, who depends so much on forgetfulness for health and vitality, has developed within himself an opposing power: memory. Memory functions to curb forgetfulness when necessary—in situations where promises must be kept.

This memory is not a mere passive inability to forget impressions once made or words once spoken. It is an active refusal to let go. It is the persistence of the will, a deliberate desire to continue what has once been decided. It creates a bridge between the original "I will" and the ultimate execution of that will. This memory ensures that even amidst a world of new and unforeseen circumstances, distractions, and desires, the chain of intent does not break.

But what is the foundation for this remarkable ability? To regulate the future in this way, man had to learn to distinguish between what is necessary and what is accidental. He had to think causally, to envision the distant future as though it were present, to anticipate, and to determine with precision the relationship between ends and means. Above all, he had to learn to calculate and to reckon. He had to become disciplined, predictable, and reliable—even to himself. Only then could man begin to promise, to guarantee himself as a being with a future.

This is, in essence, the long history of how responsibility came into being. The task of creating an animal capable of making promises includes, as we now understand, the preliminary task of shaping man to be, in some sense, necessary, predictable, consistent with his kind, orderly, and therefore calculable. The immense undertaking I refer to as the "morality of custom" (see Dawn of Day, Aphorisms 9, 14, and 16)—the actual, painstaking work that humanity has done on itself throughout its longest and most prehistoric periods—derives its meaning and justification from this goal. Despite all its inherent harshness, despotism, rigidity, and occasional foolishness, the morality of custom made man truly calculable.

If we now consider this colossal process from its endpoint, where the tree of humanity finally bears its mature fruit—when society and its morality of custom have achieved their purpose—we find the sovereign individual. This individual is unlike anyone else, having freed himself from the constraints of the morality of custom. He is autonomous, a being who stands "beyond morality" (for autonomy and morality are mutually exclusive). He is, in short, a man of personal, enduring, and independent will—a man capable of making promises.

This individual possesses a proud awareness, felt in every fiber of his being, of what he has achieved and brought to life within himself: a genuine sense of power, freedom, and human perfection. This person, who has grown into true freedom and who is capable of binding himself with promises, is a master of his own will, a sovereign. How could he not be aware of his immense superiority over all beings incapable of committing themselves to promises or acting as their own guarantee? How could he not recognize the trust, reverence, and awe he inspires? He has earned all these. With mastery over himself, he is also granted mastery over circumstances, over nature, and over all creatures with weaker wills and less reliability.

For the free man, the man of the enduring and unbreakable will, this strength becomes his measure of value. From this vantage point, he looks outward, evaluating others. He honors and respects his equals—the strong and the reliable, those who, like him, can bind themselves with promises. Such individuals promise sparingly, carefully, and deliberately. They give their trust rarely, and when they do, it is an act of conferring honor. Their word is reliable because they know they possess the strength to uphold it, even in the face of calamity or fate.

Conversely, the sovereign man has no patience for the empty and thoughtless, for those who promise without reason or capability. He stands ready to crush the hollow fools who make promises they have no business making and to chastise the liar who breaks his word even as it leaves his lips.

The proud knowledge of this extraordinary privilege—the privilege of responsibility—and the deep awareness of this rare freedom, this power over oneself and over fate, become ingrained in him as an instinct, a ruling instinct. What does he call this instinct, this governing force within him, if he feels the need to name it? There can be no doubt: the sovereign man calls it his conscience.

His conscience? One quickly realizes that the idea of "conscience," seen here in its highest and most striking form, must have undergone a long history of development. The ability to guarantee oneself with pride, to say yes to oneself—that is a mature fruit, but also a late one. How long this fruit must have hung sour and bitter on the tree! And for an even longer period, there was no sign of it at all. No one had yet dared to promise such a thing, even though everything on the tree had been preparing and ripening for that very purpose.

"How does one create a memory in the human animal? How can an impression be so deeply fixed in this fleeting, half-thoughtless, and half- oblivious creature—this embodiment of forgetfulness— that it remains present permanently?" It is easy to imagine that this ancient problem was not solved with gentle answers or kind methods. Perhaps nothing in early human history is as dreadful and sinister as humanity's first system of mnemonics.

"Something must be burned into memory to ensure it stays there: only what continues to cause pain is remembered." This axiom comes from the oldest—and, unfortunately, the longest- lasting— psychology known to the world. One could even say that wherever we now find solemnity, seriousness, mystery, and grim colors in the lives of people and nations, we see remnants of the terror that once accompanied all promises, pledges, and obligations. The past, with all its vastness, depth, and cruelty, breathes its influence into us when we grow "serious."

When humanity deemed it necessary to forge a memory for itself, it did so through blood, torture, and sacrifice. The most horrifying sacrifices (including the sacrifice of first-born children), the most repulsive mutilations (such as castration), and the cruelest rituals of religious cults (for all religions, at their core, are systems of cruelty) all originate from this instinct that found its strongest mnemonic tool in pain.

In this sense, asceticism itself can be understood as part of this process. Certain ideas had to be rendered indelible, ever-present, and fixed in such a way that they could dominate the nervous and intellectual system. Ascetic practices and lifestyles served to eliminate competing ideas, ensuring these chosen ones became "unforgettable."

The less capable humanity was of remembering, the more horrific the signs and customs it employed. The harshness of ancient penal laws, for example, reveals how difficult it was for humans to overcome forgetfulness and hold a few basic social principles firmly in mind. These laws were directed at people ruled by every fleeting emotion and passing desire, those incapable of maintaining even the simplest agreements.

We Germans may not see ourselves as particularly cruel or hard-hearted, and certainly not as frivolous or careless. But a glance at our old penal codes reveals the tremendous effort required to evolve into a "nation of thinkers." By this, I mean the European nation that still today represents the pinnacle of reliability, seriousness, bad taste, and pragmatism—a nation that, thanks to these traits, claims the right to train Europe's intellectual elite, its mandar ins.

The Germans employed horrific means to create for themselves a memory strong enough to overcome their deeply ingrained plebeian instincts and the raw brutality of those instincts. Consider the old German punishments: stoning (as described in legend, where a millstone crushes the guilty man's head), breaking on the wheel (an original and uniquely German invention in the realm of punishment), dart-throwing, tearing or trampling by horses (the infamous "quartering"), boiling criminals in oil or wine (practiced even into the 14th and 15th centuries), the gruesomely popular flaying ("slicing into strips"), cutting flesh from the chest, and besmearing the offender with honey before exposing him to flies under the blazing sun.

It was through such vivid and horrifying images that humanity learned to retain in its memory a mere five or six "thou shalt nots," essential for societal coexistence. These were promises that man had to remember in order to enjoy the benefits of living in society. And it was, indeed, through such methods that man eventually attained r eason! But alas, reason, seriousness, control over emotions—all those somber and weighty achievements we now call reflection, all the supposed privileges and crowning glories of humanity—what a steep price they have demanded! How much blood and cruelty have laid the foundation for all the so-called "good things" in life!

But how did that other bleak phenomenon—the consciousness of sin, the pervasive sense of a "bad conscience"—enter the world? This question brings us back to our genealogists of morality. For the second time, I must say—or perhaps for the first time—that they are utterly inadequate. They possess nothing more than a few narrow spans of modern experience, lacking any deep knowledge of the past, and showing no real desire to gain such knowledge. Even less do they possess the historical instinct, that essential "second sight" needed for this kind of inquiry. Yet, despite this, they attempt to write the history of morals, and their conclusions are inevitably far removed from the truth—so far that their efforts deserve no more than a condescending glance.

Have these so-called genealogists ever entertained even a vague understanding, for example, that the fundamental moral concept of "ought" originated in the very material idea of "owe"? Or that punishment initially developed as retaliation, entirely independent of any consideration of free will or determinism? It was only when civilization reached a high level of development that humans began making more subtle distinctions such as "intentional," "negligent," "accidental," "responsible," and their opposites— distinctions which are now used in evaluating punishment.

The idea that "the wrongdoer deserves punishment because he could have acted differently," though today it seems self-evident and foundational to the notion of justice, is in fact a very late and highly refined form of human judgment. To retroactively project this idea back to the origins of human society is to commit a crude violation of the principles of early psychology.

For the vast majority of human history, punishment was never based on the offender's responsibility for their actions. It was never about punishing only the guilty. Instead, punishment functioned much like the way parents still punish their children: out of anger for a wrong suffered. This anger, often raw and instinctive, would mechanically vent itself on the source of the injury—the wrongdoer. Over time, this anger became moderated and shaped by the notion that every injury has an equivalent pr ice that could be repaid, even if the repayment took the form of pain inflicted on the perpetrator.

But from where does this deeply entrenched and seemingly indestructible idea of equivalence between harm and pain draw its strength?

I have already traced the origin of this idea to the contractual relationship between creditor and debtor, a relationship as old as the concept of legal rights itself. This points further back to the most basic forms of purchase, sale, barter, and trade.

The recognition and enforcement of these contractual relationships naturally provoke suspicion and resistance toward the primitive societies that created and upheld them. In such societies, promises were made, and mechanisms were devised to ensure the promiser would remember and honor them. These societies, as we might expect, often resorted to harshness, cruelty, and pain to achieve their goals. To instill confidence in their promise to repay, to affirm the seriousness and sanctity of that promise, and to etch the duty of repayment into their own conscience, debtors would pledge something they still owned or controlled. This might include their life, their spouse, their freedom, their body—or under certain religious frameworks, even their salvation, their soul, or their peace in the afterlife. In ancient Egypt, for example, even the corpse of a debtor could be denied rest in the grave if the debt remained unpaid—a particularly grave matter from the Egyptian perspective.

Moreover, creditors were often granted the legal right to inflict pain or torture on the debtor's body as a form of repayment. They might cut off an amount of flesh proportionate to the debt owed. This practice gave rise to elaborate, often grotesque systems of valuation for different body parts, which were meticulously detailed and legally sanctioned. Such schemes reflect the harsh precision with which early societies attempted to ensure the fulfillment of obligations.

A step forward in legal thinking—and an indicator of a freer, less pedantic, and more Roman perspective on law—can be seen in the Roman Code of the Twelve Tables. It stated that the amount creditors could cut off in such cases did not matter: "si plus minusve secuer unt, ne fr aude esto" ("if more or less is cut, it shall not be considered fraud").

Let us unpack the logic behind this entire system of equivalence. It is, indeed, a strange and revealing logic. The equivalence here does not consist of direct compensation for the injury— no payment in money, land, or goods. Instead, the creditor is compensated with a kind of emotional satisfaction. This is the satisfaction of exercising power over someone powerless, the perverse pleasure of inflicting harm simply for the sake of doing so—" de fair e le mal pour le plaisir de le fair e" ("to do harm for the pleasure of doing it"). This joy in cruelty is often most intense for creditors of lower social standing, as it allows them a fleeting sense of power and superiority. For them, it might even feel like a foretaste of a higher social position.

By punishing the debtor, the creditor momentarily participates in the privileges of the ruling class. For once, the creditor experiences the gratifying sense of being able to despise and mistreat another being as an "inferior." Even when the power to punish has already been transferred to authorities, the creditor still enjoys witnessing the debtor being despised and punished. Thus, compensation for the creditor is effectively a claim to cruelty—a right to exercise or benefit from the infliction of suffering.

It is within the realm of contractual law that we find the origins of the entire moral framework surrounding ideas such as "guilt," "conscience," "duty," and the "sacredness of duty." As with all great beginnings in human history, this moral world is steeped in blood. Should we not also acknowledge that this world has never entirely lost its connection to blood and torture—not even in the philosophy of old Kant, whose categorical imperative carries the faint yet unmistakable scent of cruelty?

In this same domain of contracts arose the dark and perhaps inseparable link between the ideas of "guilt" and "suffering." But why, again, can suffering serve as compensation for "owing"? Because the infliction of suffering brings an intense kind of satisfaction. The injured party receives, in exchange for their loss (and the frustration accompanying it), an extraordinary compensation: the pleasure of inflicting pain. This act becomes a feast for the senses—a reward that grows all the more delectable the greater the disparity in rank and social standing between creditor and debtor.

These are speculative thoughts, of course, for it is difficult, both intellectually and emotionally, to delve into such depths. The crude notion of "revenge" often introduced as a connecting concept only obscures the issue rather than clarifying it. Revenge merely redirects us to the same question: Why does inflicting suffering bring satisfaction?

It is unsettling—perhaps repellent—to the sensibilities of modern, "tame" humans (ourselves included) to fully confront how deeply cruelty once permeated human joy and pleasure. Ancient man, with a simplicity and innocence we might now find shocking, openly embraced cruelty as a natural and delightful part of life. He even institutionalized "disinterested malice" (what Spinoza calls sympathia malevolens) as a fundamental trait of human nature, something the conscience could unreservedly approve.

The more insightful observer will already have recognized this primal and enduring joy in cruelty. In Beyond Good and Evil (Aphorism 188) and earlier in The Dawn of Day (Aphorisms 18, 77, 113), I have cautiously hinted at the ongoing "spiritualization" and "deification" of cruelty that runs through the entire history of higher civilizations—indeed, that largely defines it. The time is not so distant when royal weddings or grand national celebrations were unthinkable without accompanying executions, tortures, or perhaps an auto- da-fé. Similarly, aristocratic households often required the presence of a victim—someone to be baited and tormented for the amusement of the household.

Consider Don Quixote at the court of the Duchess. Today, we read Don Quixote with a bitter taste in our mouths, almost as if we are enduring a form of torture. This reaction would have been utterly foreign to Cervantes and his contemporaries, who saw the book as one of the most joyful of all comedies, a work to laugh at until they could laugh no more.

The sight of suffering soothes; the act of inflicting suffering soothes even more. This harsh principle is ancient, powerful, and fundamentally human. Perhaps even apes would agree, as they seem to demonstrate in their own inventions of bizarre cruelties— acts that prefigure and foreshadow their future humanity. Without cruelty, there can be no feast. This lesson comes from the oldest and most enduring history of mankind. Even in punishment, there has always been something of the festive.

Considering these ideas, I must clarify—let me say this in passing—that I am fundamentally opposed to providing pessimists with more fuel for their mills of dissatisfaction and despair. On the contrary, it should be emphasized that when humanity was unashamed of its cruelty, life was brighter and more vibrant than it is now, in this age of pessimism. The darkening of human existence has always paralleled the growth of man's shame in himself. The weary, pessimistic outlook, the suspicion that life itself is a problem, the icy denial born of boredom and disgust—these are not the signs of humanity's most depraved era. Rather, they bloom, like swamp flowers, only when the swamp itself comes into being— when diseased refinement and over- moralization take root, teaching "animal man" to feel ashamed of his instincts.

On the path to becoming "angelic" (to avoid using a harsher term), humanity has developed a kind of moral dyspepsia, complete with a sickly stomach and coated tongue. These have rendered not only the joy and innocence of animal existence repugnant to him but also life itself. At times, humanity stands before itself in revulsion, pinching its nose as though life stinks. Pope Innocent III's infamous list of human horrors—"unclean generation, loathsome nutrition in the womb, the vile material from which man develops, the stench of excretion, saliva, urine, and feces"— captures this attitude perfectly.

Today, suffering is trotted out as the ultimate argument against existence, the most damning indictment of life. How different this is from earlier times when people thought quite the opposite. They valued the infliction of suffering, seeing it as something magical and even a seductive lure to life itself.

Perhaps, for the more sensitive souls among us, it will be comforting to hear that pain may not have hurt as much in those days as it does now. Any physician who has treated individuals of less "refined" cultures (for instance, some African groups taken to represent prehistoric man) might confirm this. These patients, even when suffering from severe internal inflammations that would drive a modern European to the brink of despair, often endure their pain with surprising resilience. Pain simply does not have the same impact on them.

Indeed, the curve of human sensitivity to pain seems to drop dramatically, almost suddenly, once one steps beyond the narrow band of over-civilized humanity. I am personally convinced that a single painful night endured by a highly-strung, cultured woman might well outweigh the collective suffering of all the animals subjected to scientific experiments with knives.

Even now, the human craving for cruelty has likely not disappeared—it has merely been transformed. With pain now more keenly felt, this impulse has undergone a kind of sublimation and refinement. It has been redirected to the realm of imagination and the psyche, camouflaged by euphemisms so artfully contrived that even the most delicate and hypocritical consciences remain oblivious to their true nature. Terms like "tragic pity" and "the nostalgia of the cross" are among these deceptive labels, concealing the enduring appetite for cruelty beneath a veil of moral respectability.

What truly stirs indignation against suffering is not the suffering itself but its apparent senselessness. This sense of meaninglessness, however, was absent in Christianity, which framed suffering as part of a grand, mysterious system of salvation. Nor did it exist for the naive ancient peoples, who found meaning in suffering from the perspective of the spectator or the one inflicting the pain. To remove the notion of hidden, unseen suffering from the world, it became almost essential to invent gods and a hierarchy of beings—figures who could wander through secret places, peer into darkness, and never miss an intriguing or painful spectacle. Through these inventions, life managed a remarkable feat: the justification of itself, including its evils.

In our time, such justifications might require different devices (such as framing life as a riddle or a problem to be solved). But for primitive people, the logic was simple: "Every evil is justified if a god can find it edifying." And was this sentiment truly limited to primitive people? Hardly. The idea of gods as connoisseurs of cruelty extends deeply into our European civilization, even today. One might recall the perspectives of Luther or Calvin in this context. It is certain, at any rate, that even the Greeks found no greater spice for the happiness of their gods than the delights of cruelty.

What mood, one wonders, does Homer ascribe to his gods as they gaze upon the fates of mortals? What ultimate meaning lies behind the Trojan War and other such tragic horrors? There can be no doubt: these events were conceived as festival games for the gods. Moreover, since poets are of a more "godlike" breed than ordinary men, such events were also games for the poets themselves. Later, in the same spirit, Greek moral philosophers envisioned the gods' eyes fixed upon the moral struggles, heroism, and self-torture of virtuous humans. Heracles, embodying the duty-bound hero, performed on a stage and was fully conscious of his audience. For this society of actors, virtue without witnesses was utterly unthinkable.

Indeed, how could one not conclude that the bold and fateful invention of "free will"—a concept then entirely new to Europe—was created specifically to justify the notion that the gods' interest in human virtue and vice was boundless? This invention ensured that the stage of the free-will world would never lack truly fresh, novel, and exciting situations, dramatic conflicts, and catastrophic endings. In contrast, a world governed entirely by deterministic principles would be too predictable for the gods and would quickly bore them. This was reason enough for the philosophers of the time—those loyal allies of the gods—to reject the idea of a deterministic universe.

All of ancient humanity was steeped in consideration for the spectator, embodying a world where public display and theatricality were central. For them, happiness was inseparable from spectacles and festivals. And, as mentioned before, even in acts of great punishment, there was something inherently celebratory, a ritual festivity woven into the spectacle of human suffering.

The sense of "ought," of personal obligation (to return to our inquiry), originated in the oldest and most fundamental personal relationship: the relationship between buyer and seller, creditor and debtor. In this context, one individual confronted another, measuring themselves against each other. No stage of human civilization, however primitive, has been found to lack some trace of this relationship. Setting prices, assessing values, calculating equivalents, and exchanging goods—these activities dominated the earliest human thoughts so thoroughly that they essentially constituted the very act of thinking itself.

It was in this sphere that the first form of human intelligence developed, along with humanity's earliest sense of pride and superiority over other animals. Perhaps even our word "Mensch" (manas) retains a hint of this self-pride: it identified man as the creature who measures and values, the assessing animal par excellence.

Commerce—sale and purchase—along with the psychological processes they entail, predates any organized form of society or community. Instead, the awareness of exchange, trade, debt, obligation, and compensation first emerged from the most basic forms of individual interaction. This consciousness was then applied to the earliest social groups, particularly in their relations with one another. It extended the practice of comparing force against force, measuring, and calculating.

Man's focus was shaped by this perspective, and with the unyielding consistency typical of ancient thought—slow to start but relentless in its course—humanity soon arrived at a sweeping generalization: everything has a price, everything can be paid for. This concept formed the oldest and most straightforward moral code of justice and laid the foundation for ideas of fairness, goodwill, and objectivity in the world.

In this early stage, justice was essentially an agreement between individuals or groups of roughly equal power to settle disputes and restore balance through mutual understanding. As for the weaker parties, justice often involved compelling them to accept terms of settlement imposed by the stronger. This basic willingness—or enforced necessity—to come to terms marked the beginnings of what we now call fairness and equity.

When viewed through the lens of antiquity (and this kind of antiquity can arise or reemerge in any era), the relationship between the community and its members resembles that of a creditor to its debtors. Man lives within a community, enjoying its benefits—what tremendous benefits these are, though we sometimes underestimate them today. He lives protected, spared, in peace and trust, shielded from the dangers and hostilities that constantly threaten those outside the community, the "peaceless" ones. (A German might recognize this from the original meaning of the word Elend, signifying "exile" or being without a homeland.) This security is granted because the individual has pledged himself to the community, entering into obligations in exchange for this protection from harm and enmity.

But what happens when this agreement is broken? When the individual fails to uphold his obligations, the community—now the wronged creditor—will demand repayment, one way or another. In such cases, the specific harm caused by the offender becomes almost secondary. The true transgression lies in his breach of trust, his breaking of the pact with the entire community, which had granted him its protection and benefits. The criminal is not just someone who fails to repay his debt; he actively attacks his creditor. Consequently, he forfeits not only the advantages and security of communal life but also receives a forceful reminder of just how valuable those benefits were.

The wrath of the injured community strips him of his rights and casts him back into the "wild" status he had previously been protected from. The community rejects him, and in doing so, opens the door for all manner of hostility and vengeance to be unleashed upon him. At this stage of civilization, punishment serves as a grim mimicry of how one treats a despised, defeated enemy. Such an enemy is not only stripped of all rights and protection but also shown no mercy. Here we see the full enactment of vae victis— "woe to the vanquished"— in its most brutal and unrelenting form.

This perspective also explains why war itself, along with its associated sacrificial rituals, has shaped all the forms of punishment that have emerged throughout human history. The treatment of the criminal mirrors the treatment of a conquered foe, embodying the mercilessness and cruelty of a victorious celebration over the defeated.

As a community grows stronger, it begins to view individual offenses as less threatening to its overall stability. The misdeeds of individuals no longer seem as revolutionary or dangerous to the existence of the group as a whole. As a result, the wrongdoer is no longer cast out or subjected to the unrestrained wrath of the community. Instead, the community actively shields and protects the wrongdoer, particularly from the anger of those directly harmed by the offense.

With the evolution of penal law, certain patterns become increasingly evident: efforts are made to moderate the wrath of the injured party, to contain the conflict, and to prevent it from escalating or spreading. The focus shifts toward finding equivalents, settling disputes (compositio), and ultimately attempting to separate the offender from the offense itself. The more powerful and self-assured a community becomes, the more its system of justice softens. Conversely, when a community's stability is threatened or its power diminishes, the harshest and most severe forms of justice tend to resurface.

This dynamic parallels the relationship between creditors and debtors: as the creditor becomes wealthier, they grow more lenient and humane in their dealings. The true measure of their wealth becomes the degree of harm they can endure without genuinely suffering. One can even imagine a society with such immense confidence in its power that it embraces the luxury of allowing wrongdoers to go unpunished. Such a society might say, "What harm do these parasites do to me? Let them live and thrive—I am strong enough to handle it."

Justice, which began with the principle "everything can be paid off, everything must be paid off," eventually transforms into something that allows even those who cannot pay to escape punishment. Like all good things on Earth, justice ultimately undoes itself. This self-destruction of justice bears a charming name: Gr ace. And as is evident, grace remains the privilege of the strongest— their super- law.

A word of caution is necessary here regarding recent attempts to trace the origins of justice back to resentment. Allow me to offer a suggestion to psychologists who wish to study revenge up close: this particular emotion thrives most vibrantly today among anarchists and anti-Semites. Like the hidden violet, it blooms discreetly—though it carries a vastly different scent. Given that similar forces tend to create similar outcomes, it's hardly surprising that such circles often attempt to glorify revenge by rebranding it as justice. The claim seems to be that justice is nothing more than an advanced form of the consciousness of injury, which serves to validate revenge and elevate reactive emotions as a whole.

I have no fundamental objection to reevaluating these reactive emotions— indeed, from a biological perspective, their value has likely been underestimated. However, I wish to highlight that the very spirit of revenge underpins this so- called new scientific "equity." This perspective, while appearing fair at first, quickly dissolves into outright hostility and bias the moment other emotions, particularly those of higher biological value, come into play. These active emotions—like personal ambition and the drive for tangible achievement— deserve far greater scientific recognition than reactive feelings such as hate, envy, and resentment. (E. Dühring's writings, such as Value of Life and Course of Philosophy, are key examples of this bias.)

To address Dühring's claim that justice originates in the realm of reactive feelings: the truth requires us to assert the exact opposite. The final domain that justice conquers is the sphere of reactive emotions. When a truly just individual remains impartial even toward their injurer—when they go beyond being merely calm, restrained, or indifferent—this represents a rare and extraordinary achievement. True justice is an active state. To maintain an objective, clear, and balanced perspective even in the face of insult, contempt, or slander is an extraordinary form of mastery. Such an individual exhibits a profound, gentle clarity—a perfection that is almost beyond human capacity.

That said, even the most just among us is vulnerable to small provocations. A mere hint of malice, hostility, or innuendo is often enough to cloud their objectivity and inflame their emotions. Justice, for all its loftiness, is a delicate and challenging ideal to sustain.

The active man, the attacking, aggressive man, is always a hundred degrees nearer to justice than the man who merely reacts; he certainly has no need to adopt the tactics, necessary in the case of the reacting man, of making false and biased valuations of his object. It is, in point of fact, for this reason that the aggressive man has at all times enjoyed the stronger, bolder, more aristocratic, and also freer outlook, the better conscience. On the other hand, we already surmise who it really is that has on his conscience the invention of the "bad conscience,"— the resentful man! Finally, let man look at himself in history. In what sphere up to the present has the whole administration of law, the actual need of law, found its earthly home? Perchance in the sphere of the reacting man? Not for a minute: rather in that of the active, strong, spontaneous, aggressive man? I deliberately defy the abovementioned agitator (who himself makes this self-confession, "the creed of revenge has run through all my works and endeavours like the red thread of Justice"), and say, that judged historically law in the world represents the very war against the reactive feelings, the very war waged on those feelings by the powers of activity and aggression, which devote some of their strength to damming and keeping within bounds this effervescence of hysterical reactivity, and to forcing it to some compromise. Everywhere where justice is practised and justice is maintained, it is to be observed that the stronger power, when confronted with the weaker powers which are inferior to it (whether they be groups, or individuals), searches for weapons to put an end to the senseless fury of resentment, while it carries on its object, partly by taking the victim of resentment out of the clutches of revenge, partly by substituting for revenge a campaign of its own against the enemies of peace and order, partly by finding, suggesting, and occasionally enforcing settlements, partly by standardising certain equivalents for injuries, to which equivalents the element of resentment is henceforth finally referred. The most drastic measure, however, taken and effectuated by the supreme power, to combat the preponderance of the feelings of spite and vindictiveness—it takes this measure as soon as it is at all strong enough to do so—is the foundation of law, the imperative declaration of what in its eyes is to be regarded as just and lawful, and what unjust and unlawful: and while, after the foundation of law, the supreme power treats the aggressive and arbitrary acts of individuals, or of whole groups, as a violation of law, and a revolt against itself, it distracts the feelings of its subjects from the immediate injury inflicted by such a violation, and thus eventually attains the very opposite result to that always desired by revenge, which sees and recognises nothing but the standpoint of the injured party. From henceforth the eye becomes trained to a more and more impersonal valuation of the deed, even the eye of the injured party himself (though this is in the final stage of all, as has been previously remarked)—on this principle "right" and "wrong" first manifest themselves after the foundation of law (and not, as Duhring maintains, only after the act of violation). To talk of intrinsic right and intrinsic wrong is absolutely nonsensical; intrinsically, an injury, an oppression, an exploitation, an annihilation can be nothing wrong, inasmuch as life is essentially (that is, in its cardinal functions) something which functions by injuring, oppressing, exploiting, and annihilating, and is absolutely inconceivable without such a character. It is necessary to make an even more serious confession:—viewed from the most advanced biological standpoint, conditions of legality can be only exceptional conditions, in that they are partial restrictions of the real life-will, which makes for power, and in that they are subordinated to the life-will's general end as particular means, that is, as means to create larger units of strength. A legal organisation, conceived of as sovereign and universal, not as a weapon in a fight of complexes of power, but as a weapon against fighting, generally something after the style of Duhring's communistic model of treating every will as equal with every other will, would be a principle hostile to life, a destroyer and dissolver of man, an outrage on the future of man, a symptom of fatigue, a secret cut to Nothingness.

A word more on the origin and end of punishment—two problems which are or ought to be kept distinct, but which unfortunately are usually lumped into one. And what tactics have our moral genealogists employed up to the present in these cases? Their inveterate naivety. They find out some "end" in the punishment, for instance, revenge and deterrence, and then in all their innocence set this end at the beginning, as the causa fiendi of the punishment, and— they have done the trick. But the patching up of a history of the origin of law is the last use to which the "End in Law" ought to be put. Perhaps there is no more important principle for any kind of history than the following, which, difficult though it is to master, should nonetheless be mastered in every detail.

The origin of the existence of a thing and its final utility, its practical application and incorporation in a system of ends, are completely opposed to each other— everything, anything, which exists and which prevails anywhere, will always be put to new purposes by a force superior to itself, will be commandeered afresh, will be turned and transformed to new uses; all "happening" in the organic world consists of overpowering and dominating, and again all overpowering and domination is a new interpretation and adjustment, which must necessarily obscure or absolutely extinguish the existing "meaning" and "end." The most perfect comprehension of the utility of any physiological organ (or also of a legal institution, social custom, political habit, form in art or in religious worship) does not for a minute imply any simultaneous comprehension of its origin: this may seem uncomfortable and unpalatable to the older men, for it has been the immemorial belief that understanding the final cause or the utility of a thing, a form, an institution, means also understanding the reason for its origin: to give an example of this logic, the eye was made to see, the hand was made to grasp. So even punishment was conceived as invented with a view to punishing. But all ends and all utilities are only signs that a Will to Power has mastered a less powerful force, has impressed thereon out of its own self the meaning of a function; and the whole history of a "Thing," an organ, a custom, can on the same principle be regarded as a continuous "sign- chain" of perpetually new interpretations and adjustments, whose causes, so far from needing to have even a mutual connection, sometimes follow and alternate with each other absolutely haphazard. Similarly, the evolution of a "Thing," of a custom, is anything but its progress to an end, still less a logical and direct progress attained with the minimum expenditure of energy and cost: it is rather the succession of processes of subjugation, more or less profound, more or less mutually independent, which operate on the thing itself; it is, further, the resistance which in each case invariably displays this subjugation, the Protean wriggles by way of defense and reaction, and, further, the results of successful counter-efforts. The form is fluid, but the meaning is even more so—even inside every individual organism, the case is the same: with every genuine growth of the whole, the "function" of the individual organs becomes shifted—in certain cases a partial perishing of these organs, a diminution of their numbers (for instance, through annihilation of the connecting members), can be a symptom of growing strength and perfection.

What I mean is this: even partial loss of utility, decay, and degeneration, loss of function and purpose, in a word, death, are part of the conditions of genuine progress; which always appears in the form of a will and way to greater power, and is always realized at the expense of innumerable smaller powers. The magnitude of a "progress" is gauged by the greatness of the sacrifice it requires: humanity as a mass sacrificed to the prosperity of the one stronger species of Man—that would be a progress. I emphasize all the more this cardinal characteristic of the historic method, for the reason that in its essence it runs counter to predominant instincts and prevailing taste, which must prefer to put up with absolute casualness, even with the mechanical senselessness of all phenomena, than with the theory of a power-will, in exhaustive play throughout all phenomena. The democratic idiosyncrasy against everything which rules and wishes to rule, the modern misarchism (to coin a bad word for a bad thing), has gradually but so thoroughly transformed itself into the guise of intellectualism, the most abstract intellectualism, that even nowadays it penetrates and has the right to penetrate step by step into the most exact and apparently the most objective sciences: this tendency has, in fact, in my view already dominated the whole of physiology and biology, and to their detriment, as is obvious, in so far as it has spirited away a radical idea, the idea of true activity. The tyranny of this idiosyncrasy, however, results in the theory of "adaptation" being pushed forward into the van of the argument, exploited; adaptation— that means to say, a second- class activity, a mere capacity for "reacting"; in fact, life itself has been defined (by Herbert Spencer) as an increasingly effective internal adaptation to external circumstances. This definition, however, fails to realize the real essence of life, its will to power. It fails to appreciate the paramount superiority enjoyed by those plastic forces of spontaneity, aggression, and encroachment with their new interpretations and tendencies, to the operation of which adaptation is only a natural corollary: consequently, the sovereign office of the highest functionaries in the organism itself (among which the life-will appears as an active and formative principle) is repudiated. One remembers Huxley's reproach to Spencer of his "administrative Nihilism": but it is a case of something much more than "administration."

To return to our subject, which is punishment, we need to make two important distinctions: first, the relatively permanent element, the custom, the act, the "drama," a fixed sequence of steps in the process; and second, the more fluid element, the meaning, the purpose, and the expectations that come with the way the procedure works. At this point, we should assume, by analogy (following the historical method we've talked about earlier), that the procedure itself is older than its use in punishment. This use was added and interpreted into the procedure (which had been around for a long time, but with a different meaning). In short, the situation is not what our naïve moral and legal historians have thought—that the procedure was created specifically for punishment, just as the hand was once thought to have been made for grasping. Now, when we look at the second element of punishment, the more fluid one—the meaning of punishment— it's clear that in very advanced societies (for example, in contemporary Europe), punishment doesn't just have one meaning, but rather a complex mix of meanings. The general history of punishment, and how it has been used for many different purposes, eventually comes together in a kind of unity that's difficult to break down into separate parts, and this unity, it should be emphasized, can't be easily defined. (Today, it's impossible to say for sure the exact reason for punishment: all ideas that lump together a whole process in one definition tend to escape definition; only things that have no history can be clearly defined.) In earlier times, however, that collection of meanings was much less fixed and much more flexible; we can see how, in each case, the elements of the meaning shift in importance and position. Sometimes, one meaning will stand out and dominate, and in certain cases, one element (like the goal of deterring crime) might even seem to take over and eliminate all the others. To give a clearer picture of how uncertain, extra, and accidental the meaning of punishment can be, and how one procedure can be used and adapted for very different purposes, I will now provide a list based on relatively small and random examples.

- Punishment as making the criminal harmless and unable to harm others.
- Punishment as a form of compensation for the injury suffered by the victim, in any form, including sentimental compensation.
- Punishment as isolating what disrupts the balance, to stop the disturbance from spreading.
- Punishment as a way to inspire fear in those who decide and carry out the punishment.
- Punishment as a kind of compensation for the benefits the wrongdoer had enjoyed up until that point (for example, when the wrongdoer is forced into slavery in the mines).
- Punishment as removing an element of decay (sometimes even a whole part, as in Chinese laws, for the purpose of purifying the race or preserving a social type).
- Punishment as a festival, where an enemy who has been defeated is violently oppressed and humiliated.

- Punishment as a reminder, either for the person being punished (the so-called "correction") or for the witnesses of the punishment being carried out.
- Punishment as the payment of a fee, required by the power that protects the wrongdoer from the excesses of revenge.
- Punishment as a compromise with the natural act of revenge, in so far as revenge is still seen as a privilege of the stronger groups.
- Punishment as a declaration of war against those who oppose peace, law, order, and authority—those who are fought by society with the weapons of war because they are seen as a danger to the community, as someone who breaks the social contract, as a rebel, a traitor, or someone who disturbs the peace.

This list is clearly not complete; it is obvious that punishment is packed with a variety of purposes. This makes it even more reasonable to dismiss one supposed purpose, which is often considered, at least by most people, to be its most essential purpose. This idea is also the one that still provides the strongest support for the belief in punishment, a belief that is already unsteady for many reasons. Punishment is believed to have the value of awakening in the guilty person a sense of guilt; punishment is seen as the proper tool to create that psychological reaction known as a "bad conscience" or "remorse." However, this theory, even from the perspective of the present day, does not reflect reality or psychology. It is even more inaccurate when we consider the long stretch of human history, particularly the early, primitive periods.

Genuine remorse is undeniably rare among wrongdoers and those who are punished. Prisons and correctional facilities are not the environments where this "worm of remorse" tends to flourish. This is the unanimous conclusion of all honest observers, many of whom arrive at this judgment reluctantly and against their personal expectations. In general, punishment tends to harden and desensitize people. It causes individuals to become more focused and sharpens their awareness of their alienation. It strengthens their ability to resist. When punishment does succeed in breaking a person's spirit and reducing them to a pitiful state of submission and misery, the result is even less healthy than the more typical effects of punishment, which are marked by harshness and grim stubbornness.

When we consider those prehistoric times, we are led to the clear conclusion that punishment actually delayed the development of the sense of guilt—at least among those subjected to the power of punishment. Moreover, we should not underestimate the extent to which the spectacle of legal and enforcement actions prevents the wrongdoer from recognizing that their deed and its nature are inherently wrong. This is because they can plainly see similar actions being carried out in the name of justice, labeled as good, and performed with a clear conscience. These actions include espionage, deceit, bribery, entrapment, and all the cunning and covert strategies employed by law enforcement officers and informants. The system of punishment itself—a system driven not by passion but by principles—relies on acts such as stealing, oppressing, insulting, imprisoning, torturing, and even killing.

The wrongdoer sees all of this and notices that these actions are not treated as inherently blameworthy or condemnable but only as problematic in specific contexts or uses. It was not on this foundation that the "bad conscience," one of the most troubling and fascinating aspects of human nature, came into being. In fact, for a long stretch of history, the idea of dealing with a "guilty person" did not even exist in the minds of those who judged and punished. They saw themselves as dealing with someone who caused harm, an unaccountable force of fate. For the individual on whom punishment fell, it did not bring about any deeper internal suffering. Instead, it was experienced as no different from an unforeseen and unavoidable event, such as a devastating natural disaster, an avalanche that struck without warning, against which no resistance was possible.

This truth crept subtly into the mind of Spinoza, much to the frustration of his commentators (such as Kuno Fischer, for instance, who made great efforts to misunderstand him on this point). One afternoon, as Spinoza sat reflecting on who knows what memories, he began to ponder what remained for him personally of the famous morsus conscientiae—the "sting of conscience." Spinoza, who had dismissed the notions of "good and evil" as products of human imagination, passionately defended the honor of his "free" God against those who blasphemed by claiming that God acted sub r atione boni—in accordance with the concept of good. To Spinoza, such an idea subordinated God to fate, which he considered the greatest absurdity.

For Spinoza, the world had returned to the state of innocence it had known before the discovery of the bad conscience. What, then, became of the morsus conscientiae? He finally defined it for himself as "the opposite of joy—a sadness accompanied by the memory of a past event that turned out contrary to all expectation" (Ethics, Part III, Proposition 18, Scholium I and II). For thousands of years, wrongdoers faced with punishment felt much like Spinoza described regarding their "offense." They thought, "Here is something that went wrong, contrary to what I expected," rather than, "I should not have done this." They accepted punishment in the same way one endures illness, misfortune, or death—with a fatalistic and resigned stubbornness. This kind of acceptance, even today, gives people like the Russians an advantage over Westerners in dealing with the challenges of life.

In those times, if actions were judged critically, the standard was prudence. Punishment's actual effect was primarily to sharpen the sense of prudence, strengthen memory, and encourage a more cautious, secretive, and suspicious approach to life. It taught people to recognize their limitations and inspired a form of self-criticism. Punishment's broader effects on both humans and animals included increasing fear, sharpening cunning, and controlling desires. In this way, punishment tamed people but did not make them "better." In fact, one could argue the opposite: "Injury makes a man cunning," as the saying goes, and as it sharpens cunning, it often makes people worse. Thankfully, it also often makes them less intelligent.

At this point, I must offer a tentative and provisional explanation of my own hypothesis about the origin of the bad conscience. This idea is difficult to fully grasp and requires careful thought, sustained attention, and reflection. I consider the bad conscience to be the serious illness that humanity inevitably developed during its most radical transformation: when people found themselves confined within the structures of society and forced to live in peace.

Just as water-dwelling creatures faced a crisis when they had to either adapt to life on land or face extinction, so too did early humans, who were like half- animals. These creatures had thrived in a world of war, roaming, and adventure, perfectly suited to that wild life. Suddenly, their instincts became useless and "switched off." From that point on, they had to support themselves, to "carry themselves," just as water creatures had to walk on land after being carried by the water. This shift brought a crushing weight upon them. They struggled to obey even the simplest commands. Faced with a new and unfamiliar world, they could no longer rely on the instincts that had unconsciously guided them to safety in the past. Instead, they were forced to think, to reason, to calculate, and to connect causes and effects—relying on their weakest and most unreliable tool, their "consciousness."

I doubt there has ever been such a profound sense of misery in the world, such a feeling of leaden discomfort. Meanwhile, those old instincts did not disappear overnight. They continued to demand satisfaction, but it was now difficult, and often impossible, to fulfill them. Broadly speaking, these instincts were forced to find expression in new, covert ways, like a shadow of their former selves. When instincts cannot find an outlet in the external world, they turn inward. This is what I call the process of man's growing "internalization." It was through this process that what we later called the soul first began to develop.

The inner world of humanity, originally as thin and fragile as if stretched between two layers of skin, now burst open and expanded. It gained depth, breadth, and height as the external outlets for human instincts were blocked. The powerful defenses created by social organization to suppress the old instincts of freedom—especially punishment—forced these instincts to turn back against the human being himself. Feelings like hostility, cruelty, the joy of hunting, the thrill of surprise, destruction, and change—all these were now directed inward, against their possessor. This, I believe, is the origin of the "bad conscience."

Human beings, no longer facing external enemies and obstacles, found themselves trapped in the suffocating monotony and narrowness of social customs. In their frustration, they lashed out at themselves, tormenting, punishing, gnawing at, and terrifying themselves. It was like a wild animal in captivity, smashing itself against the bars of its cage. It was this being, longing desperately for the wild freedom of the past, who turned their inner life into a place of adventure, a chamber of torture, a dangerous and unpredictable desert. This homesick and despairing prisoner created the concept of the "bad conscience."

With this invention, humanity introduced a profound and sinister illness— one from which we have not yet recovered. This is the suffering of humankind caused by its own nature, a sickness born from the violent severing of humanity from its animal past. It was like a sudden, wrenching leap into a new way of life, a rejection of the instincts that had once been the source of human strength, joy, and fearsome power.

Yet, this turning of the human mind against itself produced something so new, so deep, so unprecedented, so complex, and so full of potential that it transformed the very face of the world. This was a phenomenon so dramatic, so paradoxical, so filled with possibilities that only divine observers could truly grasp its significance. The drama that began then is still unfolding, with no clear end in sight. It is too intricate, too extraordinary, too paradoxical to have happened meaninglessly or unnoticed on some random, grotesque planet.

From this moment onward, humanity must be seen as one of the most unexpected and astonishing outcomes of the game played by Heraclitus' "great child," whether you call it Zeus or Chance. Humanity now inspires interest, excitement, and hope. It even gives the impression that it is not the final goal, but a stepping stone, a bridge, an interlude—a great promise of something yet to come.

The hypothesis about the origin of the bad conscience begins with the idea that this transformation was neither gradual nor voluntary. It was not an organic adaptation to new circumstances but rather a rupture, a sudden break, a necessity imposed by fate. This change came without resistance or even a spark of resentment. Furthermore, this transformation—the shaping of a previously unrestrained and chaotic population into a rigid form—was initiated through violence and could only be maintained through violence. The earliest "state" thus emerged as a horrifying tyranny, a relentless and grinding machine that molded the raw, semi-animal masses into something pliable, structured, and disciplined.

By "state," I mean what is self-evident: a herd of blonde beasts of prey—a race of conquerors and rulers. This race, armed with all the tools of war and organization, descended with ferocious claws upon a population that, though numerically much larger, was unformed and nomadic. This is the true origin of the "state." The fanciful theory that the state began with a social contract is easily dismissed. Those who can command, who are natural masters, those whose very being is forceful and decisive—what would they have to do with contracts? These individuals are beyond calculation. They arrive like fate, without cause, without justification or warning. They are like lightning:

too powerful, too sudden, too undeniable, and too alien to even inspire personal hatred.

Such beings instinctively create and impose forms. They are the most involuntary, unconscious artists to exist. Their arrival immediately establishes a living order of sovereignty, one in which roles and functions are defined and assigned. In this order, no part exists unless it serves a meaningful role in relation to the whole. These born organizers are utterly unfamiliar with concepts like guilt, responsibility, or consideration. They embody a terrifying, artistic egoism that shines like polished metal, fully convinced of its eternal justification in its creations, just as a mother sees her child as her unquestionable right.

It was not in these individuals that the bad conscience first grew—this is a fundamental point. Yet, the bad conscience could not have developed without them. For all its repulsiveness, the bad conscience arose because their hammer blows, their violent artistry, expelled a tremendous amount of freedom from the world. This freedom was not destroyed but rendered invisible and latent.

This instinct for freedom, repressed and confined, is the key. The instinct for freedom, forced back, trampled down, imprisoned within itself, and eventually finding expression only within its own confines—this is where the bad conscience begins. It is this imprisonment, this inward turning of freedom, that marks the origin of the bad conscience.

Do not dismiss this phenomenon lightly just because of its initially painful and ugly appearance. At its core, it is the same active force at work on a grander scale in powerful artists and organizers who build states. Here, however, this force operates internally, on a smaller, more personal scale, with a tendency to turn backward on itself. It becomes a bad conscience in what Goethe calls the "labyrinth of the breast." It constructs negative ideals. This is, as I've said, the very same instinct of freedom (or, in my own terms, the will to power). The only difference is the material on which this force is unleashed.

In the grander, external phenomenon, the material is other people— other men. But here, it is man himself, his entire old animal self, that becomes the target.

This secret self-tyranny, this artistic cruelty, this pleasure in shaping oneself as though one were a difficult, resistant, and suffering material—this burning desire to impose a will, a critique, a contradiction, a disdain, or a rejection upon oneself— this dark and dreadful labor of love performed by a soul divided against itself, inflicting suffering upon itself for the delight of suffering, is what we call the active bad conscience. It is this same bad conscience, brimming with creative energy as the source of idealism and imagination, that has ultimately produced an extraordinary wealth of new and astounding beauty and affirmation. Indeed, it might even be said to have given birth to beauty for the first time.

What would beauty be, after all, if its opposite had not first been made conscious? If ugliness had not first declared, "I am ugly"? With this realization, the problem of tracing idealism and beauty in ideas such as selflessness, self- denial, and self-sacrifice becomes much less perplexing. It becomes clear that the original character of the pleasure felt by the selfless, the self-denying, and the self- sacrificing is rooted in cruelty.

This, then, is a preliminary explanation of the origin of "altruism" as a moral value and an outline of the soil from which this value has grown. It is the bad conscience—the will to self-punishment— that creates the conditions necessary for altruism to emerge as a value.

Undoubtedly, the bad conscience is an illness, but it is an illness in the same way that pregnancy is an illness. If we examine the conditions under which this illness reaches its most extreme and profound heights, we can begin to uncover what first brought it into the world. To do this, however, we must take a deep breath and return once more to an earlier perspective.

The relationship in civil law between debtor and creditor (which we have already discussed in detail) has been interpreted in a way that is both historically fascinating and deeply suspicious. It has been reimagined as a relationship between the current generation and its ancestors—a concept that is perhaps more incomprehensible to us today than to any other era. In the original tribal associations of primitive times, each living generation recognized a legal obligation to the generations that came before, especially to the earliest ancestors who founded the family. This obligation was far more than a sentimental one. During the longest period of human history, the mere idea of sentimental obligation was far from certain.

Instead, these early generations believed that their very existence depended on the sacrifices and efforts of their ancestors and that this debt had to be repaid through sacrifices and services. The debt was considered ongoing, growing ever larger, as the ancestors, now regarded as powerful spirits, continued to grant new privileges and advantages to the tribe. Did these benefits come for free? Certainly not, according to the harsh and "mean-souled" mindset of that era. What could be given in return? Sacrifices—at first, nourishment in its most basic form—then festivals, temples, tributes of reverence, and above all, obedience. For all customs, as works of the ancestors, were also seen as their commands and precepts. But was it ever enough to repay the ancestors? The suspicion lingered and grew over time. This suspicion occasionally demanded great acts of atonement, extravagant repayments to the creditors—such as the notorious sacrifices of the firstborn, or the spilling of blood, including human blood.

The fear of the ancestors and the sense of indebtedness to them grew stronger in direct proportion to the success of the tribe. As the tribe became more victorious, independent, respected, and feared, so too did the fear of the ancestors' power increase.

This, not the reverse, is the truth. Every step toward decay, every disaster, and every sign of degeneration or collapse diminished the fear of the ancestors' spirits and eroded the belief in their wisdom, foresight, and presence.

Imagine this crude kind of logic carried to its extreme: the ancestors of the most powerful tribes must, in proportion to the increasing fear they inspire, grow into immense, almost unimaginable figures. They become shrouded in the darkness of divine mystery and are ultimately transformed into gods. Perhaps this is the very origin of the gods: born out of fear! And for those who wish to add, "but also out of piety," it would be difficult to support that claim in relation to the earliest and longest period of human history. It is even harder to maintain with respect to the middle period—the formative era of aristocratic races. These aristocratic races repaid their founders, their ancestors (now seen as heroes or gods), with interest, attributing to them all the qualities they themselves developed over time—the qualities of the aristocrat.

Later, we will briefly examine the process of ennobling and elevating the gods (which is quite different from their sanctification). For now, however, let us follow to its conclusion this development of the consciousness of "owing."

According to historical accounts, the sense of owing a debt to the deity did not vanish with the disintegration of clan-based social structures. Just as humanity inherited the concepts of "good" and "bad" from the aristocratic nobility—along with their tendency to create social distinctions—it also inherited from the racial and tribal gods the oppressive burden of unpaid debts and the enduring desire to repay them. This inheritance was transmitted through vast populations of slaves and bondsmen, who, whether by force or through submission and imitation, adopted the religions of their masters. Through this channel, these inherited obligations spread across the world.

For centuries, the feeling of debt owed to the deity grew steadily, keeping pace with the growing prominence and exaltation of the idea of God among humanity. (The entire history of ethnic conflicts, triumphs, reconciliations, and amalgamations— everything leading to the eventual merging of social elements into grand racial syntheses—

is reflected in the chaotic genealogies of their gods, in myths of battles, victories, and reconciliations. Progress toward universal empires consistently corresponds to progress toward universal deities; despotism, by crushing the independence of the nobility, always clears the path for some form of monotheism.)

The advent of the Christian God, the most exalted deity to date, simultaneously brought with it the greatest degree of guilt consciousness. Now, if humanity has begun a reversal of this trajectory, there is reason to believe that the gradual decline in belief in the Christian God has corresponded to a significant decline in humanity's sense of moral obligation. Indeed, we can foresee the complete triumph of atheism as potentially liberating humanity from this feeling of obligation to its origin—its causa prima. Atheism might usher in a kind of second innocence, a fresh beginning free of this burden.

This, then, is a rough outline of the connection between the concepts of "ought" (owing) and "duty" with the foundations of religion. Up until now, I have deliberately avoided addressing the moralization of these concepts—their integration into the bad conscience, or more specifically, the fusion of the bad conscience with the idea of God. In the last paragraph, I even implied that such moralization did not occur and that these ideas would naturally dissipate as faith in the "creditor," in God, eroded. However, the reality is far grimmer.

The moralization of "ought" and "duty," their absorption into the bad conscience, marked the first attempt to reverse the development we have described—or at least to halt its progress. At this point, even the hope of eventual redemption is locked away in the prison of pessimism. Here, humanity's gaze recoils hopelessly from an unyielding impossibility. The concepts of "guilt" and "duty" turn backward—but against whom? There can be no doubt: they turn primarily against the debtor, the "ower," in whom the bad conscience takes root, expands, and consumes everything like a parasitic growth.

As the impossibility of repaying the debt becomes undeniable, so too arises the idea of the impossibility of atonement. This leads to the concept of inexpiable guilt—the notion of "eternal punishment."

Eventually, the bad conscience turns against the creditor as well. Whether this creditor is seen as the causa prima of humanity— the origin of the human race, its father, now cursed ("Adam," "original sin," "the bondage of the will")— or as Nature itself, the womb from which humanity emerged, and which is now held responsible for the principle of evil (the "demonization of Nature")—or as existence in general, viewed as an absurd and unbearable burden. This logic leads to nihilistic despair: the rejection of life, the desire for nothingness, or for some other form of existence, as seen in Buddhism and similar philosophies.

It is here that humanity arrives at a paradoxical and terrifying solution: the ingenious creation of Christianity. In this system, God sacrifices himself for humanity's debt. God pays himself by offering his own flesh. God, the ultimate creditor, becomes the scapegoat for his debtor—all out of love. Can you believe it? Out of love for his debtor!

The reader may already have guessed what unfolded both on the stage and behind the scenes of this drama. The will for self- torture— the turned-inward cruelty of human beings, who, once introspective and frightened by their confinement (caged within the framework of "the State" as part of their taming)—gave rise to the bad conscience as a way to hurt themselves when their natural outlet for cruelty was blocked. This man of the bad conscience seized upon the religious hypothesis to drive his self-inflicted torment to unimaginable extremes.

The idea of owing a debt to God became his tool for self- torture. In God, he imagined the ultimate antithesis to his own ineradicable animal instincts. He reinterpreted these instincts as offenses against what he "owes" to God—as hostility, rebellion, and defiance toward the "Lord," the "Father," the "Creator," the very "Beginning of the world." He trapped himself in the agonizing contradiction between "God" and "Devil." Every denial he wished to make against himself, against his nature, his naturalness, and his very reality, he twisted into an affirmation of God's existence. He transformed these negations into declarations of God's holiness, judgment, punishment, and transcendence— into eternal torment, infinite guilt, and unending hell.

This represents a madness of the will in the realm of psychological cruelty unlike anything else. Humanity's will to find itself guilty and beyond forgiveness, its will to think of itself as punished without any possibility of atonement, and its will to poison the foundations of the universe with the problem of guilt and punishment—all serve to trap humanity within this labyrinth of fixed ideas. It is a will to construct an ideal—that of the "holy God"—before which humanity can eternally prove its unworthiness.

Alas, for this despairing and deranged creature called man! What wild fantasies it conjures, what fits of perversity, hysterical irrationality, and mental savagery erupt whenever it is restrained from being the beast of action! All of this is deeply fascinating, yet it is also dark, oppressive, and draining, compelling us to resist gazing too long into these depths. Here is a sickness, undoubtedly the most horrifying disease that has ever afflicted humanity.

And if someone still has the capacity to hear—though modern man now often turns a deaf ear to such things—they may recognize that, within this night of torment and absurdity, the cry of love once echoed. It was the cry of the most intense ecstasy, the yearning for redemption through love. But anyone who truly listens to this cry recoils in unspeakable horror. For within humanity, there is so much that is monstrous. For far too long, the world has been a madhouse.

Let this be sufficient, once and for all, regarding the origin of the "holy God." The idea of gods does not inherently lead to the degradation of human imagination that we have just described. The fact that there are nobler ways to use the concept of gods—ways that do not involve the self-crucifixion and self-debasement of humanity, which has characterized the last two thousand years of Europe— remains clear. We only need to look at the Greek gods to see this. These gods were reflections of noble and grand men, mirrors in which the animal within humanity felt deified rather than destroyed by inward madness.

The Greeks used their gods in a completely different way. For them, the gods served as buffers against the "bad conscience," allowing them to preserve their inner freedom. This stands in stark contrast to Christianity's approach to its god. The Greeks, those magnificent and courageous people, embraced this principle wholeheartedly. Even the Homeric Zeus himself occasionally reminded them not to take life too lightly. Take, for instance, his commentary on the case of Aegisthus, a truly egregious example:

"Wonderful how they grumble, the mortals against the immortals.

They claim all evil comes from us, yet in their folly, They fashion their own doom, against all fate."

Yet note how this Olympian observer and judge is neither angry with mortals nor condemns them. Instead, he views their misdeeds with a certain amused detachment. "How foolish they are," he seems to think. For the Greeks, even in their strongest and most valiant era, the causes of evil and disaster were not rooted in sin but in folly, in imprudence, in a kind of temporary disturbance of the mind. Folly, not sin—do you see the distinction?

Even this "brain disturbance," however, presented a puzzle to the Greeks. "How could this happen?" they wondered. "How could such foolishness find its way into the minds of men like us— men of noble ancestry, men of wealth, men with fine natural gifts, men of the best upbringing, men of virtue?" For centuries, the Greek aristocracy asked this question whenever one of their peers committed some incomprehensible outrage or act of sacrilege. Eventually, they settled on an answer: "It must be that a god has deceived him," they concluded, nodding their heads.

This solution is quintessentially Greek. In their worldview, the gods did not punish humanity for its failings; instead, they took upon themselves the responsibility for human guilt. This approach justified human actions to a certain extent, even when those actions were evil. In those days, the gods were not seen as dispensers of punishment but as bearers of guilt—a role far nobler than that of executioner.

I conclude with three questions, as you will notice. "Is an ideal being established here, or is one being torn down?" you may ask. But have you truly considered the cost of creating every ideal in the history of the world? How much truth has had to be distorted and misunderstood, how many lies have been sanctified, how much conscience disturbed, and how many sacrifices of "God" have been made each time? To build a sanctuary, another must be destroyed—this is an unyielding law. Show me a single instance where it has not held true!

We modern men have inherited an ancient tradition of vivisecting our consciences and inflicting cruelty on our natural, animal selves. This is where we have undergone our most rigorous training, where we have perhaps honed our artistic talents—or, at the very least, indulged our dilettantism and perverted tastes. For far too long, humanity has regarded its natural instincts with suspicion, branding them as evil. Over time, these instincts have become intertwined with the bad conscience.

Wouldn't it be possible to attempt the opposite? Couldn't we attach this bad conscience to all our unnatural inclinations—our transcendental aspirations that oppose sense, instinct, nature, and our very humanity? Couldn't we apply it to all the ideals, past and present, that reject life and defame the world? But who today would be strong enough to undertake such a reversal? To whom could one turn with such aspirations?

It is precisely the "good" people who would rise against us if we tried. Alongside them would be the indolent, the conformists, the vain, the hysterical, and the weary. Nothing is more alienating or offensive than hinting at the stern rigor with which we treat ourselves. And yet, how readily the world embraces us when we simply "let ourselves go" and do as it does. For such a transformation, we would need spirits of an entirely different caliber than those of this feeble and introspective age—spirits strengthened by wars and victories, who crave conquest, adventure, danger, and even suffering.

Such spirits would need to be accustomed to rarefied air, to the sharpness of winter wanderings, to both literal and metaphorical ice and mountains. They would need a sublime malice, a supreme and conscious audacity born of great health. In summary, they would require nothing less than this great health.

Is this even conceivable today? Perhaps not. But someday, in an age stronger than this decaying and inward-looking present, such a redeemer must come. This redeemer, a spirit of great love and great scorn, will create anew. Driven by his own power, he will rebound from every transcendental ideal, not to escape reality but to penetrate it. Diving deep into existence, he will return to the surface with the means to redeem it—redeeming reality from the curse imposed upon it by the old ideal.

This man of the future will free us from the old ideal and its inevitable companions: great nausea, the will to nothingness, and nihilism. He will be the herald of a new dawn, restoring freedom to the will, purpose to the world, and hope to humanity. He will be the Antichrist and the Antinihilist, the conqueror of God and Nothingness. He must come.

But what am I saying? Enough. Enough! At this moment, the only course left to me is silence—otherwise, I overstep into a realm that belongs to someone younger, stronger, more "future" than I. This realm belongs to Zarathustra, Zarathustra the godless.

Chapter 3
What Is the Meaning of Ascetic Ideals?

What is the meaning of ascetic ideals? For artists, they mean either nothing or far too much. For philosophers and scholars, they reflect a kind of instinct or "flair" for the conditions that best support advanced thinking and intellectual pursuits. For women, at best, they add an extra layer of charm, a faint touch of delicacy on a beautiful body, the angelic quality of a plump, attractive creature. For those who are physically weak or chronic complainers (the majority of humanity), they serve as a way to appear "too good" for the world, a holy excuse for indulgence. Ascetic ideals become their main weapon in dealing with lingering pain and boredom. For priests, they represent true priestly belief, their greatest tool of power, and the ultimate justification for that power. For saints, ascetic ideals offer a reason for retreat, a longing for the ultimate glory of nothingness—"God"—and serve as a form of madness.

Yet, the fact that ascetic ideals have meant so much to humanity reveals something fundamental about the human will: its horror of emptiness. Humans need a goal, and they would rather will nothingness than have no will at all. Do you understand me? Have I made myself clear? No? "Certainly not, sir?" Well, let's start over from the beginning.

What is the meaning of ascetic ideals? Or, to take a specific example I've often been asked about: why would an artist like Richard Wagner embrace chastity in his later years? True, he had always done so in a certain way, but only near the end of his life did he do so in a fully ascetic sense. What explains this change, this complete reversal in his attitude? Wagner turned into the opposite of what he had been. What does it mean when an artist transforms into their own opposite? Let's pause to consider this question.

Think back to the boldest, happiest, and most creative period of Wagner's life. This was when he was deeply involved with the idea of

Luther's Wedding. Who knows what twist of fate led us to have The Master singer s instead of this wedding music? And how much of the latter might still echo the former? There is no doubt, however, that Luther 's Wedding would have celebrated chastity. Yet, it would also have celebrated sensuality, and it would have been entirely fitting— entirely Wagnerian. There is no inherent contradiction between chastity and sensuality. Every true marriage, every genuine and heartfelt love, transcends this division.

I believe Wagner could have shown his fellow Germans this beautiful reality through a daring and elegant "Luther Comedy." It would have reminded them that chastity and sensuality can coexist, even complement each other. Among the Germans, there have always been many critics of sensuality, but perhaps Luther's greatest achievement was his courage to embrace it. He called it, quite charmingly, "evangelical freedom." Even in situations where the conflict between chastity and sensuality does arise, there is no reason for it to be tragic. At least, this should be true for those who are healthy in both mind and body, who do not see the balance between "animal" and "angel" as a fundamental challenge to life itself. The most brilliant spirits, such as Goethe and Hafiz, even found this balance to be one of life's greatest charms. These so-called "conflicts" can actually make life more alluring.

On the other hand, it is painfully clear that when broken, miserable people worship chastity, they do so because it represents the opposite of what they are. They see chastity as the antithesis of their own ruined nature. And when such people worship chastity, the result is tragic. You can imagine the desperate grunting and pathetic eagerness with which they embrace it. They celebrate this painful, unnecessary conflict, the very conflict Wagner seemed to want to set to music and display on stage in his later years. But why? What purpose could it possibly serve? What did these broken souls mean to him? What do they mean to us?

At this point, it's impossible to avoid asking what Wagner really intended with that rustic, unmanly character, that naïve and unfortunate soul, Parsifal, whom he ultimately turned into a Catholic through such dubious means. Was Parsifal meant to be taken seriously? One might hope not—one might even suspect the opposite. Perhaps Wagner intended Parsifal to be a lighthearted farewell, akin to the final act of a trilogy or asatyric drama. Perhaps he, the great tragedian, wanted to bid farewell to us, to himself, and above all to tragedy itself, in a manner fitting his stature: by parodying the very idea of the tragic, mocking the grim seriousness and earthly sorrows of the past. This parody would also mock the most grotesque and unnatural aspects of the ascetic ideal, a phase that he had finally overcome.

Such an interpretation would indeed be worthy of a great tragedian. Every true artist reaches the height of their greatness only when they can look down on themselves and their work, when they can laugh at their own creations. Could Parsifal be Wagner's secret laugh at himself? The triumph of ultimate artistic freedom and transcendence? We might wish it so. For what else could Parsifal amount to if taken seriously? Are we to see in it, as some have suggested, a work driven by an insane hatred of knowledge, reason, and the body? A curse against flesh and spirit uttered in one breath of bitter contempt?

Could Parsifal be Wagner's retreat into the sickly ideals of Christianity, his return to a decayed and obscurantist morality? Was it a self-negation, a complete reversal by an artist who had previously poured all his will into the highest artistic expressions of both soul and body? And not just in his art, but in his life as well? Recall the enthusiasm with which Wagner once followed Feuerbach's teachings. Feuerbach's motto of "healthy sensuality" was, during the 1830s and 1840s, like a word of salvation to Wagner and many other Germans, especially the so-called "Young Germans."

Did Wagner later change his mind about this? It certainly seems that he wanted to change his message on the subject. This shift isn't only apparent in the Parsifal trumpets resounding onstage; it echoes in the somber, constrained, and troubled writings of his later years. In countless passages, Wagner reveals a hidden desire, a hesitant and unspoken will to preach retreat, to advocate for conversion, Christianity, medievalism. It's as if he wanted to say to his followers, "All is vanity! Seek salvation elsewhere!" At one point, he even invokes the "blood of the Redeemer."

What, then, are we to make of all this? Could Wagner's Parsifal truly represent the turning point where he gave up his earlier ideals and turned toward something entirely opposed to what he once stood for? Or is it something else altogether?

This list is certainly not complete; it is obvious that punishment is overloaded with utilities of all kinds. This makes it all the more permissible to eliminate one supposed utility, which passes, at any rate in the popular mind, for its most essential utility, and which is just what even now provides the strongest support for that faith in punishment which is nowadays for many reasons tottering. Punishment is supposed to have the value of exciting in the guilty the consciousness of guilt; in punishment is sought the proper instrumentum of that psychic reaction which becomes known as a "bad conscience," "remorse." But this theory is even, from the point of view of the present, a violation of reality and psychology: and how much more so is the case when we have to deal with the longest period of man's history, his primitive history! Genuine remorse is certainly extremely rare among wrongdoers and the victims of punishment; prisons and houses of correction are not the soil on which this worm of remorse pullulates for choice— this is the unanimous opinion of all conscientious observers, who in many cases arrive at such a judgment with enough reluctance and against their own personal wishes. Speaking generally, punishment hardens and numbs, it produces concentration, it sharpens the consciousness of alienation, it strengthens the power of resistance. When it happens that it breaks the man's energy and brings about a piteous prostration and abjectness, such a result is certainly even less salutary than the average effect of punishment, which is characterised by a harsh and sinister doggedness. The thought of those prehistoric millennia brings us to the unhesitating conclusion, that it was simply through punishment that the evolution of the consciousness of guilt was most forcibly retarded—at any rate in the victims of the punishing power. In particular, let us not underestimate the extent to which, by the very sight of the judicial and executive procedure, the wrong-doer is himself prevented from feeling that his deed, the character of his act, is intrinsically reprehensible: for he sees clearly the same kind of acts practised in the service of justice, and then called good, and practised with a good conscience; acts such as espionage, trickery, bribery, trapping, the whole intriguing and insidious art of the policeman and the informer—the whole system, in fact, manifested in the different kinds of punishment (a system not excused by passion, but based on principle), of robbing, oppressing, insulting, imprisoning, racking, murdering.—All this he sees treated by his judges, not as acts meriting censure and condemnation in themselves, but only in a particular context and application. It was not on this soil that grew the "bad conscience," that most sinister and interesting plant of our earthly vegetation—in point of fact, throughout a most lengthy period, no suggestion of having to do with a "guilty man" manifested itself in the consciousness of the man who judged and punished. One had merely to deal with an author of an injury, an irresponsible piece of fate. And the man himself, on whom the punishment subsequently fell like a piece of fate, was occasioned no more of an "inner pain" than would be occasioned by the sudden approach of some uncalculated event, some terrible natural catastrophe, a rushing, crushing avalanche against which there is no resistance.

What, then, is the meaning of ascetic ideals? In the case of an artist, we are starting to understand their meaning: Nothing at all… or so much that it is almost nothing. So, what is the point of them? For a long time now, artists have not taken an independent enough stance, either in the world or against it, to make their views and the changes in these views worth paying attention to. They have always been the servants of some morality, philosophy, or religion. And, unfortunately, they have often been excessively obedient courtiers to their clients and patrons, and overly curious sycophants to the existing powers, or even to new powers that are rising. To put it simply, they always need a shield, a support, some established authority: artists never stand on their own. Standing alone goes against their deepest instincts. So, for example, when the time came, Richard Wagner took the philosopher Schopenhauer as his shield, his support. Who would even think it possible that he would have had the courage for an ascetic ideal without the backing of Schopenhauer's philosophy, without the authority of Schopenhauer, which ruled Europe in the 1870s? (This is without considering whether an artist could have even existed without the support of an orthodoxy.) This leads us to a deeper question: What does it mean for a real philosopher to embrace the ascetic ideal, a truly independent intellect like Schopenhauer's, a man with the courage to be himself, who knows how to stand alone without waiting for others to protect him, and without needing approval from his superiors? Now, let us think about Schopenhauer's remarkable attitude toward art, an attitude that even fascinates certain types of people. This is clearly the reason why Richard

Wagner suddenly turned to Schopenhauer (as we know, influenced by the poet Herwegh), turning so completely that it caused a major shift in his views, creating a sharp contradiction between his earlier and later aesthetic beliefs. His earlier ideas are expressed in his work *Opera and Drama*, while his later writings, starting in 1870, show his change of heart. In particular, from that time on (and this is the change that most alienates us), Wagner had no hesitation in changing his opinion on the value and role of music itself. What did he care if, until that point, he had seen music as a tool, a medium, a "woman" that needed an end, a "man"—that is, drama—in order to thrive? He suddenly realized that much more could be achieved by applying Schopenhauer's theory to music, in *majorem musicae gloriam*—meaning, through the idea of music's sovereignty, as Schopenhauer understood it. Music was now seen as separate from and opposed to all other arts, as the independent art in itself—not like other arts, which reflect the world of appearances, but as the voice of the will itself, speaking directly from the "abyss" as the most personal, original, and direct expression. This huge increase in the value of music (which seemed to grow from Schopenhauer's philosophy) was accompanied by an unprecedented rise in the status of the musician. He became an oracle, a priest—no, more than a priest, a kind of spokesperson for the "intrinsic essence of things," a messenger from another world. From then on, he spoke not just of music, this ventriloquist of God, but also of metaphysics. So, is it any surprise that, eventually, he spoke of ascetic ideals?

Schopenhauer made use of the Kantian approach to the aesthetic problem—but he certainly did not see it in the same way as Kant. Kant thought that he honored art by emphasizing those qualities of beauty that also contribute to the dignity of knowledge: impersonality and universality. This is not the place to discuss whether this was a complete mistake; all I want to highlight is that Kant, like many other philosophers, did not approach the aesthetic problem from the perspective of the artist (the creator). Instead, he only considered art and beauty from the perspective of the spectator, and in doing so, he unknowingly brought the spectator into the very idea of the "beautiful"! But if only the philosophers of beauty had a better understanding of this "spectator"!—an understanding of him as a great personality, as a rich experience, as a wealth of powerful and most individual events, desires, surprises, and raptures within the realm of beauty! But, as I feared, the opposite was always the case. And so, from the very beginning, we get definitions from philosophers that are burdened with a coarse mistake, like Kant's famous definition of beauty. "That is beautiful," says Kant, "which pleases without interest." Without interest! Now, compare this definition with another, made by a true "spectator" and "artist"—by Stendhal, who once called beauty *une promesse de bonheur*

(a promise of happiness). Here, at the very least, the one point Kant makes in his aesthetic theory—disinterest—is rejected and eliminated. Who is right, Kant or Stendhal? When, after all, our aesthetes never tire of pointing to the fact that under the magic of beauty, men can look at even naked statues of women "without interest," we can certainly laugh a little at their expense. In this respect, the experiences of artists are much more "interesting," and, at any rate, Pygmalion was not necessarily an "unaesthetic man." Let us think all the better of the innocence of our aesthetes, reflected in such arguments. Let us, for example, count as a point in Kant's favor the country-parson naivety of his doctrine on the peculiar character of the sense of touch! And here we return to

Schopenhauer, who was much closer to the arts than Kant was, yet still never fully escaped the Kantian definition. How can this be? The situation is remarkable: he interprets Kant's phrase "without interest" in the most personal way, drawing on an experience that must have been a part of his regular routine. Few topics are discussed with such certainty by Schopenhauer as the workings of aesthetic contemplation: he claims that it simply counteracts sexual interest, like hops and camphor. He never tires of glorifying this escape from the "will to live" as the great advantage and utility of the aesthetic state. In fact, one might be tempted to ask whether his fundamental idea of Will and Idea—the thought that freedom from the "will" can only be achieved through the "idea"—didn't stem from a generalization of this sexual experience. (And, by the way, in all discussions of Schopenhauer's philosophy, one should never forget that it reflects the thinking of a young man of twenty- six, so it carries not only the peculiarities of Schopenhauer's life but also the characteristics of that particular stage in his life.) Let us now listen to one of the most striking passages he wrote in praise of the aesthetic state (from *World as Will and Idea*), and pay attention to the tone, the suffering, the happiness, and the gratitude with which these words are spoken: "This is the painless state that Epicurus praised as the highest good and the state of the gods; during this moment, we are freed from the vile pressure of the will. We celebrate the Sabbath of the will's hard labor, and the wheel of Ixion stands still." What power in the language! What images of agony and long-lasting revulsion!

How extreme is the contrast between "that moment" and everything else— the "wheel of Ixion," "the hard labor of the will," and "the vile pressure of the will." But even if Schopenhauer was absolutely right for himself, how does that help us understand what the beautiful really is? Schopenhauer describes one effect of beauty— the calming of the will—but is this effect something that usually happens? As mentioned before, Stendhal, who had a more balanced and happier nature than Schopenhauer, highlights a different effect of beauty. "The beautiful promises happiness." To him, the excitement that beauty creates in us, the "interest," is what matters most. And doesn't Schopenhauer leave himself open to criticism here, by claiming he understands Kant's view on beauty when he really doesn't? Kant defined beauty as something that pleases without making us feel any personal interest in it. But Schopenhauer actually found beauty interesting—perhaps even through the most personal kind of interest of all, the feeling of relief from suffering, like a tortured person escaping their pain. So, if we return to our original question—"What does it mean for a philosopher to admire ascetic ideals?"—we get our first clue: he wants to escape from suffering.

Let's be careful not to overly focus on the word "torture"—there is definitely room for some criticism and even some humor here. We shouldn't ignore the fact that Schopenhauer, who treated sexuality as an enemy (and even woman, whom he saw as "the instrument of the devil"), needed enemies to keep himself in a good mood. He loved using dark, bitter, and harsh words. He often raged just for the sake of raging, out of sheer passion. Without his enemies—without Hegel, without women, without sensual pleasures, and without the "will to live"—Schopenhauer would have become ill. He would have become a pessimist (although he wasn't really one, despite wanting to be). Without his enemies, he wouldn't have been able to continue at all. He would have given up. But his enemies kept him going. They always dragged him back into life, and his anger, just like that of the ancient

Cynics, was his source of strength, his way of coping, his way of finding relief and happiness.

So much for what is most personal in Schopenhauer's case; on the other hand, there is still a lot that is typical of him— and now we return to our main question. It is an accepted and undeniable fact, as long as there are philosophers in the world, and wherever philosophers have existed (from India to England, for example, at opposite ends of the spectrum of philosophical ability), that philosophers often feel irritated or even angry at sensuality. Schopenhauer is just the most passionate, and if you can listen closely, the most captivating and enchanting example of this. There is also a real philosophical bias and love for the entire ascetic ideal; there should be no illusions about this. Both of these feelings, as I have mentioned, are common in the type of philosopher we are talking about. If a philosopher lacks both of them, you can be sure that he is, at best, only a "pseudo- philosopher."

What does this mean? This situation must first be understood: in itself, it stands there, pointless and unchanging, like any "Thing- in-itself." Every living creature, including the "philosophical beast," naturally strives for the best conditions where it can fully express its power, and experiences the most satisfaction in doing so. Similarly, and with a keen sense that is even sharper than reason, every animal, including humans, instinctively fears any kind of disturbance or obstacle that could block or prevent its ability to reach these optimal conditions (I am not talking about happiness here, but about the way to power, action, and the most powerful actions, which often lead to unhappiness). Likewise, the philosopher deeply fears marriage, along with anything that could lead to it—marriage is seen as a deadly obstacle to reaching the ideal conditions for intellectual freedom.

So far, how many great philosophers have been married? Heraclitus, Plato, Descartes, Spinoza, Leibniz, Kant, Schopenhauer—they were not married, and one can't even imagine them being married. A married philosopher is something of a joke—that is my rule. As for the exception of Socrates—he married out of a kind of ironic humor, seemingly just to prove this very rule. Every philosopher would say, just as Buddha said when he heard that he had a son: "Rahoula has been born to me, a fetter has been forged for me" (Rahoula here means "little demon"); every "free spirit" must have his moment of reflection, just like Buddha did at one point: "Life is too narrow in a house; it is a place of impurity; true freedom is found by leaving the house." Because Buddha thought this way, he left his house.

There are so many ways to seek independence shown in the ascetic ideal, that philosophers can't help but feel joy and excitement when they hear the stories of those who, with great resolve, said no to all forms of servitude and chose to live in the desert— though they may have been, in reality, just strong donkeys, far from strong minds. So, what does the ascetic ideal mean for a philosopher? This is my answer—it probably won't surprise you: when a philosopher sees this ideal, he smiles because he sees it as a perfect condition for the highest and boldest intellectual freedom. By embracing this ideal, he doesn't reject "existence" as a whole; on the contrary, he affirms only his own existence, and perhaps even to the point where he is not far from wishing in a blasphemous way, "let the world perish, but let philosophy, let the philosopher, let me, exist!"

These philosophers, you see, are by no means untainted witnesses or judges of the value of the ascetic ideal. What do they think of themselves—what does the "saint" mean to them? They think of what is most essential to them personally; of freedom from force, disturbance, and noise; freedom from work, responsibilities, and worries; of a clear head; of the flow and freedom of thoughts, like a dance or spring or flight; of good air—fresh, clear, free, dry air, like the air at high altitudes, where every living creature becomes more intellectual and gains wings; they think of peace in every room; of all the hounds neatly chained, with no barking of anger or rough hatred; no regrets from wounded pride; quiet and obedient internal organs, busy like mills, but unnoticed; a heart that is distant, transcendent, future, even posthumous— to sum it up, they mean by the ascetic ideal the joyful asceticism of a deified and newly born animal, one that sweeps through life instead of resting. We know the three main ideas of the ascetic ideal: poverty, humility, chastity; and if you closely examine the lives of all the great, creative, and inventive minds, you will repeatedly find these three qualities, to a certain extent. Not for a moment, of course, as if these were their virtues—what does this type of person have to do with virtues?—but as the most essential and natural conditions of their best existence, their greatest productivity.

In this regard, it is possible that their strong intellectualism had to first control a proud or easily irritated nature, or an excessive sensualism, or that it had to work hard to keep its desire for the "desert" against a temptation for luxury, indulgence, or even a generous and excessive nature. But their intellect did all this because it was the dominant instinct that carried out orders over all the other instincts. It still does: if it stopped, it would simply no longer be dominant. But there is not the slightest trace of "virtue" in all of this. Moreover, the "desert" I just mentioned, where strong, independent, and well-prepared minds retreat to their hermitages—oh, how different it is from the dream of a desert that the cultured classes have! In some cases, the cultured classes themselves are the desert. It is certain that none of the intellectual giants could tolerate this desert for even a minute. It is not romantic enough, not enough like the mystical, Syrian deserts they dream of! Yes, there are still many donkeys here, but the resemblance stops there. But what a desert means today is something more like this—it might be a deliberate obscurity; a way of getting away from one's own self; a fear of noise, fame, papers, influence; a small office, a daily task, something that hides rather than reveals; sometimes associating with harmless, cheerful animals or birds, the sight of which refreshes; a mountain for company, but not a dead one, one that has life (that is, with lakes); and sometimes, even a room in a busy hotel where one can count on not being recognized, and be able to speak freely to everyone—this is the desert—oh, it is lonely enough, believe me! I admit that when

Heraclitus retreated to the courts and halls of the massive temple of Artemis, that "wilderness" was worthier; why do we lack such temples? (Perhaps we do not lack them: I just think of my wonderful study in Piazza di San Marco, in spring, of course, and in the morning, between ten and twelve.)

But what Heraclitus avoided is still what we try to avoid today: the noise and endless chatter of the Ephesians, their politics, their news from the "empire" (which I mean, of course, Persia), their market-trade in "the things of today"— for there is one thing from which we philosophers especially need rest—from the things of "today." We honor the quiet, the cold, the noble, the distant, the past—everything that, in fact, does not force the soul to tense up and defend itself— something we can connect with without needing to speak out loud. Just listen to the way a spirit speaks; each spirit has its own tone and loves its own tone. That one over there, for example, must be an agitator, a hollow mind, an empty vessel: whatever goes into him, everything comes back from him dull and thick, heavy with the echo of an empty space. That spirit over there almost always speaks hoarsely: has he, perhaps, thought himself hoarse? Maybe so—ask the physiologists—but he who thinks in words, thinks as a speaker, not as a thinker (this shows that he does not think about objects or think objectively, but only about his relationship with objects—that, in fact, he only thinks of himself and his audience). This third one speaks aggressively, coming too close to us, his breath touching us—we involuntarily shut our mouths, even though he is speaking to us through a book: his tone of style explains why—he has no time, he has little faith in himself, and he thinks this is his one chance to express himself. But a spirit who is sure of himself speaks softly; he seeks privacy, he lets himself be awaited. A philosopher is recognized by the fact that he avoids three bright and noisy things—fame, princes, and women—which is not to say that they do not come to him. He avoids any glaring light: that is why he avoids his time and its "daylight." In this way, he is like a shadow; the lower the sun sinks, the longer and darker the shadow becomes. As for his humility, he accepts, just as he accepts darkness, a certain dependence and obscurity: also, he fears the shock of lightning, he shudders at the danger of a tree that is too isolated and too exposed, where every storm blows with full force. His "maternal" instinct, his secret love for that which grows within him, leads him into states where he is relieved from the need to take care of himself, much like the "mother" instinct in women has always kept women in a dependent position. After all, philosophers demand very little; their favorite motto is, "He who possesses is possessed." All of this is not, as I must say again and again, due to a virtue, or a worthy desire for moderation and simplicity: but because their highest master demands it of them, demands it wisely and relentlessly; their master who cares for only one thing, and for which he gathers and hoards everything—time, strength, love, attention. This type of man does not like to be disturbed by enemies, nor by friends; he is a person who forgets or despises easily. He finds it bad form to play the martyr, "to suffer for the truth"—he leaves all of that to the ambitious, to the stage-heroes of the intellect, and to everyone, in fact, who has enough time for such luxuries (the philosophers themselves have real work to do for truth). They use big words sparingly; they are said to dislike the word "truth" itself: it sounds too pompous. Finally, when it comes to the chastity of philosophers, the creativity of this type of mind clearly lies in a different area than that of having children; perhaps in some other area as well, they achieve a kind of immortality, a small, lasting legacy (philosophers in ancient India would be even bolder in expressing this: "What use is posterity to someone whose soul is the world?"). In this mindset, there is no trace of chastity because of any ascetic belief or hatred of the body, just as an athlete or jockey's abstaining from women is not really chastity. It is simply the will of the dominant instinct, at least during their period of deep philosophical reflection. Every artist understands how sexual activity can harm the mind during times of intense focus and preparation; for the greatest artists and those with the most refined instincts, this is not necessarily learned through hard experience—it is just their "maternal" instinct, which, in order to nurture the growing work, carelessly uses up (beyond all its usual resources) the strength of their physical life; the stronger power then takes over the weaker. Let's now apply this idea to Schopenhauer, a case we have already discussed: for him, the sight of beauty acted like a kind of irritant that triggered the main power of his nature (the power of deep thought and intense focus); so this strength erupted and suddenly took control of his consciousness. But this doesn't rule out the possibility that the special sweetness and fullness of the aesthetic state, which is linked to sensuality (just like the "idealism" seen in young girls at puberty), could also come from this same source. Therefore, it may be that sensuality isn't removed when the aesthetic state arises, as Schopenhauer thought, but instead, it transforms and no longer enters the mind as sexual desire. (I will come back to this point later, when discussing the more detailed aspects of the physiology of the aesthetic experience, a topic that has been largely unexplored and not well explained up until now.)

A certain asceticism, a serious yet joyful renunciation, is, as we have seen, one of the most favorable conditions for the highest intellectualism. And, as a result, it will not surprise us that philosophers, in particular, always have a certain affection for the ascetic ideal. A serious historical investigation shows that the bond between the ascetic ideal and philosophy is even tighter and stronger than we might expect. It could be said that it was only in the leading strings of this ideal that philosophy really learned to take its first steps and baby paces—oh, how clumsily, oh, how crossly, oh, how ready to tumble down and lie flat was this shy little creature with its bandy legs! The early history of philosophy is like that of all good things; for a long time, they lacked the courage to be themselves. They kept always looking around to see if anyone would come to their help; moreover, they were afraid of everyone who looked at them. Just enumerate in order the particular tendencies and virtues of the philosopher— his tendency to doubt, his tendency to deny, his tendency to wait (to be "ephectic"), his tendency to analyze, search, explore, dare, his tendency to compare and to equalize, his will to be neutral and objective, his will for everything to be "without anger and prejudice."

Has it yet been realized that for quite a long time, these tendencies were opposed to the first demands of morality and conscience? (Let us not even speak of reason, which even Luther called "Frau Klüglin," the sly whore.) Has it yet been recognized that a philosopher, upon arriving at self-consciousness, must indeed feel himself an incarnate "we strive for the forbidden," and thus guard himself against "his own sensations," against self-consciousness? It is, I repeat, the same with all good things, on which we now pride ourselves; even judged by the standard of the ancient Greeks, our whole modern life, as far as it is not weakness but strength and the awareness of strength, appears as pure "Hybris" and godlessness. The things that are the complete opposite of those we honor today have long had conscience on their side and God as their guardian. "Hybris" is our entire attitude toward nature nowadays, our violation of nature with the help of machinery, and all the unscrupulous inventiveness of our scientists and engineers. "Hybris" is our attitude toward God, that is, toward some alleged teleological and moral spider behind the webs of the great trap of cause and effect. Like Charles the Bold in his war with Louis the Eleventh, we could say, "I fight the universal spider"; "Hybris" is our attitude toward ourselves—for we experiment on ourselves in a way we would not allow with any animal, and with curiosity, we open our souls in our living bodies: what does the "salvation" of the soul matter to us now? We heal ourselves later: being ill is instructive, we do not doubt it, even more instructive than being well—inoculators of disease seem to us today even more necessary than any medicine-men or "saviors." There is no doubt that we do violence to ourselves today, we crackers of the soul's kernel, we incarnate riddles, who are forever asking riddles, as though life were nothing more than cracking a nut; and even through this, we must inevitably become more and more worthy of being asked questions and worthy of asking them, and in this way, we perhaps also become more worthy to—live?

All good things were once bad things; from every original sin, an original virtue has grown. For example, marriage was once seen as a violation of the rights of the community. A man used to pay a fine for the audacity of claiming one woman for himself (this idea connects to things like the jus primae noctis, the right of the priest to be the first to sleep with a bride, which is still a custom in Cambodia today, as a part of the "old traditions").

The soft, kind, yielding, and sympathetic feelings we now value so highly were once looked down upon by those who had them. Gentleness was once a source of shame, just as hardness is seen as a fault now (see Beyond Good and Evil, Aph. 260). The submission to law: how difficult it was for the noble people around the world to give up their personal vendettas and accept the law's power over them! Law was once considered forbidden, a blasphemy, an unwelcome change; it was forced upon people like a power they reluctantly accepted with personal shame.

Every small step forward in the world used to come at the cost of great mental and physical suffering. Today, the idea that not just progress, but any step forward, any movement or change, required countless martyrs sounds strange to us. I mentioned this in Dawn of Day, Aphorism 18. "Nothing is bought more dearly," says the same book a little later, "than the small amount of human reason and freedom that we now take pride in. But that pride is why it's almost impossible for us to sympathize with those vast periods in history, the 'Morality of Custom,' that shaped the early stages of the 'world's history,' and set the course for human nature. I repeat, during those times, suffering was seen as a virtue, cruelty as a virtue, deceit as a virtue, revenge as a virtue, and rejecting reason as a virtue. Meanwhile, well-being was seen as a danger, the desire for knowledge as a danger, pity as a danger, peace as a danger, being pitied as a shame, work as a shame, madness as divinity, and change as immorality and corruption!"

In the same book, Aphorism 12, there is an explanation of the burden of unpopularity under which the earliest group of contemplative men had to live— despised almost as widely as they were first feared! Contemplation first appeared on earth in a disguised shape, in an ambiguous form, with an evil heart and often with an uneasy head: there is no doubt about it. The inactive, brooding, unwarlike element in the instincts of contemplative men long invested them with a cloud of suspicion: the only way to combat this was to excite a definite fear. And the old Brahmans, for example, knew to a nicety how to do this! The oldest philosophers were well versed in giving their very existence and appearance meaning, firmness, background, by reason whereof men learned to fear them; considered more precisely, they did this from an even more fundamental need, the need of inspiring in themselves fear and self-reverence. For they found even in their own souls all the valuations turned against themselves; they had to fight down every kind of suspicion and antagonism against "the philosophic element in themselves." Being men of a terrible age, they did this with terrible means: cruelty to themselves, ingenious self- mortification—this was the chief method of these ambitious hermits and intellectual revolutionaries, who were obliged to force down the gods and the traditions of their own soul, so as to enable themselves to believe in their own revolution. I remember the famous story of the King Vicvamitra, who, as the result of a thousand years of self-martyrdom, reached such a consciousness of power and such a confidence in himself that he undertook to build a new heaven: the sinister symbol of the oldest and newest history of philosophy in the whole world. Every one who has ever built anywhere a "new heaven" first found the power thereto in his own hell… Let us compress the facts into a short formula. The philosophic spirit had, in order to be possible to any extent at all, to masquerade and disguise itself as one of the previously fixed types of the contemplative man, to disguise itself as priest, wizard, soothsayer, as a religious man generally: the ascetic ideal has for a long time served the philosopher as a superficial form, as a condition which enabled him to exist… To be able to be a philosopher he had to exemplify the ideal; to exemplify it, he was bound to believe in it. The peculiarly etherealized abstraction of philosophers, with their negation of the world, their enmity to life, their disbelief in the senses, which has been maintained up to the most recent time, and has almost thereby come to be accepted as the ideal philosophic attitude—this abstraction is the result of those enforced conditions under which philosophy came into existence, and continued to exist; inasmuch as for quite a very long time philosophy would have been absolutely impossible in the world without an ascetic cloak and dress, without an ascetic self-misunderstanding. Expressed plainly and palpably, the ascetic priest has taken the repulsive and sinister form of the caterpillar, beneath which and behind which alone philosophy could live and slink about... Has all that really changed? Has that flamboyant and dangerous winged creature, that "spirit" which that caterpillar concealed within itself, has it, I say, thanks to a sunnier, warmer, lighter world, really and finally flung off its hood and escaped into the light? Can we today point to enough pride, enough daring, enough courage, enough self-confidence, enough mental will, enough will for responsibility, enough freedom of the will, to enable the philosopher to be now in the world really— possible?

And now, after we've seen the ascetic priest, let's address our main question. What does the ascetic ideal really mean? This is when it becomes very serious— critically serious. We are now facing the real representatives of seriousness. "What is the meaning of all seriousness?" This even deeper question might already be on our minds: it's a question more for scientists, but we will skip it for now. In this ideal, the ascetic priest finds not only his beliefs, but also his will, his strength, and his interest. His right to exist depends on this ideal. No wonder we run into a fierce opponent (assuming, of course, that we are the ones opposing this ideal), someone fighting for his very survival against those who reject this ideal! On the other hand, it's already unlikely that such a biased attitude towards our problem will help him much; the ascetic priest will hardly be the best champion of his own ideal (just like a woman often fails when she tries to defend "woman")—let alone being the most objective critic or judge of this debate. So, it's clear that we will more likely have to help him defend himself properly against us, rather than worry about him defeating us too easily. The idea we're debating is the value of life from the perspective of the ascetic priests: this life (and everything it's part of—"Nature," "the world," everything that is always changing) is seen by them in relation to a different kind of existence, which it pushes away unless life denies itself: in the case of the ascetic life, life is seen as a way to get to another existence. The ascetic views life as a puzzle, where one must move backwards to find where it began; or he sees it as a mistake that must be corrected by action: he demands that others follow him; he enforces his view of existence wherever he can. What does this mean? Such a strange view is not a rare case, or a curiosity in history: it's one of the most common and enduring facts we have. If we looked at the big picture of human life from the perspective of a distant star, we might think that Earth is especially ascetic, a place full of unhappy, proud, and ugly creatures, who never stop hating themselves, the world, and all of life, and who hurt themselves out of the pleasure of causing pain—probably their only pleasure. Let's think about how regularly, how universally, the ascetic priest appears: he doesn't belong to any one group; he thrives everywhere; he comes from all walks of life. It's not that he inherited this view and passed it down—quite the opposite. There must be a deep, powerful need that makes this kind of person, so hostile to life, appear again and again.— Life itself must have a reason for letting this type of self- contradiction continue. For the ascetic life is a self-contradiction: it is based on deep resentment, the resentment of a never-satisfied desire and ambition, wanting to control not just one part of life, but life itself, with all its deepest, strongest, and most basic forces. The ascetic tries to use power to block the sources of power. The green-eyed jealousy even targets physical well-being, especially things like beauty, happiness, or pleasure, while the ascetic finds satisfaction in suffering, decay, pain, misfortune, ugliness, and even in punishing and sacrificing themselves. This is all deeply paradoxical: we're faced with a split that chooses to be a split, that enjoys the suffering, and only becomes more confident and victorious as its own basis—its physical life—diminishes. "Triumph in the greatest agony": this is the symbol under which the ascetic ideal has fought throughout history; in this mix of temptation, pleasure, and torture, it found its brightest light, its salvation, and its final victory. Crux, nux, lux—all three in one.

If a will so driven by contradiction and unnaturalness is compelled to philosophize, where will it direct its peculiar obsession? It will aim its skepticism at those things most firmly believed to be true and real. It will seek out error precisely where the instinct for life has most confidently established truth. Following the example of the ascetics of Vedanta philosophy, it might declare matter to be an illusion, dismiss pain and multiplicity as errors, and even reject the logical distinction between "subject" and "object" as falsehoods. To abandon belief in one's own self, to deny one's own "reality"—what a victory!

This is a higher kind of triumph, not just over the senses or the physical, but an act of violence and cruelty against reason itself. This ecstasy reaches its peak in ascetic self-contempt, where reason, despised and scorned, is forced to decree: there exists a realm of truth and life, but reason is excluded from it. Even Kant's idea of the "intelligible character of things" retains traces of this schism so beloved by ascetics—the tendency to turn reason against itself. In Kant's view, the "intelligible character" of things refers to a quality that reason can only understand as being beyond comprehension.

Despite this, as seekers of knowledge, we should not be entirely ungrateful for such radical reversals of perspectives and values. The mind's relentless rebellion against itself, even when it seems futile, has value. The very act of seeing the world from a different angle, the very desire to do so, serves as a form of training for the intellect, preparing it for true objectivity. Here, objectivity is not understood as "disinterested contemplation"—a concept that is impossible and absurd—but as the ability to command both sides of an argument and to shift perspectives at will, using the contrast between viewpoints and emotional interpretations to advance understanding.

However, let us, as philosophers, be cautious of the dangerous mythology surrounding ancient ideas that have enthroned concepts like a "pure, will-less, painless, timeless subject of knowledge." Let us be wary of such contradictory notions as "pure reason," "absolute spirituality," or "knowledge-in-itself." These ideas demand something absurd: they require an eye that does not see, an eye without direction, stripped of the active and interpretive functions that make perception possible. In these theories, seeing is divorced from context, and vision itself is reduced to nonsense.

There is no seeing without perspective, no knowing without a viewpoint. The more emotions we engage with, the more perspectives we apply, the more different "eyes" we turn toward an object, the fuller and more complete our understanding of it becomes—this is true objectivity. But to eliminate all will, to silence every emotion—if such a thing were even possible—what would we call that? Surely it would amount to nothing less than intellectual castration.

But let us return to the topic. The apparent contradiction seen in ascetics— "life turned against life"—is, from a physiological standpoint (and not merely a psychological one), complete nonsense. It can only seem to be a contradiction. It must be a temporary explanation, a formula, a misunderstanding—a psychological attempt to explain something deeper, something that could not be fully understood or articulated for a long time. It is merely a term placed over an old gap in human knowledge.

Let me state the facts more plainly: the ascetic ideal arises from the instincts of self-preservation and self-defense found in a decaying form of life. It is a strategy employed by a life form struggling to hold its ground and fight for its survival. This ideal signals a state of partial physiological exhaustion and decline, against which the strongest and most intact life instincts continually battle, creating new tools and strategies. The ascetic ideal is one such tool. Its purpose is precisely the opposite of what its worshippers imagine—life fights within and through this ideal against death. The ascetic ideal is a strategy for sustaining life.

History provides an important clue to this. The dominance of the ascetic ideal, particularly in times and places where human civilization and taming were most developed, reveals something significant: the diseased condition of humanity up to now. Specifically, the condition of tamed humanity shows a physiological struggle against death—or more accurately, against the weariness of life, exhaustion, and the longing for an end. The ascetic priest embodies the desire for another kind of existence, one on a different plane. He represents the highest point of this yearning, its official ecstasy and passion. Yet it is this very strength of the desire that binds him to earthly life. It makes him a tool for creating better conditions for human existence on this plane. Paradoxically, this power is what allows the ascetic priest to keep the entire herd of failures, distortions, outcasts, and self- tormentors tethered to life, even as he himself leads them forward, instinctively acting as their shepherd.

Do you see it now? This ascetic priest, this supposed enemy of life, this denier of life—he is, in fact, one of life's greatest conservative and affirmative forces.

What, then, is the cause of this diseased condition? For it is certain that man is sicker, more uncertain, more changeable, and more unstable than any other animal. He is the sick animal—there is no question about it. But why? Certainly, man has also dared, innovated, and risked more than all other creatures combined. He is the great experimenter with himself, the restless and insatiable being who challenges beasts, nature, and even gods. He is ever striving for mastery, driven relentlessly forward by the future pressing upon the present. How could such a bold and resourceful creature not also be the most endangered, the one with the longest and deepest sickness of all the sick animals?

Man grows weary of himself. Entire epidemics of this weariness have swept through humanity, as during the Dance of Death in 1348. But even this exhaustion, this disgust with himself, is transformed into something powerful. Man discharges his nausea and fatigue with such force that it becomes a new chain that binds him to life. His "no" to life somehow conjures countless graceful "yeses." Even in wounding himself, this master of destruction and self- destruction is forced by the wound itself to continue living.

The more common this sickness in humanity becomes—and we cannot deny its prevalence—the more we should honor those rare individuals who possess both mental and physical strength, the true gifts of humanity. These exceptional individuals should be protected even more carefully from the worst kind of environment—the atmosphere of the sickroom. But is that being done? The sick pose the greatest threat to the healthy. It is not the strong who harm the strong, but the weak. Do we recognize this?

On a larger scale, it is not fear of humanity that we should wish to diminish. Fear forces the strong to remain strong, even to be fearsome at times, preserving the vitality of humanity's healthiest type. What is truly dangerous is not the fear of humanity but the nausea with humanity—and just as much, the excessive pity for humanity. If these two emotions were ever to merge, they would unleash the greatest monstrosity imaginable: the ultimate will of humanity, the will to nothingness—Nihilism. The path toward this is already well-paved. Anyone who uses their senses—who not only smells but also sees and hears—can detect the faint yet pervasive odor of madness and sickness wherever they go. I am speaking, of course, of the so-called cultured regions of humanity, of every "Europe" that exists in the world today.

It is the sick who are the greatest danger to humanity, not the evil or even the "beasts of prey." Those who are flawed from the start, crushed, broken— these are the weakest among us, and they undermine the ground beneath humanity's feet. They inject the most dangerous poison into our trust in life, in humanity, and in ourselves. How can we escape it? How can we avoid the covert glance of the malformed and miserable, a glance that leaves us deeply saddened? That glance, turned away from life, reveals their inner monologue: "I wish I were something else, but there is no hope. I am what I am. How could I escape myself? And truthfully—I am sick of myself!"

|

From such soil—this swampy ground of self-contempt—springs a weed, a poisonous growth. It is small, hidden, ignoble, and sickeningly sweet. Here, the worms of revenge and resentment crawl. The air reeks of secrecy and unmentionable things. In this foul environment, a malicious web is spun—a conspiracy of the suffering against the healthy and the victorious. Here, the sight of success and strength is met with hatred. And yet, what efforts they make to conceal this hatred! What grand words and virtuous postures they adopt! What skillful lies they tell to disguise their bitterness!

These wretched beings—what a noble tone their complaints take on! How their eyes ooze sugary humility and submission! But what do they really want? Above all, they want to appear righteous, loving, wise, and superior. This is the ambition of the "lowest" and the sick. How clever this ambition makes them! You cannot help but marvel at the skill with which they counterfeit virtue, even forging the golden seal of righteousness. They have taken virtue for themselves, beyond all doubt. "We alone are the good and the righteous," they declare. "We alone are the homines bonae voluntatis—the people of good will." They move among us as living accusations, as warnings, as if health, strength, pride, and the joy of power were sins for which we must one day atone. How they long, in their hearts, to make us atone! How they thirst to become our executioners!

Among them are countless vengeful individuals masquerading as judges, constantly invoking the word "righteousness" as if it were a venom they are ready to spit. Their mouths are always pursed, prepared to attack anything that does not wear a mask of discontent, anything that dares to move through life with cheerfulness and ease. Among them, too, is the most repulsive type of the vain and deceitful—those twisted creations who present themselves as "pure souls," peddling their warped sensuality disguised as "purity of heart," wrapped in poetic verses and other such coverings. They are the self-comforters, the ones who indulge in their own illusions, masturbators of their own souls.

The sick have a relentless will to project some form of superiority, to seek out devious paths that lead to power over the healthy. Where can this will to dominate—the will to power of the weakest— not be found? Especially in the sick woman: no one surpasses her in inventiveness when it comes to ruling, oppressing, and tyrannizing. The sick woman spares nothing—neither the living nor the dead. She digs up even the most buried and forgotten things. (As the Bogos say, "Woman is a hyena.") Look into the private lives of families, communities, and institutions: everywhere you will see this ongoing, silent battle of the sick against the healthy. It is often fought with subtle poisons, pinpricks, and spiteful grimaces disguised as patience. Yet sometimes, it escalates into a diseased kind of self-righteousness, a pure pantomime of "moral indignation."

This battle even reaches into the sacred spaces of knowledge, where the yelping of these sick hounds can be heard. Their lying and frenzied moralism infect even the noblest pursuits. Think, for instance, of that Berlin preacher of revenge, Eugen Dühring, who shamelessly exploits the most vile moral refuse in modern Germany. He stands out even among the Anti-Semites as the loudest and most repugnant moral hypocrite of the age.

These individuals are consumed by resentment. They are physiological distortions, worm-eaten remnants of humanity, a kingdom of festering revenge. They are tireless, insatiable in their attacks on the happy and equally ingenious in finding ways to disguise and justify their revenge. When will they reach their ultimate triumph? Likely when they succeed in planting their misery—and all misery— into the minds of the happy. At that point, the happy might begin to feel ashamed of their happiness and say to one another, "It is wrong to be happy when there is so much suffering."

But there could be no greater or more disastrous misunderstanding than for the healthy, the strong, and the joyful to doubt their right to happiness. Away with this "perverse world"! Away with this sickly sentimentality! Preventing the sick from infecting the healthy—this must be our highest goal. To achieve this, it is essential that the healthy remain separate from the sick, guarding themselves even from their gaze, avoiding any association with them. Is it their mission to play nurse or doctor to the sick? Certainly not. To do so would be the grossest denial of their true purpose. The higher must never degrade itself into becoming a tool for the lower. The pathos of distance must always maintain this separation.

The right of the happy to exist, the right of full-toned bells to ring above the discordant cracked bells, is infinitely greater. The happy, the healthy, and the strong are the true guarantees of humanity's future. They alone are bound to its destiny. What they can and must do, the sick cannot and should not attempt. But for the healthy to fulfill their unique role, they cannot waste themselves as the doctors, comforters, or "saviors" of the sick.

…And so, good air! Good air! Let us move away, at all costs, from the madhouses and hospitals of civilization. Let us seek good company—our own company—or, if need be, solitude. But at any rate, let us escape the foul stench of inner decay and the rotting corruption of the sick. This, my friends, is how we must defend ourselves, if only for a little longer, against the two worst afflictions that could ever befall us: the great nausea with man and the great pity for man.

If you have truly grasped—deeply and profoundly—the reasons why it is impossible for the healthy to act as nurses for the sick, to take on the task of healing them, then you must also understand another necessity: the need for doctors and nurses who are themselves sick. And now, with both hands, we hold the essence of the ascetic priest. The ascetic priest must be understood as the predestined savior, shepherd, and defender of the sick herd. It is only through this lens that we can comprehend his terrifying historical role. His domain is the rule over sufferers; this is his kingdom, his instinct, his unique art, his craft, and even his form of happiness.

To fulfill this role, he must be sick himself, a kin to the sick and the deformed, so that he can understand them and communicate with them. Yet, at the same time, he must also be strong—stronger than both himself and others. He must possess an unshakable will to power to win the trust and reverence of the weak. He becomes their anchor, their bulwark, their guide, their overseer, their tyrant, even their god. His duty is to protect the herd—but against whom? Against the healthy, of course, and against the envy the herd feels toward the healthy.

The priest naturally opposes every form of untamed, wild, predatory strength and power. He is the first embodiment of a more refined creature, one that scorns more easily than it hates. He will inevitably find himself in conflict with the beasts of prey, but his weapons are not brute force; they are cunning and spirit. He may even need to summon from within himself, or at least project, a new form of predator—a hybrid monstrosity, part polar bear, part stealthy panther, and part fox. This combination is as mesmerizing as it is terrifying.

When necessary, the priest appears with the gravity of a bear—serious, wise, cold, and full of deceitful superiority. He presents himself as the voice of mysterious powers, even venturing into the realm of other predators. His goal is to sow suffering, discord, and self-doubt among them, and he is certain of his skill to remain the master of sufferers at all times.

The priest arrives with salves and balms, but before healing, he first wounds. And as he soothes the pain of the wound, he poisons it further. He excels at this, this wizard and beast-tamer, who turns everything healthy sick and makes the sick docile. He guards his herd well—this strange shepherd—protecting them even from themselves. He shields them from the sparks of malice, deceit, and wickedness that smolder within the herd, for these are the ailments of the sick.

He fights tirelessly, using cunning, harshness, and secrecy, to stave off anarchy and the ever-present danger of the herd's collapse. For within the herd, resentment—the most dangerous and volatile of all explosives—constantly accumulates. It is the priest's task to manage this brewing storm, to keep the herd together and obedient, even as he strengthens his own rule.

Diverting this volatile resentment in a way that prevents it from destroying both the herd and the herdsman—this is the true achievement of the ascetic priest. It is his most significant function. If one were to summarize the value of the priestly life in the briefest formula, it would be this: the priest is the diverter of resentment. Every sufferer instinctively seeks a cause for their suffering. More specifically, they seek a doer—an agent they can hold responsible. Even more precisely, they long for a sentient, accountable being upon whom they can place the blame. In short, they need something alive, something tangible, upon which to direct their emotions. Whether this target is real or symbolic, it serves the same purpose: it provides an outlet for the sufferer's pent-up emotions.

For the sufferer, venting emotions becomes their most desperate attempt at relief—a kind of self-induced numbness, a narcotic they turn to in their struggle to deaden any kind of pain. This phenomenon, in my judgment, reveals the true physiological root of resentment, revenge, and related emotions. These are not merely defensive reflexes, as they are often misunderstood. They are not the protective reactions that help one avoid further harm, like the way a decapitated frog might reflexively react to corrosive acid. No, the purpose here is different. It is not about avoiding harm but about numbing a deep, persistent, almost unbearable pain by replacing it with a more violent emotion—any violent emotion will do.

For this purpose, an excuse is needed to provoke such emotion. The more intense the emotion, the more effective it is in temporarily driving the pain out of consciousness. This is why sufferers instinctively conclude, "It must be someone's fault that I feel this way." This reasoning is universal among those in pain, but it becomes more pronounced the less they understand the true physiological cause of their suffering. The source of their pain could be anything—an imbalance in the nervous system, an excess of bile, a deficiency in vital minerals like potassium, intestinal pressure disrupting blood flow, ovarian degeneration, and so forth. Yet, instead of addressing these actual causes, sufferers turn to imaginative and emotional explanations.

Sufferers possess an almost inexhaustible creativity in finding excuses to amplify their painful emotions. They revel in jealousy, wallow in dark suspicions, and relive supposed injustices. They dig through the depths of their past and present, searching for hidden grievances that allow them to indulge in torturous doubt and drink deeply from the poison of their own malice. They reopen old wounds, make scars bleed once more, and transform loved ones— friends, spouses, children—into perceived enemies. Their inner voice constantly repeats, "I suffer; it must be someone's fault."

This is where the ascetic priest steps in. He speaks to the suffering sheep and says, "Yes, my sheep, it is someone's fault—but that someone is you. You are the one to blame. It is your fault, and it is your fault alone." Bold, even false, as this declaration may be, it achieves one critical outcome: it redirects the resentment inward.

Now you see the purpose of the ascetic priest's role, the remedy that life's instinct has attempted through him. To achieve this, the priest employed a temporary tyranny of paradoxical and extreme ideas such as "guilt," "sin," "sinfulness," "corruption," and "damnation." The goal was not to heal the sick in any real physiological sense. Instead, it was to make them harmless, to a certain extent, by turning their destructive tendencies inward. The incurable were, in effect, destroyed by their own self-accusations. The milder cases were redirected toward self-discipline, self- surveillance, and self-mastery. Their resentment became a tool for controlling and policing themselves.

It is evident that this emotional "medication" never aimed to truly heal the sick. Healing, in the physiological sense, was never the goal of this instinct of life. Instead, two outcomes were achieved. First, there was a kind of consolidation and organization of the sick—a systematized management of suffering, which we often call the "Church." Second, a provisional safeguarding of the comparatively healthy was achieved. A deliberate separation was created between the healthy and the sick—a rift that kept the two groups distinct.

For a long time, this was all that could be achieved, and yet it was significant. It was a great deal—more than could have been imagined in such a state of widespread suffering and decline. It was an accomplishment of enormous importance.

As you can see, I am proceeding in this essay from a hypothesis that, for the kind of readers I address, does not need proof: the idea that "sinfulness" in humanity is not an actual fact but rather an interpretation of a fact—a physiological discomfort viewed through a moral and religious lens that no longer holds authority over us. Therefore, the feeling of being "guilty" or "sinful" is not evidence that one is justified in feeling so, any more than feeling healthy is proof of actual health. Consider, for example, the infamous witch trials. Even the most intelligent and humane judges of the time firmly believed they were dealing with guilt. The so-called witches themselves believed it. And yet, guilt was absent.

Let me expand on this hypothesis. I do not accept the concept of "pain in the soul" as a fact. Rather, I see it as an explanation—a temporary one— for phenomena that could not previously be clearly defined. In this sense, it is still unsubstantiated and scientifically unsupported, a convenient term that takes the place of a question mark. When someone cannot escape their "pain in the soul," the cause lies not in the "soul" itself but far more likely in the body—in the stomach, for instance. (I speak crudely, though I do not mean to encourage a crude interpretation of my words.)

A strong and well-balanced individual processes their experiences—both their deeds and misdeeds—just as they digest their food, even when some morsels are tough to swallow. If they fail to "digest" an experience, this indigestion is physiological as much as it is psychological. In fact, the two forms of indigestion are often interlinked, with one contributing to the other. You could embrace this perspective and still remain, in principle, an opponent of materialism.

But is the ascetic priest truly a physician? We already have reasons to hesitate before calling him one, no matter how much he enjoys portraying himself as a "savior" and being worshipped as such. His efforts are focused entirely on addressing the sufferer's discomfort, not the root cause of the suffering or the underlying illness itself. This is the most fundamental objection to priestly "medicine."

However, if you adopt the priest's perspective, it is difficult not to marvel at what he has seen, sought, and achieved from this vantage point. His genius lies in mitigating suffering, in providing consolation. Consider the inventiveness with which he has interpreted his role as a consoler and the boldness with which he has selected the tools for his task. Christianity, for instance, could be considered a vast treasure trove of ingenious consolations. It has amassed a remarkable storehouse of remedies—refreshing, soothing, even numbing drugs. Christianity has ventured some of the most daring and dangerous psychological strategies. With unparalleled refinement, often with a distinctly Oriental subtlety, it has identified emotional stimulants capable of countering the profound depression, crushing fatigue, and black melancholy of those who are physiologically unwell.

Indeed, all religions share this common goal: combating a kind of weariness that weighs down life. It is likely, even inevitable, that in certain times and places large portions of the population would experience waves of physiological depression. Without the scientific understanding of bodily health that we possess today, such depression would not have been recognized as physiological. Instead, its causes and cures were sought within the realm of moral and psychological explanations. This, I propose, is the most general framework for what is often called "religion."

Religions, then, can be seen as grand systems of consolation, designed to manage the fatigue of life that spreads among societies. By addressing this fatigue, they provide temporary relief and create narratives that help individuals endure the burdens they cannot fully understand or escape. This is the ascetic priest's domain: offering solace for suffering while leaving its true sources untouched.

Such feelings of depression can arise from a wide variety of causes, each shaped by unique circumstances and influences. For example, depression may result from the intermingling of races or classes that are too different from each other. Genealogical and racial distinctions often manifest in class structures, and the European "Weltschmerz" or the pessimism of the nineteenth century can be traced back to absurd and abrupt class mixing. Similarly, depression may be triggered by ill-fated migrations, such as when a race moves into a climate it cannot adequately adapt to, as in the case of the Indians in India.

Other causes might include the natural decline brought on by old age and fatigue, such as the Parisian pessimism that emerged after 1850, or poor dietary habits like the rampant alcoholism of the Middle Ages or the peculiar nonsense of vegetarianism, even though vegetarianism has been endorsed humorously by figures such as Sir Christopher in Shakespeare. Further contributors include deteriorating blood health or diseases like malaria and syphilis, which devastated Germany after the Thirty Years' War and left behind a population marked by submissiveness and timidity.

When such widespread depression arises, humanity instinctively wages war against it on a grand scale. This battle unfolds in various practices and stages. For brevity, I leave aside the philosophical struggles against depression, which often accompany these efforts. These philosophical battles, though intellectually engaging, are largely ineffective and impractical. They are riddled with abstract theorizing, such as the notion that pain is merely a mistake to be corrected—an assumption that, when tested, invariably fails to make the pain disappear.

The dominant approach to combating depression is through methods that reduce life's intensity to its absolute minimum. The strategy seeks to suppress the consciousness of life itself, lowering it as much as possible. This often involves eliminating desires and avoiding anything that provokes emotion or "stirs the blood." Practitioners of such methods might abstain from salt (as in the hygiene of fakirs), avoid love and hate, embrace equanimity, renounce revenge, wealth, and labor, and sometimes even resort to begging. They shun the company of women or limit their interactions with women to the barest minimum. Intellectually, this strategy aligns with Pascal's principle, "il faut s'abêtir"—the need to dull one's mind.

In ethical and psychological terms, these practices are labeled as "self- annihilation" or "sanctification." Physiologically, they resemble a form of "hypnotism," an effort to simulate the human equivalent of hibernation in animals or aestivation in tropical plants. The goal is to achieve a minimal level of metabolism and assimilation, allowing life to persist without fully entering consciousness. An extraordinary amount of human energy has been invested in achieving this state—possibly to no avail.

Still, it is undeniable that such "saintly athletes," who have appeared throughout history in nearly every culture, often find genuine relief from the physiological depression they battle. Through rigorous training and their system of hypnotism, they have managed to escape the deepest forms of depression in countless cases. This success places their methods among the most universal practices documented in ethnology.

It is incorrect to dismiss such strategies, aimed at starving the physical desires and instincts, as mere madness. While some blunt, roast-beef-eating "freethinkers" and Sir Christophers may be eager to label these practices as insanity, their view is overly simplistic. That said, there is no doubt that such methods frequently lead to mental disturbances. These may include experiences of "inner light," auditory or visual hallucinations, ecstatic raptures, or heightened sensualism, as exemplified in the cases of the Hesychasts of Mount Athos or St. Theresa.

The victims of these phenomena often provide explanations filled with fanatical falsehoods. Yet, even in their explanations, one detects a profound tone of gratitude—a sense that their suffering has granted them a higher understanding. They interpret their final state of salvation, the ultimate goal of their hypnotic practices, as a profound mystery beyond words. To them, it is a return to the essence of existence, a liberation from illusions, desires, and all forms of action. It is seen as a state beyond Good and Evil, transcending every boundary and dichotomy.

As the Buddhists say, "Good and Evil are both chains. The perfect man is the master of both."

"The done and the undone," says the disciple of the Vedanta, "do him no harm; the good and the evil he shakes off, for he is wise. His kingdom remains unaffected by actions; he transcends both good and evil." This is a thoroughly Indian conception, shared by both Brahmanism and Buddhism. In neither Indian nor Christian doctrines is "redemption" achieved through virtue or moral improvement, no matter how much they might value the hypnotic power of virtue. This is a key point to understand—and it aligns entirely with reality. The fact that these traditions stayed true to this principle may be one of the best examples of realism within the otherwise morality-saturated framework of the three great religions.

"For those who know, there is no duty." Redemption, according to these teachings, is not something attained by accumulating virtues. Redemption means unity with Brahman, who cannot gain perfection because he is already perfect. Similarly, it is not about shedding faults, for Brahman, with whom unity constitutes redemption, is eternally pure. These ideas are well-articulated in the commentaries of Cankara, as cited by Paul Deussen, one of the first true European experts on Indian philosophy and a personal friend.

We must, therefore, give due respect to the concept of "redemption" in these great religions, but it is hard to remain entirely serious when faced with how these exhausted pessimists—too weary even to dream—praise deep sleep. To them, deep sleep is seen as a merging into Brahman, the ultimate unification with God, the unio mystica.

The oldest and most revered scriptures express it this way: "When he has completely gone to sleep and reached perfect rest, so that he sees no more visions, then, oh dear one, he is united with Being. He has entered his true self—enclosed by the Self with its absolute knowledge. He has no more consciousness of anything within or without. Day and night do not cross these bridges, nor do age, death, suffering, good deeds, or evil deeds." Similarly, the adherents of this deepest of the three great religions claim, "In deep sleep, the soul rises out of this body, enters the supreme light, and takes its true form: it becomes the supreme spirit itself. There, it moves about freely, rests, plays, and enjoys itself—whether with women, chariots, or friends. Its thoughts no longer return to the burdens of the body, to which the vital breath ('prana') is yoked like an animal to a cart."

Yet, as with the concept of "redemption," we must note that this elaborate and extravagant Oriental imagery ultimately conveys the same critique of life as did the Greek philosopher Epicurus. His approach, while clear and cold in its simplicity, expressed the same underlying sentiment. The hypnotic sensation of nothingness, the peace of deep sleep, and the numbness of complete anesthesia— this is what the suffering and utterly dejected regard as their highest good, their ultimate value.

For them, this state of absolute negation becomes something positive, the essence of what they consider the highest achievement. By this same emotional logic, all pessimistic religions declare that nothingness is God. In their eyes, to embrace the void is to find peace, and the absence of everything is exalted as the ultimate liberation.

This hypnotic dulling of sensitivity and resistance to pain—requiring rare qualities like courage, disregard for public opinion, and intellectual stoicism—is far less common than another, simpler method often employed to combat depression: mechanical activity. Undeniably, the burden of a painful existence can be significantly lightened through such activity. Today, this phenomenon is often referred to, somewhat crassly, as the "blessing of work."

The relief it provides comes from its ability to divert the sufferer's attention entirely away from their pain. By monopolizing the consciousness with constant action, little room is left for suffering to take hold. After all, human consciousness is a narrow space, easily filled. Mechanical activity, combined with its byproducts—absolute regularity, rigid and unthinking obedience, the monotony of routine, the total occupation of time, and even a certain freedom found in impersonality—becomes a powerful tool. This "training in impersonality" or incuria sui (carelessness about the self), has been utilized with great skill by the ascetic priest in his ongoing war against pain.

When addressing the lower classes—slaves, prisoners, or women (who, in many cases, exist as a blend of laborer and captive)— the priest requires little effort beyond linguistic manipulation. By renaming and reinterpreting their circumstances, he can make them view their hated conditions as blessings. It is important to note that dissatisfaction with one's lot as a slave was not a creation of the priests, but the priests were adept at redirecting that discontent.

A complementary and equally popular method for combating depression is the prescription of small joys, particularly joys that are easy to attain and can be integrated into daily routines. This remedy often works alongside the discipline of mechanical activity. Among the most common forms of this "medication" is fostering joy through producing joy—acts such as doing good, giving gifts, helping others, offering comfort, praising someone, or extending kindness. These acts of generosity are often linked with the moral commandment to "love your neighbor."

The ascetic priest, however cautiously, also prescribes a controlled stimulation of one of the strongest and most vital instincts: the Will to Power. Even the smallest feeling of superiority, which naturally accompanies acts of helping, comforting, or praising others, becomes a profound source of consolation for the afflicted. Physiological distortions and those suffering from depression wisely use this instinct to their advantage, finding happiness in the smallest affirmations of power. Where this instinct is not harnessed constructively, the same drive often leads to harmful actions, as people injure one another in their pursuit of even the most minor dominations.

An exploration of Christianity's origins in the Roman world reveals that cooperative organizations for addressing poverty, illness, and burial emerged among the lowest social strata. These groups deliberately fostered the antidote of shared, mutual benefits as a way to combat depression. At the time, this approach may have been a novel discovery—a true innovation. By promoting cooperation, family structures, community life, and gatherings in shared spaces (Caenacula), these groups stimulated the Will to Power on a communal level, albeit in modest doses. This collective drive for mutual aid blossomed into a more potent and expansive manifestation of that instinct.

The development of these herd organizations marked a genuine advancement in the battle against depression. As communities grew, individuals often found a new focus of interest that drew them away from their personal despair or self-loathing—what Geulincx termed despectus sui (contempt for oneself). Through communal bonds and shared purposes, individuals could escape the narrower confines of their own dissatisfaction, finding solace and meaning in collective life. This was, in many ways, a triumph—not only for the community but for the individuals within it, who discovered a form of redemption through their integration into something greater than themselves.

All sick and suffering individuals instinctively strive for herd organization, driven by a deep desire to alleviate their overwhelming discomfort and sense of weakness. The ascetic priest recognizes and nurtures this instinct, fostering the formation of herds. Wherever herds arise, they are the product of the instinct of the weak, who crave union, and the cunning of priests, who structure and lead them. This dynamic reflects a natural divide: the strong, by necessity, strive for isolation as much as the weak seek union.

When the strong join together, it is not out of love for community but rather a reluctant alliance aimed at achieving aggressive collective action and fulfilling their shared Will to Power. Such cooperation is often against their individual inclinations, each strong individual wrestling internally against this compromise. Conversely, the weak unite with genuine delight in the organization, feeling their instincts gratified. For them, the herd is a source of solace and strength, whereas for the "born master"— the solitary predator type of man— any form of organization is a wound to their very nature, an affront to their instincts.

History teaches us an inescapable lesson: lurking within every oligarchy is the seed of tyranny. Oligarchies are perpetually tense, as each individual member must constantly suppress their own tyrannical desires. (The Greeks exemplify this dynamic; Plato, with his deep understanding of his contemporaries—and himself—revealed it time and again in his writings.)

The ascetic priest's methods, which we have already examined— suppressing vitality, enforcing mechanical labor, offering small joys, and promoting "love your neighbor"—are all tools for herd organization. By awakening a shared sense of communal power, the priest enables individuals to find joy in the success of the group, thus overshadowing their disgust with themselves. These strategies, according to contemporary standards, are considered "innocent" methods in combating depression.

Let us now turn to the "guilty" methods, which are far more intriguing. These methods center on the deliberate creation of emotional excess, a strategy used to provide temporary relief from the chronic pain of depression. Emotional excess acts as a powerful anesthetic, dulling the sufferer's awareness of their agony. This need for intense emotion has driven priestly ingenuity to extraordinary lengths, leading to the invention of countless techniques to provoke overwhelming feelings.

This may sound harsh. One might prefer a gentler phrasing: "The ascetic priest has always harnessed the enthusiasm inherent in strong emotions." But why should we sugarcoat this for the delicate sensibilities of modern listeners? To do so would only cater to the verbal Pecksniffianism of our age. For a psychologist, to indulge in such euphemisms would not only be hypocritical but nauseating. Good taste—or perhaps what some might call integrity—demands that we challenge the sickly moralized language that infects modern discourse about humanity and the world.

Do not be deceived: the defining trait of modern souls and modern literature is not outright dishonesty but the innocence that accompanies their intellectual dishonesty. This innocence is what makes modern psychology such a distasteful and dangerous enterprise. It is a path that leads directly to the "great nausea"—a revolt against the sugary moralism and falsity saturating contemporary culture.

I am well aware of the role modern works, and modernity as a whole, will serve for future generations (should they endure and should a healthier, stricter generation eventually arise): modernity will function as an emetic. It will purge the moral and intellectual systems of those future people, ridding them of the cloying sweetness, the ingrained softness and false idealism that masquerades as high-mindedness today.

Our contemporary "cultured" men and "good" men do not lie—this much is true. Yet this is hardly to their credit. Their unwillingness to lie is not a sign of virtue but a reflection of the same ingrained dishonesty that defines them. It is not a conscious choice but a symptom of their weakness, their inability to confront or express uncomfortable truths. Such is the state of modern idealism, cloaked in moral sugar and falsehood, steeped in the sentimental idealism they mistake for greatness. And such is the legacy that modernity will leave behind: a purgative for a future stronger, healthier humanity.

The real lie—the deliberate, intentional, and "honest" lie, the kind Plato speaks of so highly—is far too bold and difficult for most people to handle. Asking them to embrace it would require them to do something they are fundamentally unwilling to do: look inward, confront their own truths, and learn to differentiate between what is true and what is false within themselves. Instead, the dishonest lie is what suits them best—a lie that fools even the "good" man. Such people are entirely incapable of being anything other than dishonorable liars, absolute liars, yet they remain innocent liars, virtuous liars, and naïve, well-meaning liars.

These "good men" are completely steeped in morality, so much so that their sense of honor has been irreparably corrupted. They are morally tainted, disgraced for all eternity. Which of them could withstand hearing more truths about humanity—or, more specifically, about themselves? Who among them could bear the weight of an honest biography? A few examples will suffice. Lord Byron once wrote a deeply personal autobiography, but Thomas Moore, being "too good" for such raw honesty, burned his friend's papers. Similarly, Schopenhauer's executor, Dr. Gwinner, is said to have destroyed many of Schopenhauer's self-reflective writings, including some that may have even been critical of himself (εἰς ἑαυὸν). And consider the virtuous American Thayer, who, while writing Beethoven's biography, abandoned the project partway through. At a certain point, even he could no longer continue exposing the truths of Beethoven's otherwise noble and simple life.

The moral here is clear: who among us, in this age, would dare to write an honest word about themselves? To do so would require one to belong to an order of holy fools, a rare breed indeed. An autobiography from Richard Wagner is promised, but does anyone doubt that it will be anything less than a carefully constructed narrative? Consider the outrage caused by the Catholic priest Janssen in Germany with his overly simplistic and harmless depictions of the Reformation. Now imagine the chaos that would erupt if a true psychologist were to present us with an authentic account of Luther—not with the timid modesty of a Protestant historian or the moralizing simplicity of a parish priest, but with the fearless precision of someone like Taine, whose boldness comes not from deference to power but from genuine inner strength. (The Germans, by the way, already have a classic example of such deference in Leopold Ranke, the quintessential advocate of every causa fortior, a master of opportunism disguised as objectivity.)

But you can see my point. To put it simply, there are plenty of reasons why we psychologists must approach even ourselves with a degree of mistrust. It is quite likely that we too are still "too good" for the work we attempt to do. Despite whatever contempt we may feel for the modern obsession with morality, we are not immune to its influence. We are, perhaps, still its slaves and victims. This moral infection seeps into even our own judgments. What else could that diplomat have meant when he warned his colleagues, "Distrust your first impulses, gentlemen! They are almost always good"? This should be the mantra of every psychologist when speaking to their peers.

And so, we return to our problem, which demands a certain level of rigor and mistrust, especially of first impulses. The ascetic ideal as a tool for inducing emotional excess—those who recall my earlier thoughts will already understand part of what I mean. This ideal seeks to unsettle the human soul completely, throwing it into states of terror, ecstasy, rapture, and despair, as though through a sudden lightning strike. This method aims to jolt the individual out of their unhappiness, depression, and discomfort. But which paths lead to such a result? And which of them are the safest?

In truth, all strong emotions hold the potential to achieve this, provided they find a sudden and dramatic outlet. Rage, fear, lust, revenge, hope, triumph, despair, and cruelty—any of these can provide a release. The ascetic priest has never hesitated to employ the entire arsenal of human emotions, unleashing them selectively to awaken people from prolonged melancholy. He chases away their dull pain and misery, if only temporarily, always under the guise of religious meaning and justification.

Of course, this emotional excess comes at a cost. It must be repaid—it inevitably worsens the condition of the sick. For this reason, such remedies are deemed "guilty" by modern standards. Still, the priest's methods are undeniably effective, even if the price is steep and the long-term consequences dire.

Fairness requires us to acknowledge that this remedy was applied by the ascetic priest with a good conscience. He prescribed it with a profound belief in its necessity and effectiveness, even though he often struggled with the very pain he created in others. The priest, as a healer of sorts, genuinely believed this was the best path forward. Even the severe physiological consequences of these methods— sometimes leading to mental disturbances— were not entirely inconsistent with the purpose of the remedy. After all, the priest was not attempting to cure diseases in a conventional sense but to combat the misery of depression and its accompanying unhappiness. The goal was to alleviate and numb the pain of existence, and in that sense, the remedy succeeded.

The central tool that the ascetic priest used to pluck every agonizing and ecstatic chord in the human soul was the feeling of guilt. As I have previously explained, the origins of guilt lie in animal psychology—it began as a primal feeling tied to the instincts of creatures struggling with survival. In its raw, unshaped form, guilt was a simple mechanism of conscience. Yet, in the hands of the priest, this crude feeling was transformed into something far more elaborate and dangerous—a masterwork of emotional manipulation.

The priest gave this new version of guilt a name: "sin." Sin became the religious reinterpretation of the animal's bad conscience, a reversal of cruelty turned inward. Up to now, "sin" has been the most monumental event in the history of the human soul afflicted by disease. It is, without question, the most perilous and fatal creation of religious interpretation.

Imagine a man already suffering, burdened by his existence, trapped in a cage of his own making, and without understanding why. He searches desperately for reasons—anything to explain his suffering—and for remedies, perhaps even narcotics, to dull the pain. When he turns to the ascetic priest, the priest provides him with his first "answer": the cause of his suffering lies within himself, in his guilt, in a piece of his past. His suffering, the priest explains, is a punishment—a direct consequence of his own actions.

The man hears and understands. But now he is trapped, like a hen that has had a line drawn around it, unable to step outside the circle. The sick man becomes the sinner. And for thousands of years, humanity has been haunted by the image of this new invalid, the sinner. Can we ever escape it?

Everywhere we look, we see the hypnotic gaze of the sinner, always fixated on guilt as the sole cause of suffering. Everywhere is the evil conscience—what Luther called the "ghastly beast"—obsessed with the past, distorting actions through the lens of guilt and fear of punishment. The sinner's suffering is endlessly misunderstood, transformed into feelings of blame and a terror of divine retribution. The consequences are everywhere: the scourge, the hair shirt, the starving body, acts of contrition. We see the sinner breaking themselves on the wheel of a restless, insatiable conscience. We see silent pain, overwhelming fear, hearts tormented by their own guilt, and cries for redemption.

And yet, this system achieved its intended purpose. The old depression, dullness, and lethargy were completely vanquished. Life, once heavy and meaningless, became deeply interesting again—so much so that it burned with an almost unbearable intensity. The sinner became a figure of endless energy, awake and sleepless, consumed by his inner fire. Exhausted but never allowed to rest, humanity, as the sinner, was thrust into a state of perpetual tension and spiritual urgency.

The ascetic priest, the master manipulator, had triumphed. His kingdom had arrived. No longer did people complain about pain; instead, they began to crave it. "More pain! More pain!" became the cry of his followers, his initiates, echoing through the centuries. What had begun as a fight against depression and despair was transformed into an insatiable hunger for suffering—a perverse new vitality born from the ashes of misery.

Every form of emotional excess that inflicted pain—everything that shattered, overwhelmed, crushed, exalted, or transported the soul—became a tool for the ascetic priest. The horrors of torture chambers, the twisted ingenuity of hell itself, and every imaginable torment were uncovered, imagined, and exploited to serve the triumph of his ideal: the ascetic ideal. "My kingdom is not of this world," he proclaimed, both at the beginning and the end of his work. But did he truly still have the right to say so? Goethe once claimed there are only thirty-six tragic situations. If we didn't know better, we might assume Goethe was no ascetic priest—because the priest surely knows more.

Regarding this "guilty" form of priestly medicine—the emotional excess prescribed by the ascetic priest to his ailing followers—criticism is almost unnecessary. The idea that such methods have genuinely helped any sick person seems laughable. Who could seriously argue that emotional extremes, wrapped in sacred language and applied under the guise of divine purpose, have ever truly cured anyone? If by "be of use" one means that these methods have reformed individuals, I won't dispute it. But let's clarify: "reformed," to my understanding, means something closer to "tamed," "weakened," "discouraged," "refined," "delicate," or "emasculated"—all of which amount to a form of harm.

When dealing primarily with the sick, depressed, and downtrodden, such treatments might indeed make them seem "better," but they also make them far worse. Ask any physician who treats mental illness: what is the outcome of systematically applying penance- tortures, acts of contrition, and ecstatic salvation experiences? The result is clear—a nervous system further shattered, piled atop whatever existing malady the sufferer endured. History corroborates this. Everywhere the ascetic priest implemented this "cure," disease spread rapidly, infecting not only individuals but entire populations.

What were the results of these methods? Time and again, they left communities and nations riddled with broken nerves and deep psychological scars. Consider the epidemic of epileptic fits in the Middle Ages, such as the St. Vitus and St. John dances—mass outbreaks of uncontrollable convulsions, born out of penance and redemption training. Another result was the emergence of chronic depression and twisted emotional states that reshaped entire cities or nations, like Geneva or Basel, transforming their temperaments into something permanently somber and repressed.

This training was also directly responsible for the witch-hysteria—epidemics of mass delusion akin to somnambulism. Between 1564 and 1605 alone, there were eight significant outbreaks of this phenomenon. Similarly, we find entire populations gripped by suicidal fervor, like the mass death-cravings of certain periods in Europe, where crowds would shout the horrifying cry, "Evviva la morte!" (Long live death!). These episodes often swung unpredictably between orgiastic ecstasy and a destructive frenzy, a pattern seen wherever the doctrine of sin and asceticism found success. Religious neuroses are unmistakably tied to these symptoms—what else could they be? (Quaeritur— we must ask).

The ascetic ideal, along with its lofty moral cult, stands as one of humanity's most ingenious, reckless, and dangerous systems of emotional excess. It has left a terrifying and indelible mark on the history of mankind, a scar that is both unforgettable and undeniable. Worse still, this history is not confined to the past. Its influence continues to manifest in the present, haunting us with its legacy of suffering and manipulation.

I can scarcely think of any force that has harmed the health and vitality of European people more than the ascetic ideal. It can rightly be called the true catastrophe in the history of European health. At most, it can be compared to the uniquely German influence: the widespread poisoning of Europe with alcohol. This plague, running parallel with the rise of German political and racial dominance, left its mark wherever their influence extended—not only their blood but also their vice was spread. Third in this grim sequence is syphilis, though the gap between these calamities is significant (magno sed proximo intervallo).

Wherever the ascetic priest has gained control, he has corrupted the health of the soul. And, inevitably, where he has corrupted the soul, he has also corrupted taste in the arts and literature—he continues to do so even now. "Inevitably," I say. I trust I will be granted this conclusion without the need to prove it exhaustively here. Allow me to offer one striking example: consider the chief book of Christian literature, their ultimate standard, their "book above all books." This book was born in the midst of the Graeco- Roman splendor—a golden age for books, when the ancient world still brimmed with literary treasures that had not yet been lost to decay and ruin.

Imagine a time when people could still read works that we, today, would trade half our modern literature to possess. Yet, in this era of greatness, Christian agitators—those we now call the "Fathers of the

Church"—had the audacity to declare: "We too have our classical literature; we have no need of the Greeks." They held up their books of legends, their apostles' letters, and their apologetic pamphlets with pride. The comparison is almost absurd, akin to how the English Salvation Army today pits its tracts against Shakespeare and other "heathens" with similar misplaced self- importance.

Let me say it plainly: I do not like the New Testament. In fact, it nearly unsettles me to admit how isolated I feel in my disdain for this highly esteemed and excessively praised scripture. Two thousand years of admiration and reverence weigh against me— but so be it! "Here I stand; I cannot do otherwise." I have the courage of what some might call my bad taste.

The Old Testament, on the other hand—that is something entirely different. It commands respect! Within its pages, I find great men, a landscape full of heroic grandeur, and one of the rarest phenomena in history: the raw, unpretentious naivety of a strong heart. In the Old Testament, I see a people, a true collective identity. But in the New Testament? It is nothing more than a crowded hostel for petty sects, a spiritual rococo with its ornate twists, exaggerated flourishes, and overly sentimental embellishments. The air of small religious gatherings permeates it, a stifling atmosphere with hints of provincial sweetness that belong more to the Hellenistic world of the Roman provinces than to anything truly Jewish.

Here, meekness and bravado stand awkwardly side by side. The New Testament is filled with noisy, emotional chatter that nearly drowns out all else. There is hysteria in abundance, but no true passion; theatrical gestures, but no substance. These "pious little people" lack all dignity. How can they make such a spectacle of their minor failings, parading them with such earnestness? Who cares about their petty sins—let alone God?

And then, they have the audacity to demand the crown of eternal life. For what? On what grounds? The arrogance of it all is almost unbearable. An immortal Peter? Who could endure such a figure?

These small, self-important provincials seem convinced that their trivial troubles and mundane lives are matters of cosmic significance, as though the universe itself were obligated to revolve around their personal struggles. They never tire of dragging God Himself into the midst of their insignificant grievances, entangling the divine in their narrow, self-absorbed misery.

This is the New Testament: a book born of small minds and small ambitions, written by and for people who elevate their everyday struggles into the grand stage of universal importance. It is impossible not to see the absurdity—and, in some cases, the insufferable insolence—of it all.

And what about the dreadful form of this constant, intrusive familiarity with God? This Jewish—and not solely Jewish— endless pleading and clawing at the divine, this desperate, shameless insistence? There are small, so-called "heathen" tribes in East Africa from whom the first Christians could have learned much, especially a bit of tact in worship. These tribes do not even speak their god's name aloud—a delicacy so refined it far surpasses anything the early Christians could have mustered. It is certainly too refined, not just for primitive Christians, but also for the loud and irreverent worshippers that came later. For contrast, just think of Martin Luther—the most "eloquent" and audacious peasant Germany has ever known. Recall the tone of Luther in his personal exchanges with God, where he felt most at home: blunt, brash, and utterly without restraint.

Luther's rebellion against the medieval saints and the Church— especially his animosity toward "that devil's hog, the Pope"— was, at its core, the revolt of a crude man offended by the etiquette of worship. That code of priestly conduct maintained the sacred distance between the divine and the profane, admitting only the initiated and reverent to the holy of holies while shutting out the unrefined masses. Luther, the peasant, could not abide this. It was not "German" enough for him. He wanted to speak directly, personally, and without ceremony to his God—straightforward and plain. And he succeeded.

Yet, as you might guess, the ascetic ideal has never been a school for good taste, much less for refined manners. At its best, it has taught a particular form of priestly decorum—a manner fundamentally opposed to all genuine civility. Its essence is one of excess, a relentless defiance of balance and moderation, a refusal to adhere to any proper limits. It is the ultimate "non plus ultra" of poor taste and unchecked fanaticism.

But the damage caused by the ascetic ideal extends far beyond health and taste. It corrupts in countless ways—third, fourth, fifth, and sixth dimensions of ruin. Listing all its effects would be endless, and exhausting the catalogue would serve little purpose. Instead, my aim is not to enumerate its outcomes but to uncover what it means, to reveal the foundation it rests on, the forces lurking beneath it, and the hidden motives it expresses—often in vague, distorted, and misleading ways.

This is why I have not spared my readers a look at its disastrous consequences: to prepare them for the ultimate and most terrifying question—what is the true meaning of the ascetic ideal? What is the source of its immense, monstrous power? Why does it wield such dominance? Why is it given so much space to flourish, and why is there no stronger resistance to it? The ascetic ideal embodies a single will. But where is the opposing will—the counter-ideal that resists and stands against it?

The ascetic ideal has one clear aim: to make every other interest in human life seem small and unimportant by comparison. It interprets entire eras, nations, and people solely in relation to this goal. It rejects and accepts, denies and affirms, only within the confines of its own interpretation. Is there any other system of meaning that has been so thoroughly worked out? The ascetic ideal refuses to submit to any other power. Instead, it claims precedence over all forces, asserting that nothing powerful in the world can exist without first being assigned meaning, value, and legitimacy by the ideal itself.

Everything is treated as a tool for its purpose, a means to its singular end.

So, where is the counterpart to this vast, all-encompassing system of will and interpretation? Why is such a counterpart absent? Where is the alternative "one aim"?

I am told that this counterpart is not absent—that it has long fought against the ascetic ideal, successfully challenging it, and has even gained dominance over it in some respects. Look, they say, to modern science—the purest form of real- world philosophy. Science, they argue, has achieved what the ascetic ideal never could: the courage to believe in itself, the will to exist on its own terms, unburdened by God, another world, or the ascetic virtues of denial and negation. Science, they say, is the true conqueror of the ascetic ideal.

All their loud, clumsy agitation leaves me unmoved; these self-proclaimed heralds of reality are poor performers, incapable of producing a sound deep enough to resonate with true understanding. They are not the voice of science's vast and profound abyss—for modern science is an abyss. In their mouths, the word "science" is reduced to a vulgarity, an abuse, an insult to its true meaning. The reality is quite the opposite of what the ascetic ideal's defenders claim. Science today has no faith in itself, much less in any ideal greater than itself. And wherever science still possesses passion, love, dedication, or even suffering, it is not an adversary of the ascetic ideal—it is its finest and most advanced form.

Does this sound strange? Perhaps, but consider this: even now, there are plenty of diligent and honorable workers among the learned, people who are genuinely pleased with their small spheres of activity. Because they enjoy their work, they sometimes become embarrassingly loud in demanding that everyone else should be content as well, especially with science. After all, they say, "There is so much useful work to do in science!"

I do not deny this; indeed, I would be the last to interfere with the joy these honest laborers find in their tasks. Their enthusiasm for their craft brings me some delight as well. But the fact that science requires hard work, or that it has contented workers, is no evidence that science as a whole possesses a unified purpose, a shared will, a single ideal, or a deep passion rooted in faith. On the contrary, the truth is precisely the opposite.

When science is not functioning as the newest incarnation of the ascetic ideal—a rare occurrence, reserved only for the most exceptional and refined cases—it often serves instead as a refuge for all kinds of cowardice, doubt, guilt, and self-loathing. It becomes a sanctuary for those plagued by a lack of ideals, those suffering from the absence of a great passion, and those tormented by their enforced restraint and moderation. Oh, how much does science obscure today? How much, at the very least, does it try to obscure?

The tireless diligence of our most accomplished scholars, their obsessive industriousness, their endless sacrifices at the altar of intellectual labor—how often is the true purpose of all this effort simply to avoid seeing a particular truth? Science, in such cases, acts as a form of self-anesthesia. Have you noticed this?

Anyone who spends time with scholars knows the experience: a single harmless word, unintentionally spoken, can wound them deeply. What you might think is a compliment can provoke an extreme bitterness, not because you intended offense, but because you failed to recognize the nature of the people you were dealing with. These scholars are sufferers—though they might not admit it even to themselves. They are dazed, unaware of their own condition, gripped by one overriding fear: the fear of becoming fully conscious.

Now, turn your attention to the other side—to those rare figures I previously mentioned, the supreme idealists among philosophers and scholars today. Could it be that we have found in them the true opponents of the ascetic ideal—its genuine anti-idealists? These "unbelievers" (for they all claim that title) believe so; they cling to this belief as their last vestige of faith. They are so earnest, so fiery in their declarations and gestures, so insistent that they stand in opposition to the ascetic ideal. But does their belief make it true?

We, who claim to "know," have become deeply suspicious of all believers, no matter their creed. Over time, this suspicion has led us to draw the opposite conclusions from those drawn by others. Where belief is strongest, we suspect the greatest difficulty in proving it; the strength of a belief often signals its actual improbability. We do not deny that faith brings comfort or even salvation; in fact, it is precisely because of this that we doubt faith proves anything at all. Strong faith, capable of creating happiness, raises suspicions about its object rather than validating its truth. Instead, it points to the likelihood of illusion.

What, then, is the situation with these figures—these solitary spirits, these self-proclaimed deniers, these champions of intellectual purity, these heroic seekers of truth? They are the pride of our age: pale atheists, anti-Christians, immoralists, Nihilists, sceptics, and "ephectics" (those who suspend judgment) as well as "hectics" (those burning with intellectual fever). These are the highest idealists of knowledge, the sole bearers of the intellectual conscience in our time. They believe themselves to be as distant as possible from the ascetic ideal, thinking of themselves as "free spirits."

And yet, if I may speak the truth they cannot see—for they are too close to themselves—this ideal is their ideal. They are, in fact, its most spiritualized embodiment. They are its most refined scouts, its sharpest weapon, and its most subtle and persuasive expression. If I am at all adept at unraveling riddles, then let me propose this: for some time, there have been no truly free spirits. Why? Because they still believe in truth.

Consider the Christian Crusaders in the East who encountered the infamous Order of Assassins—a group that epitomized free spirits, disciplined far beyond anything the strictest monastic orders could achieve. Among their highest initiates was shared a secret motto: "Nothing is true; everything is permitted." This was the ultimate expression of freedom in thought—freedom that rejected even the belief in truth. Have any Europeans, any self-proclaimed freethinkers, ever truly confronted this idea? Have they grappled with its consequences or ventured into the labyrinth it creates? I doubt it. No, I know otherwise.

The so-called "free spirits" of today are, in fact, bound tighter than ever. Their belief in truth has an absolutism that is unmatched, even fanatical. I speak from experience, having encountered it firsthand. This belief binds them to a form of dignified intellectual asceticism—a stoicism of the mind that prohibits negation as firmly as it does affirmation. They remain paralyzed before the brute fact, the factum brutum, as though standing still is their ultimate virtue.

This small-minded fatalism, this "petit faitalism" (as I term it), is especially evident in the French scientific mindset, which tries to claim moral superiority over the German approach. But this renunciation of interpretation—this refusal to modify, challenge, or creatively engage with facts—this so-called objectivity is nothing more than a modern variation of ascetic virtue. It is, in essence, another form of the same repudiation of the senses, merely disguised under a new guise. At its core, it is still the ascetic ideal in operation, perpetuating itself through intellectual austerity.

The force that drives science into its relentless pursuit of truth is none other than faith in the ascetic ideal itself, even when this faith operates as an unconscious imperative. Do not be mistaken—this is still faith, faith in the metaphysical value and intrinsic worth of truth, a belief that is legitimized and sustained only within the framework of the ascetic ideal. This ideal upholds and guarantees the worth of truth; if the ideal falls, so does the belief in the inherent value of truth.

Strictly speaking, there is no science without its guiding "hypotheses." The very concept of a science that stands independent of assumptions is illogical, even inconceivable. Before science can take form, there must first be a philosophy, a faith, something that provides it with direction, meaning, boundaries, methods, and ultimately, the right to exist. Anyone who imagines otherwise—who claims, for instance, to establish philosophy on a "purely scientific basis"—must first overturn not only philosophy itself but also truth as we understand it. This would be the gravest affront to both, an unforgivable insult to the foundations of thought.

Make no mistake: the unwavering pursuit of truth, conducted with such daring and extremity as demanded by the faith in science, inherently asserts the existence of a world distinct from life, nature, and history. By affirming such a world, does it not simultaneously reject its counterpart—this world, our world? This paradox was already noted in my earlier work, The Joyful Wisdom (Book V, Aphorism 344): "The one who pursues truth in this radical, uncompromising way presupposes the existence of another world. And in so doing, must they not reject this one— the very world in which we live?"

Even now, we so-called knowers, we godless opponents of metaphysics, remain bound to a legacy born of ancient belief. Our zeal for truth, the very fire that drives us, is drawn from a thousand-year-old blaze ignited by faith—a Christian faith, a Platonic faith. This faith declared that God is truth and that truth is divine. But what happens when this belief crumbles? What if nothing proves to be divine except error, blindness, and lies? What if God Himself turns out to be the oldest and most tenacious lie?

At this point, we must pause to consider the consequences carefully. Science, which has long appeared as self-justifying, now finds itself in need of justification. This is not to say such justification necessarily exists; rather, it highlights a fundamental problem that has been ignored by nearly all philosophers, ancient and modern alike. Why this blind spot? Because all philosophy to date has been shaped by the ascetic ideal, where truth was enshrined as absolute—whether as Being, God, or the ultimate arbiter of reality.

Truth was sanctified, removed from scrutiny, and treated as unquestionable. Do you grasp the significance of this "unquestionable"?

Once belief in the God of the ascetic ideal is rejected, a new and pressing question arises: what is the value of truth itself? This becomes a problem for the first time—a question that the ascetic ideal never allowed to surface. The Will to Truth, which has driven humanity for centuries, now demands a critique. This is the task we must take upon ourselves: to examine, even challenge, the value of truth itself.

If this seems overly concise, I encourage readers to revisit The Joyful Wisdom, particularly the aphorism titled "How Far We Too Are Still Pious" (Aphorism 344) and the entirety of its fifth book. For further reflection, the preface to The Dawn of Day also offers valuable insights into this ongoing inquiry. Through these works, one might better understand the profound questions we must now face in our reevaluation of truth, its worth, and the faith that has sustained it for so long.

No, you cannot deceive me with science when I seek the natural opposition to the ascetic ideal or when I ask: "Where is the counter-will, the opposing ideal that expresses itself against it?" Science is far too dependent to fulfill this role. In every field, science relies on an ideal, a value-creating force that gives it direction, a purpose in which it can believe. Science does not create values on its own. Its relationship to the ascetic ideal is not inherently antagonistic. On the contrary, it often acts as a driving force in the inner evolution of that ideal.

If we examine more closely, science does not attack the core of the ascetic ideal but merely its outward manifestations—its rigid forms, surface expressions, and dogmas. Science liberates the inner life of the ideal by stripping away its superficialities, but it does not overthrow the ideal itself. In fact, both science and the ascetic ideal rest on the same foundation: an overvaluation of truth, or more precisely, a shared belief in the impossibility of questioning or valuing truth itself. This shared foundation makes them allies. If one is to critique the ascetic ideal, one must also critique science. Recognize this connection; it is crucial.

Art, in contrast, holds a far more genuine opposition to the ascetic ideal. Art, where deception is sanctified, and the will to create illusions is celebrated, stands fundamentally opposed to the ascetic ideal. Plato understood this deeply; he was the greatest adversary of art that Europe has ever known. His opposition to Homer reflects the full antagonism: on one side, Plato represents the life- denying transcendentalist, the great critic of existence. On the other side, Homer stands as life's unconscious celebrant, its golden admirer. For art to serve the ascetic ideal is the deepest corruption of its essence— a sad but frequent reality, as artists are often susceptible to such compromise.

Physiologically speaking, both science and the ascetic ideal stem from similar conditions: a certain decline in vitality, a frugality of life. Both reflect a cooling of emotions, a slowing of life's tempo, and the replacement of instinct with analysis and reason. Seriousness becomes their shared hallmark—a clear sign of life's struggle, a strenuous effort to maintain balance. Consider the eras in which scholars and intellectuals gain prominence; they often coincide with periods of cultural fatigue, societal decline, and the fading of confidence in life and the future.

The ascendancy of intellectuals, like the rise of democracy, arbitration instead of war, equal rights for women, or religions based on pity, are all symptoms of life's weakening vitality. They signify moments when a society has shifted from the vitality of creation to the slower rhythms of maintenance and decline. Science, when considered as a problem, raises questions about its very meaning and purpose. For a deeper exploration of this, one might refer to the preface of The Birth of Tragedy.

Modern science, despite its celebrated independence, often acts as the unwitting ally of the ascetic ideal. This partnership is subtle and unconscious, but it is undeniable. Science and the ascetic ideal have long reinforced one another. Their apparent opposition is misleading; they serve the same underlying purpose. Even the so-called victories of science often strengthen the ideal, not weaken it. When science dismantles a theological framework, it does not destroy the ideal itself. Instead, it refines it, making it more elusive, abstract, and insidious.

For instance, did the collapse of theological astronomy herald the end of the ascetic ideal? Hardly. If anything, the need for transcendental solutions to life's mysteries has only grown stronger. Since Copernicus, humanity has seen a continuous process of self-diminishment. The idea that we are mere accidents in a random and indifferent universe has not freed us from the ascetic ideal but has intensified our longing for meaning. This relentless will to belittle ourselves, to make existence seem smaller and more inconsequential, reveals the enduring grip of the ascetic ideal.

Science, with all its achievements, has yet to confront this core issue. It has not provided an alternative to the ascetic ideal but has instead evolved alongside it, refining and reinforcing its foundations. The need for critique remains. Only by addressing the shared underpinnings of science and the ascetic ideal can we begin to question the deeper values that continue to shape humanity.

Alas, humanity's belief in its own dignity, uniqueness, and indispensable role in the grand scheme of existence has eroded. Once, man regarded himself as almost divine—"a child of God," or even a "demi-God." But now, that sense of sacredness is gone, and he sees himself as nothing more than an animal—plain, literal, unremarkable, and unqualified. Since Copernicus, it feels as though mankind has been slipping down a steep incline, rolling faster and faster away from the perceived center of existence. But to where? Into the void? Into the "thrilling sensation of his own nothingness"?

Perhaps this descent is merely a direct path back to the old ideal. Consider how all branches of science—whether astronomy or even philosophy, including the harsh self-examination of reason itself—have labored to dismantle man's lofty opinion of himself. Kant, for instance, confessed to feeling diminished by the discoveries of astronomy, admitting it "annihilates my own importance." Science seems to take a strange pride in this project, finding its satisfaction in maintaining the very state of self- contempt it worked so hard to cultivate in humanity. For science, this disdain for man becomes his final and most profound claim to self-worth—a bitter, stoic form of pride. After all, only one who understands value can truly despise something, even himself.

But does this mean science has effectively countered the ascetic ideal? Hardly. If anything, it reinforces it. Take Kant's so-called "victory" over theological dogmas concerning God, the soul, freedom, and immortality. Many theologians believed this victory marked a blow to the ascetic ideal, but has it really? In truth, transcendentalists have thrived since Kant. Freed from direct ties to theologians, they've found a new respectability under the guise of science. Kant taught them the tools and methods to pursue their deepest aspirations without theological oversight, cloaked in scientific respectability.

Consider the agnostics, who revere the unknown and the absolute mystery. These modern worshippers elevate their very questioning into a form of divinity. They have turned their reverence for what they cannot comprehend into a new kind of faith. Xaver Doudan remarked on this phenomenon, noting how the habit of admiring the unintelligible has led to confusion, displacing a simpler stance of merely accepting the unknown. Ancient peoples, he speculated, may have been spared such ravages.

Suppose that everything humanity has ever come to know contradicts or horrifies its desires. In such a situation, how convenient it is to shift the blame— not onto the desires themselves but onto the act of knowing! "There is no knowledge; therefore, there is a God."

What an elegant syllogism! What a masterstroke for the ascetic ideal! It manages to transform humanity's dissatisfaction with the world into a divine affirmation of its own worldview. In doing so, the ideal emerges not weakened but stronger, perpetuating its hold over humanity.

Or, does modern history seem to reflect a greater confidence in life or its ideals? Quite the opposite—it prides itself on being merely a mirror, rejecting any teleological purpose or claims of proving anything. It disdains judgment, deeming such roles beneath it, which it might call an act of "good taste." Instead, it avoids both assertions and denials, merely fixing its gaze and "describing." This approach, while seemingly detached, is highly ascetic and, even more so, deeply nihilistic. Make no mistake about that.

Consider the historian's gaze: it is stern, somber, and determined, much like that of a solitary explorer in the Arctic, peering outward as if to avoid looking within or back. What does he see? A barren wasteland. Life lies silent beneath the snow, and the only echoes are bleak murmurs: "Whither?" "Vanity," "Nothingness." This desolate landscape yields nothing—no growth, no vitality— except perhaps the hollow intellectualism of "meta-politics" in St. Petersburg or Tolstoy's overwrought pity.

And then there is that other, perhaps even more modern, school of historians—a group enamored with life and the ascetic ideal alike. They romanticize and fetishize the contemplative life, praising it as though it were an art form, and establishing for themselves a smug little corner of pseudo- intellectual worship. These "sweet intellectuals," with their pretentious adoration of winter landscapes and ascetic ideals, inspire in me a deep and furious longing—for action, for vitality, even for the icy mists of historical nihilism. Yes, I'd prefer the company of those historical nihilists trudging through grey, cold fog over these effete, self- satisfied contemplators.

But worse still are the "objective" historians—those detached scholars perched on their worm-eaten chairs, feigning neutrality while oozing hypocrisy.

They are neither fully priests nor wholly men of passion; instead, they are grotesque hybrids, half-priest and half-satyr, their entire existence marked by a false refinement. Renan, for instance, reeks of perfume but lacks substance, a perfect example of this type. Such figures make me bristle with irritation. They sap my patience, and their very presence enrages me more than the supposed "play" of history itself. How could one not feel disdain? These eunuchs of thought, these weak-kneed admirers of ascetic ideals, deserve nothing but contempt.

Nature, in its wisdom, granted horns to the bull and teeth to the lion. For what purpose did it give me feet, if not to kick? Yes, kick— to trample down these cowardly intellectuals, these groveling contemplators who flinch at vitality and flirt shamelessly with ascetic ideals. They are hypocrites, eunuchs, and frauds, wrapping themselves in the guise of wisdom or objectivity, but inside, they are hollow. They are tragic clowns posing as priests, agitators masquerading as heroes, and opportunists exploiting idealism for personal gain.

Take, for example, the modern Anti-Semites, who cloak themselves in the supposed virtue of "Christian-Aryan honour." They roll their eyes and posture with cheap moralistic tricks, aiming to manipulate the most gullible elements of society. Their success reveals the sad state of modern intellectual life, particularly in Germany, where the mind has been dulled by an unhealthy diet of newspapers, politics, beer, and Wagnerian bombast. Combine this with the isolationist arrogance of "Germany above all," and you have the perfect storm of intellectual stagnation, a kind of mental paralysis that grips the nation and prevents any genuine progress or vitality.

All reverence to the ascetic ideal, but only insofar as it is honest and believes in itself. When it plays no games or flirts with pretensions, it retains a certain dignity. But the insipid bugs who cling to it, feeding on its infinite aspirations, until even the infinite stinks of their corruption—I cannot abide them. Nor can I stomach the empty facades of life these hypocrites parade, the exhausted souls wrapped in hollow wisdom, or the theatrical agitators hiding their triviality behind grand ideals. They represent everything that stifles life, everything that dulls the spark of vitality and replaces it with the rotting specter of pretense and decay.

Europe today seems consumed by its craving for stimulation. It overflows with ingenious means of excitement, as if it knows no greater need than for stimulants, whether intellectual or alcoholic. This has led to a widespread counterfeit of ideals—a flood of artificial inspirations and theatrical displays of passion. The atmosphere is thick with a pseudo-alcoholic stench of pretense, suffocating and false.

I can only imagine how many shipments of fake idealism, heroic posturing, and melodramatic moralism would need to be exported from Europe to cleanse its air. How many barrels of saccharine pity labeled as "the religion of suffering"? How many props for limp-minded intellects—crutches of righteous indignation? How many actors parading as champions of the Christian moral ideal? There's clearly a new business opportunity here: a trade in small, mass-produced idols of idealism and compliant "idealists." The market is wide open! With boldness—or perhaps just a free, uninhibited hand—one might imagine rebranding the entire world under these ready-made ideals.

But enough! Let's set aside these absurdities and grotesque spectacles of the modern spirit. They elicit as much ridicule as revulsion, and our present problem—the meaning of the ascetic ideal—does not depend on them. I will address these matters in more depth elsewhere, under the title "A Contribution to the History of European Nihilism." This will appear in a larger work I am preparing, The Will to Power: An Attempt at a Transvaluation of All Values. My only reason for mentioning them here is to note a peculiar irony: the ascetic ideal's most dangerous adversaries are not its critics, but its comedians. These performers of the ideal inspire distrust, undermining its seriousness.

In all other domains where intellectual work is done earnestly and authentically, without counterfeit, the ideal is often dispensed with entirely. This abstention is popularly labeled "Atheism," but even this so-called rejection is deceptive. The will to truth, which persists even in atheism, is in fact the most distilled and severe formulation of the ascetic ideal. Stripped of its adornments and external structures, this will to truth represents the ideal's core, not its remnant.

Consider this carefully: unadulterated, honest atheism—breathed in by the most intellectually rigorous minds of our time—does not oppose the ascetic ideal as it might seem. Rather, it is one of its final, logical expressions. It is a culmination, an awe-inspiring catastrophe born from two millennia of training in the pursuit of truth. This discipline has finally forbidden itself from indulging in the "lie" of belief in God.

This trajectory is not unique to Europe. A strikingly similar development occurred in India, providing independent and therefore illustrative evidence of the pattern. The same ideal drove to the same conclusion centuries earlier, culminating with Buddha around 500 years before the European era. This evolution began in the Sāmkhya philosophy and was later popularized by Buddha, transforming it into a religion.

The parallel is fascinating: two cultures, separated by vast distances, reaching the same endpoint through the relentless logic of their ideals. Europe, following its path of rigorous devotion to truth, finds itself arriving at a stark, godless reality—not an opposition to the ascetic ideal, but its ultimate refinement. The story of this ideal is not yet finished, and its ramifications continue to unfold in ways both profound and disquieting.

What, I ask in all seriousness, has truly triumphed over the Christian God? The answer is stated in my Joyful Wisdom, Aphorism 357: "Christian morality itself has triumphed—the idea of truth, taken with increasing seriousness, the intricate subtlety of the Christian conscience transformed and elevated into the scientific conscience, into an intellectual rigor at any cost." Viewing nature as proof of God's benevolence, interpreting history as evidence of divine reason and a moral order, seeing personal experiences as though every event were orchestrated for the salvation of the soul—such ideas are now entirely overturned. The sharper conscience rejects these interpretations, deeming them dishonorable, cowardly, and false. This severity, this demand for intellectual integrity, makes us, indeed, good Europeans, inheritors of the most rigorous self- discipline Europe has ever known.

All great things, however, crumble by their own weight, by acts of self- destruction; this is the law of life, the rule of inevitable "self-mastery" intrinsic to existence itself. Even the lawgiver must eventually face the verdict of his own law: pater e legem quam ipse tulisti—"submit to the law you have made." Christianity as a dogma fell through the consequences of its own morality, and now Christianity as a morality is unraveling in the same way. We are on the verge of this event. Christian truthfulness has led, step by step, to conclusions that ultimately turn against itself. It culminates in the question: "What is the meaning of all will for truth?"

Here lies our challenge, my unknown friends (for I know of no friends yet): what is the sense of our existence if not that the will for truth has become self- aware in us as a problem? With this self-awareness, morality as we know it collapses. This is the grand drama of the next two centuries in Europe—the most terrifying, enigmatic, yet potentially hopeful of all dramas.

Without the ascetic ideal, man—the human animal—lacked meaning. His existence had no purpose, no justification. The question "What is man for?" was met with silence. There was no will for man or the world; a vast emptiness surrounded human existence. Behind every great life echoed an even greater refrain of "Vanity!" The ascetic ideal answered this vacuum. It signified that something was missing—

that man needed justification, explanation, affirmation. He suffered not just physically but from the problem of his own meaning.

Man's issue was not suffering itself, but rather the lack of an answer to the searing question: "Why do we suffer?" The bravest and most resilient of creatures, man does not inherently reject suffering; he embraces it when it has meaning. He seeks suffering if it serves a purpose. What humanity could not bear was the meaninglessness of suffering, and the ascetic ideal gave it meaning. For the first time, suffering was explained. The immense void was filled. The door to suicidal nihilism was shut.

Granted, the explanation brought new and more agonizing suffering— more corrosive, more brutal—but it gave suffering purpose. It recast suffering through the lens of guilt. Despite this, humanity was saved. Man now had meaning and could "will" something—anything. The content of the will mattered less than the act of willing itself. The will was preserved, and with it, humanity was saved from nihilism.

This ascetic ideal, however, expressed profound contempt for life. It represented a hatred of the human, a disdain for the animal, and an aversion to the material. It loathed the senses, feared reason, rejected happiness, and recoiled from beauty. It yearned to escape illusion, change, growth, decay, desire—even life itself. At its core, the ascetic ideal revealed a will for Nothingness—a will fundamentally opposed to life. Yet it remains a will.

And as I said at the start: humanity would rather will Nothingness than not will at all.

Peoples and Countries

The Europeans today see themselves as the highest examples of humanity on Earth.

A common trait of Europeans is the inconsistency between their words and actions, unlike the people of the East, who stay true to themselves in daily life. The way Europeans established colonies can be explained by their nature, which resembles that of a predator.

This inconsistency stems from Christianity having abandoned the class it originally came from.

This marks a significant difference between us and the Greeks: their morals were shaped by the ruling classes. The morality we see in Thucydides is the same as the one that erupted in Plato's time. Honesty, for example, saw an effort during the Renaissance, often to benefit the arts. Michelangelo's view of God as the "Tyrant of the World" reflected an honest perspective.

I hold Michelangelo in higher regard than Raphael because Michelangelo, through all the Christian limitations of his era, glimpsed a nobler cultural ideal than the one embodied by Christian-Raphaelite art. Raphael merely and respectfully celebrated the values handed down to him without striving for something beyond. Michelangelo, in contrast, grappled with the immense challenge of creating new values. He sought to embody the conqueror perfected, the one who must first overcome his inner hero, a figure standing at the highest pedestal, mastering even his pity, and ruthlessly destroying anything that does not reflect his vision. Michelangelo at times surpassed his age and Christian Europe. However, he often yielded to the softer, eternal feminine elements of Christianity. In the end, it seems he abandoned the bold ideal of his greatest moments—a vision too immense for anyone but a man in his prime to carry. As he aged, he could no longer bear it. To fulfill his ideal, he would have had to destroy Christianity itself, but he lacked the philosophical depth to do so.

Perhaps only Leonardo da Vinci among the artists achieved a truly post- Christian perspective. Leonardo seemed to carry within him an understanding of the East—the "land of dawn"— both internally and externally. There is something transcendent and silent about him, a trait shared by all who have seen too much of both the good and the bad in the world.

How much we have learned in just fifty years! The Romantic School and its belief in "the people" have been entirely discredited. Homeric poetry is not "popular" poetry. The powers of nature are no longer deified. Relationships between languages no longer imply relationships between races. There is no mystical contemplation of the supernatural, no hidden truth in religion.

The question of truthfulness has become a completely new challenge. I am amazed. From this perspective, figures like Bismarck seem guilty due to carelessness, and Richard Wagner seems culpable for his lack of humility. Even Plato's noble falsehoods (pia fraus) and Kant's derivation of the Categorical Imperative now appear flawed, as these ideas were not truly their own beliefs.

In the end, even doubt turns upon itself, leading to doubt about doubt. The question of the value of truthfulness and how far it should go lies before us.

What I appreciate in the German character is its Mephistophelian quality. However, to truly understand this, one must have a greater concept of Mephistopheles than Goethe had. Goethe reduced Mephistopheles to make his "inner Faust" appear larger. The true German Mephistopheles is far more dangerous, daring, wicked, and cunning—yet also more open and honest. Consider the character of Frederick the Great or, even more so, Frederick II of Hohenstaufen.

The true German Mephistopheles crosses the Alps and claims everything he sees as his own. Then, like Winckelmann or Mozart, he collects himself. He views Faust and Hamlet as exaggerated figures made for ridicule, and he even looks at Luther the same way. Goethe, during his better German moments, likely laughed quietly at such things. But even Goethe could not avoid slipping back into his more somber moods.

Perhaps the Germans simply grew up in the wrong environment! There is something within them that could have been Hellenic— something that stirs when they come into contact with the South, as seen in Winckelmann, Goethe, and Mozart. However, we must remember that as a culture, the Germans are still young. Luther remains their last significant historical figure, and their most recent defining book is still the Bible. The Germans have never truly "moralized" in a philosophical sense. Even their diet has been a curse, contributing to a certain Philistinism.

The Germans are a dangerous people, experts at inventing intoxicants of all kinds. Gothic art, rococo (as Semper described), their sense of history and exoticism, Hegel, Richard Wagner— even Leibniz, who still exerts influence today—all are evidence of this. They even turned the servile spirit into an ideal, celebrating it as the virtue of scholars, soldiers, and the humble-minded. Germans may well be the most complex and mixed people on Earth.

They are "the people of the middle," inventors of porcelain and a peculiar type of bureaucratic Privy Councillor, resembling something out of Chinese tradition.

The smallness and pettiness of the German soul were not caused by their history of small states. History shows that people from even smaller states could still be proud and independent. Nor does a large state automatically foster freer, stronger souls. A man whose spirit bows to the command, "Thou shalt and must kneel!"—a man whose very body instinctively submits to titles, medals, and favors from above—will bow even lower under a greater ruler than under a lesser one. There is no doubt about this.

In contrast, in the lower classes of Italy, there is still a sense of aristocratic self-assurance. The discipline and self-respect that come from a long history of greatness are still visible. A poor Venetian gondolier cuts a more impressive figure than a Privy Councillor from Berlin and is, in many ways, the better man. Ask the women—they know this.

Most artists, even the greatest among them, have historically come from the serving classes. Whether they served nobility, princes, women, or the masses, they remained tied to their patrons, not to mention their dependence on the Church and moral conventions.

Rubens, for example, painted the nobility of his time, but he adhered to their vague notions of taste rather than his own sense of beauty. He worked against his personal standards.

Van Dyck, however, was nobler in this regard. He elevated those he painted, infusing them with qualities he admired most. He did not lower himself to match them; instead, he brought them up to his level through his art.

The artist's submissive humility to his audience, which Sebastian Bach revealed in bold and shocking terms in the dedication of his High Mass, may be harder to detect in music, but it is deeply ingrained. If I were to explain my views on this subject, I might not even find a willing audience.

Chopin, like Van Dyck, carried himself with distinction. Beethoven had the proud spirit of a peasant, while Haydn carried the pride of a servant. Mendelssohn, too, had a natural elegance, much like Goethe.

German scholars with wit have always been few—countable on one hand— while the rest possess understanding, and some, fortunately, that famous "childlike quality" that enables them to intuitively sense things. This ability has led German science to uncover phenomena that we can scarcely imagine—and which, perhaps, do not exist. Yet, this quality of "divination" is not shared by the Jews among the Germans.

Just as French scholars reflect the wit and courtesy of French society, Germans mirror the deep, contemplative seriousness of their mystics and musicians, along with a certain naive childishness. Italians, on the other hand, exude a sense of republican refinement and artistry; they can appear noble and proud without slipping into vanity.

It is my hope that more of Germany's talented individuals will eventually gain enough self-control to abandon their poor taste for affectation and sentimental gloom. Such men will, I trust, turn against the influences of Richard Wagner and Schopenhauer. These two figures, dangerous as they are, flatter Germany's most perilous traits and lead the nation toward decline. Instead, a stronger and more promising future lies with the legacy of Goethe, Beethoven, and Bismarck, not with such deviations from the path. After all, Germany has yet to produce true philosophers.

The peasant represents the most common form of nobility because he relies primarily on himself. Peasant blood remains the strongest in Germany, as seen in figures like Luther, Niebuhr, and Bismarck. Regarding Bismarck, one cannot ignore his Slavic ancestry. German faces often reveal this mixture—those with vigorous, masculine blood left Germany for foreign lands, while the remaining population, largely docile and subservient, saw improvement through an infusion of Slavonic elements. Today, the Brandenburg and broader Prussian nobility, as well as the peasants from specific northern regions, embody the most masculine natures in Germany. It is natural for such men to rule; indeed, the future of German culture rests with the sons of Prussian officers.

Germany has always suffered from a lack of wit. Even average minds achieve high honors there simply because they are uncommon. Qualities like diligence, persistence, and a dispassionate, critical perspective are what Germany values most. These traits have allowed German scholarship and the German military system to dominate Europe.

Parliaments can be of use to a strong and capable statesman; they provide something stable to rely on, something that can bear responsibility. However, Germany should not adopt the counting obsession and faith in majorities seen in Latin nations. There is still an opportunity to innovate in politics, and universal suffrage, which is relatively new and could easily be uprooted, should not be allowed to take deeper root. It was introduced only as a temporary solution to pressing problems.

Can anyone genuinely care about the German Empire as it stands? Where is its new and innovative thinking? If it is merely a new combination of power, that's even worse—especially if it lacks a clear vision. Peace and laisser - aller are not the kind of politics I respect. What interests me in Germany is the potential to rule effectively and to champion the most elevated ideas.

The greatest threat in the world today is England's narrow-mindedness. Remarkably, I observe more ambition for greatness among Russian Nihilists than among English Utilitarians. To achieve true mastery, Germany must forge a union with the Slavic races and incorporate the skills of the Jews, who are the most capable financiers.

To achieve this, several elements are necessary: (a) A firm grasp of reality. (b) Abandoning the English principle of popular representation and replacing it with representation of major interests. (c) An unconditional alliance with Russia and a joint strategy to ensure that English schemes have no influence in Russia. The future must not be Americanized. (d) Nationalistic politics are unsustainable, and the entanglement of Christian ideals is a major hindrance. In Europe, all rational minds are skeptics, even if they do not openly admit it.

I see beyond these national conflicts, new empires, and whatever else appears on the surface. My true concern is with what I perceive slowly taking shape—the vision of a United Europe. This has been the only meaningful labor, the singular impulse in the souls of all the broad-minded and forward-thinking individuals of this century. Their aim has been to prepare a new synthesis, an effort to anticipate and shape the future of "the European." Only in moments of weakness or as they grew older did they revert to the narrow nationalism of "Fatherland" sentiments—then they once again became "patriots." Figures such as Napoleon, Heinrich Heine, Goethe, Beethoven, Stendhal, and Schopenhauer come to mind. Perhaps even Richard Wagner, with his peculiar brand of German obscurity, belongs among them, though his inclusion warrants some hesitation.

Supporting the minds that seek this unity is a significant and clarifying economic reality: the small states of Europe—our current kingdoms and empires—will soon become economically unsustainable. The frenzied, unregulated competition for control of local and international trade is pushing Europe toward amalgamation into a single power. Money is driving this necessity. For Europe to effectively engage in the looming struggle for global dominance (and it is easy to imagine against whom this struggle will be fought), an agreement with England will likely become unavoidable. England's colonies will be essential in this endeavor, just as modern Germany, in its emerging role as broker and middleman, will find itself reliant on the colonial assets of Holland.

It is clear that no one believes England can maintain its current global role alone for another fifty years. The impossibility of preventing homines novi from entering government will undermine her stability, while the constant rotation of political parties will obstruct any efforts requiring long-term planning. Today, a man must first be a soldier to secure his reputation as a merchant later. Suffice it to say, the next century will likely follow the path laid by Napoleon—the foremost figure of his era and the most innovative and visionary of modern times. For the challenges of the coming century, the methods of popular representation and parliamentary governance seem woefully inadequate.

Europe's condition in the next century will once again demand the cultivation of manly virtues, as life will be defined by constant danger. Universal military service already serves as a curious counterbalance to the softness introduced by democratic ideals, born as it was out of the nations' struggles. And what is a nation?

A group of people who speak the same language and consume the same news. These groups call themselves "nations" and are all too eager to trace their ancestry and history to a single, unbroken source. Yet, even with the help of the most outrageous falsehoods about the past, they have never fully succeeded in doing so.

What confusion and falsehood must exist for questions of "race" to even be raised in the chaotic mixture that is modern Europe! (Assuming, of course, that the origins of these writers are not in some far-off place like Horneo or Borneo.) A simple principle: avoid associating with anyone who participates in the deceitful "race" charade.

With the freedom of travel available today, people of like minds and shared heritage can gather and create communities with shared customs and practices. This is how nations can be overcome. To make Europe a true center of culture, we must rise above the foolishness of national divisions. At higher levels, there is already an interconnectedness that we cannot ignore. Think of France and German philosophy, Richard Wagner and Paris during the 1830s to 1850s, or Goethe and Greece. There is a natural momentum toward unifying Europe's past in the minds of its greatest thinkers.

Humanity still has much ahead of it—how could anyone believe the ideal lies in the past? Perhaps the past can only offer meaning when seen in contrast to our present, which might well be a lower phase of development.

This persistent uncertainty haunts us, keeping us awake, raising questions that no one wants to acknowledge. It's our riddle, our Sphinx, standing near more than one precipice. We suspect that today's Europeans are deeply mistaken about what they value most, and some indifferent, childlike force—a pitiless demon— seems to toy with our passions and ideals, just as it has perhaps toyed with all that has lived and loved before us.

I suspect that much of what we Europeans admire today—values like "humanity," "sympathy," and "pity"—might have some worth only because they weaken and tame certain powerful, primal drives. Over time, however, these virtues seem to shrink the potential of the human type, reducing us to mediocrity. If I may use a desperate phrase for a desperate situation: all of this leads to the belittling of man. For an epicurean god watching this human comedy unfold, it must be amusing to see Europeans believe, with all their moral earnestness and self-satisfaction, that they are advancing. The truth, however, is that they are sinking—lower and lower. By cultivating herd-friendly virtues and suppressing the contrary qualities that could create a new, stronger, and more masterful race, we are merely refining the herd-animal within man. And yet, man remains the animal that has not yet stabilized itself.

Genius and the times in which it arises are intricately connected. Heroism, for example, is not a form of selfishness—it often leads to ruin. The strength of an individual often finds its direction shaped by the era into which they are born, giving rise to the misconception that such a person is a product of their time. In reality, this strength could manifest in many different ways. There is always a disconnect between the individual and their time. Public opinion tends to celebrate the herd instinct—the instinct of the weak—while the strong individual fights for ideals that defy this collective mindset.

The looming fate of Europe is clear: her strongest individuals emerge rarely, and even then, often too late in life. In their youth, they are already burdened by sorrow, disillusionment, and a darkness of mind. This happens because, with the intensity of their strength, they confront the full weight of their era's despair— the despair of knowledge and disillusionment—and drain it completely. Yet, this is the ultimate test of their power: they must rise above the sickness of their age to find their own health. Their distinction is marked by their late blooming—late joy, late folly, and a late but exuberant springtime of spirit.

But here lies the danger of our time: everything we cherished in our youth has betrayed us. Even our last love—the one we placed in Truth herself— threatens to betray us if we are not careful. Let us guard this final love with vigilance, for it represents our deepest acknowledgment and our most profound hope.

The End

Thank You for Reading

Dear Reader,

We hope this timeless classic has sparked your imagination and enriched your literary journey. Now that you've turned the final page, we want to share a vision for the future of reading—one where every classic you've ever wanted to explore is at your fingertips, in a format that best suits your life.

We'd like to invite you to gain immediate, unlimited digital & audiobook access to hundreds of the most treasured literary classics ever written—along with the option to secure deluxe paperback, hardcover & box set editions at printing cost. Together, we can spark a new global literary renaissance alongside our small, independent publishing house called "The Library of Alexandria."

Thousands of years ago, the Library of Alexandria stood as a beacon of knowledge—until it was lost to history. We aim to reignite that spirit of preservation and discovery right now, in the modern age—only this time, it's accessible to all, in every language and every format.

Picture a world where every timeless classic, novel, poem, or philosophical treatise is not only available to read but also updated for today's readers—modernized, translated into any language or dialect, and ready to enjoy in any format you choose, whether that is in an eBook, audiobook, paperback, or deluxe hardcover & box set version a printing cost.

By joining our movement to rebuild the modern Library of Alexandria, you become part of an unprecedented mission to offer:

- **Unlimited Audiobook & eBook Access to the Greatest Classics of All Time**

    Instantly explore thousands of legendary works, from Plato and Shakespeare to Jane Austen and Leo Tolstoy. All are instantly ready to read or listen to, giving you a complete literary universe at your fingertips.

- **Paperback & Deluxe Editions at Printing Costs:**

  Purchase any title in a paperback, deluxe hardbound, or deluxe boxset edition at printing costs, shipped right to your doorstep. Curate your personal library of Alexandria with editions worthy of display—crafted to last, designed to captivate, and delivered straight to your door.

- **Modern translations for Contemporary Readers in all languages and dialects**

  Discover a vast selection of classics reimagined in clear, current language—no more struggling with outdated phrases or obscure references. Next to the original versions, we aim to offer translations in as many languages and dialects as possible.

  As we continue our translation efforts and add new languages, readers everywhere can connect with these works as if they were written today. By bridging linguistic divides, you're contributing to ensuring that these timeless stories become more meaningful, accessible, and inspiring for people across the globe.

- **Your Personal Library of Alexandria:**

  Over the months and years, you'll curate a unique physical archive of classics—each volume a testament to your taste, curiosity, and love of knowledge. It's not just about owning books—it's about curating a cultural legacy you'll cherish and pass down for generations to come.

- **Join a Global Literary Renaissance:**

  Your support fuels an ongoing mission: allowing us to reinvest in offering deluxe print editions (including special boxsets) at their true cost, broaden the range of available formats and translations, and extend the reach of these works to new audiences worldwide. By joining today, you're not just preserving a legacy of masterpieces; you set in motion a powerful wave of literary accessibility.

We are more than a publisher—we're a movement, and we can't do it alone. Your support lets us scale our mission, preserving and reimagining history's greatest works for tomorrow's readers.

Become a Torchbearer of knowledge.

Thank you for picking up this book and allowing us into your literary journey. As you turn the pages, know that you're part of something larger: a global effort to keep these stories alive, share their wisdom across borders and generations, and spark a true cultural revival for the modern era.

If this resonates with you—please consider taking the next step by visiting:

www.libraryofalexandria.com

With gratitude and a shared love of knowledge,

The Modern Library of Alexandria Team

Visit:

www.libraryofalexandria.com

Or scan the code below: